Burnt Offering

Burnt Offering

Vivian Zabel

 Fiction
Edmond, Oklahoma

Dedication

I dedicate *Burnt Offering* to the people who believed in me and my writing, especially Jacque Graham and the late Edna Hilburn. Thank you for supporting me.

Contents

Important People in Burnt Offering

Aaron: A priest for Yahweh

Hadara: The daughter of wealthy Egyptians, given in marriage to Tzabar to gain favor with the King Jotham of Judah, the father of Ahaz

Ahaz: King of Judah during the mid-8th Century BC, a follower of idols

Hosa: Aaron's companion

Barrack: A trusted advisor to King Ahaz, a devote follower of Moleck

Tobias: Hadara's and Tzabar's son

Nava: The young girl Hadara and Tobias found abandoned in a deserted village

Philmon: An Ethiopian body guard and close friend to Hadara and Tobias

Mazza: Hadara's retainer, nurse, companion

Amzi: A servant, thought to be a eunuch, joins rebels

Simeon & family: The chat'ran (head of household) for Tzabar, he and his family become Hadara's staff and protectors

     Rachel – Simeon's wife;

     Dan, Liam, and Liber – their sons;

     Ahuva, Noma, and Zema – their daughters

     Martha – Dan's wife

     Gafna – Dan and Martha's daughter

Tzabar: Depraved noble and advisor to King Ahaz, married to Hadara

Hemut: Hadara's brother, he and his brother Raz share the duties of the family trading business, the caravans and barges.

Raz: Hadara's and Hemut's brother

Losha: The old woman, keeper of the hidden oasis

Deborah: Nava's mother; Sofai, Jacob, and Caley's mother;

Jacob: Deborah and Ruben's son

Nathan: Son of Jacob, grandson of Deborah and Ruben

Ruben: Nava's father; Deborah's husband

Lior: Noma's fiancé at one time

Caleb/Kalif:	Once a soldier,
Abram:	one of the rebels, looks younger than he is
Naman:	Military minister under King Ahaz
Shem:	Financial minister under King Ahaz, secret supporter of rebels against Ahaz
Hezekiah:	Remaining son of Ahaz, whose mother hid him
Micah:	Kalif and Hadara's houseman
Abial:	Kalif and Hadara's cook and housekeeper
Pace:	Sergeant of the "Silent Soldiers"
Saburo:	In charge of the king's barracks
Shebaon:	Philmon's wife

Chapter 1

Aaron's house, Bethlehem :: 720 BC

I, Aaron, named by my mother for the first High Priest of Yahweh, did little to attain greatness, but I did what He led me to do. I must share what I know before I leave this life. Old age and frailty have left me unable to continue much longer. My mind wanders much, and I need to put the words down the best I can. I am thankful that Hadara's family has kept me provided with parchment over the years. A friend, whose family are traders and merchants, often helps in many ways. They created and traded parchment and other … Ah, I need to write the tale.

When Ahaz attained the throne of Judah, for the first five or so years, he followed many pagan gods, especially Baal. He became more and more involved in wickedness as if trying to prove how evil he might become. I never knew Ahaz' thoughts; therefore, I only make conclusions based on the man's actions.

One night in Israel, the few of us with Isaiah left the prophet in prayer as we sought our beds. In the depth of the darkness, we all scrambled to prepare to leave because Isaiah sent word to all we must go to Jerusalem immediately. He and his son must meet with King Ahaz of Judah.

We arrived at the palace three nights later. Isaiah, his back straight and robes flowing, marched up the steps to the golden doors of the palace. The guards stopped him.

"Stand aside," Isaiah declared, not shouting, but his voice strong and firm carried. "I have a message for the king."

The guards fell back and opened the doors.

The servants inside parted before him, and two rushed to open the doors to the throne room, where the king sat on the platform above his subjects crowded below him.

"Stand aside," Isaiah demanded, and the mass of bodies parted. The prophet and his son strode forward until they reached the steps leading to the king. "I bring a message from Yahweh. Your enemies join together to attack your borders."

King Ahaz pushed himself upward. "To attack Judah, to attack me?"

"Yes, but Yahweh will save you and smite them if you turn from your wicked ways and serve Him."

The king trembled. "I … I must speak with my nobles before I make a decision. Then I will send word."

Isaiah bowed his head, whirled around, and, followed by his son, strode back through both sets of doors and from the palace, and the other three of us hurried behind. When we reached the street, the prophet stopped and faced us.

"I feel King Ahaz already has his decision. Some of his nobles have a slight amount of goodness, but he will listen most to Tzabar, who has none." Isaiah stared into the darkness of the sky for a moment before looking directly at me. "Aaron, you need to stay here because you will be needed."

"Have I displeased you?" I asked. "I know I'm not as young as the others, but I have kept up so far, haven't I?"

The prophet placed his hand on my shoulder. "This is not a matter of my sending you from me, but Yahweh has a mission for you, here. The evil of this place will grow, and the people need guidance and comfort."

"Of course, I will do whatever the one true God commands." I struggled to hide my disappointment.

"Hosa," he called to one of the younger men, "come. You will go with Aaron and assist him, help him in every way he needs." His eyes searched mine in the darkness. "Try to find any good in Ahaz and those closest to him. I fear for Judah."

So, I stood beside Hosa and watched Isaiah, his son, and another friend walk away through the night.

King Ahaz did not accept Yahweh's offer, but he went to King Tiglath of the Assyrians for help to be delivered from his enemies. Tiglath came to his aid, but the Assyrian king took money and land from Judah, making it a vassal to Assyria.

On a trip to Damascus, Ahaz discovered the demon god Moleck and turned to him, moving even further into abandoned wantonness. I searched for any goodness in Ahaz and his noble Tzabar, but I found no sign of any. None. Evil possessed them completely, and they enjoyed being wicked. When Barrack came back to the land of his fathers, he advised Ahaz and became more involved in licentious actions than even they did, but not much. I wondered if demons possessed them. Barrack drew Ahaz to him, Tzabar followed his king, even encouraging him in his explorations into immorality. Those three men had no good in them, none whatsoever, and I searched. Evilness filled them. What those men, and the people they influenced, did sickened Yahweh and those who followed Him.

Forgive me. My mind wandered again. I must complete the story, about people who believed in goodness. I observed some of the story; others told me parts of it; and some events were revealed to me. I will concentrate and write the story as if it happened in front of our eyes. Let me begin with Hadara, a woman yoked to an evil man but his opposite.

Chapter 2

The countryside outside Jerusalem :: 734 BC

A small caravan traveled the back roads of Judah. Puffs of dust rose around the hoofs of three horses, two ridden by guards, and the feet of four men who carried a silk covered litter.

Inside the litter, a woman stared at the silk curtains blocking her view of the passing countryside. *I feel as if in another prison. I can't escape except for a short time.* She shook her head. *Hadara, things could be worse. Perhaps.*

The young man on the black horse beside the litter called, "Mother, please open the curtains. We still need to talk."

Hadara's slender hands pulled the silk back to reveal her half-reclining. "When you call me 'Mother' rather than 'Eema,' I know you're not pleased." She smiled, and her chocolate-brown eyes twinkled. "Now, what's the problem?"

"Why did you marry my father?" He dropped his head a moment before he looked at her again. "I've tried to ask you many times, but you always change the subject. You're kind, generous, and good. He's so evil: no kindness at all. Most men are at least proud of a son, but not him." He frowned. "I've heard the stories about him, what he does to girls not much more than children, then throws them away like garbage."

The woman took a deep breath and exhaled with a whoosh. "I wanted to protect you. Tobias, you're so young. How could I expect you to understand when I can't?"

"Mother! I am nearly seventeen, almost a man. I'm years older than you were when I was born. In four years or less, King Ahaz will use me for fodder as he wages war for the Assyrians or against Israel. Humph, if I weren't the son of a noble, I would already be fighting." He patted the horse's neck. "I need to know. How could you become his wife in the first place and remain married to Tzabar?" Tobias stared across the sun-parched land. "As I've learned more about him, I don't want anyone to know I'm related to him." He turned his attention back to his mother. "I, uh, yes, I *need* to know. I *must* know."

"Very well." Hadara bit her lip. "You know marriages are often used to weld alliances. My family wanted to trade with Judah and even into Israel and further east. Ahaz's father, King Jotham, offered to sign an agreement with my family and allow safe passage if they found a bride for his friend Tzabar." She wiped tears from under her eyes. "They … they couldn't know the monster Tzabar was, is. The king didn't know." She gave an unlady-like sniff, which would have drawn strange looks if she did such a thing in society. "Tzabar has been a manipulator all his life, apparently. He made Jotham believe he was a good man, but when Ahaz became king, so different from his father … How shall I put this: he and Ahaz are much alike. Once Ahaz became king, they seemed to compete to see who could be more immoral."

"Eema, please don't cry. I shouldn't have asked." Tobias stared at the sky a moment, his hands and legs guiding his horse. "Ahaz has been king a few years and has already lost – ha! – *given* part of our country to the Assyrians.

"As far as Tzabar, I know you take these short journeys outside of Jerusalem to get away from him unexpectedly entering your rooms. To give yourself a break from being his wife."

"My son, I did –"

The guard in front of the short column interrupted her as he pointed. "There is the abandoned village. The well still has water. Shall we stop?"

Tobias looked at his mother, who nodded. "Yes, Yatan, we'll stop." He turned the horse's head toward the piles of empty stones and streets.

The dirt road encircled the well in the area where the town square once existed. A child huddled near a broken rock wall, as if the meager shade might give respite from the flies swarming in the dusty air. A light shawl covered her head and most of her face. Stripes of dried mud streaked the small portion of skin revealed. Her lashes fanned across softly rounded cheeks. Even though she slept, her stomach growled with hunger.

Her eyes flew open. She tilted her head as the jingling of harness and thud of feet and hooves echoed through the vacant streets of the unoccupied village. She covered her face completely and pressed against the wall, her heart pounding. The caravan advanced through a whirl of powdered soil.

The mounted guards circled the well before they swung from their mounts, swords in hand, eyes searching the area. The four massive men lowered their burden to the ground, and Tobias slid from his horse. Hadara brushed her dark hair from her face, lowered her feet to the ground, and stood. She stretched. Her robes stirred in the breeze.

"Eema, one of the men will bring water, but we can't linger." The young man touched her arm. He towered over his mother; and although he wasn't fully grown, his broad shoulders showed he would be a large man. He smiled.

The corners of his mother's mouth tilted upward in answer. "Son, we can manage a few moments for me to bring life back to my limbs. Lying in the carrying chair can cramp one's body after hours of doing nothing else." She patted his hand resting on her arm. "Tobias, all will be well. You do worry –" She pointed. "Look." She strode away from her son toward the bundle of cloth by the crumbling wall.

"Eema, you don't know what – Wait."

"It's a child," his mother interrupted him. "Now be nice and don't scare her." She smiled. "I believe it's a girl."

Tobias heaved a sigh. "And, you would take in all the abandoned children in the world, I know, but we don't know what *that* is."

The woman knelt beside the girl and brushed the thin material away from the small face. The girl pushed harder against the wall, causing stones to shift.

"Please, I won't hurt anything." The young voice broke on a sob. Startling emerald-green eyes filled with tears as the child looked at the woman beside her.

"Come, child, you will be safe with us. My name is Hadara, and this is my son, Tobias. He may act tough, but he has a kind heart. All is well. I promise we'll not hurt you."

The child's eyelids fluttered. "You smell like flowers. My eema smells like flowers, too." The tears over-flowed, and she wiped them off her cheeks leaving muddy tracks. "I didn't do what my parents told me. Now they are gone."

"Gone? Gone where?" Hadara glanced at her son, who knelt beside her, a frown furrowing his forehead.

"Eema and Abba said we are going home, but home is that way." The child pointed a grimy hand toward the mountains in the far distance.

Hadara used her sleeve to wipe dirt and tears from the filthy face. "What is your name, and why are you here alone?"

"My name is Nava. Eema told me," the girl nodded, "when we stopped to eat, to stay close." She sniffed. "I followed a quail. I didn't mean to go so far. I … I sat under a tree. I was tired." She rubbed her nose with a fist. "I didn't mean to fall asleep." Her eyes dropped. "I didn't mind."

"I'm sure you didn't mean to fall asleep, child." Hadara glanced at her son again. "I think we need some water."

With a nod, Tobias rose to his full height, settled his short wrap-around robe skirt over his leggings, and strode to the well. He spoke to the other men before returning with a wooden bowl, which he handed to his mother. Hadara in turn lifted the water to the girl's lips.

"Eema, you need to drink, not give the water to her." Tobias reached toward the bowl, but his mother pulled it away, splashing a few drops over the rim.

She shook her head. "We can get more, and I'll drink then. Now, behave like a true noble, not one of Ahaz's."

The girl's eyes widened as she gazed at Hadara, peeked at Tobias, and returned her attention back to Hadara. She raised one thin hand to steady the bowl and sipped.

Tobias lowered his head. "I apologize, Mother, Eema." He raised his eyes and looked at the child. "Nava, I owe you an apology, too. I'm sorry." He smiled, and Nava's mouth moved into a small grin. "Now, can you answer some questions?"

She nodded and pushed the bowl away. "I'll try."

"Who are your parents?"

"Abba is Ruben. Eema is Deborah." Her eyes strayed to the bowl of water Hadara still held. "May I please have another drink? The water skin has been empty since yesterday."

"Water skin? You had water?" Hadara handed the bowl to Nava, who didn't sip but drank thirstily before handing the bowl back.

She nodded. "When I woke, I ran back here, but everyone had left." She shrugged one thin shoulder. "A skin of water and a cloth wrapped around cheese and bread sat on the edge of the well." Another tear crept down her cheek. "I didn't mean to misbehave."

Hadara wrapped the girl in her arms. "I'm so sorry, child. Where did they go?"

Nava shrugged. "They said home, but we left home."

One of the carriers, an Ethiopian, walked to stand behind Tobias. "Tobias, here's more water. We have all drank and watered the horses. When you are ready, we are — " He jerked back, staring at the girl who studied him. "A demon!"

Tobias leaped to his feet and grabbed the man's arm and shook him, although the carrier stood over a head taller and twice as wide. "Be quiet, man. What is wrong with you?"

A shaky black finger pointed at Nava. "Her eyes, full of evil."

Nava hid her face in her shawl and pushed herself further against the crumbling stones behind her.

"You fool," Tobias shouted before lowering his voice. "She was with a group of captives returning from the Caucasus Mountains. After a hundred years, many have yellow hair and blue or green eyes. If you were a regular servant, uneducated, I could understand, but you aren't."

Hadara rose to face her servant. "King David, according to writings, had red hair and a red beard. Was he a demon?" She knelt again to wrap Nava in her arms. "A fool indeed. Don't be afraid, child. Philmon talks before he uses his mind."

The huge man stood stricken. "Please forgive me, little one. I am a fool. Yes, indeed I am a fool."

Nava peeked from where she hid behind Hadara's shoulder. "Oh, no, you're a mountain. Please don't fall on me." She gulped. "I promise I'm not a demon."

Philmon moved closer to the girl and rested a ham-sized hand gently on her head. "No, little one, you are not. Forgive me. I will get a cloth wet so we can clean your face and hands." Bright green eyes followed his passage to the tent on poles.

"Now, we need to get you ready to travel." Hadara turned to her son. "We need to get her in the litter." She smiled at Nava. "The carrier chair."

"Eema, she is so dirty." Tobias stood. "I'll carry her with me." He walked toward his horse shaking his head. "She would take all the abandoned children in the world."

"I heard that, and, yes, I probably would if I could," Hadara called after him. "And, please bring something for Nava to nibble on. I'm sure she's hungry."

After the child ate a piece of bread and a tiny chunk of cheese, Philmon lifted her to sit sideways on the horse in front of Tobias. Nava sat stiff and didn't touch the young man, who to a child's eyes seemed as much an adult as the others. Her eyes rounded as she watched Hadara climb into the litter. When Philmon reached to close the curtains, the woman stopped him.

"No, let's leave them open. Nava will be less frightened if she can see me."

Philmon bowed his head and, once he checked to be sure the other three men stood in their places at corners of the litter, strode to the front of the chair. He called, "Up," and the four men raised the chair posts to their shoulders and marched past the well. The guards took their places, one in front and one behind the litter. Tobias, with Nava, rode beside the chair.

Tobias traveled a few minutes in silence before he asked, "Nava, how old are you?"

The child trembled. "I ... I will see ten harvests when grain is cut."

"I see. You seem younger."

"My savta, my eema's mother, says when we get home, I will get bigger." Her shoulders rose and lowered with a deep sigh. "I won't ever go home, will I?"

Tobias touched her arm with one hand. "We will try to find your family. What members of your family traveled together? Maybe that can help us."

Nava trembled again when the young man's hand brushed her arm.

"Nava," Hadara called from the litter, "you can say whatever you want, or you don't have to answer. No one will hurt you. Tobias simply wants to know you, and so do I."

The girl turned her head so she could look up at Tobias. Her wide eyes searched his. He smiled. A timid grin curved her lips.

"My grandfather was our leader. He's not very nice, but the king, um, King Ahaz, thinks he's important, sent a messenger to tell Grandfather to bring us back." She shrugged and heaved a sigh. "He and Abba's mother will live close to the king because he is so important." Nava turned to look across the land they passed. "Grandfather is why Abba and Eema and my brothers and sister had to go without me."

Hadara leaned toward the outside of the chair, her voice raised in anger. "What? Why would he have anything to do with them leaving you? Parents would never want to leave a child."

Her shout startled Tobias' horse, which stamped his hooves and tried to buck. Tobias gathered Nava close to his body as he used legs and one hand on the reins to gentle the animal. Nava buried her face into his chest and held to his coat tightly enough that her knuckles turned white.

"It's all right. It's all right," Tobias whispered, soothing both child and horse. "See, Nava, everything is fine. I won't allow anything to harm you."

She looked at him, eyes shining with unshed tears, and a smile spread across her face. "No one ever kept me safe before."

Tobias stared at the girl until her smile faded, and he barely heard her whisper, "Did … did I do something wrong?"

"No, no, not at all. I liked seeing you smile." He chuckled. "I don't have lovely young ladies smile at me very often."

Nava ducked her head. "My grandfather says I'm ugly."

"Is that your father's father or is that your mother's father?" Hadara asked, a scowl crossing her face.

"Oh, Eema's father died when I was but a babe. No, it's my abba's father." Nava leaned against Tobias' chest. "Eema's mother, my savta, traveled with us, and she gave me hugs and told me stories. Abba's mother doesn't like children, says we are dirty." She held up her hands that still showed dirt even after a quick wipe with a wet cloth. "I guess I am, but Eema makes us clean ourselves, all my brothers and me. She really does. She *is* a good mother."

Tobias grinned. "Even when we first saw you, you were cleaner than I was at your age."

"Oh, yes, all of six and a half years ago," his mother contributed with a laugh. "Actually, after you practice your battle skills with your friends, you are still that dirty or worse."

When a smothered giggle erupted from the girl, Tobias glanced down. "Are you laughing at me?"

She jerked away and stiffened her back. "I … I am sorry," she whispered, her head bowed.

Tobias hugged her one-armed. "Oh, don't be. I was teasing."

"Are you sure? I … I …" A sigh shuddered through her thin frame. "My savta says I talk and then I think."

Hadara's soft laugh caused Nava to look toward the chair. The woman smiled at the girl. "Were you and your family the only ones traveling together?"

"Oh, no. Almost all our village came. My abba's father is going to be important at the king's court. Everyone wants to be important with him."

"Is that why your parents left you, because they want to please your father's father?" Hadara's brow wrinkled. "I would never leave my child no matter what."

The smile on Nava's face faded. "I heard him tell my abba, when one of my brothers did something my grandfather didn't like, that Abba would lose his portion if his – I can't say the word he used. But if we caused any trouble, Abba would lose his portion. Grandfather said, 'Then how will you feed those parasites of yours?' Abba walked away."

The woman gasped. "Your father just walked away? I don't understand." She shook her head. "You saw and heard all that and remembered it?"

"My eema says I collect everything with my ears and let it flow from my mouth." After a pause, Nava added, "My brothers always teased me about that, too."

Tobias asked, "How many brothers and sisters do you have?" His hand rubbed her back, soothing the tension that tightened her muscles.

"I have two brothers, one now grown, married with a son. Caley is three years older, and he teases me most." As she spoke, she leaned more against his chest, relaxing. "The baby is my only sister, Sofai."

The young man chuckled again. "My mother was the youngest and only girl in her family. She says the older, especially brothers, think their job is to tease little sisters."

They rode in silence for a few minutes, the sun beating on them.

"But, I don't understand why your family didn't stand up to your grandfather and wait for you. Surely, they could have waited and continued after you returned. Then you could have continued traveling, but together." Tobias paused. "Doesn't make sense. They had such a short distance to go."

"I don't know what a portion is, but my abba and grandfather set much importance to it." She shrugged a shoulder. "Grandfather seemed to think Abba would do what he wanted to keep the portion."

"Ah, yes, a portion would mean much to a person going to a strange place with nothing except what his father provided." Hadara sat straighter in the chair, no longer half reclining. "Nava, a father gives a portion of what he owns to his children, usually his sons. Usually, the portion comes after the father dies, but at times, the father will 'portion' out his estate while he is alive."

"Therefore, little one," Philmon's voice interrupted, "your father was willing to trade you for a portion of a promise he might never receive."

The green eyes, with their fringe of black, stared in the direction of the carrier and then at Tobias. "Abba traded me?"

"Maybe he thought he had no choice. I don't know, Nava, but Mother and I will take care of you. I have a feeling that Philmon will help keep you safe, too."

Nava turned her bright smile at Tobias, Hadara, and the huge man looking from the front of the chair carrier, its pole over his shoulder. She yawned before snuggling against Tobias. Her breathing slowed until she slept.

Once he could tell Nava wouldn't hear, Tobias met his mother's eyes. "Do you see how lovely she is? Only nine, but the beauty is there."

"I saw, and I hope we are doing the right thing. She will only grow more beautiful as she grows older. I have to admit I'm afraid."

"Mother, you must keep her hidden. We must not let *him* see her, ever." He brushed a hand over the head leaning against him before he repeated, "He must not ever see her. Ever." A minute later, he again whispered his fear, "Never see her."

He studied the child in his arms. "He would as soon as use this small girl as a target for his bow as breathe." Tobias looked at Nava and then his mother. "I have heard rumors, about how he takes young girls and … I may not know details, but I know enough. This little one must be saved from him."

"The stories you heard about your father are true, about how he … he, uh, destroys young girls. At least he hasn't used any of his cruelty on you, my son. I suppose that is one good quality."

"Only because I will be a means to please Ahaz. We must succeed in our plans to get away from him and the nobles of Ahaz." Tobias gave a soundless whistle. "We can be at least partially successful."

"You, my son, are more of a man already than Tzabar could ever be.

Chapter 3

Jerusalem, the palace of Ahaz's noble Tzabar :: three years later

An elderly woman fussed over Hadara's hair. "Be still, child. You must look your best."

"Mazza, we will be on the balcony, and no one can see us."

The retainer, who had tended Hadara since her mistress had been a child and who had been brought with her charge from Egypt, shook her head. "I will know, and I will not allow you to look anything but your most beautiful." A wrinkled hand passed over the younger woman's head.

A giggle caused Hadara to glance toward a young woman, almost still a child, sitting to one side sewing fine linen. "Nava, it is not funny. Imagine being a woman and being treated as a child."

"You're very fortunate to have someone who cares enough to follow you so far." The girl returned to her sewing. "You know where your family is and that they care."

Hadara waved Mazza away. "We still search for your family. We *will* find them some day."

Nava raised her eyes to search the older woman's face. "If they wanted me, they wouldn't have left me." She sighed. "But, you gave me a home. I'm very fortunate, and I am thankful."

Hadara stood and walked to the open windows of the balcony. "Come, it's time for the procession to begin. Tobias should be here already."

"I am." Tobias walked through the chamber's double doors from the vestibule to the women's section, followed by Philmon and one of the eunuchs. The eunuch bowed toward Hadara and then Mazza, ignoring Nava.

Tobias laughed. "Father insisted I watch him and his guest climb into the chariot they'll ride."

"I'm surprised Tzabar didn't force you to ride with him." Hadara grimaced. "Would have been like him."

"He tried, Eema, but when I mentioned that the noble who was with him might want his undivided attention, he told me to hurry away." Tobias grinned. "Apparently, his partner in the procession is King Ahaz's dear friend, and Father always does what he can to draw ever closer to the king."

After the group gathered on the balcony where each could see through the ornate metal screen, Hadara asked, "Where are Fatra and Mira?"

Mazza gave a part snort and part humph. "They insisted they wanted to be on the streets so they could 'see' all the nobles and visiting dignitaries. They want to flirt with the soldiers more than likely."

"Now, Mazza, you know we can enjoy the ordeal more without them here being such silly girls." Tobias hugged his adopted grandmother.

"Oh, look," Nava pressed her face closer to the grill with its carved scrolls and openings, "the soldiers are marching into the square. Soon will come the first chariots with dignitaries."

The group watched the soldiers march from the road at the far-left corner of the square, near a corner of the palace. They strode in unison to their right and ringed the huge square. They left an opening only in front of the king's palace, a half mile across from Tzabar's, and for the road they used to enter the square. Once the soldiers stood as a wall between the people watching and the dignitaries to come, dancing girls whirled into the area from the open road. They took places in the center of the square, continuing to dance and slither in a tight circle.

The first chariot appeared in the square and made its way counter-clockwise in front of soldiers and crowds. The odor of packed bodies rose to agonize the noses of those hidden above.

"Those chariots look as if made from gold!" Mazza's voice held the shock all watchers felt. "People starve and are sold as slaves because they cannot feed their children, and ..." Her voice faded away.

Tobias inhaled. "Yes, they are gold, and the helmets of the drivers are also gold. King Ahaz wants to impress his visitors, especially the Assyrian representatives, with his wealth." He exhaled a puff of air.

"Made on the backs of his subjects and what he tries to hide from Tiglath-Pileser." Philmon tried to whisper, but everyone heard his rumble. "Amzi, don't look so disapproving." He lightly punched the eunuch in the shoulder, rocking the smaller man.

"If the master hears you talking so, he will add you to our numbers or perhaps kill you." Amzi glared at Philmon. "You shouldn't be here, not in the women's section."

Tobias turned toward the eunuch. "Amzi, Philmon is my bodyguard and my mother's. He is allowed wherever either of us may be."

Nava turned from viewing the pageantry below to ask Tobias, "Who is Tiglath-Pileser?"

"Humph," Mazza answered, "the king of Assyria, who now owns Ahaz and thus Judah."

"Oh, I see; I think." Nava spun back to face the screen.

The group watched in silence as chariot after chariot made its way around the square and stopped for soldiers to escort nobles into the king's palace. All the while, the dancers continued their performances. Spectators yelled and clapped as the procession continued.

Nava gasped. She pressed her face against the grill.

Hadara slipped an arm around the girl's shoulders. "What is wrong, child?"

Nava pointed, her finger passing through an opening in the elaborate design. "There, just halfway toward us, that is my grandfather in that chariot."

"Are you sure?" Tobias moved to her other side. "With my father? It's a far distance. How can you tell?"

"I would know him anywhere. See how tall and unbending he holds himself?" A tremble shivered through her. "Yes, that is my grandfather."

"I see. His name is –"

"Barrack. I know," Nava interrupted. "He is the reason my family left me alone in that barren place. I know he is. I...I don't care to watch more." She backed away from the screen.

Tobias held her to his side as he led her back into the chamber. He lowered her into a chair and knelt beside her. Hadara and the others followed and took places close by: Philmon standing behind Nava's chair, Amzi and Mazza behind Hadara's.

Nava wiped her eyes with the tips of her fingers. "I wonder what happened to my parents, my family?" She glanced at the man by her side. The shock of seeing her grandfather upset her, but she still thought, *How handsome Tobias is.* A slight inner shiver caused her wrap her arms around her waist.

Philmon's huge hand lay on her head. "I have heard guards and servants talk. There is no talk of Barrack's family, except his young wife. He and she have chambers in the king's palace. They expect a child in the near future, but there is no other family with them."

"Please, no." The girl's words echoed through the room. "He couldn't have killed them, could he?"

"He is capable of doing that and worse, Nava. I've heard my father talk about him, and cruel as Tzabar is, he is in awe of Barrack." Tobias stood. "However, the king's entranced with the man and his ideas. I dread to think what decisions will be made over there," he pointed toward the outside wall, "today and the days to come." His mouth tightened and a frown furrowed his brow. "A meeting of evil minds ... Their plans will result in much trouble and sorrow for our country."

Chapter 4

Jerusalem

Although as large as some small villages, Tzabar's place still didn't match King Ahaz's palace across the half-mile-square plaza, but Tzabar tried to create, or have others create, a close second. Morning light filtered through the ornate screen which hid the balcony from the street beyond the open doors. The sunshine cast patterns on the chamber floor and furniture. At one end of the main room of the women's section, Hadara sat at a long table with pages of parchment, an ink pot, and writing reeds in front of her; and Simeon, the chatz'ran, the head of the household, sat across the table.

Further down the table, a young woman faced parchment, ink pot, and reeds, too, but splotches of ink spotted a sheet, and a frown puckered her forehead. Her deep, dark eyes rose to glare at Hadara.

"Why do I have to learn how to do this? I'm going to marry a rich man." She brushed her long nearly black tresses from her olive face.

Hadara didn't even glance toward her. "Fatra, I am married to a rich man. See what I'm doing?" She shook her head. "With the amount of parchment you splatter, I'm glad my family is so liberal with their gifts of many sheets and scrolls."

Across the room, Mazza and another young woman worked on a loom, creating fine cloth. The retainer showed the other woman a mistake in the pattern. "There, Mira, do you remember how to remove that knot?"

Mira smiled. "Yes, I do." She turned light brown eyes to the older woman. "I *am* learning."

In a chair near the open window, Nava hemmed a garment, her light brown head with its golden streaks bowed over her work.

The doors from the chamber to the vestibule crashed against the wall. Amzi stood in the opening. "Mistress, he's …" He catapulted into the room, landing on his knees, Tzabar behind him.

"Get out of my way, you imbecile." Tzabar strode into the middle of the room, his head swiveling to view everyone. He spied Nava trying to curl into the back of her chair, reached her in two long strides, and grabbed her by one arm.

"I knew you were hiding something." He scowled at his wife, who now stood, hands fisted.

"Leave her alone. She is my adopted daughter."

Tzabar's laugh bounced off the walls. "Everything here is mine. Mine!" He jerked Nava to her feet and hauled her toward the hall. Hadara scurried to him and grabbed his sleeve. He yanked away, back-handed his wife, and knocked her to the floor.

Fatra slipped to his side and touched his arm. "Why not me?"

The huge man, with muscles still honed under layers of fat, snorted. "Why would I want used?" he whispered close to her face, and then he plowed toward the open doorway, dragging Nava behind him, who lost her footing. Nava whimpered and grasped at the slick floor while he towed her away. He left a cowering Amzi on the floor and a screaming wife and her retainer behind.

He paused and turned to face Hadara before he passed through to the vestibule. He pointed a finger in her direction. "I can't get rid of you or kill you because of your interfering family, but I can kill everyone else around you, and I can lock you away. Beware, woman." He whirled and stomped away, Nava's whimpers now sobs as Tzabar, still grasping one of her wrists, dragged her behind him.

Mazza hurried to help Hadara to her feet. The two younger women huddled together in one corner. Amzi crawled to cower at Hadara's feet. "I am sorry, mistress. I was too slow to warn you."

"You sniveling beast. You were slow on purpose. You know you must let us know quickly. Why didn't you?" Hadara's body trembled. "You know what he will do to her. You know, and you let him grab her."

"Mistress, she is evil. You are better if she is gone." The eunuch kept his face against the floor. "She is a demon."

Hadara straightened. "You *were* slow on purpose. You wanted him to get her." Her voice dropped lower with each word. "You *wanted* him to get her."

"She is a vile demon as is he. They deserve each other."

Tobias and Philmon strode through the still opened doors. "What happened?" Tobias asked. He stared at the eunuch on the floor and then at his mother.

"He," she jabbed a quivering finger at the servant at her feet, "he did not warn us your father was coming. He wanted Tzabar to take Nava." She collapsed to the floor and covered her face with her hands. "Tzabar has her."

Philmon reached down, grabbed the neck of Amzi's robe, and raised the man to his feet. He roared, "You allowed that monster to take that small one. *You* allowed him to get his hands on her." He shook Amzi like a bag of rags.

Tobias knelt beside his mother and stared at the eunuch above him. "Death will be something you welcome for what you've done." He slid an arm around Hadara and raised her back to her feet. As he spoke, she leaned against him, as if old and feeble. Tobias raged, "Nava is but a child, innocent and kind, and you sent her to cruelty beyond your ability to understand." His body shuddered with anger. "Do you not know her goodness, the love we have for her? She is my sister."

"No, I saved you. I saved all of you. She's wicked. She's the spawn of that demon Barrack. You know."

Philmon shook Amzi again until the eunuch's teeth rattled. "You don't know about what you talk. He threw her away. He is evil, but not Nava, not the little one."

"Aaaaigggghhh, eeeeiiiii, ahhhhheeee." Screams echoed through the halls and into the chamber. Everyone looked toward the open door as if they could see, could help. Tobias ran toward the opening. Philmon threw the eunuch to one side.

"No, Tobias, no," Hadara yelled. "Philmon, stop him. Tzabar will kill him."

Philmon wrapped his arms around Tobias and squeezed him close. "No, you can't help her, not now. Stay alive to care for her and save her mind and soul."

Amzi took advantage of Philmon's attention no longer on him and raced from the room.

Screams continued for a spell, then died away, only to begin again. Mazza closed the doors while Tobias led his mother to a chair. Mira and Fatra slipped from the main chamber to the hall leading to the sleeping rooms. Those remaining either closed their eyes or stared into nothingness between rounds of screams. Tobias muttered under his breath and again strode toward the doors, but Philmon pulled him back.

Sudden silence spread throughout, deafening, quiet, as unnerving in its way as the screams.

"What should we do?" Hadara whispered, looking at the closed doors.

"Eema," Tobias replied, his hand on her shoulder. "We will wait a while, and then Philmon and I will search for her. We need to be sure Tzabar doesn't know."

The group sat waiting. Hadara fought the desire to race from the room, to face Tzabar, to find Nava. She wiped tears from her face. *Too late, even if I found her … too late. I failed. Promised to take care of her, keep her safe.* A heaviness settled in her chest.

A pounding on one of the doors brought all to their feet, and Mazza scurried to open the doors a crack. She backed away as Amzi pushed through, a burden wrapped in bloody bedclothes in his arms; blood dripped on his feet and left a trail behind.

Hadara motioned for him to follow her, and she led the way down the hall into another chamber. Tobias and Philmon followed. Mazza hurried past the eunuch with his burden and helped her mistress place cloths on a small sleeping platform. As Amzi laid Nava on the bed, she opened her eyes a slit.

"Hurt … hurt." Her voice exhaled no more than a breath. "He … he … pain … want to die. Please … please make … it stop." Her voice faded into a moan as her back arched and a strangled scream erupted, her voice hoarse.

Hadara brushed the girl's matted hair off her face. "I know. I know." She looked at Mazza. "Get water and strips of cloth." Turning to Philmon, she added, "Go get the midwife. Hurry. Tobias, please send the other girls somewhere safe, but stay here, don't leave."

The head of household entered. "What may I do, mistress?"

"What? Oh, Simeon, I forgot you. Perhaps you should leave and pretend you never were here."

"I hid under the table so the master didn't see me, but I want to help. I need to help. He did the same to my daughter years ago." The man gritted his teeth. "He is like his father was, only more malicious."

Hadara held her hand to her head. "How many? What did my parents do to me?" She bent to push bedclothes against Nava's body, but the blood continued.

"Here they are, Mother. Where do you want them to go?" Tobias stood over Simeon's shoulder.

"Where? Let me think a minute. I don't have time."

Simeon spoke, "I know where to take them, to the brothel where Tzabar found them."

"Brothel?" Tobias asked, echoed by his mother.

The man bowed his head. "Yes."

"They will spread the word everywhere, though." Hadara glanced from where she worked on Nava.

"I will send them somewhere they will not be heard, the old concubine quarters. Very appropriate." The chatz'ran brushed by Tobias with a quick nod of his head.

"Mistress?" Amzi whispered from the corner where he squatted.

Tobias whirled, grabbed the man by the throat, and raised him until his toes barely touched the floor. "What are you doing here?"

"Please, forgive me," the eunuch whispered as he clawed at the hands around his neck. "I ... I ..."

"Tobias, let him go. We don't have time." Hadara ordered. "He did bring her back."

Amzi rubbed his neck. "The master ordered her thrown in the garbage. Tinlia let me take her, helped me get her away unseen."

"The tongue-less one?" Tobias backed away, but his glare caused Amzi to shake.

"Yes, he has reason to hate your father, too." He swallowed. "He has servants who can clean blood off the floors in the other wing, but I need to haul water and clean traces from there to here."

"Out of my way." The midwife pushed by the others to hurry to Nava's side, Mazza close behind with one arm full of cloths and the other hand lugging a bucket of water.

Philmon motioned for the other men to follow him back to the main chamber where Simeon waited. The black man stared at Amzi and jerked his head toward the doors to the hall. "Go clean and be glad you weren't killed just now."

Simeon raised a hand, palm toward Amzi. "You can't remove all the blood by yourself. I saw it everywhere. My daughters and wives-to-my sons are already hauling water and cleaning. They can use help, though."

Amzi bowed his head. "Thank you." He started toward the door. "I am sorry."

Tobias heaved a deep breath. "How do we make sure no one can surprise the women again?" He walked through the heavy double doors to the vestibule.

At the end of the anteroom opening to the main hall, two enormous doors pressed against the wall on each side. They reached from the floor to the ceiling twenty feet above. Each door weighed more than four large men. Across the vestibule from the doors leading to the main room of the women's area, doors opened to three other rooms, each about the size of a bedchamber.

Simeon pointed to the rooms. "We could place men who we trust in those rooms, and we could close the outer doors."

"I have never known those doors to be closed, but they couldn't be opened quietly or easily." Philmon grabbed the edge of one door and strained to close it. Even with his strength, the door closed haltingly and with a groan. "I can put the other litter bearers," he panted as he moved the door to a closed position, "in the rooms. They are loyal to the mistress."

After the one door half-blocked the opening, he leaned against it. "Any offers to help shut the other one?" He stepped over the trail of blood to the second door.

Once the doors blocked the entrance to the women's section, Simeon shook his head at the blood staining the floor of the main chamber. "Amzi may scrub forever, but the stains will remain even when not seen with eyes." He faced Tobias. "Since your mother has few servants, the rooms on the level below this, still part of the women's wing, are empty. Is there some way I can move all my family into those rooms to add more protection and to give your mother and Nava servants they can trust? My three sons are in the army, but they are attached to Tzabar's service. They have little reason to trust him."

Tobias tilted his head as he thought. "Of course. That's an excellent idea. I know of at least three secret ways into this wing; two lead to the outside. Come, I'll show you."

Philmon followed the other two. "I'll have my men move into the rooms off the vestibule. Perhaps they can enter through the secret passages, too. The less others know, the less likely Tzabar will hear."

"One leads from the back of the vestibule to the garden below. They can then pass through the garden through a secret passageway to the alley between the palace and the stables." Tobias shrugged. "They can come and go as they please as long as at least one is on duty at all times."

After Amzi finished the scrubbing and had cleaned himself, he, Tobias, and

Philmon sat in the main chamber. Except for Mazza stepping into the room long enough to order Amzi to haul more water, no word came from the room where Nava fought to live. After the eunuch carried three loads of water, he rejoined the men.

"I couldn't see anything. Mazza opened the door enough to take the water, but she said nothing." Amzi wiped his face with his hands. "I'm an imbecile. Such a fool."

Tobias stared at Amzi. "If she dies, you are dead."

Amzi nodded. "I would deserve such." He nodded again. "With your permission, I will help Simeon move his family to the lower level."

Tobias dismissed the eunuch with a wave of his hand as Philmon watched Amzi stride toward the hall to the sleeping chambers and other rooms, including the stairs to the lower level.

"Tobias, have you ever looked at Amzi, I mean actually to see him?" The big man squinted.

With a shrug, the younger man replied, "Not really. Why?"

"For a eunuch, he is much more, um, manly than other eunuchs, is he not?" Philmon quirked an eyebrow toward Tobias.

A frown furrowed the young man's brow. "I hadn't really noticed, but ... But, how?"

"I think I will find out why and how. He is not soft and womanish at all." He nodded. "Yes, I will discover why and how a eunuch is not a eunuch. First, however, we will wait and make sure I don't have to kill him.

Chapter 5

a month later

"Come, Hadara, you must eat." The dish sat as full as when Mazza placed it in front of her mistress.

The other woman glanced at her retainer before turning her gaze to the open doors to the outside balcony. "I'm not hungry, Mazza."

"Nava is improving. She will be fine in time."

Hadara rose, shook her head, and paced around the table. "But, she nearly died. I don't know if she will ever truly recover mentally. The horror and the pain she endured ..." She stopped speaking as her thoughts retreated inwardly. *My fault, my fault.*

"I know. I know. But, she is recovering, in a way more than you."

But, Hadara could only hear her internal words, *My fault. I didn't protect her.*

"Mistress?"

Hadara whirled, her hand going to her chest. "Oh, Simeon, I didn't hear you come in."

"I'm sorry. I came through the secret entrance downstairs. I don't want anyone to know I'm here." The steward took his mistress' arm and led her to a divan. "Here, sit. We have to discuss what I overheard."

"Heard?" Mazza moved a chair closer to where the other two sat.

Simeon looked around. "Where is everyone else? No one else can know, at least yet."

"Doing their duties. Nava is still in bed. Tobias stays away from his father's sight." Hadara clasped his arm. "You frighten me."

"I know, but we *all* should be afraid. You know how Tzabar seeks Barrack's favor, wanting Barrack to help him become even closer to the king."

"As sequestered as I've been, I heard that." Hadara rubbed the top of one hand with the other.

Simeon nodded. "They met today in the master's decision room. As usual, neither noticed a mere servant." He inhaled and exhaled loudly. "Since Barrack has a new, young wife who will give him a child soon, they discussed the 'need' for Tzabar to put you aside and find a young wife for himself."

"What?" Mazza rose from her seat. "What!"

"Shhh ... quiet, Mazza. Let Simeon finish." Hadara rubbed both hands over her face. "I'm not really shocked he would do such a thing. I hoped I had more time."

"Wait, mistress, you do. Members of your family will visit in the next weeks, and Tzabar will wait until they leave before he announces he wants to put you away." Simeon nodded when Hadara stared at him. "You have time to plan and make your moves before he can officially do anything."

Hadara rose and stepped to the balcony, followed by Simeon and Mazza. "Yes, I must plan." She faced the man. "Can you meet me here later tonight, when I've had time to think?"

"Of course. Now, I need to get to the main part of the palace before I'm missed." He bowed and slipped from the room.

Hadara moved to the table which held writing materials. "Mazza, please keep everyone away for at least an hour. I need quiet. Tell anyone who asks that I have felt the results of all the problems and need time." As her retainer turned to leave, she added, "Wait, if Tobias comes, have him join me."

Alone, Hadara sat for a time at the table with writing materials in front of her. Her face showed nothing. Finally, with a quick nod, she picked up a writing reed, dipped it in the ink pot, and wrote on a sheet of parchment:

My beloved parents,

    Tzabar plans to put me aside. We knew this might come, but not this soon. He wishes to wait and notify you after my brother Hemut and his family leave. He may send word to you with Hemut. Here is what I hope you will do: Tell Tzabar he is to return the dowry to me and is to wait six months after I am given notice so that I can make arrangements.
    That time will allow me to finish the plans you and I started.

My love,
Hadara

After allowing the ink to dry, Hadara rolled the parchment and sealed it with wax melted from the candle in front of her. She slid the roll into a pile of fine cloth.

"Mazza, I need you," she called. When the retainer entered the room, Hadara rose, the pile of cloth in her hands. "I need to make arrangements for this gift to be sent to my mother. Her birthday will be here soon."

The older woman nodded. She carried the cloth to a cabinet, where she removed a leather pouch. After placing the "gift" in the pouch, she tied it closed.

"I will make sure a trusted messenger takes this immediately. None will know."

"Thank you. It must get to my mother as fast as it can be carried to Egypt. Our lives may depend on it."

After Mazza left the chamber, Hadara dropped onto a divan. She brushed tears from her face. *What am I to do?* She heaved a deep sigh. She pushed herself to her feet and walked to stare through the screen between her and the outside. "I need more time. I must have more time."

Chapter 6

Jerusalem – main room of women's section, Tzabar's palace :: two months later

Shadows created by a few flickering candles and two firepots added shades of mystery as a group huddled around one of the fire pots. Each person leaned toward the middle of the circle so all could hear the whisper of each speaker.

"What's ... what's wrong?" Six heads whirled to face the slight figure standing in the hallway to the sleeping chambers. Nava backed toward the hall. "I'm sorry. I didn't mean to interrupt."

"Come, child, I know you won't spread rumors." Hadara motioned for the girl to join her. "I know you have learned to continue hearing everything but not allowing it to flow from your mouth."

The slight smile on the girl's face didn't show well in the dimness, but everyone noticed, as they noticed her halting pace. She could now walk and physically appeared healthy, yet everyone watched over her.

Tobias rose from his chair and offered it to her before pulling another one into the circle. "You should be involved in our planning any way, since you're included now."

Nava sat in the chair still warm from his body and glanced at the faces staring at her. "I am included in what planning? What have I done?"

Hadara patted the girl's hand. "First, allow me to introduce Aaron, a priest of the one true God." The tall, thin man bowed his head as Hadra continued, "Of course, you know Philmon and Amzi, who will help you and Tobias escape this madness. Beside Aaron is his assistant, Hosa."

"Escape? Me? Why? I understand you want Tobias to avoid being massacred in King Ahaz's army, but why me?"

In the wavering light, Nava watched Hadara close her eyes and bite her upper lip. With a shiver, Hadara opened her eyes. "Child, we know that you carry a child, and we all know the depth of Tzabar's wickedness. Didn't he try to make a eunuch of his own son?"

"What?" Nava rubbed her forehead. "I don't understand. He did that to Tobias?"

"No, little one, he did that to me," Amzi answered. "He used my mother before throwing her out with the garbage. I was born as a result." He lowered his head. "That is what makes my actions so much worse, what I allowed to happen to you."

"I don't understand. I do not understand." Her eyes searched Amzi's face then Hadara's. "Amzi is Tobias' brother? Tzabar did such a horrible thing to his son?"

"If I may explain," Amzi leaned forward in his chair, "I will tell you what I told the others months ago. When Tzabar heard about me, he told my mother he wished to give me a home with him. She thought it would be best and sent me here. Tzabar had me taken to the men who take boys and make them eunuchs. They thought it a fun thing to fool their master and did only half the job." His chest filled outward as he took a deep breath. "I don't belong as man or as eunuch, but I'm definitely not a eunuch."

Simeon stepped from the shadows. "Tobias and Amzi probably have siblings spread across Jerusalem, as probably does Tzabar himself. That wouldn't be surprising, but what Tzabar has done, unbelievable."

Nava leaned forward, her eyes searching Amzi's. "Your mother allowed this?"

With a humorless chuckle, Amzi said, "When I was able to slip away, I discovered she was gone. The neighbors said some men took her and all our possessions away the night I left." He shrugged. "I had nowhere else to go, but my hatred became skewed. Again, I am indeed sorry for what I allowed to happen to you."

"Amzi, I forgive you. I forgave you long before I knew your story." She looked at the others. "But, why do you want me to go away. Where will I go?"

Aaron, whom everyone forgot as he sat still and quiet, spoke for the first time. "If Tzabar discovers you are alive, if he knows you carry his child, both you and your babe will be in danger. Therefore, it is my duty to get both of you to safety."

Hadara stroked the top of the girl's hand. "Tobias will go to my family in Egypt, but you will go to a closer but safe place, where I will join you later.

Nava struggled to her feet. "I ... I believe I'll return to bed. This is too much to understand. I ... I ..." She stared at Amzi. "I don't understand. I'm confused, but I know your father must have done a terrible thing to you."

"Come, child, I will tuck you in." Hadara stood and wrapped an arm around her adopted daughter. "We will take care of everything. You have enough to do as you continue to regain your strength and carry this child."

Simeon announced as he moved toward the hall with the two, "I must return to my quarters. Please let me know what I can do to help."

As Nava moved toward her room with Hadara, she heard Amzi whisper to Tobias, "How could I explain more to her, as innocent as she is. She wouldn't understand what having one testicle removed means, rather than both or all my male organs."

Confusing, so confusing, I understand so little. Nava lay on her bed, staring upward. The fire pot in the corner of the chamber didn't create enough light to reach far, but she had faith the ceiling still hung between her and the night sky. She rubbed her hand over the pooch where a babe now cuddled.

"Little one, our future … whatever it may be … will be you and me together. How you came to be doesn't matter. You belong to me, and I will never leave you as long as I live."

Her mind whirled. "Poor Amzi. I don't understand. Others say making boys into eunuchs is painful and cruel." She rose from her bed, wrapped a cloak around her night clothes, and wandered toward the balcony overlooking the women's garden. Opening one of the doors, she slipped through the doors and leaned against the banister. She gazed into the garden below, lit by the full moon.

Restless, she ambled to the steps that led to the garden. At the bottom, she moved to a bench under a tree in the oasis in the middle of the palace. She watched the moon make its way across the sky between palace walls. With a deep sigh, she leaned against the tree, disappearing into the shadows. She jerked forward at the sound of footsteps and whirled toward the steps. Two male shapes moved toward her.

"Nava, it's Tobias and Amzi. We thought we saw you on the balcony and then come down. Are you all right?" Tobias sat beside her. "Mother told us to leave, that the adults needed to talk." A chuckle softened the sarcasm of his words.

The girl leaned back against the tree again before drawing her feet up under her cloak. "Just the adults? Are you and Amzi not adults yet?"

"Humph." Amzi strode to a bench farther away. "I believe I have been given the title of chaperone."

Nava tried to study Tobias' face in the darkness. "What is wrong? Why are you here with me?" She turned toward Amzi sitting in more moonlight. "Are you two now comrades?"

Amzi shrugged one shoulder. "We have found we have more in common than we have differences. If we work together, we both may survive."

She closed her eyes and swallowed a sob. "I do not understand this nightmare life has become."

Tobias wrapped one arm around her and snuggled her to his chest. "You might have been better off if Mother and I hadn't found you."

"No, no, I would *not* have been."

Amzi snorted. "Come on. We need to plan, not become melancholy. We can't change the past. We need to go forward."

"This from the man who keeps apologizing?" Tobias removed his arm from around Nava. "Not that you should ever stop after what you did."

"Stop, both of you. Tobias, Amzi should not keep apologizing. I forgave him. Amzi, we can't change the past, but if we forget it, we will make mistakes over again." She sighed. "Now, please tell me what is going on, why— "

BOOM! BOOM! The explosion reverberated through the women's quarters and down to the garden. Nava jumped to her feet as Tobias and Amzi followed. All stared at Philmon as he barreled down the steps.

"Someone's at the door to the rest of the palace," he said. "Amzi, go meet whoever it is. The guards will slow them as much as they can. Tobias, go to the secret passage. We will wait there. Nava, hide in the arbor." He whipped the dark mantle from his shoulders. "Use this to cover all of you. Do not let even a strand of hair show. Hurry!" He pushed Nava toward the arbor and Tobias toward the back wall as he called over his shoulder to Amzi who was halfway up the steps, "Let us know when it is safe."

Nava stumbled into the midnight blackness of the arbor, bumping into a bench. She felt her way to the other end and curled into a ball between it and the back of the small enclosure, fear causing her heart to pound until she felt it through her chest. She wrapped herself from head to toe in Philmon's mantle and prayed to the only God she knew, the one true God.

Amzi rushed to the doors from the main chamber to the vestibule. He opened the doors to find Tzabar pushing by the guards toward him. He quickly stepped back into the main chamber and bumped into one of Simeon's daughters.

"Where is she? Where is that woman?" Tzabar's roar echoed through the rooms.

"Do you mean me, Tzabar?" Hadara entered from the hallway to the other rooms, smoothing her robe. "Do you realize how late it is? It is past time to retire."

Tzabar frowned as he looked around the chamber lit by torches in the vestibule behind him and a small fire in each of three fire pots. "That does not matter. What you need to know and do is what I tell you." He strode toward a divan before turning sharply and marching back toward the doors. "The king has commanded that all his subjects appear at a ceremony in the Valley of Hinnom outside the south gate. Soldiers will search each house, each dwelling. Anyone left in the city will be beheaded when found."

He glared at his wife. "Besides, whoever owns the building will also be beheaded. You and all who serve you must be gone by the time the bells ring after the fast is broken. You and all your staff will go to a place arranged for the households of the king's nobles to stand." He whirled on his heel and stomped from the room, through the vestibule, and out the huge outer doors.

Those left in the main chamber waited until they heard the groan and thud of the huge outer doors before they moved. Amzi hurried to the doors to the vestibule. The three guards nodded to him before returning to their rooms.

Hadara gasped. "Is this ... could this be ... a trick? Has he heard that Nava— "

"No, mistress, he was too panicked himself." Simeon joined her in the middle of the chamber from where he had waited in the hallway. "King Ahaz has planned something. We must decide how to have all the people in this wing out unseen and transport everyone to the valley." He escorted her to a divan. "Sit." He glanced at his daughter Noma, who had escorted Hadara into the hall. "Please have everyone from the lower level come here. We need to know what each person is to do."

"I will get the others," Amzi announced before passing through the doors to the balcony above the garden. "This is not good news, not for anyone."

Chapter 7

Valley of Hinnom – Evil Flames

Nava exited the city on the path from the south gate with the other women and their escorts. When they reached the rim of the valley nearly a half mile from the city gate, she viewed an enormous idol of bronze which stood at the westernmost end of the valley. Its head, a bull's; its outstretched arms and hands, that of a man. The idol faced a platform where a throne of gold and smaller chairs of gold and silver held the king and his nobles, including Barrack at his right hand. Tzabar occupied a chair behind the king and his closest advisor. She noticed a woman, veiled and robed, sat in a chair to the king's left and slightly behind his throne, an infant in her arms. *She must be the queen, can't tell with her face and body covered.* Nava glanced around her and back at the valley.

Moleck priests stood at each corner of the platform and formed a double line from the statue to the ground in front of the platform. Drummers waited with their instruments ready. Ten men loaded wood through an opening in the bottom rear of the statue, jumping back to escape the flames and sparks that flew outward. From time to time, one of the men wouldn't move quickly enough, and he writhed on the ground screaming in pain. Nava closed her eyes briefly before opening them again to watch where she walked.

Nava and the others made their way downward into the valley, the women draped in veils and robes that covered their bodies. Simeon's sons in their military garb, Tobias, Amzi, and Philmon escorted the women. No one talked as they trod the winding way in single file. Masses of people packed the different sloped levels of the valley or forced their ways closer to the platform of dignitaries. A slight breeze blew toward Nava, bringing a mixture of heat, body odor, and trampled crops. The sun beat on her, creating a suffocating warmth.

Once the group from Tzabar's household reached a flat area not far from the valley's floor, Nava discovered she could hardly move with people pressed around her. She swallowed to keep bile from rising in her throat. To her right, she could see the idol. To her left, the platform with her grandfather and the other dignitaries.

When the statue glowed red from the fire within, the hundred drummers began a wild and furious pounding. The sound soared until many covered their ears, including Nava, but the beat penetrated through covering hands. One of the priests on the platform appeared to glide as he moved from his position to stand in front of the king. King Ahaz rose and reached for the infant in his wife's arms. She pulled back, but Tzabar stood and clasped her shoulders and held her fast. The squalling baby clutched the veil over his mother's face and yanked it away as the king snatched him from his mother's arms. The group on the slopes could see her mouth open in a scream, but nothing could be heard over the drums.

The king laid the babe in the priest's hands. The priest turned and marched to the edge of the platform. Another priest climbed the steps, took the infant, and returned to the ground. He walked toward the glowing statue, holding the child outward in front of him. The rest of the priests followed in lines. When he came within a distance that the heat caused perspiration to form on his face, he stopped. Two of the other robed priests picked a long pole from the earth, revealing an end that resembled a claw. After the first priest placed the babe in the claw, the other two raised the pole until the claw slipped the infant into the red-hot hands of the idol. The drums continued their frenzy, trying, but failing, to overpower the screams of the terrified, tortured babe as it burned alive. Nava stared in mindless shock as the babe turned red then black, but when the burnt scent wafting in the wind reached her, she wrapped her arms around her middle and pitched forward. Two of the other women caught her. Hadara motioned Tobias forward.

"Take us away from here. Immediately." She waved to others crowding the back portion of the area. "Come, you can see better from here."

After a short pause, no one looking toward the flat surface could tell Hadara and her group had left, Tobias carrying a limp Nava.

The silent sense of depression pressed on the inhabitants of the women's quarters. Nava sat curled on a divan hugging herself, eyes staring into nothing. Simeon's family moved through rooms as quietly as possible as they tempted Hadara, Nava, Tobias, and Philmon with food and drink. Gloom permeated the air and mood.

"Please, we appreciate your concern and that of your family, Simeon, but none of us can face food." Hadara shivered. "I keep seeing and hearing and …" she shuddered again, "the smell, that horrible smell."

With a bow of his head, Simeon replied, "I should go to the other part of the palace and discover what's happening."

Hadara nodded. "Yes, we should have all the notice possible."

Mazza entered from the back part of the quarters. "Simeon, your son Dan awaits in the kitchen."

"Mother, that smell will stay with all of us forever, but we have to face the future." Tobias stared from the doors to the garden below. "Barrack and King

Ahaz have become monsters, and Tzabar has probably given them ideas." He grasped the edge of one of the open doors. "I don't understand how men can live without any redeeming qualities, but they have none, not one."

Philmon leaned forward where he sat. "Yes, we must face the future. You realize that all the nobles will want to follow the king, do you not?"

Hadara squeezed her eyes shut. "They will, and Tzabar will be one of the first." She opened her eyes. "We must get Aaron and his assistant here immediately. We also must move up having Simeon's family disperse to the new location." She rose to her feet and moved to stand by the divan where Nava huddled. "She will not be safe at the farm now."

Tobias turned to face his mother. "She will be safe if we can get her to my grandparents in Egypt."

"We have preparations for you to travel, but not for her, too." Hadara smoothed Nava's hair. "I don't know how we can make arrangements, which must be finished within days."

Philmon said, "We must find a way. Perhaps Aaron can help."

"Mistress," Simeon rushed into the chamber, "one of my sons says Tzabar comes, and he is angry."

Tobias turned from the doors and ran to the divan where Nava half lay. He scooped her into his arms and continued to the hall leading to the lower level and safety.

Nava squealed in shock and wrapped her arms around his neck. "What ... where ..."

"We must hide. Hurry, Philmon. Amzi, you better come, too."

Philmon placed Hadara on the divan Nava had left. "He may have seen a woman faint. Lie here." He placed a cushion behind her head. "Someone fan her, and get wet cloths on her face." He whirled on his heel and trotted after the other men.

By the time the banging on the doors to the main part of the palace echoed through the quarters, Mazza sat in a chair beside Hadara, wiping her charge's face with a wet cloth. Zema, one of Simeon's daughters, waved a palm frond fan over her mistress. Hadara reclined, eyes partially closed, her breathing ragged.

"Did you dare leave before the end of the ceremony?" Tzabar raged as he stomped into the room. "I saw a woman faint. Who was she? How dare you embarrass me?" His questions spewed one on top of the other.

Mazza tilted her head to stare at the red-faced man above her. "Yes, the heat caused a woman to faint. Can you not see my mistress is poorly?"

Tzabar's jaws bunched as he gritted his teeth. His fists rose as if to pound on something or someone. "She caused me to look weak!"

"How could I cause you to look weak?" Hadara forced herself to speak softly, breathlessly. "If anything, the others would think you a man who deserved their support for having such a wife. Most would understand."

The man paced from one side of the chamber to the other before returning to glare at his wife. "If I hear one joke, one comment to the contrary, you will pay the price." He visually searched the room. "Where is Tobias? Where is *my* son?"

Hadara pushed Mazza's hand away and pushed herself to a sitting position. "I have no idea. He left here after escorting us home, left in a hurry."

"He is never around."

"I know he has duties preparing for the army. He works hard to be deserving." She wiped her forehead with the back of one trembling hand. "If I see him, I'll tell him to contact you."

"You had better." Tzabar turned sharply and strode toward the still opened doors to the vestibule. "Your brother sent word. He will be here three days after the Sabbath, not the Sabbath tomorrow, but the next one." He slammed both doors behind him.

The women froze in place until they heard the main doors groan shut with their regular thump. Hadara exhaled the breath she held. "All right, he won't do anything until after Hemut and his entourage leave. We have maybe a month." She removed the cloth from Mazza's hand and patted her perspiring face. "That's not long enough, but we have more time than I feared we had. Now, we must have a meeting of everyone involved."

Noticing Simeon joined them, she told him, "We must let everyone know that nothing is to be told or in any way revealed to my brother's wife, Sira, if she comes with Hemut. She doesn't mean to do so, but she cannot keep anything secret."

"I summoned the priest and his assistant. Tobias has taken Nava to her sleeping chamber." The chatz'ran forgot himself enough to drop into a chair without permission. "Mistress, she does not do well. I asked my daughter Zema to tend to her."

Mazza joined Hadara on the divan. "We must now work to save everyone in danger."

Tobias entered the chamber in time to hear Mazza's comment. "I have a solution for removing Nava from here. Have Aaron marry us, and she will go to Egypt as my wife. She will be protected several ways."

Hadara rose to face her son. "Marry? You would marry her?"

"Eema, why would you object? You love her, and so do I."

"But, you love her as if she were your sister. How can you build a marriage, a family on that?"

He moved to her side and wrapped her in his arms. "Eema, many good marriages have begun with less. The problem will not be whether I can grow to love her as my wife, but whether she can overcome what Tzabar did and accept me as her husband." He laughed half to himself. "Yes, that will be the problem. She's beautiful inside and out. She is intelligent and has learned so much that she is never boring. I enjoy talking with her. I'll be the fortunate one."

"But, I want you happy, my son. I want you to experience more than what you have seen between Tzabar and me."

"Ah, Eema, with the love Nava has for everyone, I'm sure she will find enough for me."

"I know you already are her hero." Hadara reached up to touch his cheek. "But, I hope that's enough to lead to true love."

Chapter 8

Jerusalem :: four weeks later

Hadara and her brother stood on the balcony behind the sculptured screen. Below in the square, people milled and greeted one another. A pickpocket "accidentally" bumped into rich merchants but avoided the soldiers, who eyed the women as the breeze flattened robes to bodies.

"If your husband, soon to be not your husband, had not kept me so busy, I would have visited earlier." Hemut whispered close to his sister's ear and in Egyptian.

Without turning her head toward him, Hadara replied, softly and in the same language, "I know. Tzabar has tried to keep us apart."

"Umm, yes. Yesterday he took me to a ceremony, had me sit with the king and his nobles, as if I should be honored." Hemut's eyes squinted, and his mouth tightened. "They had a bronze idol with a vat sitting under its outstretched arms, a vat of fire. The priests threw a half-grown boy into the fire." He shuddered. "Horrific." He dropped his head.

Raising his head, Hemut changed the subject. "The main house on the farm is finished. I left two of my men to guard it. They will find someone local to marry and will settle close by you." He chuckled. "Yes, the tunnels you insisted we dig from the main house to the other farm houses are ready, and the hidden rooms." He glanced over his shoulder at Tobias and Philmon, who stood with their backs to the balcony, guarding his visit with Hadara. "Did you receive your gift of fine linen from our parents?"

"Yes, and I have enjoyed it immensely. Thank you for bringing it to me." She touched his sleeve. "Did you check the oasis on your way? Is everything all right?"

"I did. All is ready for Tobias and his friends. The nomad tribe has left for their yearly journey south, and only the old woman and her goats are there. I left two horses. My men built a strong enclosure for the animals and a stone barn. All is ready."

She bowed her head. "There has been a change. Aaron performed the marriage blessing and prayer over Tobias and Nava. They must both go to our parents for safety. Can you manage to transport supplies for both to the oasis and inform Father?"

"Married? You approve of this?" Hemut gave a harrumph. "Of course, you did, or it would not have happened. Yes, we can gather all the supplies. I have to obtain a few more camels to take back with me; loading them will be easy enough." He turned to face her. "How soon can you have a list?"

Hadara removed a parchment from beneath her robe. "Here is what will be needed. Nava carries a child, and both she and the babe will have needs. Tobias and she must stay at the oasis until after the birth." As she placed the list in her brother's hand, she added, "Please do not ask about the babe. Nava is innocent in all ways."

"I probably know enough already. The poor child." Hemut slid the parchment under his robe.

"Another favor, brother."

"I will do anything I can, little sister."

"I need Philmon and Amzi to ride with you as far as the oasis. Tzabar must not find them or take them."

Hemut bowed his head. "Have them dressed as camel riders with their supplies and necessities in packs tomorrow night. They are to make their ways in the middle of the night, unnoticed, to my camp outside the south gate. We need to be gone before dawn. I will be sure my guards expect them." He shrugged. "Their accommodations will not be the best, but we will spirit them away."

"They must not fall into Tzabar's hands. Neither must Tobias and Nava, and especially not the babe." She laid her head on his arm. "We will probably not get another chance to talk. Tzabar will interrogate you and me about what we could talk about for so long."

"Mother's note gave you all the family news, so that's what we discussed: the births, deaths, marriages of our huge family. I, of course, was most bored having to be the bearer of such mundane things." He hugged her. "The time will come when we can visit openly. The evil king cannot live forever even if young, and Tzabar certainly won't."

He turned to leave but stopped to face her again. "By the way, I'll be taking Tzabar's request to put you aside to our parents. They will make the demands you suggested. Therefore, you have perhaps seven months to put all in order."

"Oh, I will not wait until the last moment. I will disappear within five months or less. Take care, Hemut, and give my love to our parents and to Sira."

Hemut touched her cheek before he marched across the main chamber and out the doors to the vestibule, pausing only long enough to clasp his nephew's shoulder on the way by.

After Hemut left, Hadara sent Philmon to find Amzi. "Tell him what must be done. You both have little time to gather what you must take with you and to leave. I count on the two of you to finish preparations for Tobias and Nava."

Philmon bowed his head. "We won't fail you." He strode from the room, amazingly silent for a man his size.

"Mother, Eema, I couldn't help but hear. At least no one else speaks Egyptian except Philmon and me. So, the king and his nobles sacrifice children older than babes. I hope his queen did indeed spirit away their older son." Tobias placed an arm around his mother's shoulders and led her to a divan.

"I have heard for many years the queen did send her older son to safety. In fact, Simeon said Tzabar and Barrack talked about how unfair that Ahaz can't follow through with his sacrifices." She rubbed her eyes with fingertips. "How can any parent kill their children?"

As they sat beside each other, he motioned to Mazza. "Please bring my mother some food and drink."

"No, Tobias, I cannot eat."

Mazza ignored her charge's protest. "Will you join her?"

"Perhaps something to drink. I need to take part in the military practice before someone besides Tzabar searches for me."

Hadara smiled at her son. "If I must eat, then so must you. Besides, Rachel, Simeon's wife, is an excellent cook."

After Mazza left to bring food, Hadara blew a breath through pursed lips. "We must get you and Nava away from this place of evil quickly. Tzabar will throw you or Amzi into the fire as soon as he can find one of you. Amzi did a sinful thing, but he doesn't deserve such a death." She closed her eyes. "I use the word evil so much, but no other word describes the king and his nobles."

"You have made arrangements. Amzi and Philmon will be gone before daylight day after tomorrow. Hemut will be sure they reach the oasis."

"We must now keep you and Nava from Tzabar's sight. You can come and go, but she cannot. What needs be done must be within a week after Hemut leaves."

The echoing boom at the outer doors brought Tobias to his feet. "I will take Nava to the secret room by the kitchen." He sped down the hall.

By the time Tzabar slammed the doors between the chamber and the vestibule against the walls, Hadara sat at the table. She frowned at her husband.

"Can you not enter politely?"

"May Moleck judge you, woman. Where is my son?" He pounded a fist on the table, missing her hand by less than a whisper.

"Mistress? Should I bring food for the master?" Mazza asked from behind them.

Tzabar whirled, a scowl deepening the lines in his face. "Why would I eat with her?" He leaned on the table. Staring at Hadara, he demanded, "Where is my son? I know he was here."

"Yes, but he left after Hemut did. He said something about needing to do military practice before the commander searched for him."

The man straightened to his full height. "He must not anger his commander.

Perhaps I can find him through the army." He stomped from the room. After a pause, Mazza and Hadara heard the groan and thud of the outer doors closing.

The women looked at the still open doors to the vestibule and then at each other.

"Hadara, this ordeal becomes too dangerous. He will destroy you and the children."

"I know, Mazza. I know too well." Hadara closed her eyes, folded her arms on the table, and laid her head on them. "In a week or less, Tobias and Nava will be gone. We will then begin to move those we trust to the farm." She raised her head. "If we can avoid him a bit longer, all will be safe." She heaved a deep sigh. "If …"

Chapter 9

Jerusalem

Two days after Hemut, with Philmon and Amzi in tow, left Jerusalem for Thebes by way of the oasis, Tzabar invaded the women's quarters again. "Where is he? Where is Tobias?" His roar filled the rooms.

Hadara glanced at him before returning to her sewing. "I have not seen him for days, not since before you last asked the same question."

"The commander has not seen him. The other young men training with him have not seen him. Where is he?"

Throwing the material to one side, Hadara jerked to her feet, facing him. "Our son has disappeared? Where else have you searched? Could someone have injured him, taken him? Why are you yelling in my chamber rather than trying to find him?" She wrenched away when he reached for her.

"You really do not know where he is, do you?" Tzabar studied her. "You don't know."

"What?" Hadara stared at him. "No, I do not know where Tobias is."

Tzabar frowned. "Perhaps he left with Hemut."

"Do you believe he left without telling me? Do you believe he would allow me to worry?" She shook her head. "Please leave." She walked to the open doors to the balcony.

When the outer doors finished their normal groaning and thudding, she turned back to the room. Mazza, who entered from the hall, applauded. "Perfect performance, child."

"However, he now suspects Hemut, and I can do nothing except wait." Hadara paced from balcony to balcony. "Philmon and Amzi must be safe. I do pray to the one true God that all will be safe." She wrung her hands as she paced. "Tobias and Nava leave in less than five nights. Should she travel so far? Will she and the babe be fine? Will Tobias …?"

From behind, Nava answered, "Please, Hadara, we will be safe, and I will do all within my power to see that Tobias has a good life." Nava watched her adopted mother's agitation. "The babe and I will travel as far as necessary to escape Tzabar and the king and Barrack." She walked to hug the woman. "You were cursed when you found me and brought me into your home."

"Never!" Hadara shook her head until her hair slipped from its binding. "You brought joy to us. The cruelty and pain were not *your* doing. We know who is to blame, and it is not you."

Nava's smile wobbled on the edges, and her eyes appeared a bit watery, but she did smile. "Now, does anyone know how Tobias is and what he is doing?"

Mazza snorted.

"Mazza, are you all right?" Nava asked.

The retainer nodded. "He is allowing his beard and hair to grow wild and unkempt, as if a poor man, a laborer. Therefore, he stays out of sight."

"Ahh, a way to be missed and overlooked." Nava yawned. "Makes sense." She yawned once more. "I need to sleep yet again."

Hadara sat in the women's garden, enjoying the crisp evening air and a few moments of peace. Nava and Tobias sat in the arbor, out of sight, whispering, discussing their flight. Just four nights and they would be gone. She realized she might never see them again, or ever hold the child she considered her grandchild.

"But they will live," she whispered.

"Mistress?" Simeon leaned over the half-wall around the balcony above.

"I am here, Simeon. Should I come up?"

Simeon didn't wait but ran down the steps, a parchment in hand. "This is arrived by a messenger from your brother. Another messenger brought word to Tzabar." He handed her the message. "Is there enough light? I can get a torch."

"I believe I can see well enough." Hadara unrolled the parchment. She read quietly for a short time before she gasped. "Tzabar sent men to search Hemut's caravan." She held the scroll to her breast. "Philmon and Amzi had left a short time before the men arrived. Hemut didn't trust Tzabar and had scouts watching their path through the valleys and hills. He had warning someone followed, someone who rode fast to catch them." Her hands trembled as she lowered the parchment. "The messenger to Tzabar is probably notifying him they didn't find Tobias."

She read the remainder of her brother's report and lay the missive in her lap. "Tobias," she called. "Please join me, Nava, too."

After the couple sat on the ground at her feet and Simeon still stood beside the bench, Hadara shared Hemut's message. "He ended by telling me he had sent the notice of Tzabar's putting me aside by a faster route, carried by a trusted man. Within a month, I should receive the announcement by Tzabar that I have six months to remove myself from his house and protection."

"Where will you go?" Nava moved from the ground to beside Hadara on the bench.

Hadara patted her hand. "I have a place that few know about. The day we met, I was 'traveling' to different areas, but I had inspected the farm my parents bought me. In case anyone followed, he wouldn't know what spot was important."

"Mistress, we need my sons to disappear from the army. If you will allow, I'll set up what needs to be done." Simeon bowed before striding to a door into the lower level of the women's quarters.

The others watched him leave. "That man does more behind the scenes than we know." Tobias stood and offered a hand to help his mother and then his wife. Hadara touched his scraggly whiskered face. "You no longer look like my well-groomed son."

Tobias shrugged one shoulder. "'Tis better than burning in a vat of fire for Moleck."

Chapter 10

Planning, planning

Once in the lower level, Simeon hurried toward a secret door to his workroom in the main part of the palace. "Father?"

Simeon stopped and whirled to face his son Dan.

"A problem in the town you should know," Dan answered the unasked question of his father's quirked eyebrow. "Several rich men have had their houses breeched and gold and precious jewels stolen."

"Ahh, yes, that will help me, give me the reason I need to have Tzabar request more soldiers to guard him and his house." Simeon smiled. "It is time to mix different soldiers and names and for you and your brothers to disappear." He clasped his son's shoulder. "Prepare the others." He turned back to his route. "Everyone knows what to do. You and your family will go first."

After moving the small stone that covered a peephole, he discovered one of the other servants sitting in the workroom, dozing in a chair. *I'll try a different track.* He walked to another door that opened into a hall beside his workroom. Seeing the empty hall, he slipped from the women's quarters into the main part of the palace. When he opened the door in the workroom, the servant scrambled to his feet.

"Sorry, sir, but the master wanted to see you, and if you had left for the night, I was to wait until you returned."

"Please let him know I will join him shortly. I received some news that concerns me. I need to notify him, but I need to finish some items for him to sign first." Simeon walked to a cabinet against one wall. "I will take but long enough to finish what is needed."

After the other man left, Simeon took parchment sheets from the cabinet and laid them on the worktable. *Now to add the finishing wording. I'm glad I pre-planned.* As soon as he wrote a few words and numbers to each of the sheets, he blew sand on them to help dry the ink. He placed the writing reeds and pot of ink into a chest before he gently picked up the parchment sheets and left the room.

Simeon found Tzabar reclining on a divan in one of his favorite chambers, a woman servant feeding him bits of fruit. As soon as the man spied his head of household in the doorway, he pushed the girl aside and leaped to his feet.

"Where have you been? I needed you here."

Simeon lowered his eyes to the floor. "I always leave for my home after you dine, master."

"Of course, of course, but I have received grave news. The rich are being attacked by rabble."

"Yes, sir, that news reached me. I hurried back to provide letters for you to sign demanding more protection. I feel that another twenty soldiers might be required." Simeon handed the parchment sheets to Tzabar. "You just need to make your mark and apply your seal to each sheet. Do you wish me to read them to you first?"

Tzabar waved one hand and reached for the sheets with the other. "No, no, I need that protection immediately." He searched Simeon's face. "Will another twenty be enough?"

"Yes, master, with the twenty you now have in service." He mentally subtracted his sons from the twenty-three men assigned to be on duty to protect Tzabar. "Forty men should be enough." He paused. "You may want to choose one to be in command once you have all here."

"Yes, yes, you are correct as usual." He returned the sheets to Simeon. "Take care of this. All of it. I haven't time."

Simeon bowed his head. "The commander will not be available until morning, but I shall be sure he is notified first thing after sunrise."

Tzabar ignored him as he reached for the servant girl.

Simeon hurried to his workroom and through the secret door behind a cabinet and back to the lower level of the women's quarters. He strode to the kitchen, where his wife and three sons waited. "Dan, take this sheet to the commander first thing tomorrow. Inform him that I will meet the men he sends by the gate to the back garden. After you deliver the messages, find a place to change out of your uniform and into peasant clothing, but you and your brothers need to keep your uniforms, just hidden. Then go directly to the farm. Have your wife and children leave before you do, before the sun rises."

"I will have Martha finish packing, and we shall take packs to the cart we have hidden. My oldest son can help. We will be ready to leave before sunup." Dan hugged his mother. "We will see you again soon."

Watching her son leave, Rachel wiped tears from her face. "Simeon, are we doing what we should?"

"Do you want us to stay in service to the man who destroyed our Medra?" Simeon held her in his arms. "We miss her so much, and each time I see this monster or hear his voice, the urge to kill him nearly overcomes me."

She nodded her head against his shoulder. "You are right. We must leave and help the mistress and her children escape, also." She straightened. "Even if we die in the attempt, we will remain until the last."

"Now, we sleep. We must arise while night still covers our world. We have much to do tomorrow."

Simeon watched rose streaks peek above the walls of surrounding buildings before visiting the barracks and speaking with the man he chose. The two then waited for the new troops to arrive. The back gate opened into a wide alleyway between the main palace and the barracks the troops used when not on duty. The alley could be closed off at each end with solid metal gates, but one end now allowed unhindered entrance for the expected men; the chosen guard stood beside the gates in order to close them once the new men entered. The smells of a city, with over a thousand inhabitants crowded together without a means for removing wastes except by human shoveling and hauling, caused Simeon to cover his mouth and nose with a soft cloth.

The sound of stomping feet and creaking leather signaled the arrival of the troops before they appeared in the open gates. The twenty men marched to where the chatz'ran waited. They filled the space between the buildings, and the guard at the gates had little room to swing them shut. Once he did, he slipped by the rows of men to stand beside Simeon.

"Men, Kannel will be in charge of all guards for Tzabar. He will oversee you and the other nineteen men assigned here. Behind you is where you will sleep and eat. You are to enter through the doors across from where he and I stand. A large room for your use when off duty is also used for times troops need to be addressed and directions given. At one end of the barracks building is an enclosed ground where maneuvers and exercises will be held. Welcome to your new place of duty." Simeon turned to the man beside him. "Please take over, Kannel. Be sure you notify the others of their duties and see that the two groups become one."

Kannel thumped his fist to his chest. "It will be done."

As Simeon entered the door that led to the back garden of the palace, the new officer informed the troops, "Turn about and enter the barracks. Stand in formation inside."

"We will soon know if this part of the plan works. Hopefully no one will compare numbers," Simeon mumbled as he hurried across the garden to the palace.

Chapter11

Jerusalem

Days passed as Hadara filled the hours with regular duties: sewing, checking supplies for the women's quarters, and working with Simeon, Tobias, and Aaron to finalize the plans for the escapes. She heard nothing from Tzabar, except for occasional unexpected visits demanding to know where Tobias hid, and the ordeal caused her anxiety to increase. She stood on the outside balcony and started at the king's palace on the other side of the square. "What evil is being planned inside your walls," she whispered before she shivered. "So many babes and children, even grown children, have died because of your obsession with Moleck." She raised her eyes to the sky. *Why does the one true God not save us?* She shook her head. "Ahaz refuses to listen, and the whole country suffers," she mumbled.

She turned back into the chamber closing the doors to the balcony behind her. Through a long but secret route, she received word that Philmon and Amzi awaited Tobias and Nava in the hidden oasis. She knew Hemut and his caravan arrived in Egypt safely. Aaron told her the next steps for Tobias and Nava to leave.

"One more night and day and I will be here alone, except for Mazza and the remainder of Simeon's family." She stopped in the middle of the chamber. "Only one of their sons, Rachel, and Simeon left." She walked across the chamber to the doors leading to the inside balcony.

She breathed the fragrance of the flowering plants in the garden below. "Why hasn't Tzabar said anything about putting me aside? That's not like him."

"I may have an answer."

Hadara whirled, her hand grasping her chest. Her knees weakened, and she nearly fell before she realized Simeon stood behind her. "I ... I didn't know ..."

The head of household clasped her arm and led her to a divan. "Mistress, I am sorry. I thought you saw me and you were talking to me."

"No ... no..." she gasped. "I didn't see you. I ... I thought I was alone. I must be more aware. What if someone else heard me talk to myself?"

"We are all conscious of the need to keep others away and to warn you."

Hadara put trembling hands to her mouth. "I am not as strong as I thought."

"Mistress, you are very strong, but so much is unknown, which makes us all ready to run up walls." He smiled. "You should see Rachel react to fear."

She dropped her hands into her lap and gazed at him. "Rachel? Rachel wouldn't be afraid of the king himself."

"Perhaps, but it would depend on what he tried to do." Simeon laughed half to himself.

"You said you might have an answer?" Hadara changed the subject with no pause between.

He nodded. "Yes, I overheard Barrack and Tzabar discussing how to find more sacrifices for Moleck. They worry about losing influence with King Ahaz." He moved a chair close to the divan and sat. "Barrack already promised his child, once born, and he, apparently, now searches for his first family. I'll find out what I can about that later because they began to discuss Tzabar putting you aside so he can take a more, uh, cooperative wife for children."

"I'm so thankful he fears my family and for the procedure he must follow to 'put me away' legally." Hadara rubbed her hand across her forehead. "What fools those men are." Hadara slapped a palm on the cushion beside her.

"Yes, fools," Simeon replied. "Tzabar told Barrack that he had no results finding either of his sons. Therefore, he would notify you of the conditions given by your parents. He assured Barrack that you would be gone in six months, perhaps less if he could manage a good 'accident' in less time."

She bowed her head. "As I feared. He will try to kill me." Hearing a footfall behind her, she twisted her head to see Mazza enter from the hall. "Simeon was giving me the latest news, Mazza. We may have to change our schedule so we can all be gone sooner than we planned."

"Yes, we don't want to be 'gone' permanently because Tzabar has us all murdered." Mazza walked to sit beside her charge. "I will see that everything that can be arranged is. After Tobias and Nava leave, we can push forth with all our efforts."

Simeon rose from the chair. "I must return before I am missed. We will be able to work more on the plans for ourselves after tomorrow night."

"Yes, after the children are gone." Hadara stared at the ceiling far above her. "Not knowing for months whether they are safe or not will be difficult. They have a dangerous trip ahead of them. We must ask the Lord God to watch over them."

A pounding at the doors to the main part of the palace caused all to jump. Simeon glanced toward the doors to the vestibule before running toward the hall. "He must not catch me here."

Mazza moved the chair he vacated back to its usual position as Hadara rose to face the person who would enter the room, sure that only Tzabar would be so insistent. As well, no one else visited from the main part of the house.

Red-faced and scowl in place, Tzabar, as usual, slammed the doors open and against the walls. He staggered toward Hadara, listing to one side and then the other.

She straightened her shoulders, ready to face the drunken man.

"I will soon ... soon be rid of you. Your parents and I reached a ..." His words slurred. "What ... called something. Doesn't matter. In six months, you be gone." His frown transformed into a smirk. "I have to give you the dowry but don't care. I will get a young wife. I will have children. I can please Ahaz. He wants sacrifices. If not to Moleck ... in army."

He laughed. "You caused me trouble, but no more." He started toward the vestibule but paused. Holding onto the door frame, he demanded, "What have you done ... with, with my son? I will find him some day. I will. You can't stop ... me using son to get ... more important." He tottered out the doors, grabbing at walls to keep from falling. The regular groan and thud announced his departure.

"You will never find him if I can do anything." Hadara dropped to the divan and covered her face with her hands. "How can such wickedness continue?"

"God has turned His face from Judah, as he forewarned. Isaiah warned Ahaz that the one true God would bless him if the king followed Him, but Ahaz turned to Assyria instead."

Hadara's head jerked upward to find Aaron sitting in a chair facing her, his apprentice beside him. "I never hear you because you move so quietly." She studied her hands in her lap. "What then can we do?"

"What you are doing, my child. You know where you'll find safety, and you must continue to believe. Ahaz's days are numbered, and another will take his place in time, one who will follow the one true God."

"I must get everyone who supports me out of here, and I must live long enough to do so before Tzabar can have me killed."

"Yes, I know. I suggest you give Tobias and his wife time to be away, at least to the oasis, before you are gone. You cannot wait longer than that. Tzabar will not give you but perhaps three months." Aaron stood, walked to where she sat, and laid his hands on her head. "Blessed be you, daughter of the one true God." He left as silently as he arrived.

Hadara stared into nothing for several minutes. The same thoughts swirled through her head: How to make Tzabar avoid the women's quarters. How everyone could slip away and no one notice. Simeon insisted he be last to leave. Over and over, her mind replayed the same worries.

"Mistress, will you eat?" Rachel touched her shoulder, breaking her trance.

"I'm not really hungry, Rachel, and please remember to call me Hadara."

"You need to eat, to keep your strength." The woman waved a hand toward the table. "I have fixed dishes you enjoy. I have already taken a meal to Tobias and to Nava where they hide below. Mazza will join you shortly."

Hadara tried to smile. "Thank you, Rachel. I will do my best to eat. Your cooking is tempting." She sat at the table and picked up a piece of meat. "Smells good." She replaced the meat on the platter.

"Eat, child, eat." Mazza joined her. "We may not feel hungry, but we must store energy." She began eating. After she chewed and swallowed, she pointed toward the food in front of Hadara. "Eat, then we shall discuss what to do next."

"Aaron said we must leave as quickly as we can after Tobias and Nava do."

"Eat and then we talk."

Hadara placed a bite in her mouth and choked when Simeon ran down the hall shouting, "King Ahaz desecrated the temple with Moleck."

Mazza thumped Hadara's back until the younger woman waved a hand. "Enough." She faced Simeon. "What happened?"

The man struggled for breath, panting after his run. "He had an idol built … one like that outside of the walls, with a vat under the outstretched hands … like the one before … he placed in the temple." He breathed deeply. "They sacrificed … son, a full-grown man, this morn."

Before anyone could react to that announcement, pounding at the main doors caused all to freeze. Simeon whispered, "I will wait out of sight." He hurried to the hall, disappearing before doors to the vestibule slammed against the chamber walls.

Before Tzabar could speak, Hadara screamed, "Did you sacrifice my son? Did you? Is that why you continue your demands I produce him? You enjoy torturing me, so you keep 'searching' for him. You had him, didn't you? You bound him and threw him into the flames." She trembled but strode to where he stood. His eyes widened in surprise as hers narrowed to slits. "You … you leave here now and never return. These rooms will be yours before long, but I *never* want to see you again." She whirled away. "Send the dowry, but don't *you* come back. I will send a message when I am gone."

"What nonsense do you speak, woman? I still search— "

Hadara turned her back to him. "Lies, all lies. Leave me, now."

Shaking his head, Tzabar did as she demanded. After the groan and moan and thud of the main doors closing, Hadara slumped onto a divan.

Mazza exhaled her held breath. "You were magnificent, child."

"You so surprised him, he might not return until you are gone, one way or another." Simeon rejoined the women. "I may be able to help reinforce his avoiding you."

Hadara wrapped her arms around her body. "I had to do something. I had to keep him away until everyone is gone." She drew in and exhaled a deep breath. "Perhaps I should have been braver much sooner. The shock on his face." She laughed. "Oh, I enjoyed how he looked when I shouted at him."

"He would definitely kill you now, if he hadn't already planned to." Simeon shook his head as he walked away.

The morning light peeked above the walls of the garden. The air began to warm as the night's chill retreated. Hadara wiped tears from her cheeks with her fingers. *They are gone. I pray the one true God will keep them safe.* As planned, Tobias and Nava had slipped from the palace during the night with no good-bye or final words. *I am left with friends, all who deserve to escape this place of evil with me.*

She rose from the bench and marched toward the door to the lower level. "Soon ... we will be gone soon. Much quicker than we first thought."

Chapter 12

The escape to the oasis :: a few hours earlier

Darkness spread over the city while Nava followed Tobias. They slid along empty streets, hugging walls and scurrying across open roadways and areas.

"Oooph." Nava doubled over, arms around her middle. Tobias placed an arm around her and helped her to straighten.

He bent his head close to her ear. "What happened? Are you hurt?

"Just a bit of pain. I'm all right," She whispered back. Her heart beat so loudly she feared others could hear.

Tobias took her hand as they continued in the darkness. When they reached the buildings along the outer wall, she saw an open door, a lighter spot against the blackness, which they entered. The door closed behind them.

"Hurry, hurry," a deep voice urged them. "We cannot leave the stones out of the wall for long."

"We appreciate your helping us." Tobias replied. He and Nava, covered in dark cloaks from their heads to their toes, made sure the faint light cast by a small candle didn't reflect on their faces.

Nava grasped Tobias' hand, squeezing until her fingers hurt.

"Here," a man pointed toward another room. "We must snuff the light before we open the other door. In there you will find the hole. As soon as you climb through, we will mortar the stones back in place." The man hesitated. "The wall is thick and is about half a man's height from the ground outside, so you," he pointed toward Tobias, "should back through the hole and drop to the ground with your feet first." He nodded at Nava. "The smaller can go head first to be helped out the other side. We begin replacing stones as quickly as you leave the opening, so hurry."

"We will manage." Tobias dipped his head to whisper close to Nava, "Close your eyes until you hear the door open. I'll lead you."

She closed her eyes and listened. As soon as she heard the shuffle of a door moving across the floor, she opened her eyes to a dark room. A slight sheen of lighter gray showed beyond the now opened door. She walked through, her hand safe in Tobias'.

"Be careful. We could not remove enough stones to allow anyone but a child to walk through the hole. Lower your heads and crawl along the bottom edge." The first man helped Tobias and then Nava through the ragged hole in the wall. "May the one true God guide you and be with you."

Nava sensed rather than saw Tobias crawl backwards along the rough stones. The walls pressed around her; she knew his shoulders filled the space as he made his way through the darkness. Nava followed, creeping head first, as quickly as she could without bumping into him. After she reached the end of the tunnel, she felt his hands touch her.

"Put your arms around my neck so I can lift you," he whispered. As soon as Nava's body left the wall, she heard the scrape of stone on stone behind her. She exhaled the breath she held.

The couple hurried over the rough ground and away from the city wall. They followed the slope from the wall toward the valley, taking nearly the same path as they had when King Ahaz held the sacrifice of his son. Close to the half-way mark, they angled past the spot where the platform sat. They walked farther east before heading toward the valley bottom. Nava stumbled over rocks and indentions in the grooved land. Finally, in the moonless darkness, her foot twisted enough she lost her balance and fell on her hands and knees. Nava swallowed a cry of pain.

Tobias knelt beside her. "How badly are you hurt?" he whispered as he helped her to a sitting position. "I can't see, so you need to tell me."

"Probably skinned my hands and knees." She shrugged, which he sensed rather than observed. Nava fought back tears. She held her left palm out. "I think something pierced my hand, and that does hurt."

Tobias touched her hand and smoothed his fingers over her palm, avoiding the dark spot in the base. "Yes, I can tell. Can you bear it? I don't have any way to clean a wound or to bandage it."

"I ... I can wait. I certainly wouldn't want to bleed over these *lovely* clothes." Her forced quiet chuckle showed more fear than she wanted.

"Still have that sense of humor. Good." He slid an arm around her waist and stood, pulling her beside him.

"Come. The cart and ass wait for us in the olive grove. If you squint your eyes, you can see a darker area below." Tobias kept his arm around her.

Nava stepped gingerly down the slope, wanting to run to the trees. "What if— "

"No 'what if,'" he interrupted. "The guards look outward. They don't worry about anyone leaving, just someone coming." He glanced at her head so close to his shoulder. "Most drink too much wine and aren't even awake."

"If I don't need to be concerned, why is my heart nearly jumping out of my chest?" she whispered back.

"We are beginning an adventure and our life together. We will be fine, even if we struggle." Tobias hugged her. "Now let's find that large stone in the middle of the grove."

As the moon rose lighting their way, Nava felt a slight relief when they passed the first line of trees. She leaned against Tobias as they walked several cubits toward the center, finally finding the stone. But, they found no Aaron waiting and no cart.

No, no. We can't be forgotten. Nava bit her lip to stop from screaming aloud.

Tobias called in an undertone, "Aaron?"

A tall man stepped from behind a tree. Nava gasped and hid behind Tobias, who reached under his robe for his sword.

"Wait, it's just me." Simeon's son Dan reached out, palm up.

"You scared us half to death." Tobias clasped Dan's forearm. "What's happened? Where's Aaron, the cart?" He moved to bring Nava beside him.

"Soldiers have been scouring the countryside for an escaped 'spy' and are now on the road between Bethlehem and Jerusalem. The cart would cause too many questions."

Nava leaned against Tobias. "What do we do?"

Dan answered, "We take the back way to an abandoned barn, half cave. Aaron, Hosa, and the cart wait there. Come, stay close."

The three made their way through the trees. Nava grabbed Tobias' hand with her uninjured one when she stumbled once more. He held it firmly as they continued along a rocky path. They trod below the skyline of the ridge and road, dropping and hugging the valley's rocks at each sound. As they began their trek after one such stop, Nava fell, only Tobias' hand kept her from hitting the ground. He lowered her and knelt beside her.

"Nava, did you trip?"

"No. Can't walk … anymore." Her eyes searched his face with its unfamiliar scraggly beard. "You go."

Tobias glanced over his shoulder at Dan. "How much farther?"

"We cross the road about ten long steps ahead. The barn is over a ridge on the other side."

Tobias turned his attention back to his young wife. He caressed the side of her face. "You've been brave and have come far— " Sounds above caused him to stop. He pulled his cloak over them both and covered her body with his.

"Thought I done heard voices." The course voice added a string of curse words. "This duty patrolling for some Moleck-hating spy is getting old."

"Feel the same, but I don't want to go in the fire. This be better than that," a different voice replied. "Don't know what you be hearing, but no spies here. Let's go back. By the time we reach the barracks, our shift be over."

"Good idea."

The three below continued to cower against the rocks until they heard the soldiers' footsteps retreat into silence.

Tobias straightened and whispered to Nava, "Are you ready to go a bit farther?"

"I'll … I'll try." She struggled to her feet but bent over with a groan.

Tobias grabbed her and swung her into his arms. "Sweet, what's wrong? Is it the babe?" He felt her head nod against his neck. "Let's get you to shelter." He looked toward Dan. "Go!"

The two men covered the remaining space to the crossing spot as fast as possible over the rough ground. When they climbed the rest of the incline, Dan pushed Tobias' back to aid him upward. They rushed across the road, Nava holding tight to Tobias, her head snug between his neck and shoulder. As they began downward on the other side, Dan moved in front of Tobias, bracing his back against the younger man's arm, slowing their descent.

"Just over this next ridge," he whispered. "We're nearly there."

"I hurt," Nava murmured.

Tobias brushed his lips over her head. "Hold on just a bit longer. We'll soon be there."

Several minutes later, the three began their descent over the ridge. Dan gave a low whistle. "Letting Aaron know we are here."

A faint light showed to their left. Dan led the way to an opening in the rock wall which blocked a small cave. Tobias carried Nava inside. She raised her head. An ass chomped on hay in a stall to one side. Hosa moved behind them to close the door to block both light and chill. A small fire burned in a pot in a corner. The warmth and smell of the fire and the animal deadened the chill inside and in her.

"What is wrong?" Aaron asked as he piled straw and spread a cloth over the pile, creating a bed. "Here, lay Nava so we can see if she's hurt."

Tobias laid her on the makeshift bed, removed his cloak, and spread it over her. "Nava, what happened? Are you hurting still?"

"I, uh, I became too tired, I think." She closed her eyes as Tobias loosened her cloak. "Just so tired, and then the babe began to kick, and I started to hurt."

Tobias ran his hand over the mound that covered the baby. He jerked back. "He does kick. That would hurt, I would think."

Nava shrugged. "Not really." A hint of a smile appeared, but it wobbled a bit. "Thank you for carrying us, the babe and me. I do feel better now, except for my hand." She held it up. "Can we remove whatever is stuck?"

Aaron bent over and examined her hand. "You seem to have a piece of stick embedded." He turned to Hosa. "Check and see if the pot of water is hot and bring some to me if it is. Find some strips of cloth in my bag, too." He looked at Nava. "We will remove it once we have the area clean and can bandage it."

After the sun rose above the valley walls, Aaron woke the other men. "Come, let us talk and allow Nava to sleep longer."

The men stepped into the cold morning, wrapped in their robes and mantles. Every breath created a puff in front of their faces. Aaron led the way to the partial walls of another abandoned building. He squatted in the protection of a corner. "At least this shall block some of the wind." After the others joined him, he said, "Nava is weakened and exhausted. I believe we should have you, Tobias, and her stay here at least another day and night." When Dan started to talk, he waved a hand. "I know. I know. The danger would increase, but what happens if she collapses on the road?"

Dan squirmed and stood. "I'll bring more supplies and will stand guard until I can move them to Bethlehem. She can take another rest before they continue."

Tobias nodded. "That might work. We really have no choice if Nava is to make the trip and the babe survive." He turned his head toward Aaron. "What will you and Hosa do now that plans have changed?"

"Hosa will go with Dan for supplies. Then he will accompany you, with Dan, to Bethlehem. I have a small house on the south side of the village. You will go there. I'll leave this morning to arrange everything for you." He rose. "Hosa, before you leave, please cook a meal for us to break our fast. We all need strength."

Chapter 13

From Bethlehem to the Oasis :: four days later

The couple rode in a dilapidated-appearing cart, bumped and jostled, as a lop-eared ass plodded over the rock-hewed road. Tobias piled the cart with bundles of supplies the couple would need for the many days ahead of them. His and Nava's dilapidated appearance matched the cart and the animal.

Aaron told Tobias and Nava before they left him, "If the ass and cart looked good, others would want them. But, few thieves are interested in broken down asses or carts."

Tobias sat on the bench in front, guiding the ass forward. Nava lay on the bundles behind, under the awning provided by worn cloth tacked to posts at each corner of the cart. The heat beat upon them during the day, and the nights turned cold. Dan escorted them for a day and a half but turned back. For the first part of each day, Nava sat beside Tobias, but once they finished their meal, he insisted she rest. She felt more comfortable than sitting on the hard bench, but not much. The broiling air and bumping cart made her head and back hurt. No matter which way she tossed and turned on the bundles, she couldn't find a spot that kept her from pain. She strained to sit.

"Can we stop a bit? I need to … I need some privacy and water."

Tobias pulled on the rein that caused the ass to trot to the side of the road. "There's not much privacy, but you might be able to go behind a boulder." He jumped from the seat to help her from the back of the cart. "I'll get the water." She held the small of her back as she stumbled behind a boulder. By the time she returned to the cart, Tobias held a water skin. She drank, and he poured water on a cloth. "Here, wipe your face with this. You're bright red."

"I … feel so hot." Nava used the wet cloth. "That does feel better. Thank you." She sagged down on the end of the cart. "How much longer until we reach the oasis?"

"The full trip from Bethlehem is four, at most six days. We have three behind us. If we can go longer each night, we could be there in maybe two days."

"Then, let's push longer during the night. Sleeping on the ground is no better than in the cart." She studied him a moment. "You can sleep in the back while I guide the ass some at night."

"We'll see. Now, do you want to ride up front or lie back down?"

"Up front for a while, please."

Another nearly three days of blazing sun passed, and Nava moaned in the back of the cart. Her body felt on fire. Her back ached with piercing pains. Her head pounded. Tobias told her they would reach the cutoff to their destination in about an hour, two at the most. The sound of horses and leather squeaking brought her to a half-sitting position. She peered behind them.

"Tobias, men on horses. They're traveling fast."

"Lie down and moan and sound as miserable as you are. Cover your face with the cloth, even if dry." He pulled the cart as close to the edge as he could.

"Halt!" Authority sounded in the voice of the soldier who first reached the cart.

Tobias pulled back on the reins. "Ya, sir. Be there a problem?" He dropped into a less educated way of speech.

"Where be you from, and where be going?" the man in charge demanded as the other two took positions behind and before the cart.

"Left Bethlehem 'bout five days past. My wife is sick until death and wants to be buried at her home." Tobias motioned behind him. "I been touched already, but you might want a move 'way so you won't be."

Each man moved his horse back two or three steps. The man in charge asked, "You seen a young man on your trip, on a horse or on foot, young and rich looking?"

"Nah. Few people on the road, and when I give warning, they back 'way. Don't feel good myself."

The leader waved his arm. "Let's be gone. I thinks we chasing a ghost." The three men rode away, leaving plumes of dust.

Tobias coughed and covered his face. "Keep down and your face hidden until this dirt dies down." When Nava didn't answer, didn't cough, didn't make any sound, he whirled around on the bench. She lay limp, not moving. He tore the canopy from the post, jumped onto the remaining bundles, and scooped her into his arms. Her head hung backward, the cloth falling from her face. Her chest barely moved as her breaths became shallow gasps.

"Nava, sweet, Nava." He held her to his chest. "No, no, can't stay here. Need help." He brushed his hand over her cheeks. "She's burning." He laid her on the bundles and loosened her robe and gown. "Glad we found that stream." He grabbed the water skin closest to him, opened it, and poured the contents over her body until the skin emptied. He took another and poured it over the rest of her, soaking her garments as much as possible.

He pressed his lips to her forehead. "I'm going to make that ass run as fast as he can. Hold on, my sweet, hold on."

As Aaron told them, the ass wasn't nearly as decrepit as he appeared. As if knowing the emergency, he stretched out and moved the cart forward faster than it had moved before. Right after they turned off the regular road, two men appeared around a ridge. Tobias kept flagging the ass with the reins.

"Slow down, Tobias," Philmon yelled. "That cart will never make the turn into the canyon."

Tobias pulled back on the reins, nearly putting the animal on its rear. "Nava's burning up. I've got to get her some help."

Amzi jumped from his mount. "Here, get on this. I'll hand her to you and will bring the cart."

Once Tobias mounted and held Nava in front of him, he and Philmon rode like mad men through the twisting arroyos and crevices of the mountains hiding the oasis, Philmon in the lead. By the time Tobias reached the area between the spring and the cave hidden behind bushes, the old woman waited. Philmon reached for Nava.

"Let me have her so you can dismount, Tobias."

When Tobias once again held his wife, the old woman told him, "I see she has had too much heat. Take her to the water and dunk her. Get her wet and then bring her to the cave." She pointed at Philmon. "You, take the pile of bedding from inside and wet them. Bring 'em with her to the cave." She hobbled toward the bushes.

When Tobias carried a dripping Nava into the cave, the old woman pointed to a bed in one corner. "Put her there and remove all her clothes. We must make her cool."

Tobias gazed around him, eyes wide.

Philmon placed the wet bedding on a small ledge at the head of the bed and hurried from the cave. "Do not go far, big man. I will need more cloths made wet often." The old woman hobbled after him from the cave. "Hurry, young man, take off her clothes as I get my herbs."

Tobias swallowed as he removed the wet clothing from his wife, one he had never seen except fully covered. "Stupid man," he muttered, "you need to help her and nothing else."

"Tobias?"

Tobias glanced down to see Nava's eyes opened a slit, and her voice wavered, almost non-existent as she forced herself to say, "We'll make memories, good ones, some day. I need you to do … what I can't. Please."

"Yes, sweet, I will do this and more." He stripped her clothes from her now trembling body. He touched her cheek. "We must get you cool, and we will."

"Not unless you wrap her in the wet bedding. We must exchange them for different ones as they heat from her body." The old woman came close to the bed and touched Nava's head. "She is far from safe. Hurry, wrap her in the bedding. Then you go wash in the pool below the spring. You should be clean to tend her. Tonight will be long."

And, long the night was. Philmon and Amzi would wet different piles of bedding as Tobias unwrapped the warm ones and reapplied the cool, fresh ones.

Over and over, throughout the night, the old woman helped Nava sip herbal concoctions. Finally, as the first rays of sunshine appeared over the edge of the mountain walls, Nava's temperature dropped. Rather than burning hot, she shivered with chills.

The old woman found dry covers. "Here, unwrap her from the wet clothing and wrap her in this. Sit out of the way and hold her. I will fix the bed with dry things." She turned to the other men. "You go lay out all the wet clothes and bedding across rocks and bushes to dry. We will need them."

Tobias gathered Nava in his arms after he followed the old woman's orders. He settled into the rough chair and held his wife's shivering body close to his. His head leaned back against the cave wall, and soon both he and Nava slept.

Chapter 14

The Hidden Oasis :: two months later

Nava unbent from the cooking fire and rubbed the small of her back. With a low moan, she lifted the pot by its handle.

"What are you doing?" Tobias' voice caused her to jump and nearly drop the stew. He took the pot away and carried it to the table sitting under a tree outside the cave entrance. "We've asked and asked you to leave the heavy work to us."

"I know, but I can't leave everything to Losha and you." She grimaced. "I know Philmon and Amzi would help, too, and do, but they spend nights and days guarding the entrance. They need rest."

"We would still help." Philmon walked to the table.

"Losha?" Tobias raised a brow.

Nava shook her head. "I couldn't just call her 'old woman.' She has a name and is a person." She placed serving platters around the table with utensils. "Go get whoever might be here so we can eat."

He slipped an arm around her shoulders. "Nava, seriously, you need to allow others to help. Your time grows close, or so the old … Losha says." When she turned and touched his face, he took her hand and kissed it. "Your hands show how much work you do."

Jerking her hand back, she hid it behind her. "I've never had to do the kind of things we do to survive here, but women work like this, or harder, everywhere except in the homes of the rich."

"What about the oils Hadara sent with the bundles when we came?" Philmon reached around the couple to scoop stew into a wooden bowl.

Nava stared at the big man. "What do you mean?"

The Ethiopian pointed over his shoulder. "In the alcove in the back of the cave. Hadara sent everything she could imagine you might need, for you and the babe."

"I forgot about those things." Losha moved a rough chair to the table and lowered her thin, aging body into it. "You will have time to search after you eat." She glanced from under her brows. "The young husband is correct; you must let others do the heavy work. You have learned to be a good wife."

The younger woman dropped her head. "I've only done what needed to be. I must be ready."

"Don't you realize how wealthy my grandparents are?" A frown wrinkled Tobias' forehead.

Nava leaned against him. "Life has not been what we expected several times already."

Tobias bent enough to kiss on her cheek. "You are amazing, but now, let's eat so I can relieve Amzi long enough he can eat, too."

Losha raised her head from her food. "We must enjoy the nice weather while we can. A storm comes. Within three days, you," she pointed her spoon toward Nava and Tobias, "will be staying in the cave. The others will be confined mainly … I suppose to their tent. I will be in my cave." She tried to hide a smile by ducking her head.

"What?" Philmon glared at her. "How will we manage food and washing and such as that?"

She glanced at the big man before ducking her head again. "Plan as much food as possible so that you can cook upon small fires where you stay. Washing will wait until the bad storms pass. You, huge one, were wise to place the tent against the mountain wall, in the angle of another." She rose with a grunt from the stool made from a tree trunk. "Be sure to fill vessels with water, too. Bring in as much wood and branches as you can find." As she hobbled away, she added, "This table and chairs need to go into the large cave."

"Wait! What kind of storms? I thought this place was protected." Philmon rushed after her. "That tent won't hold up under much of a storm."

Losha stopped and whirled to face him. "Yiiyiiyii. Come, let me show you. You can't find anything even under your noses." She led the way into the cave Nava and Tobias used. "There are many caves connected. Look, this can be the main room with cooking fire and where we gather." She limped to the alcove and moved aside a skin on the wall to reveal an opening into another cave. "They," she motioned at the couple, "will move into here. Come," she hobbled to the wall just inside the opening to the outside and moved aside another skin to reveal another small cave.

She faced the three behind her, cackling when she saw their expressions. "My cave can be reached through this one. We will all be inside and connected, but we must gather everything needed and fast." She hobbled back outside. "Get the pretty man. With the storms coming, no one will be searching. Beds must be set up, the tent down. Hurry, hurry, hurry. Be sure the animals' pen is closed tight and that they have plenty of food and water in their barn." She cackled as she hobbled away. "I like my little jokes."

As predicted by the old woman, a storm of whirling winds, ice, and rain battered the oasis. The five people huddled in the caves, thankful for her warning and advice. Piles of wood filled a corner of each cave; vessels of water and bags of food, also. The animals the men hunted and cleaned before the storm hit hung on the outside of the main cave, ready to be brought inside and cooked. The caves might not have been ideally warm, but close to each fire pit, people could forget the battering cold of the outside.

A week later, the winds and rains stopped as suddenly as they began, but all plant life in the oasis suffered from the freezing temperatures, all except the evergreens. At least the goats, horses, ass, and camels fared well in the enclosure and barn Hemut's men had built.

Chapter 15

Jerusalem :: before the oasis storm

The day hadn't broken yet when Hadara looked around the main chamber. Simeon and his sons removed boxes with her dowry two days previously. All her possessions, except for what she needed for a few days, awaited at the farm. She and Mazza planned on leaving for the farm outside Bethlehem within two or three days. Simeon and Rachel remained, but the rest of their family left days and weeks before.

"Mazza, the Lord has been good to us." She smiled at her retainer. "He sent us friends who have made our survival possible." With a deep sigh, she moved to look out the doors to the garden. "The one true God has indeed been good to us."

"Mistress!" Simeon ran into the room. "We must leave now!"

"What, what?" Hadara whirled around. "Why?"

"Dan slipped back to let us know our house and other older places burned last night. People died. Tzabar will think Rachel and I are dead." He took a breath. "Now, we can leave, and Tzabar will never look for me."

Mazza hurried toward the hall. "I will finish packing."

"Dan and the guards from the vestibule will load the few things left," Simeon added. "Mistress, you go to the litter at the alley door. The three regular litter bearers and Dan will carry you. Hurry."

"What about the three men. Should they know where we are?" Hadara asked as she rushed toward her sleeping chamber.

"One, Fiaz, is to marry my daughter Zema. The other two want a new life, too. They plan on seeing us safely to Bethlehem before they go elsewhere." Simeon ran past her. "Now hurry, hurry. The weather has turned nasty, but it will help hide us."

By the time the bells rang to signal the start of the regular day, the litter with Hadara and Mazza inside, a donkey carrying Simeon, and one carrying Rachel passed through the gate and headed toward Bethlehem. The winds and rain pounded them. The unprotected people lowered their heads and pulled their cloaks around them. The animals also lowered their heads and prodded forward.

"This weather is terrible. The poor men carrying us ..." Hadara commented. "At least we will not meet anyone."

Mazza opened a side curtain a slit. "Perhaps we can find a place to stop. This cold and rain will make them ill."

Simeon rode his donkey beside the litter in time to hear Mazza. "No, we must continue. The weather is difficult, but we are actually safer. We have only two hours, and we will arrive at the farm." He paused a moment. "However, if I may ask a favor ..."

"Let us stop and allow Rachel to join us." Hadara laughed at the shocked expression on Simeon's face. "But, what can we do for the litter carriers and for you?"

Simeon waited until the litter sat on the ground and Rachel seated before he answered. "We will cover ourselves as best we can and hurry as much as possible."

An early dark had fallen when the group reached the walls around the main farm buildings. Simeon pounded on the gates for some time before one side opened a crack. When the person saw Simeon and the litter, he threw the gates open. "Hurry inside," he told Simeon before calling over his shoulder, "The mistress and Simeon are here. Prepare baths and food."

Hours later, when curled into the warmth of her new bed, Hadara prayed: "Thank You, oh, Lord. We are now safe in our new home, and You brought us here. I pray now You will be with my family in the oasis. I hope they are also safe and all is well."

Chapter 16

The oasis :: two weeks after the storm

Philmon rode into the oasis camp. "Visitors coming." He swung off the horse. "One of Hemut's caravans waits at the usual place."

"Good," Tobias announced as he strode toward the enclosure to put reins on the other horse. "Perhaps we can get some more feed for the animals and news."

"Food for us, too. The old woman wouldn't like us to start eating her goats." Philmon held his horse's reins in one hand. "The storm didn't leave anything for animals to eat."

Amzi wandered from the main cave. "What's going on?" He shaded his eyes with a hand. "Where are you going?"

"To meet the caravan." Tobias turned the horse's head toward opening from the hidden valley as Philmon remounted and followed.

Losha and Nava came from the cave in time to watch the two men ride around the first turn and out of sight. Amzi joined them. "Apparently, we have visitors, a caravan."

"They better have food. The huge man eyes my goats." The old woman muttered as she loaded wood in the outside fire pit. "The goats want food. Those ugly camels eat more than the horses, and they eat too much and do too little."

Nava picked up branches and added them to the pit. "Losha, we'll be gone before long."

"Did not say anything about you leaving. We need food. That is what I said."

The women and Amzi had a fire going and a pot of stew of the last of the provisions bubbling by the time Tobias and Philmon returned. The men led a camel loaded with bundles.

"Amzi," Tobias called, "would you take one of the other camels back to the caravan while Philmon and I unload this one. Everyone will be happy." He waved Philmon on toward the enclosure. "We will unload the camel and sort everything after we eat."

"I don't get to eat first?" Amzi frowned at Tobias.

"If you rush. The caravan leader wants to travel farther before they camp for the night." He walked to the pot of stew to fill a bowl. "I'll share the news after all chores are finished."

The camels lay ruminating their cuds with the other animals in the pen, all which had been fed. The people gathered in the main cave, protected from the night chill. Tobias, as he promised, shared the information given him by the caravan leader.

"Hemut didn't come this trip. He said he would have to be careful with Tzabar still searching for me and for Eema and all our friends. Yes, he sent word that they are safe in their new homes. The caravan won't stop near Bethlehem, either, but his men there will know when it goes by and will meet with the leader in Jerusalem. They will return this way, bringing more feed for the animals and fresh provisions for us, as well as more current news." He paused and waved his hand toward the opening of the cave. "No one expected the storms to affect us as they did."

"So Hadara, Mazza, and Simeon and his family escaped and are safe?" Nava touched Tobias' knee, her eyes searching his in the flickering fire light.

He covered her hand with his. "Yes, sweet, at least according to the last messages Hemut received three weeks ago, they are safe." He looked at each person in the circle, even to Losha who squatted on the floor behind the others. "We will hear more and receive more supplies when the caravan returns. Losha, we will be sure that you will have provisions to last until things grow again."

"The peacefulness we now enjoy is good." Amzi stood and stretched. "Now, after working so hard today, I think I shall get some sleep." He stared at Tobias' and Nava's joined hands. "I believe everyone needs some privacy."

Philmon rose, too. "I pray this is not the calm before another storm. We better enjoy while we can. We will have more battles before the evil of Ahaz and Moleck is conquered."

After the others left the main cave, Tobias raised Nava's hand to his lips. He kissed the back and then the palm. "I enjoy us having some time together, alone."

Nava ducked her head. She felt a fluttering in her chest. "I ... I like being with you, too. We're so tired at night we seldom talk or anything but sleep."

He used a finger to tip her face toward his and bent to brush his lips over hers. Her breath caught and then exhaled in a soft sigh.

"You're lovely, sweet. I hope you know you are."

She pulled back and gazed at him. "I am fat and awkward, not lovely."

"Nothing can take away your glow and the softness of your skin." He caressed her cheek and down her throat. He felt her swallow and watched her eyes widen. He bent his head and kissed her again, slightly longer, before he moved back. "I think that's enough for tonight. I frightened you."

"I, uh, I ... Yes, a bit, but I liked it, too." Her eyelashes fluttered. "I have never been kissed, not like that, before."

"You like the kisses?" His lips tipped upward. "I am not very … well, I haven't experienced much more myself." He grinned. "Perhaps we can learn together, discover what we like?"

Nava giggled. "That could be enjoyable." Her face sobered. "I'll try not to be afraid." She stroked his face. "May I have another kiss?"

"Always glad to please when I can." Tobias rose, bringing her with him, and bent his head once more.

As his lips covered hers, she breathed a low sigh.

"Oooph!" Tobias jerked back and placed a hand on her abdomen. "He kicks hard."

With another giggle, Nava agreed. Suddenly she moved from his arms and turned her back to him. "Will the fact that … Will knowing … Will you hold how he was made against this babe?"

Tobias wrapped his arms around her, one hand resting on her belly. "Ah, sweet, this is now *our* babe, yours and *mine,* if you will allow me to be."

She turned in his arms and studied his eyes in the dim light. "You mean this? You will be the baby's father in every way?"

"Yes, I do."

Laying her head on his shoulder, she nodded. "Thank you. I hope I can make you the wife you deserve." She raised her head. "I'm so afraid. The pain was so horrible. I've tried to forget. I have, but I remember sometimes."

"I will always do my best to be gentle. I will never hurt you deliberately. I do know, though, if you can accept and love this child, we can make our marriage a good one. But, we both will have to love and trust."

A bright smile spread across Nava's face. "I do trust you completely. I do love this babe, and I love you more every day. You're no longer the comfortable brother, and that frightens me in a way. What I feel now, I do not understand, but …" She stroked the side of his face. "Won't we be able to become a real husband and wife?"

"Ah, I believe we will." He kissed her gently. "Now, my sweet, it is late. Let's go to bed."

As Nava drifted into sleep in Tobias' arms, Philmon's words echoed in her head, "the calm before another storm." *Please, no more storms, at least not for a long time.*

Chapter 17

three months later

Nava awoke before light shone above the mountain rims. She waddled outside, rubbing the small of her back. "I will be glad when you come, babe. I'm weary of being miserable, never comfortable."

"Nava, what are you doing up?" Amzi ambled from behind some bushes. "Is something wrong?"

Nava shook her head. "Nothing new. I'm cranky and ready to have this baby."

"Sit and I'll bring you some water. Not having to add wine because the spring is safe is good."

She gingerly lowered herself on a rock. "Thank you, Amzi. You have been kind."

He snorted. "Kind? Hardly. I try to make up for my stupidity." He handed her a wooden bowl of the nearly cold water. "Take today and rest. I will help Losha with meals. One thing about being away from civilization is I have learned to cook." He grinned. "I have also become stronger."

Nava handed him the bowl. "Yes, you have. I believe you will be able to build a life for yourself someday, as long as you never cross Tzabar's path again." She tilted her head. "Although, I doubt he could recognize you now."

"Why are you out here?" Tobias' voice interrupted, harsh and angry.

Nava whirled to face him, nearly falling off the rock. "Tobias! I couldn't sleep and didn't want to bother you. Why are you angry? Amzi brought me some water." She dropped her head. "If I did something wrong, I'm sorry."

With a glare, Amzi snapped, "Can you not see how tired and uncomfortable she is with carrying the babe? Don't be a fool." He whirled and stomped away, muttering.

As she studied her hands in her lap, Nava said, "You shouldn't be angry with Amzi. He did nothing."

"Oh, sweet, I'm sorry." Tobias took her hands and raised her to her feet. "I was concerned and a bit frightened when I woke and you weren't in the cave." He wrapped his arms around her, feeling her tremble against his body. "I didn't mean to scare you. Forgive me?"

She nodded but didn't say anything. Her body grew rigid. A low gasp escaped her. Then she relaxed.

"Nava? What's wrong?" Tobias sat her back on the rock. "What happened?"

She looked at him, her eyes wide and frightened. "I don't know. I felt like — " Her hands grasped his tight enough that he stared at her whitened hands. "Ohhhhh, I think …" A moan broke through her words as fluid gushed from her body.

"Losha! Philmon! Amzi! We need help, *now*!" Tobias scooped Nava into his arms and strode toward the cave. "Come on, help!"

Losha hobbled from the mouth of the cave. "Her time has come? Bring her to the bed." She shuffled at her fastest rate into the cave with the bed, Tobias with Nava behind her, and he practically stepped on the old woman's heels. She pulled the blankets back and smoothed the bottom bed covers. "Put her here and then get a pot of water heating. Hurry."

"I'll get the water heating," Amzi announced from the opening.

"What should I do?" Philmon asked, his face gray in the dim light.

Losha waved in his direction. "Get more bedding ready and unload the bundle from the other cave for the babe. Lay things where they can be found easily, inside this cave."

"Auggggh." Nava pulled her knees toward her body, and her back arched.

Tobias knelt beside her and took her hand in his. She clasped it in a death grip as a pain and contraction ripped through her body. When Losha tried to move him away, Nava's head thrashed back and forth on the bed. "No, no, no, please don't leave, Tobias." She grasped his hand tighter. "Please."

When he glanced at the old woman, she nodded. "If having you helps, stay, but don't get in the way." She picked up a cloth and covered Nava. "Never heard of such, a man at a birthing."

As the hours passed, Tobias wished he weren't at the birthing, wanted to be out with the other men heating water, fixing broth, doing anything but watch Nava's body fight, anything but have her squeeze his hand until it became numb.

"Sweet, I never knew you were so strong," he murmured as he watched tears stream down the side of her face. She didn't sob, but the tears flowed. He wiped them away with the thumb on the hand not being mangled by his wife. "I wish I could take the pain."

He looked at Losha. "How much longer?"

"Have no way to know. It's up to the babe and Nava." She turned away and began searching through the items piled inside the opening. "We wait."

The torches and fire in the pit created flashes of light and dancing shadows. The old woman and young man waited and watched as Nava's contractions became longer, harder, and closer together. She continued to clasp Tobias' hand. Her moans and groans increased to cries for help, for release, for the torment to end.

"You must move up by her head and hold her to sit," Losha advised. "The time has neared."

Tobias slid his arms under Nava's shoulders, lifting her until his body could move behind her. He held her upright as her body continued its labor, his arms loosely circling her waist. He closed his eyes and prayed that the babe would hurry.

With a scream, Nava dug her nails into his arms. She pushed with a force he had never seen. Finally, the babe slipped into the world and into Losha's hands.

"'Tis a boy. You have a son, young husband and wife." Losha continued her duties as midwife as Nava leaned limply against Tobias.

Chapter 18

two months later

Philmon suggested the men hone their fighting skills. "After all we do not know what we will face in months to come."

"Perhaps you might use some of this time to learn to write, Philmon," Nava suggested. "I could teach you."

"No, little one, I can read; that is enough."

The men used swords, spears, and bows to practice military maneuvers and weapon usage. They lifted boulders to increase their strength.

As *her* strength increased, Nava helped Losha with meals, washing bedding and clothing, and keeping the living areas neat.

The men aided Losha with the animals after she told them, "I will tend my goats, but those others are not my responsibility. Although, the ass is not difficult to care for."

One day, Nava gave in to her curiosity. "Losha, you speak very well, as if well educated. Where is your home? What is your background?"

The old woman glanced at Nava before returning her attention to the food on the fire. When Nava thought she wouldn't receive an answer, Losha said, "I came from a home such as your young husband did. I was married off to a man richer than my father. When I couldn't have children, I was put aside. I could read, write, take care of a large household, all the things a rich woman must do. However, my father would not allow me to return to his house. The rest, I will not tell. The one true God kept His hand on me. I survived."

The babe grew and thrived. Tobias and Nava named him Benjamin after one of the leaders of Israel, before the country split into Israel and Judah.

Life passed quietly, but the men began to wonder how they could still hide when the wanderers returned. The caravan scheduled to take them to Egypt could appear at any time. They didn't know which group would arrive first.

One morning, Nava left the cave, the baby tied to her chest in a sling of cloth. As she carried a pot to the spring, she saw Amzi piling bundles beside the animal enclosure.

"Amzi, what are you doing?"

The "pretty man," as Losha insisted on calling him, froze in place for a few moments before facing her. "It's time I left and found a life for myself."

"But where will you go? What will you do?" Nava set down the pot and walked closer to him.

Rubbing his forehead with a fist, Amzi blew out a breath. "When I've been scouting, I have also been searching. A band of rebels has a stronghold in another valley, not as well hidden as this, but well defended. I'll join them."

"Why do you have to leave— "

"Nava!"

Tobias' yell caused Nava to jump, startling Benjamin, too. The babe cried as Nava cuddled him through the cloth. Amzi scowled at his half-brother, who demanded, "What are you doing?" He glared at Amzi and then Nava. "You have no right meeting with him."

Nava stared at her husband. "What do you mean? I came out for water, saw Amzi piling his belongings— "

"You are leaving? Good. You need to leave and to leave my wife alone." Tobias stepped closer to Amzi, hands fisted.

With a sob, Nava ran from the men. Holding her infant against her body, she rushed around Philmon into the cave and bedchamber area. Both she and the babe cried.

Philmon ran as she passed him, but toward the brothers. When he reached them, he stepped between them and slapped Tobias on the shoulder, causing the younger man to stumble back three steps. "What is wrong with you? You act like a dog defending a chuck of meat simply because another dog looked at it. You are an imbecile. You already have what you want, but you are too stupid to know it." The man's voice shook with anger. "Amzi shows wisdom by leaving rather than cause trouble, but you won't allow him to do what's right. No, you have to be a fool. And, the little one, who would never look at a man but you, hurts because she thinks she did something wrong. You … you imbecile."

Amzi picked up a set of reins and walked toward the enclosure. Philmon continued to glare at Tobias, and Tobias glanced back and forth between Philmon and Amzi. The scowl on his face disappeared into a blank expression and then to confusion. "I, uh, I …"

Finally, Tobias called to Amzi, "Wait. I … I owe you an apology. What can I do?"

"Nothing," Amzi answered. "I'll take the ass and make my way— away from you."

"Take a horse. We owe you that much."

Amzi stared at the sky and then at Tobias. "You owe me nothing. I will take the ass. I want to blend in, not be robbed and killed." He opened the gate and moved toward the ass eating from a manger. He paused. "Use the brain you should have and realize how fortunate you are. Maybe if you hurry, you will comfort Nava, and she will forgive you." He began to work the harness over the ass' head. "I don't know that I could," he muttered.

Tobias turned away and hurried by Philmon, who glared at him. "You do not deserve for her to forgive you, ever. You have more of Tzabar in you than I thought."

"She probably won't, but I hope she does." He stopped and stared at Philmon. "Do I? Do I really behave like him? May the one true God forgive me if I am anything like Tzabar. I must not be, can't be." He inhaled deeply before continuing on his way, now at a run.

When he entered the cave, Tobias found Nava cuddling Benjamin as she rocked back and forth in a roughly formed chair, crying. He whispered, "Nava, will you listen to me?"

"I made you angry, and I ... I don't know why." Benjamin began to cry with her. "Hush, baby, hush." She held him to her shoulder and rubbed his back. He snuggled into the side of her neck, hiccupped, and quietened.

Tobias stood watching her for a few moments before he moved beside her legs and knelt. "I'm sorry. I am really sorry."

"What did I do? I try ... so hard to be what you want, and ... I fail." She struggled to control her sobs. "You are so angry at me. It tears my heart in pieces."

"Oh, my sweet." He curled his arms around her and the baby. "You are my life. I acted the fool."

Nava bit her lower lip, trying to stop the trembling. "I don't understand."

"I know. I don't understand myself. I saw you with Amzi, and I ... All right, I was jealous. I don't want another man to look at you like ... with longing."

Her head drew back, and a frown knotted her brows. "What are you saying? Have you lost your mind? You thought Amzi ... Amzi and I ..." Nava began to shake her head but remembered Benjamin. "You make no sense. What did we ever do to make you think such a thing? Nothing, that is what we did." Her tears stopped, and her eyes narrowed as she studied him.

"I have worried that I am not what you deserve. I know I lack much to be a wife, but I tried and tried. I now know that I will never please you. Perhaps you should put me aside as your father did your mother. Go on your way. Benjamin and I will stay with Losha." She turned her head so she couldn't see him.

"No!" Tobias clasped her chin with his hand. "No, I do not want you to leave me. Do you not see? That is the problem: I ... I'm afraid that you will find Amzi more handsome, more ... more what you want in a husband than I am. Losha calls him the 'pretty man' for a reason."

She tilted her head and studied his face. Little by little her frown eased. She reached a hand to touch his face. "Your scraggly beard and wild hair don't help your handsomeness, but I know it's still under the hair." She touched his chest. "I know the good heart, or I thought I knew the good heart that beats there." She drew her hand back to join her other one, to cradle the baby. "Those are what I love. I love *you*, not Amzi, not any other man in that way."

Tobias laid his head against her arm. "I don't deserve that love. I am glad you do, and I don't know if I could go on without it. Please forgive me. Please."

She studied him a moment. "May I have time to think over this matter?"

He drew back and stood. "Of course. I will await your decision."

"Tobias?"

"Yes?"

She motioned with a finger for him to bend down. When he did, she pulled his head down and kissed him. "I cannot *not* love you. I don't know what kind of love, but you are a part of me. For us to part would cause me to lose some of me." Her smile wobbled, but it appeared. "Does that make sense?"

"No, sweet, you sound as I feel, too." He touched her cheek. "Do you forgive me — again? I will work not to be worse than that ass Amzi rode away."

"You made him leave on the ass?"

"No, sweet, he insisted he take the ass, as a reminder of me, most likely."

Chapter 19

Four days after Amzi left, Hemut arrived. He dismounted from his black stallion, and Philmon took the reins and led the horse to a pool below the spring, allowing the animal to drink and graze nearby. Tobias escorted his uncle to the sitting area around the outdoor table where Nava and Benjamin waited.

"I see the babe arrived safely." Hemut chucked the baby's chin. "Handsome. A boy?"

"Yes," Nava answered. "We named him Benjamin."

"Good name." He sat, and Losha placed a drink in front of him. He smiled his thanks. "Are you ready to leave? The caravan will be at the meeting place in two days."

"Two days?" Nava's eyes blinked. "We …" She swallowed. "Of course, we will be ready."

Tobias grinned. "The look on your face says a different story, sweet." He reached for Benjamin. "If we all work together, we will be ready. You just make sure we have all the supplies for you and Benjamin. Philmon and I will do the rest."

Nava gazed around the oasis, her home for so many months. "I will miss this place." When Losha joined them at the table, the young woman smiled at the old one. "I will miss you most of all."

"I will be here if you come this way again." Losha touched Benjamin's arm with a knarred finger. "I will be here at least another six to ten harvests." She looked at Hemut. "You will bring them back before then."

Hemut harrumphed and said, "I will make sure they return when it is safe. Ahaz's and Tzabar's days will not last for many years." He abruptly stood. "Let's get everything ready to leave. The wanderers will be back for their stay in four or five days. We must be long gone.

"When the bundles and packs are gathered, make sure Nava's bleongings and Benjamin's go in one pile. Those will be on the camel close to the ones that will carry you and the babe. Be sure necessities are in smaller packs that can ride with you in the litter."

"The litter? I don't understand. Who would have to carry a litter all that distance?"

Hemut smiled. "No, the litter is hung between two camels. For you and the babe. Riding on a camel and caring for him would be much too difficult. We have brought a litter that has poles that fit along both sides of one camel and then along the sides of a camel behind. Between the two animals is the litter with protection from sun and wind. You will have privacy."

"I feel that this trip will not be comfortable." Benjamin began to fuss. "I must feed him. I'll put together the packs to go with us in the litter after he eats." Nava carried the baby into the back cave.

Tobias followed. He watched the infant suckle. "A beautiful view, Nava. Mother and child. I would never tire of watching you."

A blush tinged her cheeks. "I believe you must be blind, but I do like when you tell me nice things, even if not really true."

"Ah, sweet, I wish you could see yourself through my eyes." He moved to sit on a large log facing her. "I must shave my face and cut my hair close so I will blend in with others in Egypt. Most men shave their heads also, but some do leave some hair close to the scalp, as my uncle does. I didn't want you surprised when you next see me."

Nava slightly smiled. "So, I can once again see your handsome face?"

"Now who must be blind?" He rose and bent to kiss her. "I'll be back to help you finish your bundles." He ran his hand over Benjamin's head. "He has soft fuzz, more than hair." He touched her cheek before leaving the cave.

Just before the sun sank below the mountain peaks, the sounds of someone riding a horse fast echoed through the canyons leading to the outside. The men grabbed weapons and scrambled up the mountain slopes, waiting to ambush anyone who might make it to the oasis. When the rider broke through the trail, Hemut called, "It's my man." He slid down from his hiding spot, followed by Tobias and Philmon.

"Allus, what is wrong?"

"Ahaz's men … led by Barrack … halted caravan. Scouts warned … I hid distance, but … could see and hear." Allus paused to take several deep breaths. "Barrack … insane." The man breathed deeply again. "Please, water?"

"Here." Losha handed the man a bowl. "I saw you had thirst. I will take your horse to drink." When Allus handed her the reins, she led the animal to the pool of water below the spring.

"Come, sit." Hemut waved an arm toward the stools and roughly hewed chairs around the table close to the fire pit. "When you can, tell us the rest."

Philmon and Tobias took stools at the table. Nava wandered from the cave. "What has happened?"

"Join us. Hemut's man will talk when he can breathe again." Tobias brought a chair close to his stool. "The babe?"

"He sleeps."

When Losha rejoined them, Philmon demanded, "Now talk, man. Do we need to run? Do we need to block the entry to this valley?"

Allus shook his head. "I tied my horse a distance from the caravan and crept back. The soldiers scattered everything, and Barrack personally viewed each man. He screamed, threw things when he didn't find whatever he wanted. He yelled loudly enough I could have stayed with the horse and heard. He looks for a eunuch and the son of Tzabar. He said Moleck wanted them in the fire." He took another drink. "He left four soldiers, but he and the others rode to Thebes to find the two. After five days, if the two he wanted didn't appear, the four were to go to Egypt." The man shook his head. "Barrack left."

"I don't understand why Barrack would care." Nava shook her head. "It does not make sense. I might understand Tzabar searching, but why Barrack?"

Allus took another drink before he replied. "He acted like a mad man. Perhaps he is mad."

"He must be. He makes no sense. Egypt will consider that an invasion. Is the man so deranged?" Hemut leaped to his feet, his stool crashing over. "We cannot wait here. The wanderers will appear any day. We can't join the caravan now. How do we get Tobias and his family to my parents ..." He paused. "We can't take them to my parents." He leaned against the tree trunk.

"I can get word to the wanderers that coming here is dangerous. They will go elsewhere until I send word." Losha stood behind Nava. "How long before another place can be found for the huge man and the young husband and wife and, of course, the babe?"

Tobias moved closer to Nava and placed an arm around her. "At least Amzi is gone, but what can we do? Hemut?"

"I have an idea, but you most likely won't like it."

"Would my family be safe? Nava and the babe must not fall into Barrack's hands. As her grandfather once he knows she lives, he will sacrifice her and Benjamin." He stared at his brother. "Maybe he knows they're with me."

Hemut studied first Allus and then Tobias. "That would answer one question, Now, my plan: Allus would have to travel to my parents quickly. Tobias, you would have to work in the stone quarries. My father owns one at Swenet, but the work is hard, to body and mind."

"Aren't slaves used for stone work?" Philmon asked.

"Usually, but my father also hires other men."

Philmon straightened to his full height. "Would I be able to be there?"

The Egyptian gave a humorless laugh. "There are several Ethiopians. You would not be out of place, but you wouldn't have to take on such a difficult life. No one looks for you."

"I care for Tobias and the little one. Where they go, I go."

Tobias hugged Nava closer. "He and I could escape easy enough, but how do we save Nava and Benjamin? How will they travel so far?"

"Come, let's look at what's here. We will work a plan once we know what's available." Hemut started toward the barn and enclosure. "First let us see what animals we have." He glanced over his shoulder at the others. "Yes, if we can get to the sea ... If so, that will be easier and faster. But, if it doesn't work ..."

After Hemut examined the cart, the four horses, and two camels in the enclosure, He nodded. "Allus, I'll ride with you close to the caravan, where you'll slip back on foot and take another horse. We need the one you have." He walked back to the table under the tree and sat.

"Then, good man, you will ride like a man possessed to the coast and take the fastest boat or ship you can find, after arranging for a ship." Hemut took a deep breath. "Allus, that ship must wait for us no matter how long." He reached under his robe and brought out a small bag of coins. "Here is enough gold. Choose wisely because our lives will depend on the captain and crew waiting and being honest." He paused. "Here, give him half the gold and tell him I will give him the rest at the Egyptian delta, where you will wait with a barge to take us to Swenet."

"Yes, sir. Should I leave a message with Effrim?" He stopped and added, "How do I leave a message for you at Gaza?"

"With Effrim, only without bringing any attention to yourself. If you do not get away, the plan doesn't work. In fact, I'll wait until you rejoin me outside the caravan so I know you managed." Hemut nodded. "Yes, that would be wise to do. As far as a message for me, leave the name of captain at the inn we used before, just the name."

"What should we do, Hemut?" Tobias asked. "Should I ride with you?"

"No, you begin gathering materials for the cart. We want to make it into a protected traveling litter, drawn by a horse. See if Losha has materials we can use to make a divan and a place for the babe inside, curtains to surround the sides, and a canopy over the top."

He stood, "Come, Allus, we must leave." Hemut looked around. "Where is Nava?"

"She probably is with the babe. I'll let her know our plan while Philmon finds materials for the cart." Tobias clasped his uncle's upper arm. "Thank you. May the one true God go with you." He nodded toward Allus. "May the Lord go with you, also."

Chapter 20

a month later

Hemut rode before the small caravan, leading one camel piled with provisions. The cart, with Tobias guiding the horse as he rode another, came next. Philmon, piloting the other camel, brought up the rear.

Nava sat on the comfortable divan in the cart. The opened side curtains allowed the breeze to circulate. Benjamin lay sleeping in the cradle Tobias and Philmon built, which they attached in one corner. Tobias rode beside the cart, the reins for the horse pulling the cart in his hand.

"Need anything, sweet?"

"Not now. As long as the breeze continues, I'm comfortable." She flashed a bright smile at her husband. "Much different than the trip to the oasis, but I'm sure we'll hit some rough places before the trip is finished. One day's experience is but a start."

"In a way, what we thought to be a catastrophe may have worked in our favor. If all goes well, this trip will be easier. Traveling over the desert is difficult."

She watched her husband's face. "But this way, your life will be very stressful, and we do not know for how long."

Tobias grinned. "Let's agree that working harder than I ever thought I would is better than burning in Moleck's vat."

With a sigh, she agreed. "Yes, there is that to consider."

"Get off the road," Philmon rode rigorously from behind. "Soldiers are marching this way."

Hemut raced back to join them. "Take the next trail, to your left. It will be rough, so hold on, Nava, hold tight to the straps on each side."

As the horse pulling the cart trod the route with Tobias now riding in front of it, Nava discovered that "rough" did not describe the jolting and bumping and swaying.

When Benjamin awoke and began to cry, she didn't dare turn loose to hold him. "Oh, my precious, Eema can't take you right now. At least the cover holds you so you don't bounce," she babbled, hoping her voice would calm him. When he still fussed, she began to hum and sing to him. At the sound, his tear-washed eyes found her face, and a baby-grin spread across his face. For over an hour, they made their "rough" way down the path, Nava singing the whole time.

When they stopped, Nava untangled the baby from the covers and held him. Tobias walked to the side of the cart. "Are you all right?"

"Benjamin wasn't very happy, but he laughed at my singing. Now he wants to eat."

"I will close the curtains. We will camp here for the night. I will bring you something to eat when the meal is ready."

"Please help me out after I feed the babe. I need to move around and, uh, have some privacy." She blushed.

Tobias reached to touch her cheek. "Of course, sweet." He closed the curtains on both sides of the cart. "I'll be back in a short time."

Nava allowed the baby to nurse until he dozed. She held him to her shoulder until he burped and laid him in the cradle. "You are growing so much, Benjamin. I would like to keep these days for when I could enjoy. Am I not silly?" She brushed her hand over his head. "Your fuzz is changing to hair. You are so beautiful."

"Should he not be handsome since he isn't a girl?" Tobias opened the curtains on one side. "Are you ready to come out?"

"Yes, thank you." She slid her arms around his neck as he lifted her over the cart side. "Is there something I can do to help with the meal, to set up camp for the night?"

"No, sweet, you rest while you can. Philmon insists on cooking, and he learned much from you and Losha. Hemut and I cared for the animals and blocked the cart. You and the babe will be all safe and comfortable."

"You may put me on my feet now." Nava looked around. "This is a good spot. I can go behind those bushes."

After she returned, Tobias led her to a rock and brought her part of a roasted quail and a bowl. "Since we don't know how clear the water is, we added some wine. Eat. Philmon hunted and provided the quail. We'll leave early in the morn."

"Are we far out of our way since we left the road?" Nava asked.

Hemut answered her question. "Actually, no. We've been angling toward our destination all the time. The way for a while will continue like that we traveled, but we join another road after tomorrow."

"That is good news, Hemut. We haven't lost as much time as I thought." Tobias took a bite of quail and chewed. After he swallowed, he asked, "So if all goes well, how many days ahead of us?"

"If we had stayed with the road, the trip would be six days, maybe seven. Now we will be traveling an extra two days. Hopefully, we'll not have more detours."

As the cart wobbled and pitched over the narrow way through the land, the group continued toward the sea. Nava thought the trip and agony would never cease. To care for Benjamin, she would slip one arm all the way through a strap so that she and the baby wouldn't be thrown off the divan when a wheel fell into a hole or bounced over a rock. Brief stops for a chance to scurry behind a boulder or clump of bushes allowed the only time for walking and stretching. The sudden rain storms added to the misery since curtains had to be closed, and the heat collected inside. At night, after eating a light meal, she tossed and turned, tired but not able to sleep. *Will this never end?* she silently asked.

When they reached the road, Hemut scouted both directions before waving the others from where they hid in a clump of trees. The way contained ripples and rocks in the dirt, but compared to what they had traveled, Nava found the "smoothness" allowed her to nap. However, if any other travelers appeared, the curtains had to remain closed, causing her to feel imprisoned.

During a time with open curtains, Tobias rode beside her so they could visit. "You have been brave, sweet. I know it must be brutal, especially when the curtains are closed."

"I keep thinking that things could be worse, especially if we're caught. That keeps me sane." She flashed her smile. "And, Benjamin and I have great conversations. He is learning to say Abba and Eema."

"Indeed, and can he?"

Nava held Benjamin in her lap. "See, Benjamin, there is Abba. Say Abba. Abba."

The baby stared at Tobias. "Babababa," he babbled.

Tobias laughed. "He needs to work on his pronunciation a bit, but not bad. Do you think he'd like to ride in front of me for a while?"

"We would need to stop to hand him to you, but he would like that." Nava giggled.

Tobias led the horse to the side of the road. When Hemut turned to see if there were a problem, he told his uncle, "Just taking the babe to ride with me for a short time."

Benjamin's eyes grew wide when he sat in front of his father on the horse. He waved his hands and arms and laughed when the horse moved forward. Tobias grinned as he held Benjamin and listened to him laugh. Before long, the baby leaned back against his father's chest and slept.

"Tobias, should you give him back to me?" Nava called quietly.

"I should perhaps, now while no one is around." He pulled both horses to a stop, handed Benjamin to Nava, and backed his horse back a step. "Someone's coming. Close the curtains."

Finally, with permission of the owner, the small band camped outside the outskirts of Gaza in a grove of trees. The clearing in the middle of the grove had a spring and a pen for the horses and camels. The men quickly started a fire in the pit to one side of the spring.

"Philmon, since you are such a good hunter, do you think you might find fresh fare for our meal tonight?" Hemut asked after the men and woman sat on the ground around the fire. "The owner says we may hunt as long as we don't mistake his goats and cattle for wild life."

"I should be able to find something. If you'll use more dried vegetables for a stew, with a bit of the dried meat."

Nava rose. "Allow me. I need to do something. I have sat and struggled to sit in the cart until I need to see if I can still move."

By the time Philmon returned with three dressed quail, the vegetables and dried meat bubbled in a pot, the fragrance wafting through the trees.

After the meal and all the cleaning completed, silence settled over the small group as they slept, all except one. Philmon sat under a tree by the path to the road, a sword by his side.

When Nava climbed out of the cart before sunrise, she discovered him slumped in sleep. He jumped to his feet, sword in hand, when he heard her steps.

"Why are you not asleep on a pallet, Philmon? And, why the sword?"

Philmon lowered the weapon and stretched his neck and twisted his head. "I am suspicious of someone who offers so much to people he doesn't know. This could be a trap. I *will* be ready."

"Then perhaps you could have shared with us." Tobias joined them. "Hemut and I could have stood guard duty."

Hemut, who had followed Tobias, agreed. "We would have."

Philmon scratched his head. "I had no proof, just a feeling of this being too easy."

Hemut turned on his heel. "Load everything. There is a place across the road and in a canyon. It doesn't offer all this place does, but we will be hidden."

Before the sun rose over the edges of the hills, nothing remained in the camp. The group crossed the road, brushing away signs of hooves and wheels, and worked its way down and around in the shallow canyons until out of sight of anyone above. Once they arrived at the area Hemut used before, no pen existed, but the men unloaded the animals and hobbled them by a small area of grass and brush. They blocked the cart so that it wouldn't tip.

Tobias helped Nava from the cart and handed Benjamin to her. He led her to a rock under one of the few trees. "We haven't much to eat, and since we don't know if the stream is clean," he pointed toward the back of the canyon, "we will have to add wine."

Nava offered a tired smile. "We will manage." She saw Hemut mount his horse. "Where is Hemut going?"

"He heads to Gaza to find if we have a ship or not. He says we must move faster than he thought."

Nava cuddled Benjamin as he began to fuss. "I need to feed the babe, but I don't want to go back to the cart."

"Don't worry. Hemut will soon be gone, and Philmon wants to guard the entrance to the canyon. In moments, you'll have privacy. Here, let me see if I can keep him happy until you do." Tobias took the babe from her arms. Benjamin stopped in mid-sob and stared at the man holding him.

"Babababa." A wide grin dimpled his cheeks.

"Yes, Abba." Tobias walked around the camp area, talking and bouncing his son, both of them laughing.

As soon as Hemut rode from the camp and Philmon grabbed his sword and spear and marched toward the opening to their hide-a-way, Tobias returned the babe to Nava. He squatted on the ground before her as she nursed the child.

"I feel so much pride for my wife and son." A musing smile tipped his lips as he watched them. "The Lord has blessed me with you, Nava. You are lovely beyond words."

Later, with Benjamin bedded down in the cart, Nava and Tobias had a fire going and a pot boiling with the last of the dried meat and vegetables. Hemut rode in with Philmon behind him on foot.

"I took longer than expected because soldiers swarm the roads, and the place where we camped last night is under siege. I took a round-about way to get back." He slid off his horse. "Food smells good." He gave a pack to Tobias. "More food. Now, allow me to hobble my horse, and I'll give my news." He started toward the stream before he turned around. "Good job, Philmon. Your suspicions were correct."

Nava and Tobias filled bowls with stew and others with watered wine. Philmon moved small boulders under the tree for seating. Everyone drank and ate a few bites while waiting for Hemut to begin.

"I found the captain and talked with him. We can load and be gone immediately." He took another bite and chewed. "The boat can take our horses, but not the camels. Therefore, as soon as we unload the camels at the ship, I will sell them. Everyone can stay on the ship until we cast off." He glanced at the cart. "I'll have to dispose of that, too, after we remove the cradle. Now, let's eat and pack what we can. I don't like moving in the dark, but we must avoid the soldiers."

Chapter 21

Nava squeezed the straps in the cart. Benjamin slept soundly in his cradle. The bumps and rocking made her stomach roll and cramp. She knew they crept upward since the divan slopped back. *Surely, soon, we will be there soon.*

When the cart leveled, she knew they reached a road. She could hear the bustle of animals and people as well as the creak of harness and jingle of chain and metal even before sunup. She didn't dare peek through the curtains in case someone saw her. The rocking of the cart continued, but at least the thumps and bumps lessened. As light showed through the closed curtains, the cart came to a stop. Moments later, Tobias opened the curtains a bit. "Will you put on a veil and your cloak so no one can describe you if they see you?"

"Oh, indeed." She grabbed a veil stuffed behind a cushion and fastened it around her head. She slipped her cloak over her shoulders and scooped up the baby. "We're ready."

Tobias helped her and the baby to the ground. Nava looked around at the bustling mass of humanity and boats. Piles of goods created small hills on the shore. Tobias aided her up the wobbly board that acted as a gangplank and onto the deck.

A man stood waiting. "Come, I be taking you to a cabin." He took the couple to a tiny room below the sound of waves slapping the outside wall. "You be told when food is ready each day. Woman must stay from sight." He turned and left Tobias and Nava staring at each other.

"How ... how many days will I be, uh, locked down here." Her eyes searched the tight area. A narrow bed pressed against one wall. A table, attached to the floor, filled the middle of the space. Piles of bundles took up the floor against the wall opposite the bed. The only light filtered through areas at the top of the walls to the hallway and a candle flickering in a holder by the door. The cradle filled the space at the end of the bed.

Tobias hugged her until Benjamin squirmed between them. "I'll check with Hemut, but I believe with good weather and a stiff wind, we should be at the delta in a few days."

"A *few* days. A FEW days?" Her voice rose in volume with each word. "I have traveled over impossible roads. I birthed my babe in a cave. Now I am to be locked in this, this place for a few days?" She snuggled Benjamin and dropped the bed. "I thought I could do whatever needed to be done, but I don't know." Her frantic eyes glared around her. "I don't know if I can."

Tobias sat and wrapped his arms around her, but she didn't relax. She held her body stiff and unyielding.

"Sweet, please, we will manage," he pleaded.

"Manage?" Her voice became flat and without emotion. "Manage? I don't think I have anything left with which to manage. I want to sleep and never waken."

"Nava, this doesn't sound like you."

She stared at him and continued, using that dead voice, "How would you know? You have not learned about me, the real me. I am tired of being the 'sweet' one. The one who gives and takes nothing." She shook her head. "I have nothing left inside."

Benjamin wailed. "Oh, poor babe. You don't want to listen to your mother complain, do you? Come, let me feed you; then we will sleep." She brushed her lips over his head.

"Nava, what might make things better?" Tobias stood and knelt by her knees as she removed her veil and cloak while trying to balance the baby at the same time. He took his son so she could finish. He kissed Benjamin's head before handing him back to Nava. "Would something to eat and drink help?"

Nava put the babe to her breast before raising her eyes to look at Tobias. "I don't know what will help. I'm so weary, Tobias, so very weary."

He stood. "I'll see what I can discover, and I will bring something to eat." He stroked her head. "I will return quickly."

When Tobias entered the tiny cabin later, he found Nava curled on the bed, Benjamin snuggled close to her body. Setting the food and drink he carried on the table, he gathered the baby into his arms. As Tobias laid the baby in the cradle, Nava awoke.

"What ... what is wrong?" She sat and looked around. "Where are we? Oh, yes, in a prison."

"I brought you food and news." Tobias glanced around the room. "A table but no chairs. Let me see if I can find a chair or two." He left the cabin but returned shortly with a chair in each hand. "With what Hemut paid for the use of this 'ship,' we should be in the captain's cabin. At least I borrowed chairs from it."

He set the chairs at right angles at the table. "Come, sweet, I brought you roasted vegetables and lamb. I also have good spring water, cool and fresh." He lifted her to her feet and helped her into a chair. He set a platter of food in front of her and a goblet. "Please eat. I'll get mine and join you."

Nava stared at the food. "Whatever you wish."

Tobias shook his head and left the cabin. When he returned, he carried another platter, goblet, and a carafe. "I brought more water." He put the items on the table and sat. "Eat a few bites, and I will tell you what Hemut had to say."

She picked up a piece of meat and slipped it into her mouth. Chunks of vegetables followed. She took a drink and then more bites. Her eyes rose from her platter. "'Tis very tasty. This wasn't fixed on this ship, was it?"

"Actually, yes. Philmon made the 'cook' leave the cooking area on the deck and did the cooking. He is having a good supply of food items loaded and will fix our meals. The water, though, is going to be another story since it won't stay fresh long. He found a spring and large pots to store water."

Nava chewed another bite. "Philmon is resourceful, isn't he?"

"Yes, he is, and we're fortunate he wants to be with us and help." He ate for a while before asking, "Do you feel better now that you have eaten?"

She nodded. "I still have little hope, but I think I'm stronger." She gazed at him through her lashes. "I disappointed you." She shrugged one shoulder. "I have done that before."

Tobias grasped one of her hands. "You have never, never disappointed me." He huffed a breath. "If anything, I have disappointed you. I have failed you."

A frown wrinkled her brow, but she didn't reply. She continued eating until her platter didn't hold anything else. "Now, what did Hemut say? How long must I be locked in this box?"

"First, after Hemut talked with the captain, the man changed his mind. You will be allowed on deck twice a day, early morn and after sunset. Other times, the crew will be very busy. The trip, if all goes well, will last two to three days."

Nava closed her eyes, and tears streamed under her lashes. "I thought, I thought it would be longer, much longer." She opened her eyes. "I could manage two to three days locked down here, if need be."

"Ah, sweet." Tobias brought her hand to his lips. "You …" He stood. "Let me remove the platters. I will leave the goblets and carafe of water." He looked at the bed. "Do you think we can both lie there?"

A giggle broke through. "If we like each other again, we could."

"Do we?"

"If you like me after I acted like a child throwing a tantrum."

Tobias gave his grin. "You deserved more temper than you showed. You have suffered much, my sweet." He gathered up the platters. "I'll be back quickly. We need to get comfortable because the ship leaves soon."

Nava partially awoke when the pitch of the ship changed. She opened her eyes into the dark before moving closer to her husband and allowing sleep to pull her back under its spell.

Chapter 22

The delta :: a day later

The next evening, Nava enjoyed her second time on deck by standing at the rail, Tobias on one side of her and Philmon on the other.

"Hemut said we will see the delta by morning since the winds cooperated. The ship moved faster than expected." Tobias hugged Nava close. "Less than a full night and day and we will join Allus and the barge."

"That means how long until we reach the stone quarries?" Nava lowered her head to watch the foam of the water rush by the ship.

"We meet Allus at Tanis. From there to Swenet will take about seven to eight days, but we will be in comfort." Tobias paused. "If the winds are steady, it will take about seven days. If the winds die, though, rowers alone will move the boat up river."

"Rowers?" Nava searched his face in the dim light.

Philmon grunted. "Rowing barges and ships is worse than working in the quarries. The hours are long and the work back-breaking."

"I'll be joining the rowers to 'train' for the quarries," Tobias announced in a low voice.

"Why?" Nava turned her back to the rail to look at him.

Philmon answered her, "Little one, a man can't suddenly do the work required in the quarries. This way Tobias and I can prepare at least some for the pitiless work we face."

"I didn't know. I didn't think. The two of you are sacrificing much to keep us from the flames." Nava passed by the men. "I need to go to the cabin. Tobias, will you join me, please? I need to speak with you."

"Have a good rest, little one." Philmon laid his ham-sized hand on her shoulder. "Do not worry about Tobias and me. We are strong and will survive." A laugh rumbled in his chest. "Are we not warriors against the evil of Ahaz and Moleck? Ah, I must not forget Barrack."

"Yes, Philmon, you are indeed warriors and brave ones." A flash of white in the dark showed she smiled before going toward the passage to the cabins.

"I will be there shortly, Nava." Tobias touched her shoulder as she passed him.

When Tobias entered the cabin, Nava sat on the side of the bed nursing Benjamin. "I came back just in time, according to your son. He thought he was starving." She smiled at her son in her arms.

"Here is a gift." Tobias showed her a clump of grapes.

"Grapes? Where did you find grapes? It has been so long." She glanced at the baby and then at the fruit in her husband's hands. "As soon as the babe finishes, I will enjoy them."

"Why wait?" Tobias plucked one from the cluster and held it at her lips. She opened and took the fruit.

After chewing and swallowing, she closed her eyes. "Oh, so delicious."

"Here, have another." As the baby suckled, Tobias fed the grapes to Nava, taking one for himself from time to time. When Benjamin finished his meal, Tobias removed him from her arms and placed him in the cradle. "He is growing so fast. The cradle is already too small."

"Tobias?"

"Yes, sweet?"

"Thank you for the fruit."

Tobias sat beside her. "Philmon deserves the appreciation. He found them and brought them on the ship."

"I will thank him tomorrow." She lowered her head and watched her hands pick at her robe. "The sacrifice the two of you are making … the danger and torture you face … How can I ever thank you for that?"

"Sweet, we would gladly do all to keep you and the babe safe, but remember, we, or at least I am on the list to be thrown into the flames, too." He kissed her temple. "Philmon is the only one actually making a sacrifice."

She tipped her head to look into his eyes by the light of the flickering candle. "Yet, I was so hateful. You never reminded me that what I face is little compared to your future. You never reminded me that you married me, accepted my babe, and were willing to give your life to keep us safe." She wrapped her arms around him. "You *are* a warrior, a man of great strength."

Chapter 23

The Egyptian Delta :: morning

As soon as the boat docked, Hemut told the others, "Stay here. I'll find where the barge is and return."

Nava stood on deck watching the activity beyond the boat as she held the baby. Women showed their faces, unveiled as found often in Judea. Men carried burdens from ships to land, from land to ships. When the babe fussed, she pointed to the horses fretting on the deck behind them. "See, Benjamin. See the horses." She turned him to face the throng on the land. "Look, goats." She pointed and named different animals, bouncing him in her arms.

Tobias joined his family. "Hemut has been gone for longer than I expected. Philmon and I have everything packed and on deck, ready." He searched the dockside. "Seems many Egyptian soldiers patrol below." He jerked back from the rail. "Come, get behind a pile of bales." He hurried her and the babe away. Once they stood unseen from the land, he said, "I saw Judean military. A bad sign."

Philmon slipped behind the bundles. "Something is wrong. The captain tried to signal some of the soldiers. I put him to sleep in his cabin."

Glancing around, Tobias asked, "What about the crew? Do you think they will cause trouble?"

"I do not think they know what is happening. I made sure they didn't observe me take their captain for a short walk to his cabin."

Nava held the baby close to her. "What is wrong?" She drew back against the pile of packs as if to melt into it. "We've traveled so far. I still do not understand Barrack's interest in you and Amzi. If he knew about me, I could understand, but not you."

"Look, there's Hemut, slipping from pile to pile below." Philmon moved from their hiding place. "I will see if I can help." He strode to the gangplank and to the ground. Without a pause, he moved to stand in the middle of several small hills of goods and studied them. He whispered beneath his breath, "What do we need to do?"

From the other side of the pile, Hemut replied, "We must get our things and the others off the ship without anyone noticing. I have hired some laborers to remove the packs and bundles, but I don't know how to get Tobias, Nava, and the babe off unseen."

"I can get clothing from the crew for Tobias, but I do not know what to do about the little one and her babe." Philmon moved around to another pile of bundles. "Perhaps ... We need a huge fight or something that takes the attention of the soldiers away from this area. I see a group of women looking at lengths of silk not far away. I will visit with them, see if they will help save a young mother and her child."

Philmon and Hemut visited, fine tuning their plan as much as they could. Philmon then meandered through the piles of goods until he reached the women and the seller.

Minutes later, as Philmon moved toward the ship, he nodded at Hemut.

After Philmon rejoined Nava and Tobias behind the bundles on the deck, he explained his plan for Tobias to dress as a crew member and for Nava to hide Benjamin under her cloak and hurry to the women at the silk vendor's when a fight took the soldiers away from their ship. He told them Hemut had laborers who would remove their provisions. "The laborers' arrival will signal the escape. You, Tobias, will carry a load off with the laborers and walk past the silk vendor. Hemut will await you with a horse and cart. Nava will lean against me as if ill. We will join you at the Inn of the Sun as quickly as we can."

He shook his head. "If we could keep the babe quiet. That will be a problem."

Nava stared into space. "What if I feed him a bit? He might sleep."

"Go to the cabin and do so. Come back with your cloak about you and the babe." Philmon looked at Tobias. "Let us get your 'new' clothing."

When Nava returned to the deck, Benjamin slept in her arms, hidden under her cloak. "Sorry, my baby, I hope the heat doesn't awaken you," she whispered.

"We are ready any moment. Lean on me." Philmon moved beside her. "The laborers arrived. See? Tobias and they leave with a load and leading two horses. Wait, don't see. It is better you keep your head lowered."

Yelling and screaming caused Nava to raise her head despite his warning. She peered from the hood of her cloak as they hustled down the wobbly gang-plank and onto solid land. She leaned against the solid force that was Philmon, and he hurried her through the piles of goods to the silk vendor's stall.

"Go with these women. They will take you to meet Tobias. They only speak Egyptian, and I told them you didn't. Therefore, just smile. I will go with the laborers and bring the horses."

Within the hour, the group gathered in a barn at the back of the Inn of the Sun. They squatted or sat in one corner, each describing his and her escape.

"The women were so kind. They all wanted to hold Benjamin." Nava pulled two lengths of silk from under her mantle. "They insisted I take this. At least I think that's what they meant since they hid the silk under my cloak."

Philmon chuckled. "I told them you were escaping slavery. They know about slavery."

"At least we are all here," Hemut said. "Now, I'll signal my brother Raz to join us."

"Raz is here?" Tobias sat on the ground and pulled Benjamin into his lap. Nava sat on a bag of feed beside him.

Hemut nodded. "He is the reason we are not all on our way back to Judah. Barrack reached the local officials, told them I am a spy, that we all are escaped prisoners and should be returned to face our fates."

"So far none realize I am part of you," Philmon said, "but once they release the captain, they will know. Since no one watched for me, I led the horses past several soldiers."

"Pssst."

Hemut rose and moved to the opening of the barn. "Come inside, quickly, Raz."

A slender man in flowing robes slipped through the pens of the barn. When he spied Tobias, he squatted beside his sister's son. "I see you have your hands full." He spoke Hebrew, as did the others.

"Nava, this is my uncle Raz. He and Hemut take turns with the caravans and the shipping business." He turned to answer his uncle. "Yes, very full. How are you, uncle?"

"Angry." He jerked to his feet and paced in a circle. "My family has been important in this country for hundreds of years, and now a foreigner arrives, telling a wild story, and the officials believe him."

"What about up river?" Hemut asked. "Will we be safe at Thebes?"

Raz nodded. "Of course, we will have to send Tobias to the quarries as you planned, but you and I will be all right. Our father's influence is still strong at the head of the Nile." Raz turned to Tobias and squatted beside him again. He studied the baby sleeping in his nephew's lap. "Our father is unhappy about not being able to see his grandson or his grandson's son. He is not happy at all."

"We are not happy, either, Raz. My wife and son should be living in luxury, not facing life in a hut at a quarry. Tzabar has lost his mind and follows King Ahaz and this Barrack, who dares bring a small force into Egypt, all because they want to please Moleck, a bronze idol."

"We must wait until dark before we go to the barge. The bundles and horses are already loaded." Raz rose. "We will prevail, if not today, soon."

Chapter 24

On the barge :: after sunset

Nava looked around her. The cabin had a window with shutters. The bed, large enough for several people, held soft pillows and covers. A different cradle filled a spot in one corner, larger with a thick pad in the bottom. After feeding Benjamin, Nava placed him in his new bed, and he snuggled into its comfort.

In a large chest, she found modest robes and sandals that fit her, plus jars of creams and oils. In another chest, she discovered clothes that looked the size for Tobias. Not elaborate, they would meet the couple's needs in the life they faced. A smaller chest held items for the baby.

"Wonderful. Someone cares." She twirled in the center of the cabin. "I could stay here and never leave."

"Oh, you think you would like to be a vagabond?" Tobias stood in the open doorway, one shoulder propped against the frame, watching as the candles threw light and shadows over her body. "Benjamin asleep?"

"Yes, and I want to thank whoever thought of providing a larger cradle."

"I believe we can thank Raz for that. He has several children, and all are older than Benjamin. He brought the cradle used for his youngest." He grinned as she smiled. "Hungry? A meal is waiting on deck. Will the babe be all right here?"

She waved a hand toward the open window. "Surely if he fusses, I will be able to hear." She laughed. "As demanding as our son is, he will be sure I hear." Tobias escorted her from the cabin and up the steps to the deck. Under an awning with torches providing light, a low table, covered with dishes and bowls filled with food, sat between divans. The blended fragrances caused Nava's stomach to growl.

"I believe I am hungry." She walked to where Philmon and both brothers half-reclined on couches. She and Tobias shared the remaining one.

Servants brought more dishes as the people visited and laughed and ate. Nava gazed at the passing shoreline, a darker shadow along the river. The breeze cooled those on deck. Stars twinkled above the horizon. When offered more drink, she shook her head.

"I have eaten and drank all I can hold. Thank you." She smiled at the slight woman holding the jar. She rose and turned to Tobias. "I need to sleep. Will you be long?"

"No, sweet, not too much longer. Raz needs to tell Philmon and me our rowing schedules for the days to come. When we finish, I'll be down."

"Rowing schedules? I forgot. If you don't mind, I will wait." She returned to her seat. She wrung her hands in her lap until Tobias laid one of his over hers.

He smiled. "All will work, sweet. Don't fear."

Her emerald eyes, darker in the torch light, searched his. "I cannot help but fear. What you will do for us ..." She paused and looked around the table at the men watching her. "I am sorry. I'm weak sometimes. Please conduct your business, and I will listen."

Raz sat straight and bowed. "You are most welcome to join the discussion if you wish."

"Let's hear what hours we will labor, Raz, and what else we should know." Philmon stood and walked to the edge of the awning, his massive arms folded over his chest as he stared toward the sky.

Nava watched the stiffness, the tension in the Ethiopian's shoulders and back.

"Yes, we should begin." Raz drank from his goblet. "To start, for the first two days you will row one half the first shift and then one half the third shift. You will dress as the other rowers. You will have most meals with them. When not on a shift, you may rest in your cabins or on this part of the deck—after changing to your regular clothes. The third day, you will row a full shift and half another. Our rowers are expected to man the oars three of four shifts each day."

"We will be expected to row three shifts by the time we arrive?" Philmon didn't turn as he asked.

Raz and Hemut both laughed. "Hardly," Hemut answered, "but you will be stronger by the time we leave you at the quarry." He stared at Tobias. "This will be harder than anything you can imagine. I hope you can endure, but if you can't, Raz, our other brothers, and I will find another way to keep you safe."

The night grew old, but Nava could not sleep. She rolled to where she could watch her sleeping husband. She touched the frown between his eyes as she mentally told him, *You worry, too, but you won't let it show.* She grimaced in the dark. *Most men your age are beginning their lives and don't have to worry about a wife or child for years. Yet, young as you are, you are indeed a man.*

Chapter 25

Tobias awoke while the night still covered the land. He tried to find his clothing in the dark but stumbled against a chest. Nava struggled up from the covers.

"Is it time already?" She stood. "Why didn't you light a candle?"

He chuckled. "I tried not to wake you." He took a flint and lit a candle on the wall. He picked up a length of white cloth and a garment with short sleeves. After wrapping the cloth around his middle until part flowed behind him, he bent over and grabbed the end and pulled it between his legs, tucking it into the front of the wrapped material. He slipped on the other garment, which covered part of his back and chest as well as his shoulders.

"We break our fast with the rest of the crew and then begin our first shift." Tobias wrapped her in his arms and brushed a kiss across her lips. "Hemut said he would be sure you had meals." He kissed her again. "Do *not* worry. We will survive."

Three hours later once relieved by another rower, Tobias wondered if he would survive or not. The sun beating down on him, the constant pull on his muscles to ply the heavy oar, the lack of movement other than rowing caused him to shuffle in a bent position as he made his way to the cabin. Philmon followed, in better shape, but still Tobias could see the pain etched into the man's face.

"Tobias, do not look at me with pity. We know what we must do, and we will do it. The little one and the babe must be kept from the claws of Moleck." Philmon's voice still carried its boom.

"I look at you in wonder, friend. You don't have to go through this torture, yet here you are." Tobias rubbed the small of his back. "I thought I had built muscles and strength. How foolish of me."

"Rest and eat and drink. We must be back at our oars at sunset. At least the next shift will be out of the sun's heat." Philmon left the younger man and continued to where he slept.

Nava threw open the door. "I thought I heard you. Oh, let me help you."

She put an arm around her husband's waist and took some of his weight. Once inside, she eased him into a chair. "What's wrong? I mean what hurts you the most. I can tell you're in pain."

With lowered head, Tobias muttered, "All over, but mostly my arms, my shoulders, my back, and across my chest."

She scurried to the chest with oils and creams. She opened a few jars before choosing one. "Sit still. This helped heal my hands, and perhaps it will help your aches. Here, remove this," she plucked at the light shirt he wore. Once he removed it, she took a small amount of the oil and spread it over her palms. She then rubbed the oil over his shoulders and down his back. After adding more to her hands, she smoothed it over his arms.

"Ummm, that feels good, so good." Tobias relaxed under her ministrations.

"I, uh, I need you to lean back so I can help the muscles in your chest." A blush streaked her cheeks. "I've … I've never …"

He took her hand in his and kissed it. "Sweet, we need to get accustomed to each other's bodies. At least, for me, this is pleasurable. Is it unpleasant for you?"

She ducked her head. "No," she whispered. She repeated, "You need to lean back, now."

Once he did, she smoothed the oil over the muscles in his neck and down his chest. Finally, she spread oil over his face and head. When she finished, she backed away. "Now, lie in the bed and rest. I will bring food –"

A knock at the door interrupted her. She opened the door to find two serving girls carrying several platters of food and two goblets on large trays. "The master said to bring food and drink," one of the servants said in Egyptian.

Nava looked at Tobias, who answered in the same language, "Thank you. Please place the trays on the table." He stood and moved to sit on the side of the bed.

The two girls giggled as they slanted glances in his direction. They placed the food on the table before backing toward the door, still staring at Tobias and giggling. Nava grabbed an arm and pushed the girl attached out the door. Before she could clasp an arm of the other girl, that one rushed through the door.

"They … they …" Nava sputtered. She stared at Tobias, not able to finish.

He sprawled across the bed, asleep.

Chapter 26

Nearly to Tentyris, north of Thebes :: three days on the river

Tobias forced himself from the bed. Two days of manning an oar for parts of two shifts each day left him with muscles that screamed in pain with every movement. His shoulders, elbows, and wrists creaked and cracked for hours after he arose. The massage of oil provided by Nava after each session eased the major cramps and agony, but he still moved like an old man until he stretched and moved for several minutes.

"Tobias?" Nava crawled from the covers.

He waved a hand in her direction. "Go back to sleep. Benjamin will be awake before long, and at least one of us should rest when possible." He bent his back and felt the popping.

"Today you must row the full shift. How will you manage?" She moved behind him and began to work her fingers into his back muscles.

"Ummm … feels good." He bent forward and grabbed his ankles, listening to more pops and cracks. "Yes, a full shift this morning. I'll manage as well as I can."

"I'll get you food." Nava started toward the door, but Tobias grabbed her hand.

"No, Philmon and I must eat with the others." He clasped his arm around her. "I will manage and grow stronger. At least I have your hands," he lifted and kissed them, "and the way you use that oil. Poor Philmon has nothing."

She glanced through her lashes. "Should I use the oil on him, too."

"What? Of course not." He chuckled. "However, if you have enough of that oil, he might find his own method to rub it in." He moved to where his "clothing" lay and dressed. "I will see you at the mid-day meal." Twisting and maneuvering his arms and shoulders, he left the cabin.

After the men on the shift ate their gruel, they took their places on the benches, ten rows on each side of the barge. The oar each man used stretched longer than five men and weighed twice as much as a heavy man. Tobias sat and lifted his oar, giving a low moan. He knew Philmon did the same behind him.

As the sun began to peek over the horizon, Tobias heard a thump followed by several other thumps against the side of the barge. He twisted his head to glance at the overseer who made sure the rowers kept in unison. The man leaned over the side and spoke to someone below him in the water. He straightened and hurried between the benches to the ladder leading to the deck above. Tobias and the other men at the oars continued rowing. In a few minutes, the overseer appeared at the top of the ladder.

"We will change directions. Hold oars up until I am back in position. We will head for Tentyris as soon as the sail is lowered."

Tobias dipped his head as he held his oar in an upward posture. He spoke so that Philmon behind him could hear. "Wonder what is wrong?"

"What makes you think anything is wrong? Perhaps it is good." A laugh followed the big man's words.

Raz appeared at the top of the ladder with two of the regular rowers. As the two men descended, he called to Tobias and Philmon. "Come up. We need to talk."

When they reached the top deck, Hemut sat with another man under the awning. Nava watched from where she held Benjamin.

"Ferris! Philmon, meet another of my uncles, Ferris." Tobias reached the man who jumped to his feet to embrace his nephew. "But what brings you here?" Tobias faced Hemut. "What has happened?"

"Sit, Ferris will bring you up to date." Hemut waved a hand toward the couch where Nava sat.

As soon as Tobias dropped beside his wife, Ferris began speaking in Egyptian. Nava watched as a serving girl moved closer to the group, obviously listening to what the man said.

"Please, I am sorry, but would someone tell me what is wrong?" She looked at each of the men. "I hope I'm not interfering."

"No, no, we were rude not to use Hebrew so you could understand," Ferris said. "I'll begin again."

The serving girl frowned before she turned away. Nava thought no one but she noticed until she saw Philmon watch the girl's movement toward the passage below the deck. Nava forced her attention back to what Tobias' uncle had to say.

"So, Barrack tried to turn Pharaoh against my grandfather and you and my other uncles?" Tobias asked. "What is wrong with the man? Why does he hunt us so relentlessly?"

"I overheard something that may explain something. I'll share that later," Ferris replied, "but Pharaoh has known Father too long to take 'the word of someone who dares bring an invading force into my country.' I was there when Father brought his petition before Pharaoh. Barrack became furious, but he had no choice but leave." Tobias' uncle rubbed his hand over the top of his shaved head. "But nothing seems to faze Barrack. He hired a barge and declared he would find you on his way back to the delta."

When Ferris paused, Raz spoke. "We must get off the river and find a way to keep the mad man's attention away from you, a way to hide you."

"Father sent me to warn you and to find more workers for the quarries. If we pull into Tentyris, the crew can work on pretended damages to the barge while I search for workers. Tobias, his family, and friend can hide at Mother's brother's home in the city until we can leave again." Ferris turned to Hemut. "What think you of that plan?"

Hemut stood and walked to look at the water flowing past the side of the barge as the vessel moved toward the port. "It might work if we can be sure no one talks about them being on board. I cannot trust everyone on this barge or those who would see our passengers leave and return."

Philmon left his spot behind the brothers to stand behind Tobias and Nava. "There are spies here. One serving girl has tried to overhear every conversation, even when told to tend to other duties. She listened carefully while you spoke in Egyptian. What she heard, if passed to the wrong person, will destroy all hope for our survival."

"I must think." Raz rose and paced under the awning. "I can have us pull between two of our barges already at Tentyris, barges loading to sail down river. I do trust all on both of those. I will have men guard everyone on this barge we cannot vouch to be for us."

Returning to sit, Hemut added, "We would move Tobias, Nava, the babe, and Philmon in the deep of night, in a mass of trusted workers, and we would return them the same way." He stared at Nava. "Do you think you could wear men's clothing long enough to get to safety?"

"But, of course. I would cut my hair, if that helped us escape Barrack's notice. But what of the babe?" Nava cuddled Benjamin to her chest.

"No need to cut your hair. We would have you wear a head dress. Do you think the babe would be quiet if he were placed in a basket that you or Tobias carried?" Raz asked.

Nava nodded. "If he had been fed just before placed in the basket."

"And, we will speak only in Hebrew when anyone we don't know well is around us." Ferris stood. "I will tell the pilot where to dock us." He headed toward the ladder to the rowing deck and turned back. "Ah, what I heard: Barrack was in disfavor with the king because his young wife and their child disappeared before the sacrifice. He is trying to return to Ahaz' good favor."

As his uncle leaped downward, Tobias slid his arm around Nava. "Let me take Benjamin, and we'll go to our cabin. We'll be arriving at Tentyris in a few hours, and we should be out of sight." His eyes met Philmon's across the back of the couch. "Philmon, why don't you join us?"

"I will be there in a short time. I wish to have a visit with a serving girl."

"No, Philmon, I will do that errand." Raz started toward the companion-way. "It is my responsibility."

Nava could tell by the movement of the barge and the sounds outside that the barge docked. An hour earlier, Tobias closed the shutters over the window so no one could see inside. Philmon went to his cabin to pack his belongings as Nava nursed the baby, and Tobias packed items for himself, Nava, and Benjamin. When Philmon returned, he carried a large basket with a lid and some clothes for Nava to wear.

"While you change into the boy's clothes, the smallest Raz could find, I will check with Raz." Philmon laid the clothes on the table and placed the basket and a bundle on the floor before he left again.

After laying a sleeping Benjamin in the padded basket, Nava examined the blousy pants and shirt. "I'm to wear these?"

"Yes, sweet, but you'll have a sleeveless robe to cover them." Tobias picked up some cloth and what appeared to be a thin rope. "We'll create a head dress from this to cover your hair. Now, let me help you."

By the time a band of seven "men" left the barge, Nava looked like a young boy surrounded by muscular workers. Each man carried a bundle, including the "boy." One man, walking next to the boy, carried a large basket. The group slipped silently through the darkness and along the dirt road leading from the dock area.

The boy pulled on the arm of the man carrying the basket. When he bent, Nava whispered, "Someone watches us, Tobias."

He rose to his full height again and replied in Egyptian, "The boy fears what he be facing." His voice, quiet as it was, carried in the stillness.

"Remind him, as the master told us, we return by dark tomorrow or face the whip. That is a fear we be facing if late." Raz's answer, also in Egyptian, reached all in the group.

Tobias leaned close to Nava and repeated what he and his uncle said so she could understand. "We have been too quiet, which is suspicious to any who might watch."

Nava lowered her head and kept walking as the men around her continued to make occasional comments as they moved toward the center of the city. *Soon, we'll be safe again, soon.* Her thoughts kept pace with her steps. *Please, my Lord, bring us to safety.* She flinched with every creak and shuffle in the shadows of the moon-lit night.

Chapter 27

Hadara's farm, a half-hour-walk from Bethlehem :: two months later

The night cloaked the land as a cold wind whipped around corners of the exterior walls of the compound. Inside the house, occupants huddled around fire pots and pits. Women had cleaned the kitchen after the night meal, and they joined family members in their sections of the compound. Hadara and Mazza sat together by the fire pot in the main chamber of their rooms. While Hadara shared a message from her parents, Mazza sewed. The lamps and fire pot provided flickering light.

After finishing the story of the "escape" from the barge in Tentyris, Hadara laughed. "Can you imagine Nava dressing as a boy?" She smoothed her fingers over the parchment. "My mother has to use what others tell her to pass on to us. I know she wishes to see Tobias and the babe, to meet her granddaughter by marriage, but she can't without endangering them."

"I assume they finally left Tentyris." Mazza glanced from the cloth in her lap.

Hadara chuckled. "I'm sorry. Let me continue." She held the parchment so the light would shine directly on the wording.

"We do have an idea why this Barrack is so determined to find Tobias and someone named Amzi. Ferris overheard that Ahaz is angry because Barrack's young wife and child disappeared. But, we believed the problem over when Pharaoh sent him back to Judah. As he left, though, he promised a huge reward to anyone who returned the two men and their companions to Jerusalem," Hadara read. "We thought Tobias, his family, and his friend could stay with us and avoid the quarries, but with criminals searching for them, they must hide."

Hadara raised her eyes from the message. "My son working as a laborer. My Nava and the babe living in a hovel." She heaved a sigh. "Tzabar and Ahaz have much for which to answer, and so does Barrack."

She sighed again and began reading once more. "Since this Barrack has used Tobias' name and has given the information they speak Hebrew, Nava is learning Egyptian, and my grandson's name is that of your favorite uncle."

"Your favorite uncle? Was that not Tor?"

"Yes, Tor." Hadara sighed again. "She ends with her love." After laying the parchment on a small table beside her chair, she covered her face with both hands. "My son working in the quarries. Nava and the babe living like the poorest, the neediest. I can do nothing to help. No one can except to pray they are hidden well."

"Your family will keep guard over them, as well as possible." Mazza looked up from her sewing to frown in her charge's direction. "I'm surprised Tzabar isn't leading the search for them."

Hadara opened her mouth to respond but a tap on the door interrupted her. Simeon opened it without waiting for anyone to invite him.

"Hadara, we have an emergency." He opened the door farther to allow a man and a young woman carrying a child about two years old to enter.

The man threw back his hood to reveal a scraggly beard and long, unkempt hair. "Do you not recognize me, Mistress."

Hadara leaped to her feet. "Amzi, it's good to see you, but, but why are you here?" She walked toward him and the woman. "Who is this?"

As Simeon closed the door, Amzi replied, "I'm with a band of rebels, and lately we've been helping women hide their children from being sacrifices." He touched the woman's arm. "This is Adi, Barrack's second wife, and her son."

"Barrack's wife? I don't understand. Why did you bring her and her son here?" Hadara backed away a couple of steps. "Do you not know Barrack is still searching for Tobias and, yes, you as replacements for her and the child?" She shrugged one shoulder. "Although, he would never recognize you now."

The woman raised her eyes from searching the floor. "Please, do not blame my child for what my husband does. Mika is innocent, and I want to keep him from being burned alive." Her eyes filled with tears which she fought as she pleaded with Hadara. "Amzi tried to move us from a hiding place that was no longer safe to one that is when … when the soldiers discovered us. They are close, please help."

"I didn't know what else to do, Mistress." Amzi shrugged. "Adi's son grew too large and vocal to stay where they were. I hoped you might hide us until the soldiers leave the area." He huffed a breath. "I'm sorry because now we've put you in danger."

Simeon spoke from behind Amzi. "Hadara, they cannot leave without being found by the soldiers."

Hadara nodded. "I know. I know." She dropped to her chair. "I cannot allow another babe to burn to death if I can save him." She looked at Adi, the child in her arms, Amzi, and then Simeon. "Simeon, fix pallets in the hidden room off the kitchen. Help them settle in and give them food and drink." She paused before adding, "Your sons will be found. You must have them hide."

"Hadara, they are safe." Simeon nodded. "We had noticed soldiers in the area earlier today."

Adi sobbed and hugged her son until he wiggled and fussed. "Thank you. Thank you."

"No, do not thank me. I pray Amzi will be able to lead you to complete safety after the soldiers are gone." Hadara smiled, but her lips trembled. "Now, please go with Simeon. There must be no sign of you nor any sound when the soldiers come. I'm sure they will be here before long."

"Mistress, please know I would not have brought Adi here if I could have found anywhere else." Amzi paused. "We will leave as quickly as possible."

Hadara turned to face her son's half-brother. "Please visit with me before you leave the farm, but now go before you are found. Also, no one must call me 'Mistress' as we all must be considered part of the family here."

The man nodded and followed Simeon and the woman from the room.

"What have you done?" Mazza demanded. Her frown and glare empathized her anger. "We are safe, but you have endangered yourself and us."

Hadara bit her upper lip before answering. "I know, but I saved my son. Should she not be able to do the same?"

"Your actions didn't put innocents at risk."

"Yes, they did. Philmon is now sought. My family would be in great danger if they weren't necessary to Pharaoh." She picked up the parchment from her mother, rose, and dropped the missive in the fire. "I hate we must always erase all trace of my family, of our old life. We must check that nothing is left. I'm sure the solders will turn the compound inside out as they try to find our guests. I will pray they hurt no one while searching."

From the now-opened door, Simeon replied, "Yes, and I have sent my family members to search and destroy anything dangerous. Amzi, Barrack's wife, her son, and traces of them are hidden." He paced around the room. "When a person is familiar with something, it is easy to miss an item that could expose us."

"I know, Simeon, and Hadara and I burn any message after it is read." Mazza placed her sewing on the floor beside her. "If she wishes to keep anything, we place it in the hidden room off this room."

"And, everyone thought me mad to insist on having secret places in this house, never mind the tunnels from our cellar area to the outside farms," Hadara retorted. "Yet, here we are, using them."

Mazza gasped. "No, no, I could understand your fears, but— "

"Don't, Mazza. I know you and my family, who actually saw to the building and adaptations, believed me a bit mad, but one can ever tell what might be needed." Hadara took a deep breath and exhaled. "Perhaps I was given a premonition. Perhaps a new task was to be mine."

A booming, thundering pounding on the gates caused the three to freeze in place. More pounding followed.

"I will go. The soldiers have arrived." Simeon hurried from the room, pulling the door closed behind him.

"Mazza, pick up your sewing and work. I'll get mine from the chest. We must look normal but surprised by unexpected visitors."

Moments later, Simeon tapped on the door before opening it. "Hadara, soldiers search for escaped criminals." Behind him, three burly men stood, swords in hand.

Mazza and Hadara rose from their chairs, laying the cloths and threads on the seats. Hadra asked, "Why do you look here? I do not understand." She waved a hand toward the weapons. "Are we dangerous that you need swords?"

One of the men answered, as he replaced his sword in its scabbard, "No, ma'am, we don't believe you be dangerous, but we be told the criminals must be found. I be Caleb." The tall, muscled man motioned toward the men with him, and they also returned their weapons to their scabbards. "We must search the house and all buildings inside the walls. Orders."

"I see. But you think these 'criminals' could have invaded our home?" She swallowed. "And, what kind of criminals are they, how many? Are we in danger from them?"

"They be three. They escaped the king's decree. We will do our search fast and be gone." As Caleb talked, he walked around the room, peeking under tables and chairs, pulling aside drapes over windows, and even removing cushions.

Mazza clasped her throat with a wrinkled hand. "Do you believe we hide them here?"

The soldier's eyes narrowed as he stared at her. "No, old woman, but when the king asks I be able to say I looked everywhere." His eyes narrowed more as he stared at Hadara, a frown formed between his brows. "Madam, you be safe."

"Oh, I see. That does make sense." Mazza dropped back into her chair.

"Where do those doors lead." He pointed to two closed doors.

"Our sleeping chambers," Hadara answered.

Caleb turned to the men at the door. "Go join the others in their search. Nothing nor no one is to be harmed. Take all the people to the kitchen and wait with them there. I will finish here and bring these two."

As she noticed the change in Caleb's speech from rough soldier to that of a more educated man, she said nothing about it. "Do you destroy our home?" Hadara slid an arm around Mazza as they watched the two soldiers whirl and march away.

"No, you heard my order: no harm." Caleb stared at Hadara again. "No one will be harmed here. No one."

Hadara tilted her head. "You send me another message, don't you?"

"Let us say a person needn't take all things as they seem. Come, let us join the others."

Mazza glanced at Hadara then Caleb and back at Hadara. "I don't understand."

"I will explain what I think I know after we're alone. Stay calm. I believe we're safe. Now let us go with Caleb." She smiled at him. "Our lives are in your hands, and I have a feeling that we will see you again, perhaps often."

Caleb nodded and motioned for the women to precede him through the door.

As the small group moved along the inner courtyard, on the path beneath the roof overhang, a crash and a woman's scream froze Hadara and Mazza. Hadara turned to the soldier who appeared to be in charge. "Are we more in danger with your men or the rebels you seek?"

The man swore. "Go to the kitchen. I'll follow after I tend to this problem." He jerked open the door to the chamber beside them.

Mazza and Hadara entered the large corner kitchen area, with its fireplace large enough to hold a full goat or sheep, working tables, cabinets, and a large table with stools and chairs circling it. Many of Simeon's family, but none of the grown men, sat huddled around the table. Soldiers stood around the sides of the room, hands on weapons in case any of the frightened group should decide to escape or attack. Simeon stood and offered his chair to Hadara as one of his daughters did the same for Mazza.

Silence blanketed the room until Caleb opened the door and escorted a sobbing woman in. "Alber," he ordered a man by the door, "Evan is outside in the hall. Take him to camp and put him under guard for disobeying orders."

Rachel hurried from her seat to wrap arms around her daughter. "Let me see. Where are you hurt?"

"I ... he hit me, but ... the other soldier came in before ..." The young woman shuddered and buried her face in her mother's shoulder.

Rachel looked at Caleb. "You, you a soldier, saved our daughter?"

"He disobeyed an order." Caleb waved off her comment. "Now, where is the rest of your household, the men?"

Simeon stepped forward. "They are pasturing the rest of the sheep and goats."

One soldier laughed. "Look at all the women around this man. Of course, he be sure to send other men away."

Caleb turned to stare at the soldier. "Men with the means offer a home to widowed mothers, sisters, and sisters of wives. This man does the same."

The soldier ducked his head, "Be that possible."

With a shake of his head, Caleb added, "Wonder if Tzabar's widow have any brother or father or some other to give her a home now."

The soldier raised his head. "Not if she be from where I heared."

Caleb shrugged. "Just remember that all is not clear from what be seen."

"Yes, sir." The soldier nodded.

Hadara sat stunned but forced her vision away from Caleb.. *He does know who I am.* She swallowed the shock and fear. *Tzabar is dead. He's dead.* She raised her eyes from her twisting hands to see Caleb watching her. He nodded before turning to his men.

"We be finished here. Let's go. We have other places to search." As his men filed out, he spoke to Simeon. "I hope we did little damage. You will be safe." He glanced at Hadara and smiled, changing his rough-honed face to one more attractive. "You are safe."

Hours later, after the squad of soldiers left, Simeon, Rachel, Mazza, and Hadara sat in the kitchen. In the partially open door to the secret room, Amzi could be part of the conversation but slip back into hiding within a second.

Behind him, Adi and Mika slept.

"They left little mess, but I will wait until after dawn to have workers put things aright." Simeon glanced toward a window. "Just three or four hours from now."

Hadara studied Amzi long enough that he squirmed before she asked, "How did you become involved with aiding women to save their children, and especially involved with Adi?"

Amzi bowed his head and then raised it to face her. "I've been part of a band of rebels fighting against those who force Moleck on people, especially sacrificing their children." His lips pressed together. "Did you know Ahaz declares that statues of Moleck will be erected at every town and village and that all citizens are to 'volunteer' their children as sacrifice to the god?"

"The people of Bethlehem are refusing to allow a statue in the town." Rachel stood and walked to the stove where a pot of water boiled. "The king's men built it outside the walls away from us."

"I joined the rebels because I know the evil found in Ahaz and his court. I wanted to do something to strike back at Tzabar." He shrugged one shoulder. "What better way than to thwart their plans to sacrifice children? Then when Adi escaped soon after she gave birth, and she stayed hidden in Jerusalem until her family couldn't keep the child out of sight and quiet enough, word was sent to us." He grinned. "What Ahaz and his nobles don't know is we have men within their ranks."

"Amzi, this life you now lead must be full of risks." Hadara twisted her fingers together. "If you had been found tonight, you would die a terrible death."

Amzi chuckled, but no humor could be heard. "If I am found any time, as Tzabar's 'son,' I face a fiery death. I would be another ember in Moleck's collection. At least with the life I live and danger of death, I can take some of the wicked with me." He frowned. "If I heard right, Caleb let us know Tzabar is dead."

"We heard about Ahaz and Barrack but nothing about Tzarba until tonight," Simeon said. "He is not the one searching for Tobias and for you; Barrack is. All seems strange, especially now that Tzabar is apparently gone."

Leaning a shoulder against the wall, Amzi wiped a hand over his face. "I think I need sleep." He nodded. "Yes, our spies within the city say Tzabar hasn't been seen at official functions or anywhere for weeks. His staff has been reduced, the number of soldiers guarding him down to two. It is strange." He straightened. "Yes, I need sleep. I need rest so that I can take Adi and Mika to their new home."

"We all need rest." Simeon stood. "My sons, who have returned, will guard the compound in shifts, and two husbands of my daughters will keep an eye on what the soldiers do, make sure they don't return without warning."

"Caleb recognized me," Hadara said. "I knew when you brought him to our room, Simeon. He hid the knowledge from his men. I don't understand. He could have gained much if he had turned me in to his superiors."

Amzi glanced over his shoulder. "I said we have men in their ranks. Caleb shared a dangerous secret with you, dangerous to him."

"Amzi, don't forget to visit with me before you leave," Hadara reminded him as he slipped into the secret room, shutting the opening behind him.

Simeon stood. "Let's all get some sleep. We need to make plans to be sure we are not taken unaware."

"What do you mean?" Mazza asked as she pushed herself to her feet.

"I feel we are about to become a part of saving women and their children." His mouth twisted into a partial smile. "Am I right?" He looked at Hadara.

Hadara heaved a deep sigh. "Am I so easy to read?"

"Only to one who knows and understands you," Rachel inserted. "We have gone through much together, and I know *I* need to help those fleeing Moleck's evil."

Hadara searched each face. "If we do this, our lives will be at risk every moment. Even if our names are unknown, soldiers will search for us. If we are discovered, we will probably be sacrificed to Moleck or worse. We must all agree or not do this."

"Hadara, are you insane?" Mazza's voice and body shook. "We escaped danger only to jump into more?"

Placing a hand on Mazza's arm, Hadara answered, "Can we hide in our safety while Ahaz and his nobles throw more and more children in the fire?"

"I ... I am afraid, oh, more for you than for me. I am old, my life close to the end. But you," she waved a hand at Hadara and the others, "you have a full life ahead. Are you truly ready to throw it away?"

Rachel pulled Mazza into a hug. "How can we not, Mazza? If we do nothing, are we not as guilty as those who throw the babes onto the burning hands or into the flames?"

The retainer bowed her head. "You are correct." She raised her head. "We will do what damage the one true God gives us time and ability to do."

An hour after the noon meal, Amzi joined Hadara in her sitting room. "We will leave within minutes, Miss ... Hadara."

"I thought you wouldn't be safe to leave until after dark." Hadara rose to face her former servant.

"A group of villagers are going to the hills for a ceremony of some kind. We can join them and be less noticeable. One of Simeon's son's wife and children are going since her parents live close to the spot the others will have their retreat." His dark eyes crinkled in a smile. "Hopefully, we will be lost in the crowd."

"Amzi, you have changed so much and have grown into a man of courage and character. I hope you will stay in contact as much as you can without endangering yourself." She paused. "If we can help ..." She dropped her head. "I'm afraid to offer our help, but I feel I must."

The former part-eunuch's smile reached his lips. "Hadara, I promise not to use your offer unless absolutely necessary. Thank you for offering." He reached to touch her hands fisted together at her waist. "You could have had me killed but didn't. You trusted me with your son and Nava, even after I had done the unthinkable. You owe me nothing, but I owe you more than I can ever repay."

Hadara took his hand in hers. "May the true God go with you. I am honest when I say we will help if needed. Remember we are here."

"This is dangerous, beyond what you can imagine. I will not accept your offer unless I have no choice." He removed his hand from hers, smiled, and left the chamber.

Hadara watched him leave. "I don't know whether to feel relieved or disappointed."

Chapter 28

Nearly two years later

Over a year passed with Hadara's household occasionally working with the rebels to help mothers escape with their babes. Caleb visited often, saying he wanted to see if they needed anything. He and Hadara often talked about things they found interesting, even if they had but a few minutes together. Now after five months of no word about the hiding of mothers and children, Hadara enjoyed the warmer weather by working in the vegetable garden located in a corner of the compound.

"Hadara, you should have others do this work." Mazza placed her hands on her hips. "You are the mistress, not a servant."

Hadara straightened and rubbed the small of her back. "Mazza, Mazza, we are now one family. I'm not the mistress, and no one is a servant." She smiled. "Besides, I enjoy working with plants. Rachel knows so much about raising food items, and she has graciously revealed some of her knowledge to me."

"Graciously revealed, indeed. She saw someone to use, to take over some of her duties."

"Mazza! What is wrong with you?" Hadara strode from between the rows of vegetables to face the woman who had mothered her most of her life. "I have never heard you be so hateful towards someone who has been good to us."

Mazza opened her mouth, then closed it. Tears streamed from her eyes, and she wiped at them with her gnarled fingers. "You, you are a lady, almost royalty. Now you live like a peasant."

Hadara put an arm around Mazza's shoulders. "Oh, Mazza, you've gone from being the governess and retainer of someone important to having to live like a peasant with me."

The elderly woman jerked away. "You believe I'm upset for me? Never. I do not like how *your* life has changed so drastically."

Hadara's laugh carried across the compound. "This life is paradise compared to living as Tzabar's wife. I'm free."

"But, if you continue with your idea to help the rebels, to hide women and children, your life is even more in danger than with him."

With a shake of her head, Hadara replied, "What help have I been? We have not heard much from or seen Amzi or … not anyone for months."

"Hadara," Simeon called as he hurried across the open ground between the house and the garden area.

She turned to face him as he neared where she and Mazza stood. "What's wrong, Simeon?"

"Please come to the house. You are needed."

"Why?"

He took her arm and started back to the house. "We can't speak out here. Come." He lowered his head to whisper, "Amzi and Caleb are inside."

"Oh, my dear." Hadara held her other hand to her chest. "Then let us hurry."

Amzi and Caleb sat in the kitchen at the table. Rachel placed a bowl of stew in front of each man. She looked up when her husband and the two women entered. "Would you like your noon meal as you visit?"

"Yes, Rachel, that would be good. I could also use a drink of cold water." Hadara sat across from the two men after washing her hands over the slop bucket. "Now, what can we do?"

Caleb swallowed a bite. "We have a problem with a current group of women and children. I've heard a rumor that Ahaz has managed to insert a spy among the women."

"That woman could destroy all we do if she discovers how and where we take those we help …" Amzi's voice trailed off, and he stared at the bowl.

Hadara drank from the goblet of water Rachel sat by her hand before she asked, "How many women in this group …" She paused and waved her hand toward Simeon and Rachel. "Please join us." After they had brought bowls of stew to the table, she continued, "As I started before I interrupted myself, how many women in the group and how many children?"

Amzi raised his head. "There are six women and nineteen children. One woman has six; one has five; two have three each; the other two have a child each." He lowered his head again and took another spoonful of the stew.

Caleb frowned. "I don't like bringing you into this situation, but Amzi thought you might have some ideas as to how we can unveil the spy."

"Then you should have stayed away," Mazza retorted.

"Mazza, enough." Hadara patted the older woman's hand before she looked at each man. "Please continue eating. I need to think. But, before we do, where are the women and children now?" She followed her own advice and began to eat.

"We have them in an abandoned, half-fallen barn not far from here," Caleb answered before giving his meal his full attention.

After everyone had finished and Rachel cleared the table, Simeon started to leave. "No, Simeon, stay. You, too, Rachel. What we do concerns you and your family as much as it does Mazza and me." Hadara stood and walked to look through a window. "I may have an idea, but we would have to find a way to move the women without them knowing where."

"Move them where, Hadara?" Amzi asked. "If not far, we can always cover their eyes."

She returned to sit at the table. "I think we need to hide them in one of the tunnels until I can 'question' each mother." With a half-smile, Hadara added, "We need to make the spy believe we will turn the others over to the soldiers."

Caleb's laugh erupted loud and forceful. "I believe you have the making of a spy yourself, my lady."

Hadara studied the ruggedly handsome man. "Perhaps I do."

"You are both insane." Mazza wrung her hands together as they lay on the table. "How can you find any of this funny? It is dangerous. We all could die."

"Dear lady, we either laugh, or we die inside. Yes, we all could die. This life is dangerous, but more people, especially children, will suffer and die. What else can we do and live with ourselves?" Caleb covered Mazza's hands with one of his. "We are all afraid. If we weren't, we would indeed be insane, but we must do something to help these poor women and their children."

Mazza's eyes searched Caleb's face. "But, I am so afraid. I am no help. I am old."

"Mazza, I will attempt to send you somewhere safe." Hadara slipped an arm around her retainer. "You have suffered enough staying with me."

The elderly retainer shook her head. "I can't leave you. I can't."

"Mazza, what if staying here with your fear puts Hadara in danger?" Rachel asked. "If Hadara and we do this dangerous deed, we must not reveal anything through our behavior."

"I … I don't know what to do." Tears streaked down her wrinkled cheeks.

Caleb patted the hand under his. "Could you act like a deranged person? Then when anyone came around, you could use your fear to become mad and hide in your room."

A slight smile tipped Mazza's lips. "Who says I would have to pretend?" She pulled her hand from under his as she stood. "I will be in my room, allowing my madness to cause me to hide."

After the elderly woman left, Hadara told Caleb and Amzi, "Simeon will take you out through the tunnel you will bring the women and their children." She turned to Simeon. "Do your sons still have their army uniforms and the helmets that cover most of their faces?" She glanced at Caleb. "Do you have a helmet?"

Simon nodded as Caleb answered, "Yes."

"Then we have some soldiers that the woman can't recognize or identify later."

Chapter 29

Late that night

Women huddled on the packed dirt floor of a tunnel, their children close to them, all except for one woman. Her child joined the children around a woman with six of her own while the mother sat by herself, scowling at the dirt wall in front of her, watching the flickering shadows caused by the torches placed on each side of a wooden door at one end of the tunnel.

A man, with his mantle partially covering his face, entered through the door and motioned for the woman with the six children to come with him. She stood, pressing her back against the packed wall behind her.

"My children?" Her voice quivered.

"Bring them, all of them," a gruff voice answered. He used his arms to shoo the children through the door, closing it behind him after everyone entered.

One of the young mothers began to cry, causing her baby to join her. The woman who allowed her child to be taken with the mother who left, turned her scowl on the crying mother and child. "Be quiet and stop that brat's crying. We don't need you adding to our troubles."

The mother sniffed. "We all be burning 'fore all is over." She cuddled her baby to her chest and comforted him. "Hush, babe, hush, Eema's here." Another sob broke through her resolve.

The door opened, and the hooded man motioned for the crying woman and her baby to go with him. She left, sobbing as she clutched the child in her arms. The remaining women gathered their children closer. Fear could be seen in every face, but they soothed their youngsters with an outward courage.

The man returned and removed woman after woman, each with her child or children, until only the one remained. When the door opened again, a helmeted soldier entered. "Come with me," he demanded.

"About time. By the fires of Moleck, I wondered when someone from the army would show up, thought I be stuck with that drooling brat forever." She hopped to her feet and strode through the door into a dim room.

A robed and veiled woman sat in an ornate chair in the middle of the room. Three soldiers stood behind her. The one who brought her from the tunnel marched to stand beside the seated woman, his sword drawn.

The veiled woman asked, her voice soft enough the young woman moved forward to hear, "Are you the one we were told to expect?"

"Yes, 'bout time someone found me. What did you do with them that brought us? Where are the traitors with their brats?"

"That is not your concern. You will now be taken to the army battalion where you will receive your reward." A slender hand waved toward the soldier beside her.

The man picked a sack from the floor and moved toward the spy, who backed away.

"What ... what you be doing?"

Two other soldiers grabbed her arms. She fought, but she couldn't overcome their strength. The soldier pulled the sack over her head, and three soldiers forced her back through the door to the tunnel.

As soon as the door to the tunnel closed, Hadara stood and removed the veil and hood of her robe. "Now, please move the rest of the women and children to safety, but make sure they have no idea where they have been."

Caleb removed his helmet. "Amzi and his men have already begun their removal. I need to get back to camp to stir up trouble when our spy appears wanting her reward."

Hadara turned to face the muscular soldier. She smiled. "We should meet some normal way some day."

"I would like that." He grinned at her. "You probably couldn't recognize me dressed as a 'normal' person."

"If that times comes, I'm sure you will introduce yourself." She reached her hand to touch his arm. "May the one true God keep you safe. You walk a dangerous path."

He covered her hand with his. "Be safe yourself." He studied her eyes in the twilight of the torch-lit cellar before he carried her hand to his lips. "I must go." He turned and hurried to the door and through it.

Hadara stared at the closed door for a bit before walking to a different door and the steps that led to the house above. "Never thought I'd feel ... just results of the excitement," she whispered to herself.

After leaving her veil and robe in her bedchamber, Hadara entered the kitchen where Simeon, Rachel, and Mazza waited.

"Mazza, your idea of watching for the 'mother' who neglected her child was a good one. The spy was easy to 'spy,' and she gave herself away immediately, wanting her reward."

Mazza twisted her hands together on the top of the table in front of her. "It worked this time, but what about other times? What if she can tell the soldiers how to find us? We— "

"Our sons will take her around in circles for at least two hours before they leave her close enough to see the fires of the army camp." Simeon rubbed his hands over his face. "They will try to see what happens, but they can't afford to get too close to the camp and must get back and out of their uniforms in case the army does believe her story."

Hadara laughed. "Caleb said he would stir up trouble for her. Perhaps someday we will hear the whole story."

"I don't want to hear the whole story. I hope everyone forgets us." Mazza rose and hobbled out of the kitchen, muttering as she left.

Rachel also stood. "Her behavior and fear could put us all in peril." She looked at Hadara. "We either must stay away from the escaping mothers and children or find a way for Mazza to be excluded."

"I know, but I am not sure what to do." Hadara bowed her head. "She's afraid for me, but I've never known her to be so …" She raised her head and gazed at first Rachel and then Simeon. "Her fear controls her now. We must not talk about our activities where she can hear. She is not to be involved in any way."

Simeon nodded. "We should also watch for any changes in what she does. She might not be able to control other things."

"She has gone through so much and been so brave." Hadara pushed herself to her feet. "She felt safe here, but nothing is as she expected. I don't think she can take changes that bring threats." She turned tear filled eyes to Rachel and Simeon. "Please let me know when your sons return. They'll need rest before they tell their story, but I'd like to know they're safe. However, Mazza is to know nothing." She shook her head. "This activity scares me, but I *know* I must help."

Rachel hugged her former mistress. "We're all afraid, and we still have a need to help save those children."

Chapter 30

The next morning

Hadara entered the kitchen where Rachel and two daughters cooked the mid-day meal. Simeon and Dan sat at the table, a goblet with wine-water in front of each.

"Where is Mazza?" Simeon picked up his goblet. "Dan is ready to give us a report."

"My working with the vegetables so upset her I allowed her to 'persuade' me to allow her to do the work." Hadara sat on a stool. "So, what happened last night?"

Dan chuckled. "By the time we left her on a hill where she could see the camp fires, still with her hands loosely bound and the sack still over her head, she was so confused she will never remember her path."

"Do you know what happened after?"

"We hid clothing in an abandoned barn not far from the camp. Liam and I changed and crept close while Liber brought our uniforms back here." Dan took a drink. "We were in place before our 'spy' made her way to the camp." He shook his head. "We could hear Caleb telling someone about some woman who was boasting that she could fool the army into giving her a big reward."

"Ahhh, then when she arrived with her story, no one would listen to her, if Caleb was able to spread the word so it found the right person." Hadara smiled. "Caleb is very devious, isn't he?"

Dan nodded. "Indeed, and the word did spread. No sooner had Caleb left one group of men than two or three of them left and moved to other groups. By the time she arrived, the welcome she received was *not* what she expected. We slipped away when she was being 'escorted' to a cage. Of course, she actually had nothing to share since she knew nothing."

Simeon arose from his stool. "I need check on the figs, see how long until harvest. Dan, you be sure all is ready if we have any unwelcome visitors. We have no way of knowing but what the woman remembered some small thing that triggers a memory in someone else."

After the men left, Hadara sat a moment before addressing Rachel. "You've been quiet, you and Zema."

Zema turned from cutting up vegetables. "We have heard the story at least twice, only in more detail, step by step and breath by breath." She scowled. "I believe Mazza may be the only sane one around here."

"Hush, Zema. You know we do what must be done." A giggle erupted from Rachel, surprising Hadara. "Men can make such exciting stories of anything, and my sons are not excluded."

Before Hadara could reply, Mazza entered the kitchen, her hands dirty and full of leeks and black radishes. "Here. This should help vary our meals some." She laid her bundle on the worktop before she grabbed the handle of a pitcher and poured water on each hand as she held it over the drainage hole in the floor.

"Thank you, Mazza." Hadara patted the stool beside her. "Come join me. I would offer to help Rachel and Zema with the meal, but they don't trust my cooking."

"Why … why, Hadara, no one ever suggested such a thing." Rachel's face showed her shock as she stared at the other woman.

Hadara laughed. "Oh, Rachel, of course no one has. However, every time I offer to help, you never allow me. What else am I to think?"

"You need to think that we can manage to give you some small thing due a noble woman. You should be doing the supervising and sewing, things a rich woman does, not work as a servant." Rachel nodded after she finished.

Mazza nodded, too. "I've told her that, but will she listen?" She harrumphed and gave her charge a stern look.

"Both of you know I must pass as a farm woman. Anyone who might come by needs to see me doing at least a semblance of farm work. We cannot afford to call any undue attention to me or my position in the household."

Zema carried a platter of lamb to the table. "Everyone knows, but we all know you would rather not be working as hard as you do. After all, *we* do most of the work."

"Zema!" Rachel stared at her daughter. "Hadara has never treated us as anything but family."

Mazza interrupted. "How long will we be safe; will you be safe? You endanger us all with your meddling with the escape of those women and children." Mazza wrung her hands. "Any time the soldiers could pound on the gates and take us all away or kill us."

Hadara patted her retainer's hands. "We're fine. No one will be here except perhaps visitors."

"What visitors? We live far from everyone, even from a town. We can't go to the market because someone might recognize you. The only visitors we have had are those who put us in jeopardy." She stood. "I am not hungry. I will be in my bedchamber sewing."

"Mazza, wait." Hadara stood beside her oldest friend. "Let's go to the market next week. I need some cloth, and I'm sure Rachel could use supplies, too."

Mazza stopped and lowered her head, frozen in place for several seconds before facing Hadara. "Are you sure? Going could put you in peril."

"Oh, Mazza, we've been out of view from people for so long that I doubt anyone would remember me. We'll go not next week but the week after, and you need to write a list of what you would like to have."

Rachel, Zema, and Hadara watched Mazza leave the kitchen with a slight spring in her step. Rachel placed a platter of roasted vegetables beside the lamb. "I hope you will eat."

"Of course, I will. Where are the others?"

Zema muttered, "Coming through the doors. You know no one misses a meal if they can avoid it."

Chapter 31

over two weeks later

Streaks of gold peeked across the hill tops as a small group left the farm. The donkey-pulled cart held several clay jars filled with figs. Mazza sat on the bench beside Simeon, who held the reins. Hadara and Simeon's youngest daughter dangled their legs off the back of the cart, watching two of his grandsons run after unseen things along the rough roadway.

Hadara inhaled deeply. "The air smells so fresh this morning. We had better enjoy the coolness before the sun reaches the top of the sky."

Noma smiled. "As usual, we will begin to wish for the sun to set so we can escape its heat."

"Anxious to see Lior?"

"Oh, yes. With his work in the carpenter's shop and me not able to visit him but perhaps once a month, we don't see each other often." Noma dipped her head to study the ground passing under her feet. "I will be glad when we can marry."

"Haven't your parents set the date?" Hadara studied the young girl beside her.

Noma nodded. "I thought so, but we must wait until we have a house. Bethlehem has few places, and Lior saves to purchase some land just outside the town. Plus, Lior's mother ..."

"Lior's mother?"

With a sigh, Noma continued, "Since his father died, she has clung tightly to Lior, her only child. We both assured her she would have a home with us, but she finds excuse after excuse for us not to marry."

"Surely, Lior will reason with her."

"I'm ... I'm afraid he is more interested in keeping her happy than with our marriage." She dropped her head to study her fingers gripping the edge of the cart floor.

Hadara reached to pat the hand nearest her. "Perhaps he isn't the one you should marry."

"Where and how shall I meet any other man?" Noma shook her head. "I really don't want to marry him, but he is the only man around not married."

Hadara watched Moshe, Dan's twelve-year-old son, push his younger brother into the ditch. Ilan scrambled back on the road and slugged his brother's shoulder. Before the boys' actions could escalate, Simeon called, "Moshe, Ilan, do you wish to return home?"

The boys' heads whipped to face their grandfather, but he didn't look in their direction. "No, sir, we wish to go to town," Moshe answered for both. "Ilan acts a bit young sometimes."

"Ah, so Ilan does, does he? Who began the pushing, Moshe?" Simeon continued to watch the road in front of the donkey.

"Uh, I guess I did, Saba."

"Let's have no more. You are the older, and you should act the older."

Moshe and Ilan trudged beside the cart, heads hanging. Hadara hid a smile behind her hand. *Boys are boys everywhere.*

The sun peeked above the hills when the group reached the outskirts of the village. Simeon stopped the cart in front of a house. "I need to deliver two jars of figs here. Then we'll go to Aaron's house. He said we could leave the other jars for customers to pick up there and that we could leave the cart and donkey in his barn." He paused. "I shall leave you at the square so you may begin your shopping before I continue to Aaron's."

As he walked to the back of the cart, Hadara and Noma dropped to the ground and moved to one side.

"Come, Moshe and Ilan, you can carry the smaller jar while I take the larger." He pulled the jars to the back of the cart and handed one to the boys. With the other jar in hand, he led the way to the door of the house.

Noma touched Hadara's arm. "Will you go with me to Lior's house? Once I'm there, his mother will chaperone us." She gave a short laugh sound. "Oh, indeed she will."

"Of course. Where does he live?"

"His house, rather his mother's with his shop attached, is a short distance from here, a few houses from the square."

"Then we'll go once we reach the square, before I search the market."

"Why don't I take us past the house and shop on the way to the market?" Simeon asked as he returned in time to hear the last of their conversation.

"Abba, that would be wonderful, but won't you have to go out of your way?"

"Not but a few minutes. I will also feel better to know you are safely delivered." Simeon huffed a loud breath. "I do not like Haggi's attitude toward you, either, daughter."

As the group continued to the square after receiving no answer to their knocks on the carpenter's shop or the house, Noma walked beside the cart in silence for the short distance. She brushed an escaped tear from her cheek.

Hadara, who hadn't climbed back into the cart either, touched her shoulder.

Noma sniffed. "I don't understand. He knew I was coming. He said …" She stared at the ground.

"Perhaps he isn't the man for you, child." Hadara hugged the girl. "But, we don't know what may have happened. Let's enjoy the market, and then we'll revisit his shop. Maybe he will be back."

With a nod, Noma attempted a smile. "Yes, let's enjoy the market."

Once the cart reached the square, Simeon helped Mazza down and motioned with his head toward Hadara. As the others ambled toward the stalls and booths, Hadara hung back.

"What is it, Simeon?"

"I heard voices in Lior's and Haggi's house when Noma went to knock on the shop door." Simeon shook his head. "They deliberately ignored us."

"I heard them whispering, too, something about they should have left hours earlier, but now they had to hide." A frown marred her forehead. "Surely there is some worthy young man for Noma."

"We must tell her," Simeon muttered. "She needs to know why I will not allow her to marry someone dishonest. He is too old for her anyway, nearly my age."

Hadara heaved a heavy sigh. "I will tell her as we shop. I don't believe she will be upset about not marrying him, though."

"Hadara, are you coming? One stall has some interesting vegetables." Noma grabbed Hadara's hand and pulled the older woman with her.

With a little wave toward Simeon, Hadara followed the girl to discover new vegetables.

A sense of impending doom enveloped Hadara. *What's wrong with me?* Her eyes searched the market. *What is amiss?* Mazza visited with one of the women by the spot with herbs for sale. Ilan and two friends ran through the area, weaving around different booths. She touched Noma's arm. "Where did your father and Moshe go?"

The fourteen-year-old turned to face the older woman. "They took our bundles to the cart. Abba said he would come here for us soon." She bit her lip. "I … I didn't take what you said about Lior well, but my pride was hurt. I wanted to be married. The one man who …" She shrugged. "I will be fine."

"Mistress." The whisper close behind her caused Hadara's heart to falter. No one called her that any more. She started to turn toward the voice, but a hand on her shoulder caused her movement to stop. "You must get away from here."

"Amzi? Is that you? What …" Noma asked as she looked at the man.

"Can't be helped now. Please, Noma, gather those with you together and bring them to that pathway." A dirty hand pointed toward an alley winding through the houses at one side of the square. "Quickly."

As the girl hurried to her brother and his friends, the fomer sevant told Hadara, "Danger comes. Where is Simeon?"

Swallowing the fear lodged in her throat, Hadara answered, "He and his older grandson have gone for the cart so we can leave."

"Where?"

"Aaron's stable." She swiveled to face the man two years older than her son. "Amzi, what is wrong?" The man looked more ragged than the last time she had seen him. Dust crusted his face and beard.

Amzi nodded toward another man who said, "I'll bring them to the roof," before he moved with quiet speed toward another part of the square.

"Good, Abram," he said to the departing man.

"Amzi?"

"You can't leave in time, so we will hide you—who are these children?" He frowned at the two boys and one girl beside Noma and Mazza close to the alley. "Never mind, they are in danger. Come." He took Hadara's arm and moved her toward the others.

"Amzi, is that you under all that dirt and rags?" Mazza asked when he and her charge joined her and the children.

"Please, please, I will explain later. This situation … Come, hurry, just hurry." After escorting them into the alleyway, he opened a door past several connected houses and pushed one person after another through before he closed it behind him. They stood in another alleyway, barely wide enough for a person to stand between the walls rising on each side. "Now, we head toward the other end. When we can go no farther, I'll stop." He led them down the narrow way.

Hadara held the little girl's hand as they squeezed between the walls. *Who is this child?* she asked herself.

Her longtime retainer grumbled as they made their way along the twisting path, "I knew helping women escape with children was bad. Knew you shouldn't be involved. I knew."

"Hush, Mazza," Hadara hissed at her. "Now is not the time."

Opening another door at the end of the twisting alley, Amzi lead the group through two rooms to a door hidden behind a cabinet. They climbed steep stairs to the roof. Once on the roof, Hadara noticed that the door closed to become part of the wall, no sign of the opening.

"Mistress … Hadara, you and Mazza can crouch or sit wherever you wish. Noma, I suggest you huddle in the back corner under the awning with the children." Amzi shook his head. "Why did you come to market today?" he muttered before addressing the others. "Now, listen carefully. No one can see you through or over the walls around the roof, but they could see movement through the slits in the upper portion. Therefore, if you move, stay behind the solid part. Be very quiet. Sounds carry."

"I want my eema," the small girl whined.

Amzi knelt beside her. "What is your name?"

"Sofai."

"I'm sorry I can't take you to your mother right now. Something really bad is going to happen, and you are safe here. Your eema would want you to be safe, wouldn't she?"

Sofai nodded her head.

"Now, be very quiet. Play a game to see which of you can be the most silent."

Noma slipped an arm around the little girl. "We'll be fine, Amzi. Thank you for helping us."

A sound caused heads to whip toward the door to the hidden stairs. Simeon, Moshe, and Abram stepped onto the roof, quickly stooping and crawling to the group under the awning. Abram and Moshe carried water bags, and Simeon held bundles in each hand.

"The other men went to spread the word for all to hide their children, but I'm afraid we're too late. We don't have time." Abram laid his water bag on the rough surface.

"Abram, we do what we can. We didn't get word soon enough, but perhaps we will save some."

"Amzi, what is happening?" Hadara touched his sleeve and puffs of dust rose in the air.

"We received a message at the camp late last night that Barrack is bringing soldiers to Bethlehem today. King Ahaz is angry because too few parents volunteer their children as sacrifices to Moleck." The man no longer looked like one who once worked in a noble's house. "We rode as hard as possible, but we arrived just a short time ago. Soldiers whose families are in Bethlehem were sent at least a two-days' march from here." He squinted at his former mistress. "Why, of all times, did you come to market today?"

"Barrack? Who is Barrack? Why would the king be angry?" Ilan, Simeon's younger grandson, whispered.

Simeon looked at Hadara and Amzi. "The children do not know." He turned to his grandson. "King Ahaz ... the king wants children sacrificed to the idol Moleck, a horrible death. Barrack is one of his nobles who *burns* with a passion to throw children into the fire, with an even greater desire, perhaps, than the king."

"But, but, they burn children?" Ilan stared at his grandfather, as did the other children.

Hadara hugged the young boy to her. "They are cruel, cruel men. Now, do you understand why you must be absolutely— "

The thump of many feet, jangle of metal, and creak of leather broke through the laughter and voices in the square. Hadara, Mazza, and the men scooted to the outer wall. Hadara's eyes widened as she stared through the slotted top section of wall. The road toward Jerusalem overflowed with soldiers, a few mounted, and one man driven in a chariot. Simeon bowed his head before crawling back with the children. Hadara turned to follow him, a frown between her brows.

"They need me," he mouthed. He pulled his daughter, grandsons, and the other two children to him, reaching his arms as far around them all as possible.

The thud of feet grew louder and swirls of dust filled the village, as the small army thundered past. Hadara watched the enemy pour into the square to the right of where she hid. People scattered before the wave of swords: laughter and idle chatter became screeches and shouts of alarm.

A child whimpered from the protected corner of the roof. Hadara spun on her heel, but Simeon waved one hand as he placed his hand over the child's mouth, bent his head close to her ear, and whispered. The girl's eyes filled with tears. Noma pulled the child into her arms and rocked her.

We all could die, Hadara thought as she reached beside her to pat Mazza's wrinkled hands. *Why* did *we ever come to market today?* She glanced back toward the man and children grouped behind her. Her heart pounded, and her throat tightened. A trembling began deep within her body and spread outward, even to her fingertips

A scream forced her attention back to the scene below. Her brain couldn't grasp what her eyes saw. One of the soldiers ripped an infant from a woman's arms. More shouts and yells joined the first woman's. Soldiers grabbed children as they tried to run. They wrestled youngsters and infants from the arms of fathers and mothers. The din of screams, cries, and wails caused some on the roof to cover their ears. Mazza wiped her cheeks with fingers that trembled. Hadara bit her lower lip to stop herself from screaming. *A nightmare. It's a nightmare.* Her eyes squeezed shut, but the sounds of horror caused them to fly open again. Her mind continued shouting, *No! No! No!* Her heart thundered in her chest.

She watched the soldiers round up the children as if they herded goats bleating for their mothers. The soldiers around the group of children marched them from the square to the road leading away from town, toward the idol of Moleck, prodding the uncooperative children with a poke from a sword or fist to the head or back. Parents and grandparents followed crying for the soldiers to stop, to let their children go.

No! No! They can't. Surely, they won't … Tears flowed down Hadara's face as pain pierced her chest and the salty taste of blood from her bit lip stung her tongue. Her thoughts returned to the one sacrifice ceremony her late husband forced her to watch. The smell of burning flesh; the wails of the infant so loud the 100 beating drums could not drown out the sounds; the heat beating upon them from the sun and radiating from the red-hot brass idol – all flashed through her mind as she stared below, unable to turn away.

A woman grabbed a leg of one of the mounted soldiers who carried a babe by one leg. "Please, don't take my baby," she begged. The soldier slung the infant by its leg and wacked the mother in the head before drawing his sword and decapitating her. Her body crumpled in a bloody heap. The soldier rode on, swinging the squalling baby.

A man ran from a house, a metal rod in his hands, and struck any soldier he could reach. One soldier laughed before plunging his sword into the man's chest. Chaos reigned as men and women fought to save their children; children and infants screeched and bawled; soldiers marched out of the village with their "spoils," at least twenty children, with a mob following.

The chariot remained on the road toward Jerusalem, the driver staring straight in front. Hadara stared at the noble in his flowing robes watching, a sneer visible. *It's Barrack. He has to inspect his dirty work.* A rage built in her, drowning out the nausea that she fought. Feeling as if in the middle of a horrible dream, she glared with hate at the man. With hands curled into fists, she started to rise.

"No, Hadara," Amzi whispered. He pulled her back to the roof top. "We must live to fight when we can make a difference."

As if sensing eyes on him, Barrack glanced around him and then toward the tops of the houses. He bent over the side of the chariot and spoke to a soldier acting as one of his four body guards. The soldier motioned for another to join him. The two marched toward the nearest house. After breaking open the door, they entered. In moments, they left that house and moved to the next.

Amzi motioned for everyone to lie on the surface. "Cover your faces, hands, every part of your body," he said so softly those by the wall barely heard him before he crawled on his belly to Simeon and the children. Hadara couldn't hear what he told those under the awning, but she saw them drop flat and cover faces and hands. Amzi stood quickly and yanked the light awning down, covering Simeon and the children and leaving no cloth flapping in the breeze. He crawled back to the wall. When he saw Hadara watching, he shook his head and pulled her mantle over her face. With a hand on the back of her head, he pushed her face to the roof top. Blind, Hadara strained to hear what might be happening below. Screams, shouts, keening echoed through the town, but she couldn't understand any words. Doors crashed, and feet stomped.

A rough voice yelled, "Don't see anyone on any roofs."

Another, more cultured voice, called back, "Return. We need to oversee the sacrifices. The fires should be hot enough." After a pause, he shouted, "Leave guards at each road so no one with children younger than twenty harvests leaves."

Above the pounding of her heart, Hadara heard the departure of marching feet, hooves, and wheels. She crawled from the mantle covering her as the shrieks, the bellows of pain, the whimpers of those left to grieve and face the destruction of their lives filled the streets of the village. Sitting with her back against the wall, she gazed around the roof, dazed.

Mazza grabbed her hand. "Horrible, horrible," she whispered. "I can't believe … those children …"

"I am glad we can't see the idol from here." Hadara pressed her elderly woman's hand. "I don't …" Her voice faltered as an invisible band tightened around her chest, cutting off her breath.

Between sobs, Mazza said, "I will … not say … anything about … helping those poor mothers. Never … again. I will help."

Amzi untangled Abram from his cloak. "Help me get the others from under the awning cloth." He glanced toward Hadara and Mazza. "We need to back up to that far corner until we know what happens."

The two young men lifted the material from the bodies hidden beneath. The four children sat up and gazed around them, their eyes wide and filled with terror. Noma wrapped her arms around herself and kept her eyes tightly closed.

Simeon exhaled loudly. "We can be thankful the wind blows away from us so we won't smell the burning sacrifices."

Sobs burst from Noma. She buried her head in her hands as her weeping wracked her body. Amzi touched her arm. "Noma, please, I know you're frightened, but we must remain as quiet as possible. Please, don't cry."

The young girl lowered her hands. "If not for you … my nephews … and I could be in the fires today. No one is safe. No one." Tears glistened on her cheeks.

She is still a child, yet she hopes she will marry soon. At least she won't marry Lior. Hadara sighed deeply. *I was but her age when married and with a child.*

Amzi studied his hands a moment before rising to his knees. "I will return quickly, then we will eat something before the soldiers and Barrack return. Come, Abram." He and his friend crawled to the door and left.

Hadara scooted closer to Noma and hugged her. "We live during a demanding time. Being strong is difficult, but if we survive, we must be strong." She looked at the three boys and one small girl who stared at her and smiled at them. "We may talk if we whisper. Moshe, Ilan, who are your friends? How did you meet them?"

Twelve-year-old Moshe answered. "This is Nathan. We met last fig harvest when Grandfather brought us to market." He shrugged. "Each time Ilan and I come with our saba, we play with Nathan. This is the first time Sofai has been here."

Ilan broke in. "I don't understand how Sofai can be his aunt. She is younger than he is."

With a shy smile, Nathan explained, "My abba is the oldest of his parents' children. I was born before my savta, Deborah, gave birth to her."

"I see." Hadara studied the two children. "Where are your parents, Sofai?"

The small girl twisted her fingers together and watched them. "They are at our farm. I visit with Nathan sometimes, when Abba and Eema let me. Eema doesn't want me to be away from her much. She's afraid I will disappear like my sister did." She glanced at Hadara, then Mazza, at Simeon, and back at Hadara. "Are you Moshe and Ilan's mother?"

Hadara bit her lip so Sofai wouldn't think she laughed at her. "Uh, no, their mother and grandmother are at home. Simeon is their grandfather. I am …" She paused to decide how to word the relationship. *I can't tell these children that I once was the mistress of a palace just smaller than the king's, that I was married to a noble, that Mazza has been my governess and retainer since I was a child, that Simeon was the head of the household and my servant, as was Amzi.*

She smiled at Sofai. "Simeon's wife has become my sister. Therefore, I am Noma's aunt." She patted Mazza's hand. "Mazza is my grandmother." *My adopted grandmother.*

"Oh." Sofai nodded. "I'm hungry."

"You are …" Hadara smothered her laugh with her hands. "Of course, children do get hungry. Amzi said he would be back and we would eat."

"How can anyone eat at a time like this?" Noma asked, a frown bringing her brows together.

Mazza brushed her hand over the girl's head. "We must keep up our strength, child. We have no idea what we must yet do before we're away from here and safe."

"Mazza is right, Noma," her father added. "Most of us don't want to eat, but we must anyway. We must find a way to escape here, and we will have to walk."

"Some of us will walk," Amzi stated as he crawled from the door, his face and hands clean, and he wore clean clothes. "However, Simeon, you, Hadara, and Mazza will go back to the farm in the cart. The soldiers are told only to stop anyone with children up to adult age." He laid a cloth on the roof top and opened a bundle filled with cheese, dried meat, and bowls.

"No," Hadara replied, "I will walk with the children."

"Hadara, that would be too dangerous!" Mazza shook her head vigorously. "You must ride in the cart with us."

"Dear Mazza, I will be as safe as these children and Noma. I'm sure Amzi will escort us, and I can help."

"Of course I will be with them, Mazza." Amzi set bowls on the cloth while Simeon poured watered wine from the water skins into them. "Come, let us eat and drink before the soldiers and Barrack return."

After they finished eating, the group half-dozed in the sunshine. The four younger children napped. Silence settled like a shroud over the town.

"What will the people do?" Mazza whispered.

"They will either give their children to be sacrificed and save their own lives, or they will fight to the death to try to save their children." Amzi rubbed a hand over his face. "Unless the soldiers with family here return, Bethlehem is doomed."

Noma stared at the young man. "You and your band, can't you do something?"

Amzi shook his head. "We will all probably die with the rest of the town, dying to save children, but we are too few to win against the troops supporting Barrack. At least he doesn't have the entire army, just the ones with him today."

"You sound so accepting of death. How can you not be afraid?" The girl studied his face.

The man gave a humph before answering. "I don't accept death. I struggle every day to stay alive and to help mothers and their babes and children escape death. Sure, I want to live, but I can't live knowing what King Ahaz and his followers are doing to children, not without fighting with everything I have to save them."

Hadara listened and watched the interaction between the young man she admired and the girl she loved as if her own. *Ah, Noma doesn't realize she admires Amzi, but this dangerous time is not one for love.* She glanced around the roof. "Where's Abram, Amzi? I didn't realize he didn't return."

A thundering roar caught her attention. Her head swiveled toward the roar and marching feet moving from the idol site toward town. "They return," she whispered as she gently woke the child in her lap. "Shhh, Sofai, be quiet and move back into the corner with Noma."

Simeon shook his grandsons and Nathan. "Wake up, boys. The soldiers return, and we must stay hidden."

As Simeon and Noma moved the children as far against the corner of the roof as possible, the others scooted or crawled to the front wall where they could watch for the returning soldiers and townspeople. The people arrived first. Some stumbled as if asleep, eyes staring blankly at nothing. When a woman fell, another pulled her to her feet. Men shook their heads as if denying the experiences of the day. Faces showed shock, grief, and anger. Behind the towns people marched the soldiers, swords and spears in hand. The chariot with Barrack standing straight and regal, even in the dust bellowing around him, followed. Last rode the mounted soldiers.

How arrogant and despicable. Hadara found herself rising to her knees. *If I had a bow and arrow—*

Her thoughts stopped as an arrow flew through the air, striking Barrack in the throat. His hands reached to clasp the shaft protruding from his neck while blood spewed around the front and back wounds.

One of the mounted soldiers shouted, "Halt." All the soldiers stopped. Those marching turned to face behind them. The people never paused but stumbled toward their homes.

Chaos erupted among the mob below. Soldiers ran or rode to circle the chariot. Hadara watched as Abram swung from a roof top across the road, followed by five other men. They ran among the people, shouting and pushing.

"Get into your houses."

"Bar your doors and windows."

"Hurry, hide."

"Protect yourselves."

Amzi grabbed her arm. "Get everyone downstairs. Hurry before the soldiers get organized." He hurried to the group in the corner and repeated his message before heading to the door himself. "Hurry!"

Time became confused and blurred as Hadara helped Mazza and Sofai down the steep stairs. Amzi aided everyone out the back door of the building. "Let me lead. Follow me closely." He retraced their path through the narrow alleyway. Passing through the door at the end, he turned the direction opposite from the square.

He fell back to put an arm around Mazza as she struggled to breathe and half-run. "I'll help as much as I can, but I also need to show everyone our route to safety."

"Could we not … have stayed … on the roof," the old woman gasped.

"No, the soldiers will search all roof tops, even if they have to climb up the walls."

Simeon paused on Mazza's other side. "I will help her. You go show us the way."

Hadara pulled a whining Sofai into her arms. She scampered after the others as quickly as she could with her burden. Noma held Ilan's and Nathan's hands, sprinting behind Moshe and Amzi. From behind, screams and shrieks pierced the air as well as thumps and banging on walls and doors. In minutes, the twisted way through the houses and buildings opened into a ravine.

"We must be quiet. Just over that ridge," Amzi pointed upward, "is the road leading from town. Soldiers will be patrolling as soon as organized."

A scattering of dirt and rocks slid down from above as Abram slithered to join them. "The soldiers from Bethlehem arrived and are protecting the town. Let's leave. Barrack's troops will be scouring the countryside to do what damage they can."

As they scrambled their way away from Bethlehem, bits and pieces of information spun through Hadara's head: a child who went missing, a woman named Deborah, a little girl named Sofai, all familiar after hearing Nava's story so many times.

A trip that usually took thirty minutes on the road became three hours as the small company made their way over rough terrain, pausing anytime a sound came from the direction of the road. Finally, they staggered through the gate of the farm.

After cleaning the dust from her and Mazza's hands, face, and feet, Hadara helped Mazza into a clean gown and into bed. "I'll be back. You rest."

Before she could leave the room, the other woman's eyes closed. Hadra hurried to change her own robe and hasten to the kitchen where everyone else waited. Simeon's wife and oldest daughter served bowls of stew and cups of water to those sitting at the large table.

"Mazza is already sleeping," Hadara said as she sat on an empty stool. Looking at Amzi and Abram, she asked, "How did the soldiers from Bethlehem arrive if they were so far away?"

Abram answered, "They ran the whole distance." He shrugged. "Their families were endangered. Fear and love can work miracles."

"Who shot the arrow that killed Barrack?"

"One of the soldiers who arrived first. His wife was the mother decapitated. He offered and will sacrifice himself by surrendering so that others will not suffer." Amzi shook his head. "Evil is cruel, but love is stronger."

Chapter 32

The next day, at the farm

Hadara sat on a large boulder in the yard between the house and front wall. The sun's warmth did little to thaw the fear, the horror remaining from the day before. Mazza constantly muttered about something or another, but Hadara tuned out the sound of her voice. However, Simeon's rushing from the house caught her attention.

"One of the men came through the tunnel. Aaron and Hosa come, bringing the cart and our supplies." He patted her shoulder as he continued toward the gate.

After the gate opened, the cart, pulled by the ass, rolled into the yard. Hosa held the reins while Aaron sat beside him on the bench seat. Baskets and jars rattled in the back.

"Spent all that money for vegetables we don't know anything about," Mazza grumbled for the tenth or twelfth time since awakening. "Also, who's going to do the planting? You?"

"Mazza, please, I will if necessary. We have a chance of adding to our food supplies with those potatoes and carrots."

"We can have carrots now by pulling them wild. That makes more sense to me than planting some seeds, and who knows what those 'potato' things will do?"

Amzi shook his head as he squatted beside Hadara. "I will plant these new vegetables. I will have to hide here for a while, and that's one way to pay for my keep." He glanced at Mazza as she frowned at him. "Mazza, if Hadara sees value in something, can't we at least help her."

A smile softened the lines on the retainer's face. "Yes, Amzi, you are correct. I'm being a grump." She patted Hadara's shoulder. "I don't mean to add to your burdens. Now, I'll go help Hosa and Simeon store the supplies."

"Mazza, the potatoes with sprouts, and some without, need to be taken to the kitchen, as well as some of the carrots and the little bundle that holds seeds." Hadara rose and started toward the house. "Come, Amzi, I'll explain how the merchant said to plant the potatoes. But, no need to begin until we hear what news Aaron brings." She huffed a breath. "The merchant told quite a story.

Maybe some day I'll know how much is true."

Soon several members of Simeon's family, Hadara, Mazza, and Amzi sat around the large table with Aaron at one end. Rachel and two of her daughters cooked as they listened to the conversation at the table.

"Thank you for bringing our supplies to us, Aaron." Hadara attempted to smile at the priest.

"With all the chaos and the king's soldiers invading the town, Hosa and I felt safer leaving. You needed your cart, ass, and goods, so we brought them. Thank you for allowing him to use the cart to take the two children you saved yesterday to their parents, who wait at the farm belonging to the girl's parents, Ruben and Deborah. The boy's father, Jacob, visited late last night. Apparently, the parents watched you hiding on the top of that building as they hid on the top of Jacob's house." He raised his eyes to the roof. "We live in troubling times. Families are mourning, but King Ahaz is not leaving them in peace." He returned his attention to those around him. "We have no idea what will happen. We can only pray the Lord God watch over us."

Simeon leaned forward. "Didn't the soldier who killed Barrack confess? Why would the king send more soldiers?"

"Yes, he did and has already paid the price. King Ahaz, however, is caught in a quandary. His finance minister has family in Bethlehem and wants Barrack's men punished. The military advisor wants the town wiped from the land because the people are uncooperative and a soldier resident dared kill the king's dear friend and advisor." Aaron blew a silent whistle.

"Who's winning?" Amzi rubbed his hand over his scraggly beard.

Aaron turned to face the younger man. "Naman, the military advisor, is questioning the people in Bethlehem. He believes a conspiracy caused the 'rebellion,' his word, and he wants to find everyone involved. The finance minister, Shem, is also questioning people, but he seeks proof that Barrack had gone rogue. The people are frightened and angry and grieving."

Hadara frowned. "What will happen now?"

"All depends on which man King Ahaz needs more, I imagine." Amzi stood. "For the present and near future, we all better stay out of sight." He gathered sprouted potatoes and a knife from a counter as well as the small packet of seed. "I will begin my new position as gardener. Staying busy may help me not worry about those children Ahaz and his followers will sacrifice until we can help them again."

Aaron shook his head. "We all must be careful. If either man should find Hosa on the road or that I am here, you could be in danger. However, we must find a place to hide. Anyone known to worship God Jehovah is on a list of those to be eradicated."

Simeon turned to Hadara. "What about the small dwelling behind the farm house to the east? It could be cleaned inside but left ragged looking from the outside."

"That could work." Hadara stood and walked to the hidden door. "From this concealed room are stairs leading to the maze of tunnels running between all buildings we own. One goes to the dwelling Simeon mentioned. You could travel between here and there without being seen, and if someone should 'find' your hiding place, you could slip into the tunnels for safety."

Aaron nodded. "We don't need much as long as we have protection from the weather and a place to lay our heads. Hosa is very adept at managing with little. Much of the time, if Hosa didn't care for me, I often wouldn't notice what I have." He stood. "Would someone find Hosa and let him know where I will be?"

"Of course. I will send one of my sons as soon as we take you to your hiding place. My daughter and I will go with you to help clean the building." Simon led Aaron to the open door.

After the men and one of Simeon's daughters left through the hidden chamber, Hadara sat back at the table. She waved a hand at the pile of potatoes and carrots. "The merchant told me quite a story. He didn't know for sure how the potatoes and carrots arrived in our part of the world. He said he heard a storm took a ship to some strange land and when it found its way back, the crew brought odd and different foods. He said the vegetables can be peeled, cut up, and placed in stews. The peelings can go to the fowls, so no waste. I would think we could roast the potatoes, when not peeled, in the coals. We can –" Her eyes widened as her eyes searched the room, glancing one way and another. Her mouth opened and closed twice, but no sound came out. Her hands covered her mouth as she stared at the people still in the kitchen.

She surged to her feet, causing the bench to fall over. "What … what is wrong with me? I'm blathering and, and … the horror, the madness … all those children, their parents." She rushed from the room and out of the house, sobs shaking her body. In the outer courtyard, she stared around her before stumbling toward the stable. Inside, she crumpled on a pile of hay, pulled her knees to her chest, and pressed her forehead against them, allowing her tears to soak her robe.

"Hadara? Hadara?" A man's hand pushed a soft cloth into hers.

"Thank … you, Caleb." Hadara raised her eyes as she wiped tears from her face. Her cries stopped abruptly when she spied the man dressed in fashionable robes, his hair and beard neatly styled. "Who … who? You sounded like, like Caleb. Who are you?"

The man stooped to face her, took the cloth from her hand, and wiped the tears from her face. "Look at me, Hadara, look in my eyes. You know me."

She stared into his eyes before shaking her head. "You are Caleb, yet you're not." She closed her eyes. "This world is gone all wrong."

"Hadara, I am Caleb, or was. Now, I am Kalif, the dealer in fine cloth and rugs." He brushed her cheek with a finger. "I know your heart and mind hurt from what you witnessed yesterday, but we have much to do. I can't give you time to work through the pain." He stood and pulled her to her feet. "Come now, my sweet. Amzi will be here soon with Simeon, and we must plan before the military advisor arrives."

Rubbing her forehead, Hadara mumbled, "Plan, plan? What … I don't understand anything anymore."

"I wanted to court you, to give you time to learn to care for me as I care for you; but with all that's happening, we haven't time. Naman is brutal, and he takes whatever he wishes. You will be in danger since you are a rich and unmarried woman."

Her eyes, still tear filled, searched his. "Court me?" She shook her head. "I don't … What do you mean? We don't have time for what?"

Kalif gathered her into his arms. "I don't have time to court you before we marry."

Hadara jerked backward. "Marry? What? Cal … Kalif, have you lost your mind?" She shook her head again. "Maybe I've lost mine."

"No, neither of us have lost our minds. I've admired you for a long time, but in the army, I had nothing to offer. Since my brother's death, I now have my father's business and can take a wife. Please, we have little time. I will court you after we're married, but we haven't time now." He touched her cheek. "Can you trust me?"

"Trust? I, uh, of course. You could have destroyed all of us, but instead you helped." She studied his face, familiar yet new, before she shrugged. "Lead on, Cal … Kalif. I will follow." Dropping her head, she whispered, "I'm so lost, so tired, I need someone to show me what to do."

"What is happening? Amzi found me and said … Who are you?" Simeon grabbed Kalif's arm, swinging him around. "Let go of her."

"Don't, Simeon, he's Caleb, uh, now, uh, Kalif." Hadara forced a half-smile on her face. "He, he was comforting me."

Simeon stared at Kalif. "You really are Caleb." He frowned. "Why all the mystery, the change of appearance and name?"

Kalif chuckled. "A long story, but a quick version is Caleb needed to leave the army; my brother died leaving my father's business without a true head since my father is old and feeble. With my becoming the owner of record of a rich company, different doors opened, allowing me to aid in my other career." He kept one arm around Hadara as he continued. "I tried to explain to Hadara that the military advisor, Naman, is as dangerous or more so than Tzabar or Barrack ever were. She would be safe from him if he were in Jerusalem, but not with him here and visiting all the farms in the area. He takes any woman who is not married and confiscates property her family may have."

"He can do that, and no one stops him?" Amzi asked.

Kalif took a deep breath and exhaled with a whoosh. "Ahaz has given him too much power."

"Then to save everyone here, I need to be married so he can't, won't take everything?" Hadara peered at the man beside her. "Why do you think he would want me, even if he should come here?"

The three men laughed, but Amzi replied, "You are a lovely woman, and you 'appear' to be part of a wealthy family, even if the world doesn't realize the wealth is yours." He guffawed. "Oh, yes, you would become a target for such a man."

"How do we stop him?" Simeon asked.

Kalif pulled Hadara closer to his side. "Hadara and I will marry as soon as we can find a priest to perform the marriage blessing."

Simeon stared at first Kalif and then Hadara. "I knew that the two of you, rather Caleb and Hadara had grown close over the past year, but I didn't realize you had decided on marriage."

As Kalif explained his previous plan to court Hadara until learning of Naman's appearance and plans to investigate every home and farm around Bethlehem, Hadara studied her feet, her mind wandering over the past two days. *Madness. Madness.* She pressed her free hand against her chest. *It hurts.*

"Hadara? Hadara?"

She raised her head and looked around.

"Hadara, are you all right?" Kalif asked as he tipped her face so she noticed him.

"I, uh, I think so … no, I'm not." She exhaled a soft sigh. "So, what do I do now?"

"Amzi will remain here as your son while –"

"My son?" Hadara interrupted.

"Yes, legally he is since his father was your husband."

She nodded. "Yes, that's true."

"Look, Ca … Kalif. Having Hadara claim me as a son is not fair to her, not what I did." Amzi frowned. "I can return to the rebel camp."

Kalif grabbed the younger man's shoulder. "I need someone here who can and will protect her. Naman will be here any time, and I don't have time to explain everything. You will be Hadara's son. Simeon can pass as her late husband's brother. Mazza is her grandmother or nurse, whatever works. I am her betrothed." He studied Amzi before turning to Simeon. "Can you get him some clothes? He needs to look presentable as a son of your sister by marriage."

Simeon snorted. "I don't have to 'pass' as Tzabar's brother. Ironic, isn't it that we shared the same father." Three sets of eyes stared at him. "Remember years ago, when Amzi told Nava about being Tobias' brother? I said Tzabar's father was the same, that both fathered children across the land."

"Simeon." Hadara shook her head. "How much you've suffered."

Kalif hugged her. "Yes, he has, but the Lord God put him in the right place to help you. Now, Hadara, you and Mazza need to hide in your rooms and not come out until I return." He wrapped her hand in his. "I need to leave before Naman arrives, but I'll be back shortly. If for some reason, you can't avoid him, tell him your betrothed is expected any minute."

With another quick embrace, Kalif started to the stable opening. "Hurry, men, he will arrive any time. Be sure no surprise visitors arrive."

"You mean Aaron and Hosa?" Hadara smiled when her "betrothed" whirled around to face her. "Yes, they arrived this morning. We have them hidden, but we will send word for them to remain hidden." She touched his arm. "Now, hurry yourself. I don't want you to be a martyr before we marry."

After Hadara calmed Mazza and both women picked up their sewing, Simeon tapped on the door before sticking his head through the opening. "I know you'll want to know what Naman says and does. I'll bring him and any guards with him to the inner courtyard. With your window slightly open, you should be able to hear most of what anyone says."

"Thank you, Simeon. Mazza and I will remain extremely quiet."

"I sent all my daughters and wives of my sons to the hidden tunnels with all the children. Only Amzi, Rachel, you two, and I are here. I sent my sons to keep watch." He started to withdraw before looking back toward Hadara. "Amzi looks the part of a son of the house now." He pulled back and closed the door.

Hadara stood and placed her cloth and thread on the chair. She walked to the shuttered window beside the door. She opened one shutter a slit and peeked at the inner courtyard of the house, the place where the family gathered for rest and visiting when not gathered around the table in the kitchen.

"What's wrong?" Mazza started to stand, also.

Her "adopted" granddaughter waved a hand. "No, don't get up. I'm, well, I guess a bit nervous, what Tobias used to call feeling as if ants crawl over my skin." She closed the shutter and paced to the other window on the far side of the door. She opened one side of a shutter and peeked into the courtyard again.

Potted plants scattered over the large area divided divans grouped together. Firepots dotted the space, as did tall rods with lamps hanging from the top hook. The peacefulness of the open lounge soothed her jumpiness. She watched the shadows of the palm awnings play across the items below them, creating shelter from the hot sun or occasional rains for divans and people who might relax beneath.

So calm, she thought, *but soon another of the king's monsters will sit there.* With a sigh, Hadara closed the shutter, leaving a slight opening where she could hear conversation if the men didn't speak too softly. She continued to wath through the crack.

A loud booming at the gate vibrated through the compound and into the house. Simeon half-ran across the courtyard and through the door to the outside. The two women heard male voices raised in anger, but they couldn't understand any words. Minutes later, Simeon opened the main door and held it so a massive man, followed by two soldiers, could enter.

"Please, Advisor Naman, sit. I will have someone bring refreshments." He motioned to the soldiers who peered around the courtyard. "What would your men prefer?"

Naman waved his hands as if shooing flies away. "They need nothing." He plopped onto a couch, which groaned but held under the weight. "They will search the premises for others and bring them to me."

"Advisor –" Simeon began.

"Go get those refreshments immediately. I want everyone here by the time you return."

Hadara closed the shutter and motioned to Mazza to join her. "Come, we must go to the courtyard as soon as a soldier comes to the door." The two clasped hands and waited.

Naman swallowed wine, dribbling some into his gray and black beard. A tray of small cakes sat on a low table beside him. Simeon and Rachel perched on the edge of a couch at right angles to Naman's. Mazza sat stiffly on another couch with Hadara standing behind her. After one look at the minister's face, Hadara looked down to avoid eye contact with him.

Hadara stared at the rug under the minister's feet. She swallowed a giggle. *No, no, not now. He looks … funny … don't laugh … don't laugh … his eyes … so much evil.* She clasped the back of the couch in front of her until her fingers hurt, but her thoughts kept whirling, blocking out the conversation around her. *Too much … death … hate … need help …*

"Simeon, I like the looks of that one." Naman used his goblet to point toward Hadara. "What is she to you?"

"She is my brother's widow. She and her grandmother, her nurse since she was a babe, have made their home here."

"Ah, yes, as should be, caring for your brother's wife. So, she is free for the taking."

"Um, no, sir, she is betrothed. She will marry within a few days." Simeon moistened his lips. "Her husband-to-be is a bit influential, in fact."

The door slammed open, startling Hadara from her daze. A soldier pushed Amzi inside, causing him to stumble a few steps before he regained his balance. "Sir, I found this one in the barn, feeding livestock."

The military advisor set his drink on the table as he glared at the young man who moved behind Hadara to stand beside her. "Who is this?"

"He is my son." Hadara straightened her back and stared at the man across from her a moment before dropping her gaze. "Amzi helps around the farm as needed." Sensing another presence, she glanced toward the door. Kalif strode toward her and pulled her to his side, wrapping an arm around her waist.

"I hurried as fast as possible." He turned to face Naman, leaving his arm around Hadara. "Naman, I see you are making your way across the countryside. Have you found any rebels?"

The advisor struggled to rise to his feet. One of the soldiers offered an arm to aid the once strong, muscular but now obese man to a standing position. "Kalif, why are you here? I was about to put claim on this woman."

"Ah, Naman, she is not available, for she is to be my wife."

"You are not yet married, so she can still become mine." Naman faced Simeon. "Name your price."

Simeon stood. "I cannot say yay nor nay. She is promised. They are as bound as if married."

The advisor's face grew red, and his several chins quivered. "I … I …"

"Before I forget, Naman, Shem is on his way. He received a message from the king for you and for him. He should arrive within seconds."

The minister's head whipped toward Kalif. "Shem? Here? Why did the king send a message to him for me?" The man grabbed the arm of the soldier by his side. "Get the troops ready to leave and bring my chariot. If the king needs me, I must be ready to go to him."

A pounding on the door caused everyone to start and stare in that direction. A soldier opened it. A man, tall as Naman but thin, almost gaunt, strode into the courtyard.

"I see everyone is here, good." He glanced around the area. "Where might I sit?" He turned his head to one side to cough. "I'm not strong today."

"Today? You are a weakling everyday. Now, why do you have a message for me from the king, and why did you read my message?"

Shem sank to the chair Simeon brought to him. "I did not open your message, only my own." He handed Naman a folded parchment sealed with the king's personal wax image. "Here is yours. King Ahaz told me in my message that the Israelis encroach from the north, and he needs you in Jerusalem immediately. I am to return as soon as I bury my dead and find a home for my orphaned grandchildren."

"Yes, yes, whatever you are to do, do. I must hurry." The man marched through the door now held by his guard, who slammed it behind him as he followed the advisor.

"Now you know his and my orders. He nor I will be frightening the people in or around Bethlehem. Israel will keep Naman occupied for months and perhaps years." Shem sipped from the cup of wine Rachel handed him.

Kalif blew the breath he had held. "I hope he can't get back before Hadara and I marry. Naman has his eye on her."

Simeon interrupted, "Aaron is close by. You can receive the marriage blessing and prayer this day, even if we must have the marriage feast tomorrow."

"I forgot Aaron being in the area. Yes, that would protect Hadara." With a nod, he continued, "Simeon, you have done so much, but would you set up the ceremony?"

Simeon gave a slight snort. "Of course, I will. Come, Rachel, we have much to do both for the blessing and prayer ceremony and for the marriage supper tomorrow."

"Allow me to go for Aaron and Hosa," Amzi suggested as he moved from behind the divan on the other side of Hadara from Kalif.

Rachel touched Hadara's arm. "We know Nava's parents are close, Sofia's parents. Do you mind if we invite them to the marriage supper?"

Hadara took a deep breath and closed her eyes a second. Opening her eyes, she nodded.

After the three left the courtyard, Kalif sat on a divan close to Shem's chair, pulling Hadara beside him. "Can I do anything to help?"

"No, my friend. I have made preparations for both my daughter and her husband's burial. Aaron took care of that late last night. My wife and the grand-children Barrack didn't burn will live outside Jerusalem, perhaps at Bethany. We have a summer home there." A skeletal hand wiped across his forehead. "I haven't been well lately, and I carry this burden of grief now." He reached to touch Kalif's arm. "Thanks for offering aid, but I must find a way to do all I need do by myself."

"Must you leave immediately, Advisor?" Hadara whispered as she leaned around Kalif. "I know Kalif and I would both be honored if you could stay for the marriage blessing and for the supper tomorrow, if you are able."

"Yes, Shem, do stay. You look as if you could use some rest before you go back."

Simeon stepped forward. "Rachel has sent for our daughters and sons' wives to fix a light meal for tonight and start the preparation for the marriage supper. I will show you to a room for your use for as long as you wish."

Shem lowered his head for a moment before raising it. "Let me tell my men we will stay. May they set up camp inside the walls of the compound? I have only three with me."

"Of course. I will send one of my sons to help them, and we will send out drink and food. Couldn't I ask one of the men to come to you?" Simeon waited for Shem to answer.

The advisor gave three short nods. "Yes, that would work. Thank you."

Chapter 33

After Aaron performed the marriage blessing and prayer, the group sat around the table in the kitchen for stew, with the new vegetables included, and fresh bread.

Hadara struggled to eat a few bites before she addressed the advisor. "Thank you for joining us, Minister. You are gracious to agree to eat with us so informally."

The man chuckled. "My family often take our meals the same. I appreciate your taking me into your family and friends." He nodded at Aaron. "Thank you for all you do for the people of the true God." Shem used his spoon to scoop up a chunk of potato. "What is this? It's very tasty."

Rachel pointed toward Hadara. "She will have to tell you about these new finds of hers."

Kalif's new wife ducked her head. "Everyone thought me mad." She lifted her head. "I found a merchant at the market who told me a wild story. According to him, a ship caught in a storm ended up on a strange land, with oddly dressed natives. While the seamen worked to repair the ship, the natives gave them potatoes and carrots and other eatable things, told the sailors how to plant and keep them. The vegetables made a long and strange trip from the ship's home country, to the far east, and finally to here." Hadara giggled. "That's what I was told." She jerked her head toward Kalif. "I ... I actually laughed."

Everyone at the table chuckled or laughed. "'Tis nothing wrong with some joy even in the midst of sorrow, Hadara," Aaron told her. "This should be a joyous time for you and your family since you married Kalif. Even with death surrounding us, life does go forward."

"Come, wife," Kalif rose and held out his hand, "let's walk in the olive grove and relax."

Hadara placed her hand in his and stood. "Yes, yes, I would like that." She glanced around the table. "Thank you all for sharing this day with us. I wish you a good evening."

The moonlight peeked through leaves and branches of the olive trees, creating shadows that shaded the two figures who ambled between the sometimes-twisted trunks. After a few minutes of walking, Kalif leaned against a tree and pulled Hadara into his arms.

"Here, rest against me. Let your tension seep away. You're safe now." Kalif wrapped his arms around Hadara's stiff body, drawing her against his chest. "The air is so still, no wind, no storms. Hear the night birds call? We will listen to their songs and learn more about each other."

As her new husband whispered the descriptions of the night around them, his voice eased Hadara. Soon she lay against him. She felt the beat of his heart under one of her hands, and the low rumble of his voice echoed against her cheek.

"I ... I ..." she began several times before finishing, "I believe you made a bad bargain taking me as your wife."

"Oh? I believe I am the better judge of that."

She drew back far enough to peer at him in the shadows. "You're laughing at me, but I'm serious. I don't know anything about being a wife, not really."

Kalif brushed his knuckles down one cheek before bending to kiss her. Hadara froze but a second before her lips softened against his. A sense of peace, of belonging settled in her chest.

"Amzi! Amzi! Wait!"

Hadara jerked back as Kalif stood upright, his arms still holding her. "Noma?" she whispered.

"Noma, go back to the house, now. You don't know what you're asking. You don't want anyone to find us here, with you 'ruined'."

"Ah, Amzi, who would be ruined? Not me. Do you feel you would be?" The young woman's voice softened. "Look at me and tell me I'm wrong. I have seen how you looked at me. Am I wrong?"

The taller shadow walked away from the shorter. "Anyone can dream, but that is all I did, dream. Nothing can come of it."

"Why? Just tell me why?" A sob broke from Noma. "Please, tell me."

Hadara whispered close to Kalif's ear, "Should we let them know we're here?"

"Probably," he murmured, "but let's wait a moment."

In the dim light cast by the moon, Hadara saw Amzi look at the night sky peeking through the tree branches. "I can't take a wife, Noma. I have no way to give her a home. I'm a nobody, with nothing." He turned to face her. "You deserve a real man, one who can give you all you need and deserve. I can give you nothing, most likely not even a family."

Noma laid a hand on his arm. "Amzi, I don't understand. You have so much to offer." Her voice broke on a sob. "And, why would giving me a family matter?"

"Women want babes, as far as I've been able to tell. I may not be able to father a child." He shook his head. "Please, go back into the house. As soon as possible, I will leave."

"No!" Noma grabbed his arm as he turned away. "As far as children, there are children everywhere in this family. I can borrow a sister's or one of my brother's wife's child for as long as I feel the need. But, what I need is a man who would love me and I can love." She thumped her fist against his arm. "If you don't love me, say so, and I will never embarrass either of us again."

Kalif cleared his throat. Amzi pushed Noma behind him and faced the sound.

"It's Hadara and me, Amzi." Kalif moved closer to the younger couple, his arm around Hadara's waist to bring her with him. "I may be able to help with one of your problems, if you want a solution."

Amzi muttered something under his breath before answering. "What 'solution' would that be and to which problem?"

"Since I now have a wife, and I need someone close by to help my father with the shop in town, would you be interested in living in the house next to the shop and to help him?" Kalif paused. "Wages would be enough for you to have a wife and however many children you might have or borrow."

Noma moved away from Amzi before facing him. "You don't have to take Kalif's offer because of me, don't feel obligated because of me." She strode toward the house. "I'm sorry I put you in this awkward position."

"Wait!" Amzi started toward her before turning toward Kalif. "I'll take your offer. Now, I better talk to her father." He hurried after Noma, caught her, and pulled her into his arms.

Hadara leaned her head against Kalif's shoulder. "Have I wandered into a crazy dream? Death and horror and everything turned upside down and a young couple deciding they belong together."

"What about an older couple deciding they belong together?" Hadara heard the smile in his voice.

She peered at him. "I believe I hadn't much to decide, did I?"

"Hmm …" A few seconds passed as Kalif studied her face in the dimness of the night. "I told you I wanted to court you first, but I needed to keep you safe. Was I wrong about us becoming close over the past, at least, past year?"

Hadara leaned her head against his arm once more. "No, I thought for some time that you were the type man I could respect and love. We may have a good life together. But, I'm not sure *I* know how to be a wife."

"I don't know how to be a husband. Let's learn together. Now come, the day has been long and tiring after the iniquity of yesterday." He exhaled a hiss into the darkness. "The future is as murky as night, but many children will die before Ahaz's reign finishes."

"We will face that too soon, but for tonight, we shall get some rest. Your man, Barris, put your bundles in our rooms. Mazza has moved to another room, and Simeon arranged a room for Barris. Tomorrow will be long as we organize our marriage supper." She stumbled and would have fallen if Kalif hadn't caught her.

"Yes, let's rest." He scooped her into his arms and carried her to the main door to the interior courtyard. "A very hectic beginning to our life together."

Chapter 34

The sound of voices in the other room awakened Hadara. She stretched and felt the empty spot beside her on the sleeping mat. *Wha …* She sat up and swung her legs over the side of the platform. *No, not a dream.* A smile spread across her face as she stood and ambled to where a robe lay across a chest. As she slipped the robe over her gown, her smile wavered and disappeared. "How can I be happy? So much evil … evil everywhere," she whispered. "There's that word again, evil."

The voices from the sitting room caught her attention once more, and she inhaled deeply and moved to open the door. Simeon stood at the open door to the courtyard. Kalif strode to her side.

"Good morn, my love. We didn't mean to wake you."

"No, Hadara, we didn't. I discussed the supper, and we brought each other up to date. Nothing more." Simeon nodded and left, closing the door behind him.

Hadara glanced around the room. "Impossible so much has happened in two days past, yet nothing seems changed." She looked at her husband. "My world was destroyed, but you put things back together." Her smile brightened her face. "I … I feel safe with you."

Kalif threw back his head and laughed, a deep, hearty hoot. Hadara tilted her head to one side and stared.

"I didn't mean … I'm sorry." When she started to move away, he took her into his arms, and she leaned against him, allowing him to snuggle her to his chest. *How embarrassing.*

"No, no, I wasn't laughing at you or what you said. Knowing you feel safe with me is delightful, my love." He ran his hand down her cheek. "Safe is a step toward feeling loved completely. You are, you know." He rubbed her back until she actually relaxed, allowing all the stiffness to flow from her. "Now, we are to have today for ourselves. Simeon informed me that Mazza, Barris, and Rachel agree that we are to do nothing but be together."

Hadara repositioned herself until she could peer at his face. "There is much work to do. I can't allow them to plan everything for tonight."

"Yes, you can. My parents sent word that my mother is preparing honey cakes, the one thing she can make well. My father sent a butchered sheep to be roasted. Rachel called in her daughters and sons' wives to help, as well as the wives of several workers. We shall have a feast, but you will be an honored guest not one of the servers."

"Kalif, I'm not a titled lady to be waited on and haven't been for years now."

"Today you are. The time will come when I expect you to clean, cook, and even plow, but not today."

The woman frowned. "Plow? Are you not able to hire someone at least to plow?"

Together they laughed as Kalif led her to a table laid with breakfast. "Here, sit, and enjoy. Simeon brought this before we discussed plans for today."

After they finished their meal, Hadara began to pile the dishes. Kalif grabbed her hands. "Go sit. I will pile these and set them outside the door." She watched him scrape leftovers into one vessel and stack the rest. In two trips, he had everything outside and the table cleared.

"What are we to do?" she asked.

Kalif looked around. "Do you have any writing materials? I need to make a list for your brother of things I need his next trip." He raised his brows as he asked, "Did I forget to tell you? Your younger two brothers and their wives will be here tonight."

With a squeal, Hadara jumped to her feet and hugged him around the neck. "You're serious. They are really going to be here? But, how, how did they know about our marriage, that they should be here?"

Whirling her around and around as he circled the room, Kalif tried to answer between light kisses over her face. "I didn't know when we would marry, but I told Hemut his last trip that we would be. He said then he would try to bring his wife, Sira, and as many brothers and wives as he could persuade." He held her away from him. "Apparently only one other brother, Raz, and his wife could come."

"You wanted writing material?" Hadara pushed him back. "I keep parchment, ink, and quills here. My family keeps me supplied." She moved to a chest in the corner and opened it. "Oh," she spun to face him. "I need to write a letter to my parents so they know Barrack is dead. Tobias, Nava, and the babe may return home."

After sealing her letter, Hadara leaned back and covered her mouth as a yawn erupted. Kalif grinned as he drew her to her feet. "I believe a rest is needed. Come, let's lie down and take time to refresh ourselves. The marriage supper will last long into the night."

"Rest, during the day? Can you be serious?" She smiled.

"Of course." He scooped her into his arms and carried her to the sleeping room where he laid her on the bed. "We mustn't cause anyone to think we are so old we can't enjoy our own marriage supper." He lay beside her and pulled her close. "Now, close your eyes and rest."

Her eyes closed and her breathing slowed. Kalif supported his head on one hand and watched his new wife as she slept. *So lovely. She feels safe with me … safe.* He lowered his arm so his head lay on the bed. "Guess I am getting old. I'm tired," he muttered as his eyes closed. Silence filled the room.

Hadara awoke to an empty room again. She slipped from the bed and walked to the chest where she kept her clothes. "What do I wear for my own marriage supper?" She removed one robe after another, shaking her head after each one. She sat on the edge of the bed platform, the robes lying beside her. Her head jerked up when someone knocked on the door to the room.

"Yes?"

Mazza called back, "Hadara, please open the door. I don't want to crumple what I carry."

"Very well." She hurried to the door and swung it open.

Mazza walked in carrying a silk robe and a gown of deep blue. "Here, this is your clothing for tonight. I'll help groom you. A bath is being prepared." She laid the gown and robe over the bed. "Come now. I already placed a robe to wear after the bath to return here. Bath cloths are ready, too. Now, come."

Brushing her fingers over the softness of the robe, Hadara turned to her old-time retainer. "Where … who … where did you get this?"

"Oh, child, Kalif had this made months ago and saved it. He had no idea, he said, that it would need to be used so soon. Enough talking, we have to get you ready."

As they walked across the courtyard to the bath, Hadara noticed no one occupied the courtyard. "Where is everyone? Where is Kalif?"

"Everyone arranges for tonight. Kalif had his bath and is now dressing in Barris' room. He wanted you to have privacy."

With a short giggle, Hadara declared, "Mazza, I have been dressing and bathing myself for many years. You needn't help me."

"For this occasion, I do. Now, no more from you. We will make you even more beautiful."

After the women returned to the bedchamber, Hadara dressed in the silk gown and robe. In front of a polished metal mirror, Mazza brushed the younger woman's hair, slightly wavy, flowing past her hips.

"I will plait a section on each side of your face and bring the plaits to the top of your head and attach jewels to hold them in place." Mazza explained as she sectioned hair for the first braid. "Kalif asked for your hair to remain loose, and the back will be."

Within twenty minutes, Hadara stood in front of the mirror again, trying to see her whole self. "Mazza, which jewels should I wear with this gown and robe?"

"These," Kalif's voice caused her to whirl to see him inside the door, holding a small wooden chest.

The gown and robe flowed around her as she sauntered toward him. "Kalif, you already gave me this lovely gown and robe."

"Ha!" Mazza half-snorted. "You are not used to receiving gifts from a husband, as a wife should."

"Mazza," Kalif interrupted her rant, "I believe I can handle everything now. Would you mind leaving us? We will join everyone in the courtyard briefly."

"Yes, Kalif." Mazza strode from the room, muttering to herself, "Finally someone who will care for my girl. Finally …"

Kalif's smile flickered when he looked at his bride. "So lovely." He opened the chest and removed three gold chains. Placing the chest on the bed, he turned Hadara around so she faced away from him. He slid two chains one after another around her neck. He moved her robe to one side. She jumped and tried to turn, but he held her in place.

"What … what are you doing?"

"This chain goes around your waist over your gown." He brushed her hair aside, bent his head, and placed a kiss on the side of her neck. "The gown and robe needed something elegant but not overpowering." After hooking the chain around her waist, he spun her around and stepped back three steps. "Ah, yes, perfect."

Hadara ran her hands over the chains around her neck before touching the one which hung loosely around her waist, one section of links dangling from where the chain joined. "I wish I could see, but I do feel quite … elegant."

Her husband drew her into his arms and kissed her. Pulling back, he studied her face. "You are lovelier than words can say, my love." He touched her cheek. "Now, let's go meet our guests."

Hadara's sight wandered around the courtyard. Groups of people clustered in different locations, talking and laughing. Her stomach rumbled in protest. *Maybe I can find some leftovers later.*

Kalif joined her in time to hear her stomach complain. "You didn't eat, did you?"

"Too many people talking to me and expecting answers. No, I didn't." She glanced at him. "How did you manage to eat anything?"

"I'm not as polite as you." He took her hand and led her toward the far end of the courtyard. "Someone wants to visit with you, and I told them only if they allowed you to eat."

They entered the kitchen where a variety of dishes covered the top of the table. A couple sat on one side, with a setting of dishes and utensils waiting for Hadara on the other.

"Hadara, these are Nava and Sofai's parents Ruben and Deborah. They wished to visit with you, but you mustn't forget to eat. Here, sit." Kalif began to fill her plate with food and her cup with drink.

Deborah nodded before she said, "You saved our young one's life, and that of our grandson. We thank you. Rachel said you know our other daughter, Nava. We have worried about her for so long."

When Hadara started to rise, Kalif placed a hand on her shoulder and pushed her down. "Eat. You can voice your anger later."

"Please, ma'am, you don't understand," Ruben pled. "I was weak, under my father's control. I kept thinking I would stand up to him once we arrived." He swallowed. "I did but too late. He was so domineering and dictatorial, and I, well, I was weak as I said."

Hadara chewed a bite and took a drink, studying the couple in front of her. Both had tears in their eyes and misery pasted across their faces.

"Ruben went back a few days later, but Nava was no longer there. He saw signs of people, but no way to know what had happened." Deborah touched her husband's arm. "We have suffered more than you can know."

"I can see you have, and I learned all too well how cruel Barrack is, rather was. I watched what he did in Bethlehem —" A sob interrupted Hadara's speech. "I, uh, I hid my son and Nava from him, and he still did everything he could to find my son, to use him as a sacrifice." She pushed her plate back. "But, how did you escape him?"

Kalif brought a small plate with a honey cake. "I won't push you to eat more, if you'll eat one of my mother's honey cakes. She would be hurt if you didn't."

With a smile, Hadara took the plate and set it on the table. She used a spoon to take a small bite, and her smile widened. "This is delicious." She looked at the others. "Have all of you tried one of these cakes? If not, you must." She ate another bite as Kalif served the other couple and himself a cake.

After swallowing her last bite, Hadara gazed at Nava's parents until they began to squirm. "Once I thought if I ever saw the two of you, I would let you know how angry I was at anyone who would leave a child on her own." She stood and walked away from the table. "I kept telling her that I would find her parents, but I didn't want to ever find you. She became *my* child. I love her; we all love her."

Returning to the table, she sat back in her chair. When Kalif held out his hand, she clasped it and brought it to her cheek for a moment before speaking again. "That anger died completely the day I met your youngest and your grandson. Sofai talked about her sister and your grief." She shrugged. "I realized how fortunate I was that you had left her for me."

Deborah's tears overflowed her eyelids and streamed down her face. Ruben gathered his wife into his arms, and his tears joined hers. "My wife … argued with … me, but … I thought … I could come back and … but took too long to get away from him."

"How did you get away from him?" Kalif repeated Hadara's question.

Deborah wiped her face and eyes. "My eema hadn't told us … that her brother, who left our village … when I was still a child … returned to Bethlehem. She didn't tell us that he sent messages when … he could." She glanced at her husband.

"I will finish, even though this, too, shows my weakness." He inhaled deeply and continued, "Deborah's uncle discovered that members of the family, his great-grandmother's older brother's grandson, still farmed in this area. The man had no children, and he and his wife took Tomas into their lives and left him the farm when they died." He reached for his cup and drank.

"Eema knew that Tomas would take us, that he had no family. She told us after we arrived at Jerusalem." Deborah tried to smile, but the grimace wavered. "We have been at the farm ever since." Her voice wavered as her smile had. "A part of us died, though, because we allowed Barrack to control us, and we allowed him to decide we leave our child."

With a nod, Hadara agreed. "However, she is alive, and so are you." She smiled. "She's a mother. She and my son married, not only to save her, but also to escape Barrack completely. In time, he would discover she lived. Then the babe had to be away from his reach. They left for Egypt before the babe was born."

"A babe? Nava has a babe?" Deborah's eyes widened. "She and your son?"

"I wrote my parents to tell them Barrack is dead, that Tobias, Nava, and the babe can return home." Hadara laughed. "We keep calling him a babe, but he is nearly three-years old now."

Deborah laid her head on her husband's shoulder. "She is alive and has a child. We will pray that she can forgive us." A sigh sent a shiver through her. "I … I need to go home now."

Kalif rose and helped Hadara to her feet. "We will escort you from this door and around to the front gate so you may avoid other guests in the court yard."

"Thank you." Ruben aided Deborah from her seat. "We hope we may visit you again, that you'll tell us more about our daughter."

"Yes, of course," Hadara replied. "We all love her, and I will share all I know."

The newlyweds lay in bed. All guests had left for their homes, and those who lived at the farm had retired to their rooms. Hadara snuggled close to her husband. "I wanted to hate them, Kalif, but I couldn't. They appeared so sad, almost broken. Barrack hurt so many with his hate, his obsession. Ruben lived under that mad man's control so much of his life."

Kalif's arms tightened around her. "You are not meant to hate, my love. You did what is right by forgiving. They need acceptance and a chance to live free of Barrack." He kissed her forehead. "We have more than enough evil to battle. Many children have been sacrificed, and many still to save." He kissed her. And, we have a new life to build together."

Chapter 35

Egypt – the stone quarry :: three months later

The heat rose like simmering waves from the sand. Nava once again silently thanked Tobias for building a cart for the water jug so she didn't have to carry it and keep up with a rambunctious nearly three-year-old. Since the boy knew they would go directly to the community well when Eema pulled the cart, he ran ahead, kicking sand dust into the air.

"Nava! Nava!"

The young mother turned as one of the quarry women ran toward her holding out a poetry shard.

"What do you need?" Nava couldn't remember the woman's name. The group of women who cooked, fixed meals, and sometimes provided "company" for the men changed numbers and faces often. This woman, older than most, looked familiar, though.

"Your Ethiopian friend asked me to give you this message." The woman tried to force the shard with writing on it into Nava's hand, but the younger woman pulled back without taking the missal. The woman tried again. "Please, he said I must deliver this to you, just to you."

"I know no Ethiopian who would write me. Now leave me alone." Nava continued toward the well, sprinting as fast as she could while pulling the cart.

The woman grabbed Nava's arm and again attempted to press the message into her unwilling hand. Nava jerked away and pushed the woman out of the way.

"Leave me alone! I don't know you, and I don't know what you try to do." She glared at the woman. "Leave me alone, or I will report you."

"Report? What is wrong here?"

Nava and the woman jumped apart before Nava faced the quarry manager, Faud. She pointed at the other woman. "She keeps trying to force me to take some message she says is from a friend, but I know no one who would write me. I also do not know her."

The manager held out his hand. "Give it to me."

The woman cringed and backed away. "Don't kill me, please don't. I tried to deliver it to her and no one else. I tried."

Faud grabbed her arm and shook her. "I will kill you now. Give it to me." His scarred and brown-burned skin intensified his frightening appearance as he loomed over the trembling woman. She placed the small, dirty piece of broken poetry in his hand.

The man, known for his temper and brutality, looked at the message. "It is not Egyptian." He turned his frown on Nava and handed it to her. "What is this?"

Her heart thumped loudly enough she thought Faud would hear. "I ... how would I know? She said an Ethiopian wrote it. I do not know that language, even to speak."

The manager reached down and grabbed the boy, who watched the actions of the adults. Holding the child with one hand, Faud strode to the well and hung Benjamin over the opening of the well.

"No! No, don't! Don't." Nava ran and clutched Faud's other arm, tugging with all her might. "Please, please don't!"

The quarry woman backed away several steps before she whirled and ran.

"What goes here? Bring that child away from the well!" A commanding voice caused Faud to jerk Benjamin over the rock wall and drop him on the ground.

Nava dropped to her knees and gathered her crying son in her arms, soothing him with quiet sounds, hugs, and soft kisses before she looked around with quick glances. Fear pounded in her chest. A man in uniform sat on a horse glaring at Faud.

Another mounted military man stopped the quarry woman, who dropped to the ground in a huddle, sobbing.

"Sir, I just tried to find the truth." Faud handed the shard to the military man beside him. "I didn't hear you come up."

"So, you torture a child and his mother?" Another man strode past to drop beside Nava, whose brows rose in surprise.

"Raz? Where, why?"

Raz ran a hand over Benjamin's head. "Is he hurt?"

Nava's lower lip trembled. "Frightened, as I am. Faud would have dropped him. He would." She used one hand to brush tears from her face. "What is happening? Why are you here?"

"Tell me first what happened." He listened without comment as she gave him a brief summary of the morning.

After helping her to her feet, Raz hoisted his nephew into his arms. He turned to face the manager. "Where is the quarry supervisor?"

"He ... he's probably in the hut," the manager stammered, pointing toward a stone hut on a ridge above them. At that moment, a man ran from the door with flapping robes flying behind him. "There is Ammon, now."

The supervisor huffed and struggled for breath once he reached the group waiting by the well. "Sir," he partially bowed, "I did not know," he gasped a breath, "you had decided to visit us."

"Apparently, you notice little. You didn't notice your manager harassing this woman," Raz nodded toward Nava, "or his torturing her and her son."

"But, but, sir, there is often yelling and commotion in the camp area. I would waste time checking on all of them."

"We will discuss this in more detail later. Now, summon all the workers, families, and camp women. I want to tell everyone what I need to say." Raz glared at Ammon. "Why do you still stand there? Did I not give you an order?"

"I thought … yes, sir." The supervisor ran to a pole with a huge metal circle attached to the top. Picking up a mallet, he banged the circle, which sent a boom echoing through the gullies and open areas of the quarry.

People ran from all directions: women and a few children from the hovels scattered around the flat area surrounding the well; more women from a section behind the supervisor's hut; men from the gullies that led to areas where they worked. Arriving first, a bronzed Tobias rushed to his wife, child, and uncle, closely followed by Philmon.

"Raz? Why are you here, and with Nava? This is dangerous." He observed the tear marks on his wife's and son's faces. "What happened? Are you hurt?" His fingers touched the wet tracks on first Nava's face and then Benjamin's. When the boy reached for him, he gathered the child into his arms, ignoring the dust and sweat on his own skin.

Raz clasped his nephew's shoulder. "Give me time to announce to everyone, but all is well, Tobias. Yes, you are no longer Tor but are again yourself." He then boosted himself on top of the low wall around the well. When he nodded at one of the mounted men, that man brought a horn to his lips and blew; the sound caused all conversation, mutters, and shuffling noises to stop.

"My name is Raz, and my family owns this quarry. We have done all we can to treat you as people, not as animals. We gave you food, shelter, and pay, even for the few slaves here. Yet, some of you have been dishonest and have tried to harm one of us."

"No, no, never."

"I never."

"Not true." Various denials resonated throughout the crowd, most loudly from the manager and supervisor.

Raz held up his hands, and the crowd grew quiet again. "A fiendish man from Judah visited Egypt, offering a huge reward for my nephew. The man had no right, no authority to do so, but many tried to find Tobias for the money."

Another wave of denials arose, until Raz again raised his hands. "Denial means nothing. I know most of you would never turn a man over for money, but some will and do. This man you knew as Tor is Tobias. This morning someone tried to trap his wife, to prove her husband and friend were the men hunted."

He motioned to the military man with the camp woman, and she was brought to face Raz.

"Tell me, woman, who had you take the message to Nava?"

She fell to her knees. "Please, master, I can't. He will kill me."

"I will protect you. Now, tell me."

Her head whipped around, her eyes wide and frightened, as she searched the people around her. Faud began to slip away from the well.

"Stop him!" Raz pointed at the manager, and several men grabbed him and forced him to stand before Raz. "Is this the man?" He asked the quarry woman, who nodded.

Faud fell to his knees blubbering.

"Stand up like a man and listen to me. Everyone, listen to me. That man Barrack is dead. Even if you captured Tobias, you would *not* be paid one piece of money. The man with the money, and the only man who would or who could pay you, is dead."

A murmur spread until it became a low roar. Faud shook his head back and forth. Raz allowed the mutters to quieten before he spoke again.

"Now, all workers have a day for rest. A cart has fresh supplies, even though earlier than you expected, and it holds a special feast for today. My nephew and his family will be leaving with me, but some of the military will remain to be sure no more trouble interferes with your lives the next few days. The manager is under armed arrest, and my family will investigate whether to replace the super-intendent or not. For now, Ammon will be acting manager." He stepped from the wall and took the few steps to where a guard stood over the blabbing Faud. "Take him back to my family's home and lock him in the prison cell."

The guard nodded before he pulled Faud to his feet and marched him toward a cart parked a distance from the people.

Nava watched the people hurry toward a larger cart where servants opened a side and loaded the makeshift table with platters of food. She turned to her husband, who still held their son in one arm while the other encircled her. "Your family is good to their people, as your mother is."

With a smile cracking through his dirt-caked face, Tobias said, "Yes, they are. They taught me any goodness I may have."

Raz told them, "Well, we are given much so we owe others, must help them. Now, my nephew, are you ready to take your family to your grandparents to be pampered some before you return to Judah?"

Chapter 36

Bethlehem :: six months later

The wind swirled clouds of dirt through the silent streets. The stars gave shadowy light, but the moon hid. In the house, next to the fine cloth and carpet shop, a young wife finished cleaning after a late supper while her husband wrote on papyrus.

"There, all ready for morning." Noma bent over her husband's shoulder. "Have you finished with your list?

Amzi glanced at her. "Just need to blot the ink and I am." He laid the list and writing supplies to one side and stood. "It's ready to go tomorrow."

"Are you taking the list to Kalif yourself or sending a messenger?"

"I'll talk to Gideon tomorrow before I decide. If he can manage, I'll take it myself. If Ruth's caregiver can't be with her, he can't spend time in the shop." Amzi smiled. "Kalif forgot to tell us that I was hired to be on hand when his mother needed his father's care. The old man can outwork me any day."

"If you take –" A tapping on the door to the alley interrupted Noma. "Who at this time?"

"I'll see. You stay here." Amzi rushed to the door at the back of the house. "Who's there?"

"Me, Abram." Amzi's friend whispered. "I have important news."

As soon as the door opened and Abram slipped inside, the men continued to the front of the house to join Noma.

"I'm sorry to disturb you so late, but Shem sent me. Naman's nephew is in Bethlehem to spy for his uncle, and he has been in Bethlehem for several months now. In fact, he used to live here with his mother."

"Who is this nephew? We may know him." Amzi frowned as he considered the men who arrived in town the last year.

"Lior."

"What? Lior is Naman's nephew?" Noma frowned before she turned to her husband. "Then, then Naman knew Barrack was bringing soldiers, knew Bethlehem would be attacked."

Amzi sat beside her and took her hands into his. "What? How do you know?"

"You know I was betrothed to Lior," she pulled her hands away and waved them in the air, "and it was a mistake. That doesn't matter now. When we stopped by for my visit with Lior and his mother that morning, they refused to answer when we knocked." She jumped to her feet and paced back and forth. "Abba heard whispering after we knocked. Lior's mother fussed at him because her brother told them to leave much sooner."

She dropped back in her seat. "They knew because Naman knew and told them to be gone before Barrack arrived." Her eyes wide and frantic, she stared first at Amzi and then at Abram and back to Amzi. "He already knew and didn't warn anyone."

Amzi hugged her. "We do have a problem, more than I thought." He regarded his friend. "We need to get this information to Kalif as quickly as possible. Are you up to taking the message to him tonight? I can't get away until tomorrow, if his father is able to watch the shop."

With a nod, Abram replied, "Of course, but the Lior problem is just part of Shem's message. Naman managed to slip two women into those trying to escape with their children. The women are spies, too."

"More spies? We found one already." Amzi closed his eyes and groaned. "I hope they haven't discovered the farm's secrets. Kalif, Hadara, Simeon, and his family ..." He paused. "Yes, Kalif *must* know tonight." He gazed at Abram for several seconds. "Will you manage?"

Abram stood. "Of course. I'll hurry so I can reach the farm before everyone is abed."

As Amzi let his friend out the alley door, he said, "Tell Kalif I will be there tomorrow as soon as I can let his father know I must leave. I will take Noma with me so she can visit her family, make the trip look even more normal."

Returning to the front chamber, Amzi stood, staring into nothing, glanced at Noma, and announced, "I'm going to visit Gideon right now. We need to leave early in the morning for the farm." He started toward the door to the alley before he turned back. "Pack a small bundle for both of us. We may need to stay more than a day."

The farm

Hadara spun around the bright white room, squealing. "I am so happy to be in our own part of the enclosure, our own home." She stopped and threw her arms open. "I can stop worrying, at least until others are here, about being too loud."

Kalif laughed. "I am sorry it took the workmen so long, but we had to be careful adding the tunnels and hidden rooms, only use our men." His eyes crinkled with laughter as he watched his wife stop and walk toward him.

"Ah, but this is worth the wait, especially since Tobias, Nava, and Benjamin will join us before long."

"And, within months, our own babe." He hugged her close. "I pray that the one true God will watch over us." He grunted. "Who would have thought we would live in the middle of so much danger and still live as if our life is normal? Very strange."

"I know. Perhaps people can live with fear just so long before simply accepting it." Hadara stared at his eyes, knowing he wouldn't avoid telling her the truth. "How are the group hidden at the old ruins? I hate that we sent them there."

"Ah, my love, they manage. In two days, we can move them into the hidden tunnels and rooms and allow them to rest before taken to the next stop." He ran a finger over each of her brows. "We had no choice. We couldn't have them here until all was complete and the workers gone."

She laid her head on his chest. "I know. I know. It took so much longer than we thought to join our back wall to the hidden area in the back wall and all of that."

"Shall we try our new bedchamber? We have a busy day tomorrow arranging our new home, and the night is late." Kalif twirled her around before leading her to the door to the other chamber.

Before they could leave the room, someone knocked on the door to the courtyard. Kalif motioned for Hadara is stay where she stood and walked to the door.

"It's Simeon," the man told them before Kalif opened the door. "We have a serious problem."

When the door opened, Simeon and Abram entered. "Abram will give you the message from Shem and Amzi while I get the man something to eat and drink." He slipped out, closing the door behind him.

"Please, Abram, sit." Hadara motioned to a couch. "Simeon will be a while since he has to go to their kitchen. Ours is empty at present."

"I was surprised to find you over here." The young man glanced around the room. "Is this part just like the other side?"

"Yes, except with an opposite arrangement." Kalif leaned forward. "Now, what is this important message?"

"First, Naman has sent two women as mothers wanting to save their children, and they have infiltrated at least one group, one that may already be here."

Hadara gasped.

"Let me finish, please." Abram told them about Naman's nephew sent to spy in Bethlehem, Noma's information about Lior. "All the pieces fit. Naman is involved in destroying at least Bethlehem and the underground movement. Amzi will be here as early as possible tomorrow, using his list of needs for the shop as his excuse."

Kalif started to speak, stopped, and began again. "Shem needs to know immediately. Let's decide –" A thump on the door caused him to stop and rise to let Simeon and Rachel in, each carrying a tray with food and goblets.

As the younger man ate and drank, Kalif paced the room. Hadara watched him, recognizing his need to think and not be distracted. When Simeon and Rachel began to gather up leftovers and utensils, he stopped.

"Let that wait. What we need to discuss affects you, too. So, please join us." Kalif moved a small table. He put writing materials on the table and motioned for everyone to join him as he set himself on a stool. He began to write on a sheet of papyrus. "I'll first list the different areas we need to address and will leave room under each for ideas.

"Let's see, the first problem is as Abram said, the women spies infiltrating the women seeking to save their children. Any ideas of what we can do to discover them this time and what to do when we can?"

"Since you are no longer with the army and since we don't know how the spies will report their findings, the stunt we pulled to find the spy before won't work." Simeon rubbed his forehead. "I guess first we need to find them."

Hadara wrapped her arms around herself. "Thankfully we have the current group at the ruins and not here." She shivered. "Thank the one true God we didn't finish the house before now."

"Yes, very fortunate." Kalif wrote as he talked. "Find spies." He looked up. "How do we tell a woman who is concerned for saving her child from one pretending?"

Rachel spoke for the first time. "I believe another mother could tell. A mother concerned for her child has a different attitude, a reaction that always put the child first. That helped us find the first one. One not really afraid would be more relaxed when anything has to do with the child. Any fear would be for herself, I think."

Everyone nodded in agreement. "I believe you have given us a starting point so we can begin our search. Who could join the mothers without causing any suspicion?" Abram looked at the others. "It would have to be a woman with at least one child."

"She would be in danger, as would her child." Simeon continued to rub his forehead. "I will be honest, I'm most concerned because I know it will have to be one of the women in my family, as would the child."

"Simeon, if I had a child I would …" Hadara paused as an idea dawned. "Not all the women already have their babes. Some expect a child." She ran her hand over her bulge. "I could be afraid for my child to be born and sacrificed."

"No!" Kalif exploded off his stool. "No, you can't."

His wife stood and slipped her arms around him. "Kalif, I must. Simeon's daughters and sons' wives with children would not know what to do. They have only been around our mothers briefly and at a distance. They would not know how to act." She sighed. "I wouldn't like going among the women, spying on a spy, but I know we will never be safe until we find the ones snooping for Naman."

"I hate to agree, Kalif, but who else can?" Rachel whispered. "We must have men close by, unseen, while she is with the women, in case of trouble. But, I don't see who else could go."

Kalif bowed his head and leaned it against Hadara's. "I don't see any other answer either." He led his wife back to their seats and pulled her down beside him. "We will need to work out the details in the next two days, but we know what must be done." He exhaled loudly. "I guess the next problem will be notifying Shem about Naman knowing about the attack on Bethlehem. All we can do is send a message."

"If I could sleep a few hours, I will take any message ready to Shem."

"Thank you, Abram, that would be good of you, especially after all the miles you have walked already." Kalif noted on the list that Abram would take the message on the Shem. "You already know what to tell him and add our plan for trying to trap the spies."

After everyone left. Kalif and Hadara finally climbed onto their bed platform. Hadara fell into an exhausted sleep almost immediately, but Kalif lay watching her, afraid that she planned to walk into a situation where he would lose her. He turned to prayer, begging his God to keep his wife and unborn child safe.

Chapter 37

Bethlehem

As dawn broke, Amzi and Noma made their way through the nearly empty streets of the village. A familiar face appeared occasionally, and the couple exchanged greetings with a few people.

"Noma? Noma, is it you?" a man called as they reached the edge of town.

Noma scowled at the dumpy man with a tall, elegant woman beside him. "Lior?"

The smile across his chubby face seemed strained, but he held the smile for several moments. "Oh, please, allow me. This is my wife, Jacoba."

Amzi bowed his head slightly. "Glad to meet you. I am Amzi, and this is my wife Noma." He shifted the bundle he carried under one arm. "Hope you have a good day. We need to be on our way."

"Wait, can't we visit for a bit? Noma and I were once quite close, weren't we, Noma?"

"Perhaps another time, Lior, but Noma and I have a bit of a walk ahead of us. We wish to be at our designation before they break fast."

Lior drew himself up to his highest height. "I had hoped we could be at least friendly."

Jacoba shifted from one foot to the other. "Shouldn't we go? They need to be somewhere, and so do we."

Lior turned his glare to her. "We will go when I decide."

"Your uncle?"

"Of course, of course. We must not keep him waiting." He glowered at Amzi and then Noma. "I'm sure he will be interested in our morning experience." He seized his wife's arm and forced her away from the younger couple.

"I believe we may have made an enemy," Amzi muttered as they continued toward the farm. "How in the world did you ever think you could marry him?"

"Frankly, I didn't think you would ever settle down and would ever want to marry me." She grinned. "He was all that was left unmarried, and I thought I had to marry."

They walked through the early morning, often in silence but occasionally discussing the problems Lior might cause.

"Perhaps we shouldn't have angered him," Noma wondered. "I let my anger at what he's doing overcome any good judgement. I'm sorry."

"Don't be concerned. I did the same." Amzi let some time pass before he added, "I will think of a way to 'smooth over' this poor beginning." He chuckled. "I'll let 'my jealousy' be known."

"Oh, Amzi, that will cause him to look down on you even more."

"As long as you and I know the truth, nothing else matters."

They arrived at the farm as the combined family began their first meal of the day in the older kitchen.

"Come in, come in." Kalif called when he saw them at the kitchen door. "As you can see, Hadara and I still don't have a working kitchen."

"Also," Rachel added, "we need to find them a working house staff."

Hadara heaved a sigh. "No one will allow me to be what I now am. I'm not a noble woman."

"But you are a rich one, none the less," Rachel argued. "Mazza is too elderly to do all the work the house will require, and she will not allow you to work that hard."

With a humph, Mazza stated, "No, I will not."

"Please, let's eat," Hadara said. "We can argue this later."

As the family squeezed together around the table, they listened to Noma and Amzi's story about meeting Lior and his wife.

"I let my anger affect my actions," Amzi admitted, "but I'll let it be known I'm jealous." He shrugged and said, "Actually, I was jealous at the time. That old ugly man with the beautiful Noma upset me, even if I didn't understand why until later."

Noma stared at him. "You weren't."

"Yes, I was."

Kalif laughed. "We men do strange things at times. However, now, if everyone is finished, we need to discuss our current situation. We could all be in as much danger as we were with Barrack running around."

"You all go to the courtyard. I have sons' wives coming in to help clean up here. As soon as we finish, I will join you." Rachel began to scrape scraps off platters.

"If we all help, you could join us sooner." Hadara stood and stacked empty vessels. Mazza and Noma helped. "You men go on to the courtyard; we will be there in a few minutes."

As the men waited for the women, Kalif told Amzi about the plan for Hadara joining the group of mothers. "I don't like the idea, but as she said, some of the escaping women haven't had their babes yet." He rose and patrolled the courtyard. "If anyone can think of a better idea, please speak. By the way, Abram slept two or three hours before leaving for Jerusalem to take word to Shem."

He halted and met the eyes watching him. "When we began this job, helping save little ones, we thought we were endangering ourselves at most. We wanted some excitement and to do something that fought King Ahaz and the Moleck worshippers. We never thought we would put people we love at risk. Please, if you have any thoughts of how we can be successful, share." He dropped to a divan.

Amzi leaned forward. "If anything happens to Hadara ... Of course, you know we can't allow anything to happen. We will have to have guards hidden everywhere, not ever allow her out of sight of someone."

"It's a difficult situation," Simeon stated, "but if anyone can manage to succeed, Hadara will. She survived living with Tzabar, escaping him, building this complex, helping women to escape for over two years." He shook his head. "Yes, if anyone can succeed, Hadara will."

"One point I have in my favor is I'm not well known in Bethlehem or Jerusalem. I stayed out of sight when I lived in the capital city, and I only went to market in Bethlehem that one time. No one knows me who might be in a cluster of escaping mothers." Hadara walked to sit beside Kalif as she talked. "Now, we need to decide how I'll find clothes that won't cause me notice and when I'll go."

"I'll find clothes," Rachel offered. "I expect you'll not go until enough protection is scheduled."

"Too bad we can't slip a man in with her." Amzi wiped both hands over his face. "Why not a 'son' that passes for not-yet a man, one who knows how to protect but wouldn't seem threatening. I know I look too old, but Abram appears ten years younger than he is. He doesn't even have a beard yet."

"Ahaz's priests are taking children up until the age of eighteen years, sometimes twenty, so that might work," Noma agreed. "I have seen Abram few times, but he seems capable. Hadara, what do you think?"

Kalif chucked. "I know I'd feel better. I have seen that young man in action more than once. Hadara would be almost as safe as if I were with her. Now, we need to know if he would be willing."

"Did he say he would return here after he told Shem about our plan to find the spies and about Lior?" Amzi asked.

"Yes, in fact he did. As he left early this morning while still dark, he said he would bring back word from Shem. He didn't say when, though." Simeon frowned. "How can we keep the women at the ruins much longer?"

Hadara heard the discussion spin around her, but she withdrew into her own thoughts. Unconsciously, her hands rested on her stomach. *Am I making a mistake?* She rubbed the area where her babe rested. *If I don't ... we could all die.* Her chest rose and fell with the deep sigh that escaped. *How will I pass as a poor woman? Afraid for her son, her unborn child?* She raised her hands. *Don't show hard work.* She closed her eyes. *I am afraid, so afraid.*

A pounding on the outside gate caused her heart to leap, and she grabbed her chest. *Calm down. Calm down. Nothing wrong.* She silently laughed. *Yet.*

By the time Simeon returned with Abram, Hadara had herself under control, especially after Kalif leaned close and whispered, "You don't have to go through with this. We can find another way."

Her lips twitched, tried to smile. "No, I can do this." She hesitated before she said, "Either way, we're in danger."

Simeon stood in the center of the group. "As we came in, I explained our plan to Abram, and he agrees to pass as Hadara's son. We can put our plan into motion as quickly as we have everything in place."

Abram inserted, "I will be more able to keep her safe than any truly young boy. No one will hurt her as long as I live."

"Abram, thank you, but I don't want you in harm's way, not more than you will anyway." Hadara heaved herself upright and took the few steps to where he sat on the ground. She laid a hand on his head, and everyone saw the flush on his beardless cheeks. "You are perhaps a year or two younger than my own son, and I would hate for anything to happen to you, just as I would if anything happened to him."

"Ma'am, I am used to the risks of my life, and I know the chances my life will be short." He swallowed loudly. "I know I must help. No one came to my mother's aid when she needed it." He ducked his head. "I apologize."

"Abram, no need to apologize. You are more a man than most." Kalif didn't leave his seat. "I feel better knowing that you will be watching over my wife and unborn babe."

Hadara nodded toward her husband. "I do, too. Now, we need to finish, and thank you, Abram." She returned to her place beside Kalif.

Simeon announced, "If this is to be successful, we must have Hadara and Abram in place tonight. We can't leave those mothers and children at the ruins much longer."

Hours later, Kalif and Hadara sat on the side of their bed. Spread across a chest on the other side of the room, a gown, robe, and mantle from a farm worker's wife made a drab puddle of cloth.

"Since we couldn't make you look older, hopefully, the story of a husband who liked young wives works." Kalif drew her closer. "I don't want you to go."

"I don't either, but if I don't, what will happen?" She gulped a sob. "We need to be saved from Naman." She stood. "I guess I'd better change. Abram will be here soon." With a small laugh, she said, "Why would I need to look older. I'm rather old to be having a child."

"You look at least fifteen years younger than you are. I feel ancient beside you."

She gazed at him. "Right now, I wish Caleb were here."

Kalif leaped to his feet and grabbed her. "Caleb is still here, under the fancy clothes and neat beard. Believe me, he's here, and he will be close by all the time you are in the ruins. I will not put your safety only in the hands of others." He touched her cheek. "The fighter, the warrior is still here, my love."

Chapter 38

A cold wind wafted around crumbling walls, creating shivers over everyone's skin. Bodies huddled in clusters: two women plus a few children in the largest group. Three covered fire pots provided the only heat. A man walked around the area, keeping watch, as two others slept close to one of the fire pots.

A whimper from a child broke through the cry of the wind as Hadara and Abram followed one of the night guards into the encampment.

"We can't have open fires because the light would cause someone to find out why," the guard loudly whispered. "We also try to keep quiet as possible with babes and young children. Glad no one much comes around here." He motioned to an empty spot not too far from a fire pot. "Make yourselves as comfortable as you can." He marched away toward the other guard.

The newcomers dropped to the ground with their backs to a wall. "Maybe we can be protected some from the wind." Hadara wrapped her mantle closer around her body. "Those fire pots don't give much heat."

The guard returned with two blankets, which he threw to them. "Sorry we can't offer more." He turned back to his duties.

Abram and Hadara wrapped themselves in the thin blankets, but the wind cut through the cloth as if nothing. Abram removed the blanket around him. "Here, you use this. I will be fine." He began to cover her with it.

She stopped his hands. "Let's at least share. I will remain covered with the one around me, and you and I will share this one. Just cover me, sit close, and tuck the other side around you." She covered one of his hands with hers. "We are supposedly mother and son, you know. I would be proud to be your mother, Abram. Maybe as we pass the time, you will tell me your story, if we talk quietly."

Soon, the site grew quiet except for the wind's shriek and an occasional cry of a child, which a mother quickly hushed. Hadara fell into a fitful sleep until sunlight peeked over the hills surrounding their hideout. Children fussed as everyone awoke and began to move around.

"Eema, I'm hungry," a little girl whined.

"Hush, Lotia, I know." Her mother pulled the girl into her lap. "We will have something to eat before long."

One of the guards walked over. "We will have some food soon, some legumes and a few vegetables."

"We will be glad for anything," the mother said.

Abram approached them. "I have a snare with me. I could catch some quail to add to the vegetables."

"If you can, we would all like some meat for a change." The guard pointed toward the closest hill. "I saw some in that direction yesterday."

When the "boy" dropped his blanket on Hadara's lap, she reminded him in a whisper, "Be careful. We don't know what soldiers or Naman's men may be around."

With a quirky grin, Abram responded, "Yes, ma'am, uh, mother. I'll be careful."

After Abram left, Hadara wrapped both blankets around herself and waddled over to one of the fire pots, where she squatted and soaked in the small amount of heat given off by the metal.

Another woman joined her. "Miserable way to help us, I say." Her pretty face twisted into an unpleasant scowl. "We was to be able to escape the burning, but this is worse."

"Do you really believe having your child burnt alive would be better than going through some uncomfortableness?" Hadara glanced around. "Where is your child? A boy or a girl?"

The woman pointed at a child curled up on a blanket and wrapped in another. "A girl. I really don't want her to burn, but I can't see anything good happening to her. You trying to save your boy? Seems to me he could'a made his way on his own."

"He probably could and be successful, but I will be giving birth in a few months. We want to save this one." Hadara looked around the camp. "Everyone appears to be scattered. If we all moved close together, we'd be warmer."

"Some of them think they be better than some of us not from some rich household." She gave a dry laugh. "You should be hearing them complain, and not because of their young ones, but for themselves."

"Really? I only see six of us plus the guards and children. Where we came from shouldn't make any difference." She studied the other four women and their children. Two sat even farther away than two others who huddled not far from this woman's daughter.

"Huh!" the woman hmphed. "You be one of them uppity ones, but you don't act so uppity as them does."

"I know we don't share much information about each other in case we're ever taken, but maybe we could talk with the others about our children."

"Might pass some of the time as we freeze. Where you want to start?"

"Hmmm ... The woman with the two little ones looks as if she could use some help. Let's offer to help her."

Within a quarter of an hour, the women, except for the two off by themselves, sat around one of the fire pots, with their children snuggling together.

No matter what Hadara said, the two loners ignored her. The guards passed out dried meat and cups of water when the children began to fuss again. Mothers soaked some of the meat in the water to soften it and to make a broth for the little ones who couldn't chew. One of the loners gave a piece of meat to her child, the other sat and ate as she held her babe.

After chewing the jerky and drinking a cup of water, the sleepless night caught up with Hadara. She found the two blankets allotted her and Abram and curled up in a corner where two partial walls met. Sleep closed her eyes, and she knew nothing until excited voices awoke her. Sitting up, she looked around, dazed. Abram knelt in front of her, three dressed quail in his hands.

"A pot of legumes and vegetables are cooking already. I wanted to show you my catch before I added them to the pot." Abram grinned, allowing his pride show.

"Oh, Abram, how wonderful." She grinned back. "My son, the hunter."

"I also found some dead tree branches and trunks to help keep us warm tonight." He grinned again before rising and taking the quail to the pot on the fire.

The women crowded around the fire where the huge pot sat bubbling with vegetables. One of the men helped Abram cut up the quail and drop the chunks of meat into the stew.

"Them quail would taste better roasted than in with the vegetables," the woman with whom Hadara had first visited remarked.

Abram glanced up at her. "Yes, but everyone couldn't even have a bite. This way, the meat provides broth for the little ones, too."

"Guess so." The woman stomped away but returned in a few minutes. "I'm sorry. I am cold and hungry, but I shouldn't be hateful."

Hadara frowned at the woman. *Something isn't right. What?* She shook her head. *Maybe the answer will come later.*

She watched as the guards took turns patrolling the area. Some of the women cared for their children and stirred the pot, and one woman sat off by herself, holding her babe so it could nurse. *We're not to use our names but we ...*

"Ladies," she said as she joined the group around the fire, "we need to be able to call each other something. What if we went by the color of our robes? Mine is closest to brown, so I'll be Brown." She nodded at the woman she visited with earlier. "Yours is a reddish color, so we could call you Red." She went around the circle with Yellow, Green, and Dark Blue. She pointed to the woman by herself. "She can be Light Blue."

Yellow laughed. "I be glad to be something beside 'woman' until I be able to use my name again." The others smiled or laughed, too.

"I agree. Red is a strange name, but I prefer that, also, to 'woman'."

Hadara, on the other hand, closed her eyes to keep from staring at Red. *I can't let her know I suspect. I can't.*

One of the men brought out two loaves of bread. "I'll tear this into pieces when the food is ready. It won't give any one much more than a small bit of bread, but that way little ones can sop up the broth even if they can't chew."

Later, Hadara and Abram sat eating across the space from where Light Blue leaned against a wall. A short distance away, Red and her daughter sat with their bowls of stew, facing toward Hadara but at a right angle from Light Blue. Hadara could see both their faces. She kept her face lowered, as if concentrating on her food, but she still watched the other two women.

"What are you doing?" Abram whispered. "I know this stew does taste good but watching it won't change anything."

"I think I may know who our two spies are, and I was wrong about one." She took another bite. "You know," she said around the food, "this is very good." She ate the rest of her bread after dipping it in the soup. "Red and Light Blue are avoiding each other too much. Watch them without them noticing."

The two continued eating without talking, but each slyly observed Red and Light Blue as they tried to be discreet. When they finished, Abram took their vessels and utensils. "I'll clean these and put them where they go."

"Abram, you hunted and helped fix the meal. You don't need to wait on me."

"Mother," Abram winked at her so that no one else could see, "you know I would be in serious trouble if I don't care for you as much as I can. Besides, I may know how to help everyone stay warmer tonight and need to talk to the guards about my idea."

With a smile and shake of her head, Hadara followed him with her eyes as he made his way to the fire pot where the other men sat. As she did, she observed Red looking at Light Blue. Red lifted one eyebrow, and Light Blue nodded. Both women then turned in other directions.

Night began to fall, but the freezing wind didn't. Abram explained how large rocks could be heated and piled so that the heat didn't create a flame. He found a section of walls that created almost a complete but roofless room. He piled stones and built a fire around and under them.

"Once the flames die down, we should have enough heat in the rocks to last us most of the night." He placed Hadara's and his blankets in a corner of the area so that the crumbling walls most protected them from the wind. "This won't be as comfortable as home, but we should be more comfortable than we were last night."

He left the enclosure and returned with his arms full of grasses. After piling them by the blankets, he used one blanket to cover the grasses. He gave a mocking bow. "There, my lady, you will be much more comfortable."

Hadara bowed her head in acknowledgement. "Thank you, kind sir." She studied him. "Where will you be?" She sat on the "bed" Abram had made her.

"I'll put grass in another corner, but I'm used to sleeping in the open. I'll be fine, especially since I'll be closer to the hot stones." He sat crossed legged on the ground and faced her. "Did you learn anything more?"

"Yes, I believe I have." She placed two fingers on her lips and glanced around. "Do you think we can talk here?"

"If we whisper. I helped everyone locate in places not very close to ours. Do you want to go first, or do you want me to share what I've discovered?"

She raised her brows. "Really? Maybe what you know is more than the suspicions I have. Let me tell you first." She held up one finger. "I thought Dark Blue and Light Blue might be the spies because they stayed away from others. After visiting with Dark Blue, though, I found she was shy, especially about nursing her babe around others." She held up a second finger. "Something about Red concerned me, although she was friendlier than the other women at first. Then, this afternoon, I knew. She tried to talk like the more uneducated, poorer women, but she would slip from time to time. She wasn't what she pretended to be." Finger number three joined the other two. "When we were eating, Red and Light Blue sat where they could see each other, but they stayed far enough apart that most wouldn't notice. When they thought no one watched, their eyes met. Red raised one eyebrow, and Light Blue nodded." She held her hands flat, palms up. "I have nothing definite, just oddities."

"If we didn't have to be quiet, I would give a yell. You put some good signs together." He scooted closer. "The one you call Light Blue took her babe and left camp for a while after the mid-day meal. She wrapped a scarf around herself and the babe. She didn't go far, but she also didn't take an easy path, but climbed over rocks and hills."

"Oh," Hadara whispered, "as if practicing to be able to make her way if she left."

Abram nodded. "I will watch her closely tonight."

"Ma'am, young man, do you need anything before we put away what food is left?"

Hadara raised her head to stare at the guard in the wide opening. "Dan?" she whispered.

"Of course. Kalif would never let you go far without trusted guardians." Simeon's oldest son nodded at Abram. "Much as we all trust you and know your many talents. Now, allow me to bring you something to eat and drink so we can visit at least a short time."

Abram leaped to his feet. "I will walk with you, and I'll bring you up to date and bring," he glanced around at the ears still attuned to what happened before increasing his vocal volume slightly, "my mother food and water. What is left that I can take her?"

"There are a few pieces of quail and some bread." Dan then returned to a whisper. "Tell me quickly."

As the men placed quail and bread on a wooden platter, Abram told Dan what Hadara and he had discovered. "And, we think Light Blue will try to leave, perhaps tonight."

"Good, good, now take this to your mother. If you need help, ask one of the other men. I came to bring more bread. I may return tomorrow, but if I don't, may you find your way to safety."

When Abram returned to Hadara with the platter, she smiled. "Thank you. I had no idea much food was left." She moved over. "Here, join me. You need to eat, also, and you brought plenty."

"I believe Dan brought more food to add to what we had left. I know he brought bread, and this quail was roasted, not scooped from stew."

As the two wrapped the meat in the chunks of bread, Abram told Hadara what he passed on to Dan. "If Light Blue does try to leave, I doubt she goes far. I will, however, still watch."

Sometime after the night became sprinkled with stars, Hadara sensed Abram left their spot without a sigh of sound. She lay wrapped in the blanket, glad she didn't have to lie on hard ground. "I wonder how long ..." she mumbled to herself. "I will wait until he returns." She tried to fight the power of sleep, but she lost.

"Mother." Abram's voice brought her awake. When he saw her eyes open, he sat close to her. "Success. Light Blue and her babe were taken by Dan and two others. Now, we watch Red, but perhaps we should give her a reason to act."

Hadara rose to a sitting position and smoothed her hair back from her face. She pulled her mantle over it. "I wouldn't do well living like this for long." She moved from under the blanket. "What is your plan?"

"I believe we need to reveal who you are, indirectly."

"What!" She clamped her hand over her mouth and listened. When she didn't hear anything except Abram chuckling, she murmured, "We can't do that. Besides how would that help?"

"No, no, no," he whispered, "not you as wife to Kalif, but a hint that you might be wife to Naman."

"Are you insane? How can we do that?"

"Just expect the unexpected, Mother." Abram grinned and walked out of the opening.

Hadara rose and straightened her "bed." The stones still radiated a small amount of heat. *Smart young man is that Abram.*

Yellow first noticed Light Blue missing. Everyone who could checked the area close to the ruins. "You must not go far," one of the guards told the women and Abram.

"Why don't I hunt again and look for signs of where she went?" Abram offered after everyone returned.

"That would be helpful," a guard said. As he walked toward the edge of the ruins, the guard asked loud enough that his words carried back to the women around the fire, "Your mother seems very young to have a son your age."

Abram stopped and stared at the older man. "Some men like to take young girls to wife."

"And, you were the result?" The guard slapped Abram on the back and laughed.

"Men like Naman care about no one but himself." Abram glared at the guard and strode from camp.

The women turned as one and stared at Hadara. Red narrowed her eyes and stepped toward the shocked woman.

"I ... I ..." she tried to talk, but the shock of Abram's words left her mute. She shivered at the hate in Red's eyes. "I, uh, I have nothing to do with anything Naman ever did. I don't."

One of the guards touched Hadara's arm. "Your son didn't mean to let anyone know."

"Of course, he didn't, but I think everyone misunderstands."

Red uttered, "I am sure we all understand completely, but you don't worry. I'm sure you will be fine." She grabbed her daughter by the hand and strolled away, her gait unhurried but her back stiff.

Abram returned with four quail cleaned and ready to cook. "I think these are large enough that we can roast them and have with the vegetables and bread." He looked at one of the guards. "We will have bread, won't we?"

The guard nodded. "Yes, and the pot is already boiling. As soon as the quail are ready, we can eat."

"Then, let's get with it." Abram went behind a wall and brought some large palm branches, wet them, and wrapped them around the quail. He dug holes in the sand beside the open fire allowed in daylight, buried the packs, and pulled some of the burning branches over the places where the quail lay.

The sun began its descent behind the hills. Piles of red hot stones created areas where people could curl up and sleep. Hadara entered the enclosed area where her bed of grasses waited when an arm looped around her neck. Something sharp pressed against her neck.

"Be still," Red's voice hissed next to her ear.

"Let her go!" Abram's yell brought guards and mothers running toward them.

Red whirled Hadara toward those rushing to her aid. "I'll slice her throat if you don't stay away." She slid sideways, keeping her prisoner close in front of her, the knife pressing into Hadara's neck enough that a trickle of blood oozed out. Once the two women left the enclosure, Red pushed Hadara ahead, forcing her to run.

Abram glared after Hadara and her kidnapper. His brain froze in horror. "What did I begin," he asked aloud. "What have I done? Kalif will kill me."

"Both of us," Dan agreed from where he stood outside the opening. "Come on, we can't let her get too far ahead."

As the two ran in the direction one of the guards pointed, Dan gave a shrill whistle, and two men in military dress joined them already at a full run. They reached the top of the first hill when another man joined them.

"What happened? Where is Hadara?" he demanded.

Abram groaned. "Kalif? We didn't know the other spy ... had a knife ..." he huffed between words, "and she grabbed ... Hadara."

Kalif faltered and almost stopped before he burst forward even faster. The others followed. After racing into the night nearly a quarter mile, Kalif halted. Dan rammed into his back before able to stop.

"Listen," Kalif whispered. "Just be quiet and listen. We can't tell where they are in the dark; we can't see their tracks, nothing. Let's use our ears since our eyes aren't much help."

For a few moments, the men heard the whine of the wind, the rustle of bushes, and the scurrying of night life.

"I can't!" The shout ricocheted off the surrounding hills. "I must rest."

"Hadara." Kalif spoke the name all recognized even at a distance.

An angry voice threw a string of curses into the night. The hunters listened closely, locating the direction. Without a word, they moved in tandem on the same course – toward Hadara and her captor.

In a shallow valley between the rolling hills, Kalif knelt and examined the scuffed ground before he rose to face the other men. Abram continued to study the surrounding terrain, anything to avoid meeting Kalif's eyes.

"Hopefully, Hadara will help us again. I can't see any foot prints. The spy brushed over the soil, erasing them." Kalif's shoulders sagged.

"Wait, look." Abram grabbed the other man's arm and pointed to a bush. "Hadara did help us again. She broke some branches to show the way."

The men restarted their hunt, but this time they spread out, watching the ground as they moved toward their goal. After they covered nearly a mile, Kalif motioned for a pause. "They are headed for the olive grove by the small farm." He glanced at the other men. "Who are the fastest runners?" When two answered, he told them, "Run at full speed to the right side of the grove and make sure no one goes that direction." He motioned to two others. "You take the left side. Get there in time to make sure no one goes that direction. Abram and I will continue and go into the grove from this direction." His sagging shoulders straightened. "Go!"

As the four men dashed to take their places, Kalif twisted his head and stared at Abram. "If you help save my wife, I will try to forgive your putting her in danger." His mouth twisted into a grimace. "Do you not think I spent all my time outside that encampment, watching and listening? Do you think I would not keep an eye on my wife?" Kalif trotted toward the grove. "What keeps you? Come on and fast."

Earlier at the camp

When Red grabbed her and pricked her neck with a knife, Hadara couldn't move. Her breathing stopped. Her heart beat skipped. Her brain kept telling her, "Fight! Get away! Fight!" but she stiffened and could no longer control herself. Her brain screamed, "No, no, don't let her pull me away." But, her body wouldn't respond.

Red walked the two of them from the encampment, keeping the knife at Hadara's neck and her captive as a shield.

As soon as they were outside the ruins, Red pushed Hadara away from the others and stuck her with the knife. "Run, if you want to live, run."

Hadara tripped and fell to her hands and knees but scrambled to her feet and loped in the direction Red herded her with swats of the knife's flat side or pokes with the tip. "Hurry. Before they get organized." She pushed Hadara again, who stumbled and nearly fell.

Kalif, where are you? Kalif, I need you. Help me. Over and over she begged, as she slipped, slid, and stumbled in front of Red. Her prayers to her God mixed with the pleas for Kalif, hoping, praying for rescue. Finally, her mind did more than pray and silently scream. *They don't know where to look. Must let them know where I am.* She allowed the next stumble to throw her to the ground.

"Get up! Get up!" Red gripped her arm and tried to lift her.

Hadara broke the grip and yelled, "I can't. I must rest!"

Red trembled. Her hands reached for Hadara's throat, but just before she strangled her victim, she managed to stop. She swore, using terms Hadara had never heard. "Get up now before I do kill you. Get up."

On shaky legs, Hadara began walking. Red broke a branch off a bush and brushed their foot prints away. As she passed another bush, Hadara broke a branch so it pointed in the direction they walked. Every time she noticed Red looking away from her, Hadara broke another bush branch. *All I can do. All I can do.* The dark allowed her to blaze a trail that she couldn't during daylight.

The rough ground leveled to a barley field. The women walked along the edge of the field, and once again, every time she could drop behind Red a few steps, Hadara broke stocks of the grain. She gazed ahead where she saw darker shadows past the lightness of the grain. *I know where we are.* She peered to her left, straining to see through the night. *So close to home.* She felt a buoyancy fill her as she prodded toward the shadows ahead. *Olive grove by small farm. Kalif, I'm here.*

She tripped and staggered until she regained her footing. Her awkward body rebelled at the physical endeavor. Red's prodding her with the knife and exhaustion battled. She began to mentally force herself to continue.

Keep walking ... don't hurry. Take step ... Step, step, step .... Step, step, step ... Come on, another step. I can't. I can't go on ... step, step, come on ... step ... step. Tired so tired. She fell into an olive tree on the outside edge of the grove. Her arms wrapped around the trunk, and she rested her face against the bark.

"We can't stay here. Get going. Get to the center of the grove." Red jerked Hadara's arms from around the tree, and the spent woman tumbled to the earth. Her hand smacked into something hard.

Hadara moved her hand over the solid object. *A branch.* She pushed herself upward until she rested on her feet and hands, one of which wrapped around the branch. *I can do it. I can do it.* She stood upright and whirled, swinging the branch with every bit of strength she had left.

WHACK! Red's head snapped back. Her body flew backward, hit the ground, and bounced once before not moving.

A sound. Hadara twirled, the branch pulled back and ready.

"Hadara, wait."

"Kalif?" Hadara dropped the branch and propelled herself into the waiting arms of her husband. She clutched his neck, and the tears and sobs burst from her.

"You're safe. You're safe. I have you." Kalif rubbed one hand up and down her back until he touched a moist place and she flinched. "What, what's wrong?" He tried to turn her, but she refused to let go of him. "Can't see a thing any way." He asked Abram, "Can you see anything on Hadara's back?"

Abram nodded. "There's a dark spot, actually several on her back. They look," he touched one of them, "they are wet."

Kalif swooped his wife into his arms and marched out of the grove. "Run ahead and open the back gate so I can take her directly to our rooms." He hugged her with care. "I'll get you home. You'll be all right now."

"Yes, I'll do that." The young man ran faster than he ever had, brushing by another man when leaving the trees.

Hadara whispered, but Kalif heard, "I know. I'm safe. You have me." Her words came in quiet bursts broken by sniffs and occasional sobs.

"Kalif? It's Dan. Do you have her?"

"Yes, but she's hurt. I have to get her home." He increased his speed. "I used to be able to do a fast march with full battle gear. I hope I still can. Dan, that monster hurt Hadara. She's hurt." He stopped. "Dan, make sure that trash back there is locked up somewhere."

"Already taken care of. Now, let's go."

Hadara's sobs completely stopped as she pressed her face into the spot where her husband's neck joined his shoulder. Kalif felt her body relax until she lay against him completely slack. He lowered his head to her face. She breathed silent puffs of air.

"She, she sleeps."

Dan chuckled without missing a step. "She has gone through much tonight, and you did tell her she was safe."

Half-way to the house, the sun peeked over the horizon. Kalif spied a boulder to the side of the path they followed. He sat, shifting Hadara so he held her more securely. "Can you see the places on her back? Does she still bleed? Is it heavy?"

Dan knelt in front of the couple. "Yes, 'tis blood in several places, and it looks wet. Nothing is flowing, though."

"Let's go. The sooner I have her home, the sooner her wounds can be dressed." He rose and continued his fast march, Dan by his side.

An hour later, the farm compound appeared in the distance. "May I give you a break carrying Hadara?" Dan offered.

"No … no, we're … doing well. Just … a short … We will … soon be … home." Kalif's words broke as he spoke between pounding steps. "Wish I had told … Abram to … have someone … have warm … water … dressings waiting."

"I can run faster than you right now. I'll go ahead and have things ready." Dan cuffed Kalif on the shoulder before he sped forward.

Kalif stayed on his course, holding his wife and concentrating on the goal moving ever closer.

Inside the house, Mazza and Rachel waited with towels, cloths, dressings, and clean garments for Hadara. A cloth spread across the bed also waited. Kalif laid her on her side and began to undress her.

"We will do that, Kalif," Mazza told him.

"No, Mazza, I will. I must know how badly she is injured. I have to check for myself." He took his knife and split her gown in front. "Wet the places where blood oozed through the cloth. I don't want the cloth to pull anything open that may have closed." He knelt beside the bed and touched Hadara's face before helping soak the back of her gown.

After the women soaked the bloody areas and Kalif pulled the rest of the gown and robe away, Mazza gasped. Rachel covered her mouth with both hands and backed away. Kalif grit his teeth until the muscles in his jaw protruded. Dozens of bleeding pricks covered Hadara's back. He rocked back on his heels, and his gaze dropped to her face. Her wide-open eyes returned his gaze.

"You're awake," he muttered.

"I have been for a while. I couldn't open my eyes yet. Too weak. Too tired." She reached for one of his hands, hers quivering. "She kept sticking me. I couldn't go fast enough." A small grin moved her lips. "I refused to go fast."

Occasionally, Hadara allowed a soft moan to escape as they cleaned and dressed the punctures on her back and the nick on her neck.

"Thankfully, none of these are very deep." Mazza shook her head.

"Uhh." Hadara winced. "How deep is not very?" another soft groan, "Each hurts like it goes through me."

Finally, she lay in a clean gown, with the soiled cloth removed so she nestled on a spotless bed. Mazza and Rachel removed all the dirty pieces of material as well as the bloody water. Kalif bent over his wife and kissed her temple.

"I need to wash myself and take off this leather armor. I'll go to the bathing room when Mazza returns."

She seized his hand. "Please don't leave me."

He knelt beside the bed. "I won't be gone long, and Mazza would be here.

Abram and Dan are right outside. No one could get to you."

Her breathing quickened. "I ... I don't know what's wrong. I am usually not so cowardly." She swallowed. "I will ... I will be strong."

Watching the color wane from her already pale face, Kalif frowned. "No, you are not cowardly, but yesterday and last night would make anyone anxious." He studied her as she closed her eyes and fisted her hands. "I will ask the men to carry in warm water and wash myself here." He touched her nose, and her eyes flew open. He grinned. "Think you can tolerate my cleaning and dressing in front of you."

A splotch of pink stained her cheeks. "I, uh, I think I could manage." She lowered her lashes. "But, but if you would rather, I will be fine while you bathe."

When a laugh erupted from Kalif, she raised her eyes to stare at him.

"What is funny?"

"Oh, my love, you are a joy. I will never be bored even if we live together for a century."

Kalif opened his eyes sometime later to find Hadara gazing at him. "Umm, did we sleep long?"

"Since it is nearly time for evening meal, yes, we have. Mazza looked in just a bit ago, said they would have us something to eat shortly." When her stomach rumbled, she laughed. "You can tell *I* am hungry."

She scooted over to the edge of the bed and swung her legs over the side so she could sit, all without having to put any pressure on her back, her movements awkward and stiff. "I am sore in more places than my back. I didn't expect that."

She started to stand: Kalif cried, "Wait," and she wailed, "Oooohhh," at the same time her feet reached the floor. She dropped back to the bed.

"They hurt. My feet hurt." She drew them up into her lap and examined the bandages covering them. "What happened to my feet?"

When Kalif didn't answer, she turned to stare at him. He had a half grin on his face as he watched her. "Kalif?"

"Oh, I'm sorry. I was wondering how you could twist your body around like that. I ..." He jerked. "Your feet, yes, your feet. The sandals you wore weren't made for walking outside or for long distances. They didn't protect your feet; in fact, they wore wounds on your skin." He touched one foot with a finger. "They are covered with bruises, cuts, blisters. I hadn't noticed, but Rachel did. While Mazza and I worked on your back, Rachel tended to your feet."

He hopped off the bed. "Now, my lady, if you will allow me, I will help you dress as soon as I slip on a robe."

After he dressed both himself and his wife, Kalif brought Hadara's brush to the bed. "Trust me to brush your hair?"

"I would trust you for anything, but I'm surprised you'd want to brush my hair."

He exhaled a low groan. "I know; you feel safe with me."

Hadara crawled to her knees on the bed. "Kalif, why do you make that sound bad?" She touched his arm. "I have never felt safe with anyone before," she lowered her eyes, "because I've never loved anyone before or felt loved. To me, love must be a part of safety, or safety a part of love."

"I see. Then I will always do my best to help you feel safe because I do love you, too." He grinned, and with a shake of his head, touched the plait of chocolate colored hair, with twigs, wisps of hair, and leaves caught in it. "I also love your hair, usually. Let's make it beautiful again."

Kalif finished the neat re-plaiting of her hair when someone tapped on the door. "Yes?" he called.

Mazza opened the door and glanced around the edge. "Your meal is ready in the next room."

"Thank you, Mazza." Hadara started to stand on her sore feet when Kalif swept her into his arms and strode through the door Mazza held open.

After their meal, Hadara partially reclined on a divan in their gathering room, Kalif at her feet. Abram, Barris, and Mazza joined them for the meal and remained as Simeon, Rachel, and Dan entered and took seats. One of Dan's brother's wives removed all the dishes and scraps.

"Since my brothers and sisters' husbands are helping the men who work for us to keep watch, I'll share what we discuss with them later," Dan explained. "I suppose I'm their representative at this meeting."

Kalif nodded. "Good idea, but too bad Amzi can't be here. We could use a report on what's happening with Naman's nephew."

"I agree, and so did he," Simeon said. "He and Noma will be here before long."

"How –" Kalif began.

Abram interrupted, "I made a quick trip to Bethlehem and back. I imagined we would need to be sure we don't get caught unaware again."

"You were busy and made a good decision." Kalif gave a slight nod.

"I needed to do something to make up for putting Hadara in danger." The young man shifted where he sat crossed-legged on the floor.

"Tch, tch, Abram, you didn't put me in danger. Whatever gave you such an idea?" Hadara frowned at her husband. "Did you …"

Kalif waved his hands in the air in front of his chest. "No, not me."

"Hmm … Abram, I suggest you forget any idea of you being at fault. Besides, we got the spies, didn't we?"

Everyone began talking at one time, words on top of each other. "Yes, and …"

"We captured the men …"

"Everyone is locked away …"

"One woman and babe escorted to …"

"You could have …"

"Don't ever do …"

"Red won't be …"

"What about Red? What about her daughter?" Hadara asked.

"Shem doesn't have the power in Judah Naman does, but he can make people simply disappear. I don't know where he moves them, but they don't come back." Kalif shrugged. "One of the other women took the little girl."

A pounding on the outer gate silenced everyone. Simeon started to rise, but Dan stood first. "Stay seated. I'll see who is here."

Noma and Amzi followed Dan back into the room. As she looked around for a place to sit in the small room, Noma commented, "Wouldn't we be more comfortable in the courtyard?"

Her father nodded. "Yes, but with no roof, we could possibly be overheard. That wouldn't be likely, but possible."

"I hadn't thought of that, and I realize how dangerous anyone knowing what we're doing is." With a gasp, she stared at Hadara's bandaged feet. "I heard you were injured, but even your feet?"

Hadara sighed. "I'll heal, and 'tis a small price for what we accomplished."

"Oh, I understand." Noma pulled a huge cushion from a corner and sat. Amzi dropped to the floor beside her.

"How did you get away without causing any suspicion?" Kalif asked.

Amzi chuckled. "Your father. He has been saying how much your mother wants to visit her sister. He even managed to prompt her to complain in her caregiver's hearing. Yesterday, he told everyone we were shutting down the shop so he could take her to her sister's." He laughed. "Therefore, I told people since I wasn't needed except to check the shop occasionally, I would take my wife and visit our families."

"And, not too soon," Noma stated. "Lior followed me every time I stepped from the house. He asked constant questions about Amzi, wanted to know what he did when he left the village on his trips." She shivered. "He kept bringing up our betrothal and touching me."

"Others told me the man asks questions of many people about others and me. He also often visits farms just outside town, without warning." Amzi stood and leaned against the wall. "Many people are upset with his searching for information, but they fear his uncle."

Simeon bent forward from where he sat. "How much trouble could he cause in just a few days?"

"Unbelievably much," Amzi answered. "Neighbors distrust neighbors. Families are divided. Unbelievable."

"What can that accomplish?" Rachel wondered aloud.

Her son answered, "By causing division, anger and distrust builds until someone reveals something, even if they don't mean to."

"Your leaving is a good thing, Amzi. My father is shrewd, too. He has removed my mother and himself from the trouble in a way that no one questions, and he gives you a way to disappear and yet go back and forth as needed." Kalif patted his wife's foot. "Your and Abarm's plan has surely caused some panic in Naman's crowd, too. Now, how can we use their distractions to help victims escape and keep them confused to avoid being exposed ourselves?"

"We must find a way to investigate women wanting our help. We can't put our people and ourselves at any more risk than we must." Simeon pounded a fist on his knee. "We disposed of Barrack, but many died in the process. We can't allow Naman to gain as much power as Barrack had."

As the rest of the group discussed ways of investigating mothers wanting to escape with their children, Hadara allowed their voices to lull her into a half-sleep. *I hurt so much ... so tired ... need to listen ...* She struggled to pay attention, but she soon slipped back into her own tumbling thoughts. *Hope Red can't get away ... are others safe?* Her eyes closed; she forced them open. Her eyes closed again; she forced them open again. The next time they closed, her head slid to rest on the back of the divan, and she slept.

When Hadara awoke, she snuggled next to Kalif in bed. She turned to face him and discovered he watched her. "Hmmm ... I ..." she yawned, "I couldn't stay awake."

"I noticed. We let you sleep while we discussed."

"Will you give me a summary of those plans while I try to fix us our morning meal?"

Kalif grinned.

"What's wrong? I really can cook ... oh, we never finished supplying our kitchen before I joined the search for the spies." She swung her legs over the side the platform and jerked back when her feet hit the floor. "Ouch! I forgot. How can I do anything if I can't stand or walk?"

"Mazza and Barris will tend to our needs until Rachel and Simeon find us household help, which will be supervised by our faithful two." He brushed a lock of hair back behind her ear. "Now, let me help you dress for the day. Believe me, you will have much to do, and none will have anything to do with cooking or cleaning."

"What? What do you mean?"

Kalif simply grinned and continued helping her dress. He brushed her hair and plaited it. "I would prefer you wear it down, flowing, but I know you need it back out of the way. At night, would you wear it down? For me?"

She nodded as she whispered, "I had no idea marriage could be so good."

Once both were dressed, Kalif gathered her into his arms and carried her to the courtyard. "We thought you might enjoy some fresh air after we eat and work a while. It's too cool yet this morn." He continued along the path way under the roof hangover to the kitchen. "Therefore, we will begin this day breaking our fast in our kitchen with our household."

When he entered the kitchen, Mazza and Barris had the meal on the large table. Mazza motioned toward her coworker. "Barris is a better cook than I am, and I'm one of the best, not that I had a chance to show anyone for a long time."

Barris shrugged as he pulled a chair away from the table so Kalif could seat Hadara. "We work good together."

As the four finished their meal, Dan and Amzi entered. "We wondered where to find you," Amzi said. "Where should we work this morn?"

Kalif rose and once again swooped his wife into his arms. "Let's try our gathering room. We still need to be sure we aren't overheard." He turned to Barris. "Anybody allowed in this house must be honorable."

Before he could answer his charge, Mazza replied, "We are both intelligent enough not to accept any spy or assassin."

"Assassin?" Hadara pulled Kalif's chin so she could look at his face. "Assassin?" She breathed deeply. "I never thought … oh, no."

Dan walked on one side of the couple, and Amzi on the other. Amzi told his step-mother, "Everyone here would give his or her life for you. No one will get close enough."

She twisted in Kalif's arms. "I don't want anyone to die for me, either."

Kalif placed her on a divan in their room. "That is why we are to be very careful of whom we allow in our home." He touched her cheek. "Now, let's do what we can to keep everyone safer."

He looked at Amzi. "Anyone else joining us?"

Amzi shook his head. "Noma isn't feeling well this morning. She probably has told her parents, and I can tell you." His smile beamed. "We are going to be parents. Noma carries a babe." He chuckled. "I'm thankful those butchers wanted to fool Tzabar."

Hadara grabbed his arm. "I'm so happy for you. Bend down here." When he did, she hugged him.

He stood and studied her. "You do forgive me, don't you?"

"I told you years ago I did."

Dan laughed. "We have much good news amidst all our problems." He cuffed Amzi on the shoulder. "Now, my parents are trying to find workers for both houses and the farm that we can completely trust. They believe too many people working on ways to investigate mothers would simply hinder us, and we wouldn't accomplish anything."

Kalif moved a low table close to Hadara. "Could you use this to place a parchment and write?"

She sat upright and bent over the table. "This would work. What am I to write? And, let's use papyrus Hemut brought us, not the parchment.'

Kalif placed an ink container, a quill, and sheets of papyrus on the table before joining the other men in a circle around the table.

Dan answered, "We need a list of steps to use to approve women we help, and you could have some suggestions, too."

Until time for the mid-day meal, the four people discussed ideas, and when they reached a consensus, Hadara would write it on the papyrus. She had filled four sheets, by the time she marked out errors and rewrote many lines, when

Kalif said, "I believe we've covered all we can. If someone manages to invade our groups of escapees, they are smarter than any of us."

"Now, we need copies to send to with our different rebel groups working with these women. We'll need someone to carry the list who can and will read it to each group." Amzi touched the stacked pages.

Hadara stared at him. "Copies. Let me guess who will write those copies."

"I, uh, I didn't think who would. Surely, we have others who can write, other than you."

Dan held up one of his massive hands. "Noma does," he folded a finger into his palm, "my mother," another finger down, "I can," another finger, "my wife," another finger, "Kalif can," his thumb joined his fingers to form a fist. "There are others, too. We are educated, not ignorant."

Hadara covered her mouth as she giggled. "I know that, but I wasn't thinking. I will make two more lists that others can use to copy. If each person passes at least one copy to another person, we can soon have enough lists." She tilted her head. "How many copies would we need?"

"We have six units of rebels working independently, each with three main leaders." Amzi brushed his fingers through his beard. "So, we will probably need maybe six people to take copies to read to them, extra copies for the leaders who can read."

"Some will not be happy because they do not want to be told what to do by anyone." Dan took some pieces of papyrus and Hadara's quill. "What do we do about them?" He began copying the lists Hadara had finished.

Hadara rubbed the frown pulling her brows together. "We cannot allow anyone who hasn't been investigated to use our farm or farms. How will we know?"

"Simple," Kalif said. "We will know which rebel groups will follow the steps. The ones who won't will not be led here. After all, we only take a few groups each year."

Amzi stood. "Then we can handle writing the lists. I'll be back. I need to check on Noma." He opened the door and turned back. "We need to reinforce all our hiding areas and make all openings harder to find."

Chapter 39

A full change of the moon passed. Seven women and their children on their way to freedom hid in a tunnel, filled with fear they might be caught, that their children would become burnt sacrifices. Every pound on the gate caused all the people in the compound to hold their breaths until they knew whoever visited would not bring danger.

Hadara once again walked without hot pains in the soles of her feet, and she moved without feeling tight muscles and aches. "Now," she murmured, "if I can become used to my new household help, and the current group of mothers leave, I can feel safe again for a while." She watched the lengthening shadows formed by the torches.

Kalif dropped onto a stool next to where Hadara sat in the inner courtyard. "All the messages with investigation steps have been read or left with rebel group leaders who can read. Perhaps we can avoid more spies with the women."

The door slammed as Abram ran into the courtyard. "Good, you're here. We have problems. A few of us were scouting the exits from the tunnels and the path the women, children, and guards would take to their next stop. We found a band of rebels slaughtered by Naman's forces, we guess. One man crawled away. He's barely alive. We brought him to one of the hidden rooms. Rachel and two of the other women are tending to him." He took a deep breath. "We looked for any others, but we couldn't find anyone still alive, not in the dark."

Kalif leaped to his feet. "Let's go." He headed toward the closest door to the tunnels, Hadara behind him.

"No, you stay here," he told her. "You've been involved enough."

"I'll be with you. I will be safe."

When the three reached the hidden room, Rachel met them at the entrance. "We did what we could, but the man was too close to death when we started. He's gone."

Kalif leaned against the tunnel wall. "What do we do now? Whoever killed these men will most likely be back to check in the morn."

Abram agreed. "We will have to take this one back, replace him where we found him."

Rachel handed Kalif a piece of papyrus. "This was tucked in his clothes."

Kalif opened the folded missive. "It's a copy of the investigation steps." He gazed at Abram. "Let's get this man back where you found him. Maybe we can discover who ambushed them."

"I have an idea. I'll share as we go." Abram moved to the body and slung it over his shoulder and back. "Let's go."

"Not you," Kalif said as Hadara started to follow Abram. "Please, stay at home. This will be difficult."

She nodded as she placed her hand on his chest. "Take care and come back safely."

When Kalif and Abram reached the spot where Abram dropped the body, the dark under the trees in the area made vision difficult. Abram positioned the body as he found it.

"Let's brush away all our footprints coming and going with brush after we look over as much as we can see." Kalif bent over several bodies bunched together some distance from the one man. "They look as if they never had a chance to fight back. No weapons are drawn, nothing."

"My idea is I climb a tree and wait until whoever attacked these men return after daylight." Abram pointed to one tree. "That one is heavily leafed, has large branches. I would be unlikely seen and as comfortable as possible."

"Are you sure you'll be able to get away after?"

"I would think I could. If I haven't shown up by mid-day meal, you might find a plan to rescue me." Abram laughed as he finished brushing out his footprints.

"Here." Kalif removed his heavy mantle and threw it around the younger man's shoulders. "You will find the night cold."

Abram jumped high enough to grab a branch, pulled himself up into the tree, and disappeared into the blackness. Kalif finished brushing away footsteps to the tree and his as he moved backward toward the path to the farm compound.

Kalif paced the inner courtyard. Mid-day arrived, but Abram didn't.

"Kalif, I've been thinking, and I may have an idea how we can check on Abram without anyone being suspicious."

He watched Hadara as he pulled her beside him on a divan. "Tell me. I don't have anything."

"If I understood where the rebels were ambushed correctly, it would be on the way to the date farm. We always check on the farm every two or three months, and it's been at least two months since anyone went. Simeon's son Liam and his family live there, but Simeon does all the extra help assignments since the date farm is on the outer edge of our farms."

"That would cover anyone if any military are around." Kalif strode toward the back of the courtyard. "I'll see who can go with me."

"I will go with you. What could be more innocent appearing than a man with his wife?"

With a smile, he turned. "You are right. Get ready to take a long walk. We don't want to give anyone any reason to question our behavior."

Within half an hour, they left for the date farm, Hadara riding sideways on a donkey and Kalif walking. Both dressed in clothing they wore for every day rather than any finery. Less than an hour after they left the compound, they neared the small forest where Abram had taken refuge in a tree.

"Halt!" A burly man in military harness rode a horse from the trees and blocked the path. "Who be you and where be you going?" Ten other men also in military garb, two on horseback, surrounded the couple.

Even though she expected to be confronted, Hadara's heart jumped a beat. She didn't dare share her thoughts aloud. *These men look more like bandits than military.*

"Is there a problem?" Kalif moved closer to Hadara and the donkey, staying between them and the man on the horse.

"I be Sergeant of Minister Naman, and by the order of the Minister, you must give reason to travel here."

"We're on the way to the date farm just past these trees."

Hadara forced herself not to look toward the grove of trees. She touched her husband's shoulder.

The burly man glared at Kalif and then Hadara. "What business might you have there?"

"Well, my wife's family owns the date farm, and we are to see how the dates are progressing. We need an idea of when to gather harvesters." Kalif kept his voice calm, almost friendly.

"You travel with no attendants?"

"Her family owns all this land. We didn't see any reason to need protection."

"Huh, what it be like to be owned by a woman's family?" The man moved his horse closer to Kalif, but Kalif didn't move except to move one of his hands over Hadara's.

"I help when and how I can." He nodded toward Hadara. "She needs someone to protect her portion of the family business. Since I am a businessman myself, I am able to do that."

"You?" The man swung down from the horse and visually examined Kalif from head to toe, even though he had to tilt his head upward to see the taller man's head. "You be dressed like a commoner, not no businessman."

"I am not attending to my business but taking a walk in the country." Although Kalif's voice never changed, Hadara felt the muscles in his shoulder tighten.

"Go about your walk, then." The man swung onto the horse's back. He waved an arm at his men. "We be wasting time. We return to the city." They rode or marched back the way Kalif and Hadara had come.

"Shall we continue to the date farm compound?" Kalif asked his wife as he watched the men leave.

"We are nearly there, so we may as well. Do you think Abram was able to escape?"

"We will go by the house, speak with Liam, and then go to the tree and see if ..." He stopped. "There he is, just behind the tree line." Kalif's voice rose in volume as he glanced toward the trees. "Let's go to the farm house and talk more there."

Abram waved and disappeared among the trees.

A few minutes later, Kalif helped Hadara from the donkey. Liam and Abram awaited them at the open gate to the house enclosure.

"Please come in. We weren't expecting anyone, but we always have refreshments." Liam waved an arm toward the house inside the enclosure.

"We should enter in case some of Naman's troops watch." Kalif moved so his wife could enter first. "We told the sergeant we were making an inspection, so we need to appear to do so."

When everyone sat in the room used for visitors, Liam gave a summary of the date crop. "Now we have proof that this visit is a regular one. What is happening that men are murdered so close to my house?"

Abram lowered his head and studied his hands. "From what I heard from my perch in the tree when Naman's men returned, they didn't leave because of the dark last night. They needed to take the women and children to a holding where they would be held until sacrificed." He raised his head so he could see Kalif. "They laughed as they reminded each other of their 'enjoyment' dispatching the rebels. I thought I would be sick. The sergeant reminded them of the joys they would have with the women once they cleaned up the mess."

He stood and walked to a table with drink and food. He filled a cup and drank all the watered wine before he turned to face the others. "Those swine plan on using those women since they are to be sacrificed with their children. They piled the bodies of the rebels in a cart and hauled them away. At least two men left with the cart. The rest sat around waiting to see if anyone came to look for the rebels."

Abram slumped onto a cushion and rubbed his hands over his face. "What do we do now?"

"Did they reveal, by chance, where those women and children are held?" Kalif's voice, calm and even, caused Hadara to frown at him.

"Yes, yes, they did, indirectly. An abandoned barn not far from here meets the descriptions I heard."

"Liam, do you have any way to fortify this place, any guards to help keep your home and family safe?" Kalif gazed at their host.

"There are four men who stay in the workers' hut in one corner of this compound. They have worked for the family since we moved here. They are former military, too. Once the gates are barred from the inside, this place is almost unassailable. We'll be safe if war breaks out."

Kalif stared into nothingness a moment. "Let's get back to the main farm compound. We need to hurry. Those mothers and children don't have much time." He stood. "Abram, any more rebels we can reach?" He turned to Liam. "We need to leave now. I'm sorry we can't be better visitors."

"Liam, I'm glad to see you again, but we are living in a dangerous and evil time." Hadara smiled at one of the men who helped rescue her from Tzabar. "May the one true God keep you and yours safe."

"The same to you, Hadara." Liam escorted the three outside the house, where the donkey waited. "We will send a message if we need. Please do the same. Thanks to Hadara, we can without revealing ourselves to any enemy."

As Hadara and the men left the enclosure, they heard bars falling in place to barricade the gate. "I hope they are safe and that we can save those women." Hadara muttered half to herself.

"I need to leave for Bethlehem. I won't even stop by the farm. In fact, I believe I can make better time on my own." Abram glanced at Hadara. "I am faster than a donkey, and I need to reach a contact to get more of the rebel bands notified." He began walking faster and faster until he ran away from Kalif and Hadara.

Hadara asked, "How did the two of you make a plan without saying a word?"

A band of men milled around the outside courtyard. Kalif went from group to group giving instructions. He wore his former military garb, as did Dan and his brother Liber. The rebels summoned by Abram and his contact in Bethlehem waited for night fall.

Amzi wove his way through the twenty-six bodies to reach Kalif. "I wish you would let me go, too. Kalif, I was part of these men for years."

"I know, Amzi, but I have another job for you, one I didn't share with everyone except Dan. The others think I will lead men to attack from the back of the barn, over the hill. What others don't realize is the barn, which is built into the hill, is connected to a cave on the other side of the hill." Kalif gave a guffaw. "We will rescue the women and children through the cave."

He glanced toward the door to the house and, seeing Hadara standing in the opening moved toward her. He reached out and cupped the side of her face with a hand. "Don't worry about us. Our part of the rescue isn't the dangerous part."

"I … I know, but I still worry. I know you must do this, and I understand. I would be with you if I were able to move quickly and quietly." She smiled. "Remember, you have a wife, who loves you waiting for your return, and a child that soon will need a father."

"My love, I will remember." He bent forward and kissed her lightly. "I will be back."

As they talked, the rebels began to leave silently, some through the front gate and some through the back. Dan barricaded the front gate while Amzi ran to barricade the back.

"Time for you to go back into the house, my love." Kalif ushered her inside. "I'll go through the tunnels with Dan and Amzi as far as we can. We won't be in the open but a short time, so don't worry." Kalif grabbed a torch from a stand in the inner courtyard. "We will return."

The three men entered the tunnels network from a hidden door in the back wall. The torch threw shadows behind them and on the walls as they ran. Until they reached the end of the tunnels, they wouldn't have the need of silence that the rebels moving through the countryside did.

Still, they didn't talk, saving their energy and breath to make their way toward their goal. *Hope we aren't too late,* Kalif thought as he studied the darkness ahead of the torch's light.

The tunnel they followed had many side tunnels, but the men continued forward for a distance of nearly three miles before they reached the end. Kalif held the torch as Dan and Amzi climbed upward. At the top landing, Dan reached down to take the torch as Kalif scampered to join them in a small room.

Amzi felt around the wall opposite the ladder until he found a tiny indention. He pushed, and a door creaked open. Dan went into the hut beyond the hidden room, lighting it with the torch and finding nothing but dust and cobwebs.

"We're safe here," he whispered to the others. "Now, we go in the dark." He pounded the lit end of the torch into the dirt floor until not even a spark remained. He opened the door of the hut, poked out his head, and searched the immediate area. When he motioned, the others followed him into the darkness of the scattered trees surrounding the battered dwelling.

Kalif bent close to Dan's ear. "You are more familiar with this area of the farm than even I. Take the lead. Amzi and I will follow."

The men took careful steps, avoiding any sounds. A crack of a branch to their right caused them to stop and squat. Three sets of eyes investigated the space around them. When a hare hopped from behind a bush, they rose and began their way toward the cave once again.

Maybe I'm too old for this. Kalif's breathing roughened as he followed Dan and Amzi. *Two rough night trips so close together.*

Every sound caused the men to stop and drop closer to the ground. They constantly listened for the noise of battle, even though their strategy called for the rebels to put hoods over the head of Naman's men so they could be moved to a far location and disappear, another mystery to confound the enemy.

When the men left the sparse trees, they kept as near the ground as possible. They passed a small plot of barley by bending low and following the outside edge of the crop. A call of an animal or bird broke the silence occasionally, but otherwise they heard nothing until they entered the cave.

Dan reached into a crevasse in the wall to one side of the entrance and removed two rough rocks and a torch. "I think we can have a light inside here if we keep it to the back. The women might feel safer with three strange men if they can see us." He handed the dead torch to Amzi while he rubbed the rocks together rapidly near the torch top. A spark jumped to the pitch on the torch and a flame grew.

Kalif looked around. The cave, deeper than wide, extended past the glow of the flame. A few rough pieces of furniture and two ancient chests didn't begin to fill the emptiness. He followed the other men to the back of the cave, where Dan opened a rugged door that led to another cave, much smaller and lower than the one they first entered.

"This cave has another door at the other end, which opens into a cabinet at the back of the barn." Dan nodded at the torch. "We might want to leave that here so we won't give ourselves away." He took the light from Amzi and stuck it into a metal holder in the wall. "We need to be extremely quiet until we're safely back in the larger cave."

Dan walked about thirty steps before coming to the door. He leaned his head against the door, his ear pressed to the wood. "I don't hear anything." He opened the door, and the men could see strips of light around the edges of another door across a short expanse of dirt floor.

The three inched across the dirt to the other door. Now, the men could hear sobs, a baby's cry, and the murmur of women's voices. Dan noiselessly eased the door to the barn open a crack and peeked around the corner. He pulled back.

"There are a couple of fires going in there. I saw three women and two children but no men." He exhaled loudly. "How do we keep from scaring them all half to death?"

Kalif started whistling. As a result, eyes looked their direction before Dan opened the door and stated, "We're here to help you."

Three shocked women faced them, two with their arms around a child, the third holding a babe close to her breast. A fourth woman rose from where she lay on the ground, her body swollen with a babe yet to be born. "Please," she cried between sobs, "no more."

Kalif ambled further into the barn. "We really are here to help you. We have a safe place for you to stay until you're able to travel again."

"But the others …" one woman stuttered. "They … they hurt …"

"We know, and we came to save you. Some of our men are keeping the swine who captured you busy so we could. Now come. We must leave in case our men aren't able to keep all of them occupied." Kalif knelt by one of the children. "Would you like to come with me? We'll find some food after we walk a long way." When the little boy nodded, his fingers in his mouth, Kalif scooped him up. "Let's go."

Amzi held the door to the closet open until everyone passed through to the small cave. He then closed the door to the barn and entered the cave himself. He barely closed the door to the cave when sounds of people running into the barn, yelling and screaming, reached him. He went back to the closet and barred the door to the barn before returning to the cave and barring that door closed, too. He rushed to catch up with the others. When everyone entered the larger cave, he barred the door to the smaller cave.

"Why did you bar the door?" Dan asked.

"I barricaded all the others, too. As I was leaving, men ran into the barn. I didn't find out what all the screaming was about. I just made sure they couldn't follow us very easily." He looked around at the women and children huddled together against one wall. "Is it safe to take them on to the hut?"

Kalif shrugged. "I don't know, but that's where the food and bedding will be. The rebels leading them to the next stop will meet us there, too."

Dan moved to the entrance to the cave. "We don't have any choice." He turned to face the women. "Do you think you and the children can walk about a mile quietly?"

One woman stood. "I don't know about the two older ones. I can keep my babe quiet, but the little ones might not be able to walk that far, and I don't think we can carry them. I'm also worried about her." She pointed to the pregnant woman

"That's no problem. We can carry the young ones." Dan went to a little girl. "Would you like to ride on my shoulders?" Her eyes widened as she nodded. Dan swung her onto a shoulder.

Kalif did the same to the boy. Amzi snuffed out the torch once the others left the cave and followed. The group of women followed Dan and Kalif while Amzi protected the rear. When the woman expecting stumbled, he grabbed her and half carried her as they moved as quickly as possible, not worrying about any noises heard.

"We're doing fine," Kalif said. "We don't have much farther." All the time he listened for anyone following.

In the distance, the hut appeared, flickering light showing around the closed window shutters. "Look," Amzi told the woman he helped, "there's where we're going. See, we're almost there. The men who will help you have warm food waiting. You'll be able to rest."

The woman began to walk more on her own power, but she held his arm.

Kalif entered the inner courtyard of his and Hadara's house as the sun peeked over the horizon. Hadara leaped from the divan where she had curled under a blanket. She wrapped her arms around him. "Come to bed. I know you are exhausted."

He held her close. "Yes, but to know those mothers and their children are safe …" He leaned his head on hers. "They were brave, even after what Naman's thugs did to them. I shouldn't be surprised after seeing your courage, but most women amaze me."

After Kalif washed the night's dust and dirt off him and they climbed in bed, Hadara asked, "Did your plan to deliver Naman's men to Shem work?"

"Two almost escaped, ran back into the barn just as we went back into the cave, but rebels caught them and finished hooding and tying them. One of the rebels who aided in the capture joined us at the hut and reported." He pulled his wife into his arms. "Shem is intelligent, and his idea of having people disappear makes his enemies uneasy, and they can't blame him."

Hadara laughed. "Brilliant idea. Do you have any idea how or where he has them taken?"

"I have a slight suspicion. I wonder if Syria is having an influx of questionable people joining the ranks of slaves and menial workers?"

"Brilliant indeed." She lay her head on his shoulder. "Now, you sleep, my hero."

"No, Dan and Amzi are the heroes, and of course the rebels. I would not want those men as my enemies." His eyes closed, and his wife watched him as he slept.

Chapter 40

Bethlehem :: a week later

Amzi checked the fine cloth and carpet shop. All the piles of silk and fine linen showed no sign of moisture or bugs. The piles of luxurious carpets also appeared in excellent shape. He tested the shutters over the windows and found them secure. He barred the front door again and left by the back door, on which he placed the huge iron lock. Both his and Noma's house and Kalif's parents' house stood empty of people but also as secure as could be from outside invasion.

The young man exited the alley by the door separating it from the main road that led to Jerusalem in one direction and the statue of Moleck in the other. He walked around the shop to the front. He trod the road that led to the town square and well.

"I'll be glad to be back with Noma." His eyes searched the empty roads and paths he passed. "Bethlehem has never been this quiet." He continued to the inn, where he would wait until the caravan arrived. He entered to find few people sitting at the tables.

He sat at an empty table and ordered a goblet of watered wine with a chunk of bread and one of cheese. The innkeeper served him without speaking and returned to wherever he had been when Amzi arrived. No one talked, and after one glance when he walked into the room, the other men ignored him and each other.

Amzi finished his meal and stood, ready to leave, when Lior and two other men burst through the door.

"There he is. Take him," Lior ordered the men with him.

The innkeeper rushed forward, "May I take your order, sir. We have a roast lamb and legumes today." He moved until he blocked Lior and the other men from Amzi, who took advantage of the few moments and slipped out the door. He hiked as fast as possible to the edge of town.

"What is happening? Why was Lior after me? I could take one of them, not all three." He reached the open field where the caravan usually bedded and glanced around. "Where to hide?" To one side sat piles of feed shucks. He ran and crawled into the center of the pile. *Come on, Raz, Hemut, whoever comes this time. I need help.* His mind searched for a solution if they didn't come in time.

"Find him!" Lior 's voice echoed through the village.

"Here he is!" shouted another voice. Screams and yells continued as the searchers broke into houses and businesses.

"Look in the cloth and carpet shop," someone yelled.

"Don't bother," returned Lior . "He's not stupid enough to hide there. No, he's somewhere in town. He hasn't had a chance to escape completely."

The bellow of camels and the sound of hooves drowned out any other words. Amzi peeked between shucks as eight camels were led in a large circle. A man on horseback followed. Once in place, the handlers had the animals lower to the ground. A large cart pulled by two horses came into sight. Two other men on horseback rode beside the cart. When the caravan stopped, it blocked Amzi's hiding place from the village. He climbed out when he saw Raz, Hadara's brother, swing down from his horse and walk toward the cart.

"Raz!" he called in a loud whisper. "I'm in trouble."

Raz stopped and stared at the dusty man. "Amzi?"

"Yes, yes," Amzi stood so that he could peer over Raz's shoulder but the man blocked him from anyone in the village. "For some reason, Minister Naman's nephew is after me. This is the first I've been in town for over a month. I don't know why he's after me, but I don't like the idea. He has at least two strong-looking men helping him."

"Well, my brother, you have a few strong men ready to help you."

Amzi whirled to face one of the other men who had been horseback. The man laughed.

"Tobias? Tobias, it is you." Amzi and the new-comer pounded each other on the back, stared at each other, and then hugged. "Hadara will be delighted." He looked past his half-brother to the Ethiopian dismounting from another horse. "You are bigger than ever, Philmon. I can't believe my eyes." He stared at Tobias. "How did you get so huge, so many muscles?"

Tobias and Philmon both laughed, but Tobias finally answered. "We worked in the stone quarry. Even if you want to be stronger and have more muscles, don't follow our example."

"There he is!" Lior tried to push between Tobias and Philmon. "You won't get away this time."

Philmon snatched the man by the neck of his robe and pulled him backward. "I don't think you want to bother Amzi, little man."

"Let go. How dare you. Do you not know who I am?" Lior squirmed and twisted, trying to escape.

Philmon turned him until they faced each other. "No, I don't know and don't care. Whoever you are, I could buy you two or three times over. Apparently, you don't know who I am."

Lior glared at Philmon, at Tobias, and at Raz. "My uncle is Minister Naman."

Raz chuckled. "Apparently, your uncle failed to tell you how we make him rich. He won't want to upset us, believe me."

"That does not matter. He told me to rid this country of Amzi and all his family. He says they are enemies of the king."

Tobias removed Philmon's fingers from Lior's robe.

"At least you have some sense." Lior straightened his robe.

"No," Tobias answered, "I wanted you free so you can listen to me without being distracted. Look around you. Do you see all of us circling you? Do you realize that Philmon or I could break your neck with one snap? Raz here and even Amzi might need two or three snaps, but they would do the job. Any of our men with the caravan would gladly slip a knife between your ribs. Now, what did you want to say about my brother Amzi?"

"Brother, you would admit he is your brother?"

"Yes. Oh, a few times I would gladly help you strangle him, but that's the past. Now, he is my brother, and every person here is part of our family. Look around you carefully. Also, your uncle would not enjoy losing the fortune he made trading with us, which he will if you give us any more trouble."

Lior blustered and started to speak again, but Tobias shook his head. "Go away, little man."

"You haven't heard the last of me." Lior stomped away, his two men nowhere in sight.

"May we get out now?" Nava opened a curtain on the cart. Tobias hurried to help his wife and then his son from the cart. "Benjamin," Nava bent to her son's height, "this is your Uncle Amzi."

Amzi grinned. "You are such a big boy. I haven't seen you since you were a baby."

Benjamin put his fists on his hips. "I not baby. I big boy."

"Yes, you are a big boy." Amzi touched the boy's head. "I am very glad to see you again, and your savta will be so excited." He glanced at Tobias. "Did Hadara know you were coming?"

"Not when, just that we would come as soon as we could."

Nava rose and stood beside her husband. Amzi laughed.

"What's humorous?" Nava asked.

"The farm compound will soon be filled with babies." Amzi held up one finger. "Hadara will have a babe." He held up a second finger. "My wife, Noma, will have a babe." He held up a third finger. "Apparently, you will have another babe."

Tobias stared at Amzi. "My mother is going to have a babe? She must be so happy. She always wanted more children." He frowned. "*You* are going to be a father?"

Amzi nodded. "We were happily surprised. Noma expected to get her baby fill by borrowing nieces and nephews."

"Come, let's get everything in the cart that needs to go to the farm," Raz said. "My men need to settle for the night. The caravan will leave in the morning."

"You leaving, too?" Amzi swung Benjamin into the cart.

"I will rejoin them on their way back to Egypt." He helped load a bag into the cart. "You are on foot?"

"Yes. Riding a horse around here isn't wise during this troubled time. Barrack may be gone, but Naman is working hard to be even worse."

Tobias jerked his head toward the cart. "Climb in. We would hate to arrive at the farm before you could."

The Farm Compound

Hadara awoke three mornings later to find Kalif resting on one elbow and gazing at her. "Um, what?"

"You are beautiful, my love."

"I am so glad you cannot see clearly in the morning. My hair is like the nest of a rat."

"You are happy, and happiness makes you more beautiful than ever."

Her smile spread across her face. "Yes, I am happy. My family is all here inside the compound walls, and all are safe." She sat up on the bed, cross-legged, to face him. "Everything on the save-mothers-and-children front has been smooth and quiet. Perhaps we will survive the rest of King Ahaz's reign."

Kalif shook his head. "I pray to the one true God that this is not the calm before a storm."

"Do you know something you haven't told me? Are we facing more trouble?"

"I don't know anything, and I cannot see into the future. I simply have a feeling that we have not heard the last of Naman. The conflict in Bethlehem when the caravan arrived angered Lior, and even though Naman makes much of his riches made through trade with your family, I don't doubt he will find a way to punish Amzi for whatever reason he and Lior created."

The smile died on her face. "I, uh, I wouldn't doubt Lior wanting to punish Amzi and everyone who participated in his humiliation."

"I should not have said anything." He cupped her cheek. "I'm sorry."

"No, I would rather you share with me." She studied her hands. "You are most likely correct, and we need to get ready for something, even if we don't know what."

"Have you visited with Philmon?"

"Only with others around. He seems to avoid me."

"Let's say you need to visit with him. He has to make some major decisions, and I think he can't until he talks with you."

"More news that won't be happy news?"

Kalif sat up and pulled her into his arms. "Children and friends grow up and move into their own lives sometimes, my love."

"Promise me you won't grow into a different life without me."

"No chance of that happening. Without you, I don't have a life." He placed a kiss on her forehead. "Our life the next few days will be tricky. Shem and his trusted men will arrive this morning. We need a place for his men to bivouac out of sight of the road. Aaron and Hosa will join us as we decide what to do about Naman and the trouble he and his nephew are creating." He climbed from the bed. "Shem wanted only the four us to meet first. Then we will call in the rest of the family."

"Since we are a distance from the road, if Shem's men were behind the compound, back by the animal pens and in the trees, they wouldn't be easily seen even from here much less from the road."

"Shem should include you at our first meeting, but he asked for just the four of us." He paused. "I thought we could meet in our gathering room, if you wouldn't mind."

"I'll work outside or in the kitchen, if I'm allowed in there other than for a meal." She laughed. "Who would have thought Mazza and Barris would find us a couple to manage the house and grounds who would intimidate me, too."

Later that day, Hadara worked in her garden, checking on the new plants. She knew Mazza would be upset, so she didn't do anything heavy, no hoeing or weeding.

"Hadara?" Philmon stood at the edge of the garden. "May I speak honestly?"

"Of course, Philmon." She walked between the rows to join him. "Let's go to the little sitting area Kalif made me. I'm not allowed in my gathering room for some time."

As they sat on the benches under an olive tree, Hadara reached across the small table and laid her hand on the big man's arm. "I owe you so much for going with Tobias and watching over him and Nava. You have given so much to my family and for us. Thank you."

"You are making this harder for me."

"Philmon, I don't want to make anything harder for you, but I want to let you know you do not owe us. We owe you."

He stood and strode to the back wall before returning to kneel in front of her. "I want to go to Ethiopia and find a wife. I would like to have my own family."

"I think that is a good plan. Have you decided then to stay in Ethiopia after you find your wife?"

He threw back his head and roared with laughter. After stopping, he said, "I dreaded this talk, yet you seem to already know."

"No, I didn't know, but you needing to build your own life makes sense. We will miss you. I will miss you, but I do understand."

He sat back on the bench. "I have a fortune now. I can do whatever almost anywhere I want. I'm not sure I would want to stay in Ethiopia, unless I find a wife who insists. I have talked to Raz about joining him in the caravan business. If I do, then I would definitely stop by to visit quite often."

"We would like that, Philmon." She smiled. "I would also like to meet your family, once you have one, but Ethiopia is far away."

A shout and banging on the gate brought them both to their feet. Philmon told her, "Stay here. No, go in the house. I will see who's at the gate."

When he opened the gate, Ruben, Deborah, Sofai, their son Jacob, and the rest of Jacob's family spilled into the compound.

"We must speak to Kalif," Ruben declared as he looked around. When he spied Hadara, he started toward her until Philmon blocked his way.

"Philmon, please let them in. This is Nava's natural family." She waved Ruben to her. "Now, what has happened?"

"Is Minister Shem here, and Aaron?"

"Ruben, no one was to know that. How did you hear?"

"Not me, Jacob. We went to market, left our other son, Caley, to watch the farm." He turned to stare at this wife. "Caley will be in danger."

"Please, Ruben, we need to know." Hadara touched his shoulder. "Please?"

"Jacob needs to tell you. He heard Naman and Lior." He looked at his son. "Come tell Hadara, but we need Kalif. He needs to hear."

"Philmon, would you please go see if Kalif will come here? Tell him we have an emergency, that Naman knows Shem is here."

"Yes, ma'am." The huge man moved as fast as a small one.

"Jacob, what can you tell me? Is there enough danger that I should call for all our people?"

"Yes, you should. Telling this only once would make it easier to keep everything clear."

She walked to a bell in a metal stand and clanged it four times. The bang echoed off the walls. As they waited, Hadara moved to Deborah. "Nava is inside. She, Tobias, and Benjamin have rooms on this side of the compound."

Deborah clasped her hands on her chest. "My daughter, my grandson are here?"

"Yes, Nava is expecting another babe and hasn't felt well, or I would have sent word already. But, now, if we have danger, we needn't wait because they will be here in moments."

"Ruben, did you hear?"

Ruben wrapped an arm around his wife's shoulders. "Yes, yes, I did." He swallowed. "I hope she forgives us."

"What's wrong?" Kalif strode from the house followed by Shem, Aaron, and Philmon. "I heard the bell, so I know the danger must be great, even greater than Naman knowing about Shem."

"Yes, sir, it is," Jacob stepped forward. "He and Lior are on their way, but it's even worse. If I may tell the whole story when everyone Hadara signaled arrives, I would appreciate it."

"And, if possible, after, may we send someone to let my other son know he's in danger? He's at our farm and has no wall for protection." Ruben asked.

From the house, through the open gate between the outer courtyards, and from hidden doors, Simeon's family and the trusted farm workers hurried into Hadara's and Kalif's courtyard. Tobias carried his son as Nava walked beside them. Soon over twenty people plus Ruben and his family crowded around Kalif. Shem, Aaron, and Hosa stood with their backs against the house wall.

"Quiet, please," Kalif called. "We need to hear what Jacob, son of Ruben, has to say. Naman and Lior apparently have a plot that endangers us." He turned to Jacob. "Why don't you stand on this table so all can see and hear you?" He pulled the table from between the benches to sit in front of Shem and the others against the wall. "Nava, why don't you, Noma, and Hadara sit on the benches while we listen to Jacob and discuss what he says?"

Jacob climbed on the table and took a deep breath. "My family and I went to the market this morn. I wanted to see if my house were in good condition still. As I walked around the outside, I heard someone talking inside. I slid under one of the shuttered windows and listened. It was Naman and Lior. I recognized Lior's voice from when we both were in Bethlehem. Lior called Naman by name and as his uncle."

Jacob took another breath. "Naman has a force of fifty-five men with him. They scheme to attack every farm and household for twenty miles around the village until they find or kill Amzi, Kalif, Shem, and Aaron. They think killing them will stop the rebels from helping women and children escape sacrifices. They also think ridding the country of those men will help increase their influence with King Ahaz and strengthen his rule.

"They will leave Bethlehem right after the mid-day meal. I gathered up the family, and we ran to reach here in time."

Shem walked to stand beside the table. "I need someone to go to my men and bring them to the back of this courtyard. We must stop Naman's forces before they arrive here."

"Do you have archers?" Raz asked.

Shem faced Hadara's brother. "Yes, I do."

"Do you know about oil and sulfa soaked cloths to tip the arrows?"

"No, we don't. Tell me about this." Shem and Raz walked outside the circle of people.

Raz replied, "The damage is horrible, but using these arrows will stop any force."

Kalif took Jacob's place on the table and raised his hands to quieten the people again. "We need everyone to get with our 'leaders' Dan, Amzi, Abram, Simeon, and Liber. We will divide into squads and then decide where to set up defenses after we know what Shem's plans are." He pointed to Dan. "Pick your people first; then Amzi will; then Abram; Simeon; and finally, Liber. We need to send word to Liam and his household." He pointed to one of the trusted farm workers. "Would you?"

When the man nodded and trotted away, Kalif stepped down and turned to Ruben. "Do you and your sons want to fight with us?"

"I do," Jacob replied, "if my son and wife can be safe."

"I will do what I can," Ruben answered. "Is there anyone who can go after Caley? Can my wife and youngest one be kept safe, too?"

Philmon spoke. "Tell me where your farm is located. I am one of the fastest people here even if I go by foot. Also, how can I prove to him that I come from you?"

"Tell him that his missing sister Nava is here. Then he will know."

Tobias cuffed his friend's shoulder. "You are one of the best fighters here."

"I plan on taking two horses. Caley and I will return very quickly. Faster than Naman and his braggart nephew can."

Two hours later, before the mid-day meal, Philmon returned with Caley. Shem's archers had arrows tipped with cloth soaked in oil and sulfa, a small fire pot ready to be lit, and rough stones ready to take with them. The full contingent of fighters and archers stood ready to leave the compound at a fast march. Kalif described for Shem a place to ambush any small army coming from Bethlehem.

When Kalif offered to go with him and his troops, Shem said, "No, my friend, you have work here. If we should fail or not succeed, you must finish the job."

"Shem, you will be putting yourself in danger. Naman knows the only way he can win is if he kills you."

"Ah, Kalif, my men won't let me go anywhere near the battle. If they had their way, I would remain here." He chuckled under his breath. "Now, we must go. They at least agreed, since we're going across land not on a road, to allow me to ride a horse, not go by chariot."

"Our one true God go with you," Aaron blessed Shem. "We will have you in our prayers as you go forth to battle for Him."

Kalif and Aaron stood outside the back of the compound watching Shem ride away, his men, on foot or mounted, behind him.

"Wonder how long they will allow him to ride in front?" Kalif wondered aloud.

"I'm sure not long," Aaron answered.

While all the troops and groups readied themselves for the upcoming battle, Hadara escorted Deborah and Nava to her gathering room. The mother and daughter hesitantly talked about Benjamin as Deborah visited with her grandson. Hadara slipped from the room and went to the kitchen, where she found Mazza peeling potatoes and visiting with the new housekeeper, Abial. Abial's husband walked in the door from outside carrying a huge platter of roasted meat. Hadara hardly noticed his slight limp. Behind him, Barris carried another platter of meat.

"Do you need something, mistress?" Abial asked.

Hadara heaved a sigh. "Yes, Abial, I do. I need to feel as if I am not invading 'your' kitchen."

"Mistress, I am sure I never said any such thing."

"No, not in words, but I happen to enjoy going into any part of my home and not feel unwanted. First of all, please no longer call me 'Mistress.' Then, Nava, Deborah, and I would like to have our mid-day meal in my gathering room." She smiled at Abial. "I will return to take the food to the room so you won't have to do anything else."

As she stopped into the inner courtyard to take a deep breath, Hadara heard Mazza tell Abial, "I have tried to tell you she considers everyone part of her family. You must listen to Barris and me so you will continue to stay here. Your work, your dedication is beyond what is necessary, but your attitude is, well, rather haughty."

"What do you suggest we do?" a man's voice, Abial's husband, asked.

Barris answered, "Micah, try to think of them as friends as well as the people you serve. Right now, they are fighting so we can be safe. Try to be their friends and support them."

Hadara hurried away from the door before anyone found her listening. *Battles outside and inside.*

Shem rode at the head of his forces until they reached the spot where the road wound between hills. One boulder-covered hill rose nearly straight up from the road, a perfect place for their ambush. The fact that Naman's troops would pass at least four small farms before they reached the ambush spot worried Shem. "People will be murdered at his hands before we can have a chance to stop him," he muttered to himself.

"What, sir?" the sergeant riding beside him asked.

"Talking to myself, Sergeant, just talking to myself."

Once the archers took their places behind boulders high on the hill, their small fire pots and stacks of arrows at hand, the foot soldiers hid behind boulders closer to the road. Some took refuge in the brush and small trees on the hill across the road. While waiting, they cut some of the larger trees to use as barricades.

Shem called one of the men he used as scouts. "Aatami, I need you to go toward Bethlehem, cutting across country, and discover where Naman and his men are and what they're doing. Get back here as quickly as possible so we know how far away they are and if they are indeed attacking innocents."

Aatami saluted. "Yes, sir. I will be back very soon, and don't worry, I won't get caught."

"Wait! Take my horse."

"No, sir, I can go places a horse can't, and I run about as fast, too." He saluted again and turned, running immediately.

The Minister-turned-soldier nodded to the aide who stayed by his side at all times. "Now, Saburo, we wait, the hardest part of any battle." He sat cross-legged on the ground and stared at the boulders below him. From his angle behind tall grasses, he could see the archers resting behind their protection. *Now, we wait.*

The men ate some of their trail rations and drank from water skins as they waited, but they stayed vigilant, on guard. In less than an hour, Aatami crawled up the back of the hill to rejoin Shem.

"Sir, they have burned at least two farms closest to the village and are attacking another closer this way. What bodies outside were dead. I heard screams from one burning farm, a woman and a child." He wiped his forehead with a hand. "I be a rough man, sir, but I, uh, be sick. I can't abide killing any innocent but burning alive – nasty."

"Thank you, Aatami. Don't worry, a true man, even a hardened soldier, would be sick at such horror. Now, we must punish those who killed the innocent." He stood so his men could see him. One by one they all turned to face him, even though they didn't stand. He raised his arm above his head and moved it in a circle several times before sitting back in the grasses.

Below him and across the road, the men changed from partially relaxed to full attention. The wait became tense, but the men, professional soldiers to their cores, didn't allow the wait to take away their edge even as time dragged. Finally, they could hear the thumping of marching feet.

The archers built fire in their fire pots and arranged arrows so they could be reached easily. The foot soldiers released their weapons and loosened their shoulder muscles and stretched their arms. Everyone's eyes searched the road in front of them, looking toward the village in the distance. The marching feet came closer.

Shem closed his eyes and offered a short prayer to his God. *Oh, Lord God, we want to save your people from the evil of Ahaz, Moleck, and Naman. Please be with us.*

The first men came into view. Naman and Lior rode in a chariot at the head of the troops on foot. The archers lit their arrows and waited until the chariot traveled to the half-way mark below them. Burning arrows rained on the chariot and the men right behind it. When the arrows hit, they exploded into fireballs. The horses pulling the chariots reared and fought free from the harness, pulling the chariot driver over the front of the vehicle and through the fire wall. The man's clothes caught fire, and he screamed all the way to his death. The soldiers behind the chariot and the two men left in it became human torches, and their screams rolled to the heavens. The archers kept shooting their fiery weapons at the troops trying to escape toward Bethlehem.

The foot soldiers rushed to dispatch those of Naman's troops not caught by the arrows. Chaos reigned until the few remaining Naman men surrendered. Shem stared at the destruction below him, sick at heart, his stomach heaving at the sight of burnt and burning bodies, the blackened skin and the stench, at the complete destruction caused by fire. "This is worse than fighting with weapons and why I no longer wanted to soldier."

He faced his aide. "Would you see what men we have that are injured or killed? We will take them back to Kalif's. The remainders of the opposition, … tell them to bury their dead, to take their wounded, and to go home. Tell them to avoid following anyone who worships Moleck." He wiped his hands down his face. "I … I will ride back to Kalif's. I am sorry to leave the clean up to you, but I must get away."

"Sir, you go. The sergeants and I will take care of the rest." The aide saluted and marched down the hill as Shem mounted his horse and rode the opposite way.

Chapter 41

The Farm Compound

Much of the mounds of food Abial and Micah fixed had filled the stomachs of workers, family, and guests by the time Shem returned, shoulders slumped and head bowed. Kalif hurried to help him dismount.

"Did it not go well?" he asked his friend.

Shem raised tired eyes to Kalif's face. "Too well, but it had to be done. The fire arrows took Naman and Lior out immediately, but such a horrible death, as bad as Moleck's sacrifices." He staggered until Kalif took his arm. "Naman burned at least three farms, killing everyone. Some he burned alive. My scout heard them screaming in the fire. I guess Naman's and his nephew's death by fire was true vengeance."

"Come, let's sit before we go inside." Kalif led the Minister to a bench under the olive tree. "May I get you something?"

"No, no, I simply need to rest before I have to face anyone else. I even left my men to clean up the mess." He covered his eyes with a hand. "I know or remember why I gave up being a soldier. Oh, yes, yes, we must be able to defend ourselves and our loved ones, but I don't have the stomach for it anymore, especially when we use more powerful weapons."

"I do understand, but what do we do if we face the evil of King Ahaz?"

Shem raised his eyes to the sky. "I fight better with words and planning, so I will do what I do best. You are a man of action but cunning. You do what you do best. The men who will fight, we will give them what assistance and tools we can."

"Good idea." Kalif stood and held a hand to Shem. "Are you ready to face the others?" He looked around. "When do you think your men will return? I will make sure they are well fed and made comfortable."

"Give them a few more hours. They will send a runner to let us know." Shem pushed himself upright. "Where is everyone? I am as ready as I can be."

Night fell. Barris, Mazza, Abial, and Micah, helped by Simeon and Rachel, fed the weary soldiers. During the battle, none had received any wounds, but the tension and total destruction left them shocked more than any other battle had.

Hadara and Kalif sat in their gathering room, finally alone for the first time since early morning. "I feel as if we have lived seven days in this one," Hadara said as she snuggled close to her husband. "Are we truly safe from Naman and Lior?"

"We are unless they can come back from the grave." He held her close. "I am afraid that as long as Ahaz in on the throne, though, he will find another to take Naman's place."

"Aaron said Ahaz's days are numbered, but he didn't know for how many more. Our land is divided into two camps, and the evil side is so huge."

"I know." Kalif breathed deeply. "I know, but all good people can do is stand firm. Now, to change the subject. How are Nava and her natural parents doing? Are they finding a way to heal the pain they all felt?"

Hadara nodded. "I believe they are. Of course, they need to learn to know each other as they are now." She smiled. "Deborah and Ruben are amazed at their newest grandson. Benjamin is such a love and full of life."

"And, you want nothing to do with the boy, correct?" He laughed when Hadara pulled away and turned to stare at him. "Ah, my love, I know you love the little boy as if he were indeed yours."

"He is mine!" She stood and walked across the room before whirling to face him again. "Do I make anyone think he isn't? I became his savta long before he was born. My heart has ached wanting him to be part of my life. He is mine."

"I know. I know. I have watched you with him and see your love. Now come here and let us relax together. Before long, three more babes will be part of our family."

Chapter 42

Tobias gazed at his sleeping son. *How can he appear so quiet and still while sleeping and be so full of energy when awake?* He left the room where Benjamin slept and entered the room where Nava awaited him.

"What worries you, Tobias? Do you still wish you could have battled Naman?"

He sat on the edge of their bed. "No, after what Shem shared with us, I'm glad I wasn't there. I watched one sacrifice to Moleck, and I never want to be around anyone burning again." He propped his elbows on his knees and rested his head in his hands.

Nava squirmed until she sat behind her husband. "What bothers you?" She laid her head against his back.

"Nothing you can understand." He straightened and turned to face her.

"Tobias, I could try. We have shared everything for years. Let me at least listen." She reached for him, but he pushed her hands away. "Tobias?"

When she touched his face, he flinched. He vaulted to his feet and rushed for the door, with her cry, "Tobias, what is wrong?" following him as he strode through the inner courtyard and out of the house.

"Why wouldn't she leave me alone?" he demanded of the sky.

"Speaking of Nava or your mother?" Kalif's voice came from the dark. "No one can torment a man more than his wife or his mother, but each acts out of love. What really irks me is either one is usually correct."

Tobias brushed his fingers through his beard. "I thought I would be alone."

"I needed to calm myself so I wouldn't upset your mother. I couldn't sleep, so I left her sleeping and came here to … to try to forget the battle as Shem described to us, to think about the future."

"The future. I wonder if I have one."

The darkness hid Tobias' face, but Kalif tried to study it anyway. "What do you mean? You have a wife who loves you, a son, and a babe on its way. At your age, I had nothing but a chance of being discovered as a spy in the military and dying or being killed in battle."

"Yes, I know." Bitterness filled his voice. "I have everything. I'm rich. I have a wife and family. Aren't I fortunate?" He paced from the wall of the house to the bench by the olive tree. "I want more!" He stopped and dropped onto a bench. "*I* want more."

"Tobias, what more? What more can you want?" Kalif lowered himself to the other bench.

Even in the night, Kalif saw the suffering in the other man's face as he spoke. "I don't know. For over two years, I labored in a stone quarry. My family lived in a hut. All the money my grandparents gave me meant nothing." He pounded a fist on his knee. "You have no idea how hard the work was. The sun beating on our bodies as we cut out blocks of stone, as we lifted those heavy stones. I would go in at night so bent I thought I would never stand straight again." Lost in the past, Tobias let the words spill from inside him. "My skin burnt from the sun. My back, my arms, my legs ... the pain was constant, day after day after day. I would enter that miserable hut and ..."

Tobias gazed into the dark past for a few moments. "I would go into the hut, and Nava would be waiting. She worked in her way as hard as I did. She kept the dirt floor as neat and clean as dirt could be. She cooked over an open fire. She tended a child. She hauled water from the well. Then, when I came home, she used the oils my grandmother sent her to rub into my aching muscles." He shook his head. "For hours through the night, before and after supper, she worked the pain from my body with her hands. She never complained, but her hands must have hurt, too."

"Sounds as if you aren't quite so upset with her now."

"Upset with her? Huh, I wasn't upset with her, but she probably thinks I am." He wiped his hands down his face. "I'm a fool. I left her thinking I was angry at her. Kalif, I'm not sure what to do with myself. I ... I must do something with my life. I don't want to have anything to do with the military. I don't know what kind of farmer I would make, if I wanted to try." He threw his head back and stared at the sky again. "What can I do?"

"You know your uncles would take you into their business."

"I would not be home for long periods of time. Hemut's and Raz's children don't know their fathers. I don't think I would like that life."

Kalif stood and cuffed Tobias' shoulder. "Why don't we look into possibilities. Do you need to talk more tonight, or do you need to make peace with your wife and talk to her?"

"I probably should talk to Nava. I, uh, I heard her crying when I stormed out." He slapped his forehead. "I was cruel to the one person who has given me all her trust and love." He blew out a loud breath. "I have hurt her before, and she forgave me then. I hope she will again." He rose to stand beside his mother's husband. "Thanks for listening. Surely, I can find something to do with the rest of my life besides grow fat and lazy."

"Let others help you find ideas. That is why the one true God gave us friends and family."

Tobias chuckled. "I wondered why. Thank you, Kalif. I am glad you and my mother married. She needs someone to care for her for a change. Tzabar ... he was cruel."

"I know, and I realized I could love your mother the first time I saw her. Now, young man, you go to your wife and show her you care."

All the torches except one had been extinguished, so Tobias crossed the gathering room given to him and his family in dim light. He entered the bed-chamber lit by one fire pot in the corner. He undressed for bed in the near dark. When he lay on the bed, though, Nava moved as far from him as possible.

"I thought you might be asleep," he whispered.

She didn't answer but turned her back to him as she held to the edge of the platform.

"Nava, please, I am sorry, so sorry. I, uh, would you please talk to me?"

"Why? You made me understand you didn't want me to bother you." A sob broke through; although, she covered her mouth with her hands.

Tobias scooted over until he could wrap his arms around her. She stiffened, but he pulled her toward him. "I still have anger that bursts out at times, but I'm never angry at you." He buried his face in her hair. "I try so hard not to let my anger show around you, but I failed again. Please forgive me, my sweet."

"But, but you ..." Her tears flowed faster.

Tobias turned her in his arms and held her. "I need you even when I don't act as if I do. You complete me, make me better than I am. I am so lost right now. I don't know what to do with my life. I should have talked with you, not lash out at you."

"Why did you change your mind ... come back?"

"I was sorry before I got out the door but too stubborn to admit it. Then Kalif was in the outer courtyard where I went to sulk. He made me admit what bothered me."

He felt her relaxing as he stroked her back and he talked.

"But what is wrong? What did I do wrong?"

He harrumphed. "I felt sorry for myself. I have a loving, lovely wife, a son that thinks his abba can do no wrong, and another babe soon to be born. Yet, I felt I had no future. I need some big reason to be important to the world." He shrugged one shoulder. "I told Kalif before I left to come back where I belong that I want to do more than do nothing and grow fat."

"What do you want to do?"

"That is the problem. I don't know what I want. Now, let's sleep and tomorrow discuss ideas." He kissed her. "Do you forgive me, again?"

She heaved a sigh and snuggled close to him. "Yes, of course. I love you."

Dawn broke, and people began their day. The inner courtyard of Hadara and Kalif's house overflowed with people gathering to visit and discuss the previous day's events.

Hadara moved, rather waddled, from her seat near her son to where Kalif visited with Shem. "I thought Simeon was here. Rachel is."

"He said he thought he heard something and left."

A pounding on the door brought Kalif to his feet. "Who would be here this early," he asked as he strode to open the door to find Simeon and a man in the wrapped skirt and leggings of a military horseman. "Yes? Simeon, since when do you knock?"

Simeon nodded toward the other man. "He has a message for Minister Shem and for you, and I thought this was too important to just walk in."

"Yes, sir, a very important message."

Hearing his name, Shem joined Kalif. "How may I help you, soldier?"

"Sir, the king is dead."

"Dead? How? When?" Shem first stared at Kalif and then the messenger.

"No one seems to know, Minister, but Aaron ordered me to ask you and Master Kalif and others to return to Jerusalem so that the new king can be crowned."

"What?" Shem nearly shouted. "What new king? What has happened?"

"I am unsure, sir. The priest Aaron told me to give you the message and to say you will receive what answers exist once he sees you. You two men and men named Dan, Amzi, Abram, and Tobias are to report to the palace and soon as possible. Minister Shem, your troops are to report to the barracks behind the palace and house there." The man saluted, his right arm crossing his chest and his fist slapping above his heart.

Kalif glanced around at the startled faces staring at the group by the door. When he spied Barris, he motioned his friend and retainer to him. Turning his attention back to the messenger, he said, "Please, allow us to give you food and drink before you leave."

Barris joined them in time to hear Kalif. "Yes, please come with me."

"Barris, before you take him to the kitchen, I will be going to Jerusalem, and I need you to stay here while I'm gone. I don't believe Hadara should make a trip," he glanced at her beside him, "not at this time."

"Of course, Kalif, I will. Now, young man, follow me." He led the messenger through the courtyard.

A multitude of questions welled from family and friends who sat or stood, making little sound, while the messenger delivered his message. Now, everyone talked at once until Kalif waved his hands for silence.

"Please, please, you know as much as we do. Abram, would you take the orders to Shem's troops so they can pack up and begin their trip to Jerusalem? Did you get everything the messenger said?"

"Yes, I'll go, and, yes, I heard."

"Then, would you be ready to pack and go with us to the palace?"

"Yes, of course." Abram rushed from the house.

Shem laughed before saying, "I will go pack my things so we can go."

"Good. I'll talk to my guests and family before I have someone ready your chariot and my horse."

Kalif looked over the faces staring at him, waiting for him to talk. "Please, sit." He bent his head to whisper to his wife, "Do you mind not going?"

She shook her head. "Yes and no. I would like to go, but," she rubbed one hand over the bulge pushing out her robe, "I don't want anything to happen to our babe. I will wait here until you return and tell me everything."

With a chuckle, he again faced the rest, all who now sat, except for Benjamin, who climbed over stools and tables. "As you all heard, apparently King Ahaz is dead, and we will have a new king. Everyone can't go with Shem and me, but Aaron wants Abram, as well as Tobias, Dan, and Amzi. Tobias and Amzi, do you feel comfortable leaving your wives at this time?"

With a glance at their wives, who both nodded, both men matched their wives' nods.

"Then quickly pack what you need. I ask the rest of those who live here to watch and care for each other." He gazed over the people in front of him. "Ruben, will your family remain while we're gone, or will you return to your farm?"

"If we could be of use, we will stay."

"Since we don't know what will happen during this unsettled time, I would appreciate any help you can give Simeon." He saw Liam far to the back of the courtyard. "Liam, would you mind taking a couple of men and preparing Shem's chariot and my horse? The other men going with us can use horses from the stable so we can travel faster."

Dan turned to his wife Martha. "I'll go pack my bag."

She slapped his arm. "*We* will go pack your bag." They hurried toward their part of the compound.

Kalif smiled at the couple before he allowed his vision to travel the courtyard again. "I will return as quickly as possible and share whatever news I discover." He wrapped his arm around Hadara and moved through the courtyard to the door to their rooms.

"I am so thankful you are not like most men," she whispered.

Kalif lowered his head to whisper back, "What do you mean by that statement?"

"You acknowledge me in public. You ask my opinion. You don't act as if I am worth slightly less than your horse, rather less than a donkey."

He laughed under his breath. "You are my help-mate, my love. I would never call a donkey or even my horse that."

Chapter 43

Jerusalem

Dusk surrounded the horsemen as they rode into the stable behind the king's palace. Shem and his driver pulled his chariot into another section of the back area. Stable workers took the horses after the men removed their packs from the animals' backs. Kalif and his party walked as a group to the visitors' door and entered the palace.

"Welcome, gentlemen." A palace servant welcomed them. "Please leave your packs here. They will be taken to your rooms. Follow me, please."

The servant led them through the maze of halls to the front vestibule. On one wall, two golden doors rose taller than the height of ten men standing on the shoulders of one another. On the opposite wall, double doors made of cedar trimmed in gold and jewels stood open, held by two more servants. The room beyond held many milling men. Armed men in military garb stood around the walls, but no one else had weapons. Aaron maneuvered his way to the opened doors.

"Shem, Kalif, please join us. You and your party are the last to arrive."

"Aaron, we are dusty from our fast ride. Are you sure you don't want us to change before we join everyone?" Shem brushed a puff of dust off his arm.

"No, no, we haven't time. We need to address this situation before we have more chaos to tame. Come. I want you up …" He paused and looked at the men with Shem and Kalif. "Tobias, I heard you returned, but I didn't recognize you at first. I remember Azmi and Abram." He studied Dan a moment. "Dan, it has been a long time." He nodded. "I have a quick question for each of you. Will you do what is needed to help our new king? To help our country return to the worship of the one true God?"

When each man gave an affirmative reply, Aaron announced, "Then let's go to the throne platform. I want Shem and Kalif with me by the throne and the rest of you standing in front of the platform, facing the rest of the crowd. Come."

The over two-hundred men in the center part of the vast room and many servants and retainers parted to create a path to the throne platform. Aaron, the minister, and Kalif mounted the steps and stood to one side of the throne,

Aaron in the middle and the others on each side of him. Dan, Tobias, Abram, and Amzi stood facing the crowd, their backs to the three on the platform. Since the stage rose so high, Aaron could easily see over their heads to the assembly beyond the three. He raised his hands, and the throng quieted.

"I invited each of you because you hold some position of power in Judah. Some of you followed the demon Moleck as did Ahaz. Many of you refused to give yourselves to an idol and stayed true to Yahweh, the one true God." He paused a moment before announcing in a booming voice, "Ahaz is dead.

"When Ahaz's oldest son was very young, his mother hid him. He has been in a place not far from Judah, preparing for the time he would reign in his father's place. Allow me to present your new king, King Hezekiah."

A tall, muscular young man walked through the drapes behind the throne to the front of the platform. His deep voice carried over the murmers and mutters, bringing silence except for his words.

"I am Hezekiah, and I am now your king since Ahaz *is* dead. And, the practice of worshiping Moleck is also dead. If you refuse to turn away from this false worship, leave now." He remained looking across the sea of heads, saying nothing. A rumbling began under the marble floor, which swayed and bowed under their feet. "I said leave unless you will worship only the one true God. Go!" His voice echoed through the room.

Many of the men glowered and glared around the room. The men around the walls unsheathed their swords. One by one, men began to flow through the doors into the vestibule and through the gold doors, now held open by servants, to the outside. From over two hundred men, only one hundred remained plus the military men and servants. The golden doors closed, and the servants barred it. They closed the doors to the throne room and joined the men left.

"Please sit, except the men at front with me." Hezekiah motioned with his hands for all to lower themselves. "I will first share what I know about Ahaz, which is little. Last evening the people who were to dine with him waited for over two hours without him joining them. Finally, one of the nobles sent a servant to ask the king when he wished to have supper. The servant returned to say he found Ahaz lying on the floor of his audience room, dead.

"The royal physician was called and checked the king. He could find no wounds and found no outward sign of poison. What priests still remained in Jerusalem were summoned. Aaron says they examined the body but couldn't find why the king died. A decision was reached that because the man had been so evil, had practically destroyed our country, that he would not be buried with the other kings.

"They, with four servants, carried the king's remains outside the palace, and they buried him where other family members are buried. We can't erase him from our records and history, and the wounds remain deep and great."

He lowered his head a moment before he looked again at the men below him. "I am grateful my mother saved me from my father's wickedness. I am a follower of the one true God, and here is my first declaration: All the statues of

Moleck are to be destroyed and removed. Crews of workers have already gone forth to follow my order.

"Now, we will need leaders for each village and town who will supervise the people and assist in the rebuilding of our communities. I will rely on guidance and advice from Aaron. He and I, with the help of Minister Shem and Kalif, will speak with the men I hope will take on the responsibilities and who will support our court and live in the will of the one true God.

"As soon as possible, the tribe of the priests for Yahweh will meet, and a new high priest will be chosen.

"Rooms for all have been readied so we can work into the night as long as needed and for as many days and nights required to bring our government into order. Servants will show you to your rooms at this time and meals will be brought to you. I ask only that the men standing in front of me and with me remain."

As the men left with escorts to their assigned rooms, other servants set up a long table and stools. Hezekiah took a place at the head of the table and motioned for Shem to sit on his right side, Kalif beside him, and Aaron on his left. Hosa entered and sat at the foot of the table while the other men took places along each side.

"Our meal will be served shortly," Hosa announced.

"Thank you, Hosa." Hezekiah sagged on his stool. "We lost more men than I thought we would, but the one true God will use those we have."

"You said there are more priests?" Abram asked. "I thought Ahaz and Moleck's priests had killed all but Aaron."

"We all learned how to hide and to stay away from those wanting us dead. However, we had only five nearby yesterday when ten years ago, the priesthood had over thirty. Now, we won't have a high priest until we meet in the temple and petition the one true God. The workers said they would first clean the temple and organize it for worship." Aaron nodded toward the new king. "King Hezekiah said we would be able to add to our ranks as we find more who are of the priesthood."

Hezekiah nodded back. "We will go forward as we are able. Many changes must be made to turn Judah away from Moleck."

Servants brought in dishes and platters of food. The men began to eat once Aaron blessed them and the food.

After eating a few bites, Hezekiah turned to Shem. "Are you willing to become my first advisor? I need someone who will stand with me as I lead Judah away from the wickedness practiced for so long."

"My king, I'm not sure." Shem gazed at his plate before meeting Hezekiah's eyes. "I would do my best, but I would think others would be better than I am."

"No, my friend, you have all the qualities necessary, if you are willing. Aaron has recommended you most highly."

"I will do what Yahweh desires me do."

"Kalif, are you willing to become the Minister of the Military?"

Kalif laid down his utensil. "I gave up the military, and I'm not sure I could return to it."

"No, Kalif, I do not need another soldier, another fighter, but someone to advise me and help me know when the military is honest."

"Would I have to live in Jerusalem?"

The king studied Kalif for a few seconds. "I would think as long as you have a fast horse, you could live where you do now. At first, I would need your presence more often and for longer periods, but after the first half year or so, I will be more confident on my own for longer periods of time."

Kalif shook his head. "I will do what Yahweh wants and what will help you most." He pushed his plate of food away, his hunger gone.

Aaron joined the conversation. "Tobias, do you plan to live close to your mother and family?"

"To be honest, I'm not sure what I will do. I would like to live close to the rest of my family, but I don't know that I'm a farmer."

"Good." Aaron smiled. "King Hezekiah has asked for my advice, and he needs a good man to supervise Bethlehem, to be sure the people have someone they can petition when they think they have been cheated or mistreated, someone to be sure idol worship doesn't take over each area, someone to represent the king in each area. Would you be interested in representing the king in Bethlehem and the twenty or so miles around the village?"

"Aaron and I have spoken many long hours since he came for me after Ahaz died. I trust his judgement." King Hezekiah sipped from his goblet before he added, "I would be honored if all of you would take positions in my government."

Tobias stared at the king before looking at Kalif. Kalif said, "You are well trained physically and have a good education. You would surely have help with any duties as needed."

"I believe I would like helping people re-find their lives." He smiled. "Yes, I would do the best job I can."

"Good. I will be talking to others about the other towns and areas."

Aaron drank from his goblet. When he sat it down, he gazed at Amzi. "As I told King Hezekiah, I know you helped Kalif and his father with the fine cloth and carpet business. Do you think you could add being one of Tobias' assistants to your duties?"

"If God wills," Amzi answered. "You do know, though, that brothers often quarrel."

"Do you not think you both are mature enough to work through any disagreements? You need to realize you are not doing a good job if you don't help each other make good decisions," the king chided.

"Yes, my king, if Tobias is willing, I am."

The king turned his attention to Abram. "After all that Aaron has told me, I would like that you also work with Tobias. There will be times when he must come to the palace or he has too many events happening at one time. He will need two good men to step in where needed."

Abram nodded. "I would be honored."

"Now, Dan, you were a military man for many years. Would you assist Kalif?" King Hezekiah studied the former soldier.

Dan stood and clasped Kalif's arm. "I would follow this man and do whatever he directs."

Hezekiah smiled, his face almost glowing. "God will bless each of you. Kalif, I will need you, Shem, and Aaron to sit with me when I talk to other nobles. I can hope that they will be as agreeable as you all have been. Now, please do eat. We have long days waiting for us."

Three weeks later

Kalif leaned against the closed door of the palace room assigned to him. Weariness drained him. "I never thought talking and listening could tire a person so much." He dropped on the side of the bed platform, rested his elbows on his knees, and held his head with both hands. "I want to go home. Now I have to wait until the coronation of King Hezekiah before I can." Falling back, he slid his legs onto the bed and let sleep take over, glad that the important positions had been filled.

A pounding on the door brought him upright and off the bed. He strode to the door and asked, "Who is there?"

"Dan."

Kalif pulled the door open. "What are you doing back here?"

"Hadara. Hadara needs you as fast as you can get home. The babe is coming. She won't listen to anyone, just says you have to be there."

Shaking his head to try to awaken, Kalif grabbed his clothes. "I'll need to get my horse."

"I told the stable men to ready him before I came inside. I also sent a servant for Aaron. All you need do is grab your pack and leave as soon as you tell the priest what is going on, and he can notify the king."

"Thank you, my friend."

The door opened, and Aaron entered. "I understand you are leaving."

"Aaron, Hadara needs me. This is my first babe. I ... I must go."

Aaron chuckled. "Of course, you must. You have stayed longer than I thought you ever would. Now go. I will make your apologies to the king."

"Will he be angry?"

"Have you seen him angry in the weeks you have been around him?"

Kalif frowned. "One time, and I would rather not see his anger again. When he discovered a statue of Moleck still standing ... He became violent."

"Now, go and be there to see your babe." He slapped Kalif on the back. "You are most different from other men. You don't act like you own your wife."

"No, I don't own her. She is as intelligent as I, maybe even more so. She will probably be my closest advisor, even if not officially."

Aaron gazed at Kalif a moment. "I have known her for many years, and I have welcomed her advice and counsel at times. I would not blame you. Now, leave. All is not well."

Kalif and Dan rode up to the farm compound. "Go, I will put the horses away," Dan said. Swinging from the horse, Kalif ran into the house to find torches and fire pots casting light throughout the courtyard. He entered their rooms and found the same amount of light. The door to the bedchamber stood open, and he could hear moans.

"Hadara." He rushed into the bedchamber. Rachel and her daughter Zema stood by the bed. They whirled when they heard him.

"Out! Men are not allowed." Zema made pushing motions with her hands. "Leave now."

"That is my wife, my babe. I will be here." He bent over the writhing Hadara. "Why aren't you helping her?"

Rachel joined him by the bedside. "The babe is turned wrong. It will not be born. I am sorry, Kalif, but both will die."

"No! No, they will not. What do you mean the babe is turned wrong?"

"The head is up, not down. The head must be born first."

Kalif grabbed a piece of cloth and wiped his wife's face. "We must do something. What? Think, must think." His mind froze as he stared at his suffering wife. "What can be done? Wait, turned wrong. I … I had to turn a foal when the mare could not … Why not a babe?" He rubbed his hands over his wife's bulging abdomen. "Yes, I can feel the head." He held his hands up. "My hands are too large."

"Too large? I don't understand." Rachel stared at him.

"This is no place for him. He must leave." Zema continued to mutter over and over.

Kalif pointed at Zema. "Either get her to leave or have her be quiet."

"Is there anything you need?" Dan's voice asked from outside the room.

"Yes, yes. Bring a large bowl of wine, not watered but the strongest you can find. Also, get Mazza." He breathed deeply. "Mares died in the past when this happened until hands were washed with strong wine." He shook his head. "My hands are still too large."

"Kalif? Please don't stay. Don't want you … to see …" Hadara's voice so soft, so low caused him to bend closer.

"My love, I should be here, with you. No matter what happens, I must be with you."

Rachel picked up one of his hands and held it next to hers. "Mine are much smaller. What do you need me to do?"

He wiped Hadara's face again. "This will hurt, Hadara, but if we don't try, we will lose you and the babe. Would you please be strong and try really hard, even when the pain becomes worse?"

She nodded as she bit her lip, fighting not to scream. "Pain worse? I … will try."

"Here's the wine," Dan called from the other room.

Zema hustled to take the bowl from her brother. Kalif heard her tell him, "You at least will stay out here. Men don't belong at a birthing." She carried the bowl to Kalif and returned to the other side of the bed.

Kalif sat the bowl on a table. "Rachel, this will be awkward, but what I want to do is the only thing that might save Hadara." He grabbed one of the cloths stacked on the end of the bed. "First, wash your hands well in the wine."

After she did, and she dried her hands, Rachel sighed. "I believe I know what you expect me to do. What if I can't?"

"While you work to move the babe from inside, I will try to help from the outside."

"No, that is wrong, wrong," Zema exclaimed. "Mother, you must make him leave. What he suggests is unthinkable."

Rachel studied her daughter. "My child, nothing is unthinkable if Hadara and her babe are to have a chance to live. Stop being so unreasonable and help or leave."

"But …"

Mazza hustled into the room. "Why am I just now called? No, doesn't matter. What can I do?"

"Zema, leave." Rachel pointed toward Hadara. "This woman has given our family and you a home and a life. I am ashamed if you think you are above what is needed to help save her life."

As Zema lowered her head and left, Mazza repeated. "What can I do?"

Kalif, who already rubbed and gently pushed against the baby's protruding form, told Rachel, "You must help by trying to move the babe in the same direction I am." He glanced at Mazza. "Have cloths ready to wrap the babe once it comes."

Silence filled the room, broken only by the moans, groans, and muffled screams from Hadara. Suddenly, a scream, not muffled, erupted from her as the baby flipped, and once Rachel removed her hand, the babe slid from the birth channel into the cloth-covered, waiting hands of Mazza.

"You have a son," Mazza whispered.

Kalif moved to Hadara's head, sat on the bed, and lifted her upper body into his arms. "Hadara, are you with me still?"

Weary eyes lifted to his. "The pain is gone … oh, no, again."

Rachel told her, "This pain is normal. It will last only a minute, and all will be over."

Hadara leaned against her husband's chest. "The babe, is the babe born?"

"Yes, my love, we have a son."

"Ah, good." A bemused smile covered her face. "I like the name Josiah." She closed her eyes. "I am so sleepy."

After the other women cleaned and swaddled the babe, they finished cleaning Hadara, changed her bedclothes and the bedding. Hadara dozed a bit before awakening to watch Dan bring a cradle into the bedchamber and place it by the bed.

"May I hold my son," Hadara asked, and Kalif placed the babe in her arms. "Oh, I thought he would be smaller." She looked at Rachel. "Tobias was so tiny."

Rachel laughed. "Yes, this one is a big one, largest I've seen. However, he will need his mother and father to care for him for many years." She faced her son. "We need to leave the little family so they can have time together." She smiled at Hadara. "I'm glad Mazza was able to be here."

Hadara whispered, "Me, too." She held a hand toward her long-time retainer and friend. "Thank you. I hoped you would be able to rest before you joined us."

Clasping Hadara's hand, Mazza answered, "I am, too, glad I was here. Now, I also will leave you to be together. I will return later. Rest." She nodded at Kalif before turning toward the door and from the room.

Hadara let her eyelids drift closed. "Should we let the others know?"

Kalif took the babe and placed him in the crib. "No, my love, morn is early enough." Kalif chucked. "They will forgive us as soon as they see Josiah."

"Thank you, my Caleb, my Kalif, my warrior, my love." Sleep wrapped her in its embrace, and she slept.

Hadara started a process as Nava, with a daughter, and Noma, with a son, gave birth within a month after Josiah's birth.

Zema avoided Kalif, and he laughed to himself each time she left a room when he entered. The new king's reign progressed, but not without some conflict and angry people, especially those who lost positions of importance with the change. Kalif and Hadara's gathering room held many meetings. She would often tend to the babe while the men discussed the country's changes and troubles. One day, she fed Josiah in the bedchamber with the door open enough she could hear.

"Some want-to-be leaders declare the king should take a slower path to ridding the country of the idols and idol worship." Shem took a drink from his goblet.

Dan scowled. "We need to rid ourselves of all signs of Moleck and any other idols. Remember what Isaiah the prophet said about the one true God being a jealous god? We don't want Him to turn his back on us again as He did during Ahaz's reign."

"We have been fortunate in the Bethlehem area, but this area fought having a statue of Moleck anywhere near. The people are happy that we have a synagogue again and no sacrifices of children." Kalif rose when he heard a pounding on the door to the house. "Excuse me, I will be right back."

One of the king's messengers stood at the door. "I have a message for Kalif, Shem, and Dan."

Kalif motioned for him to enter and led him to the gathering room. "We three have a message from the king."

"Approximately fifty followers of Moleck have taken up arms and protect the idol's statue at the town of Asdod. The king wishes for you to meet with him immediately." The messenger paused. "What message may I take to the king?"

Kalif looked at Shem, who replied, "We will be at the palace as quickly as we can load our packs and ride there."

"Please, have something to eat and drink before you return to Jerusalem," Kalif offered. "We will need a little time before we can leave."

"Thank you."

"Please follow me," Joseph said from the doorway. He nodded toward Kalif. "I will have horses readied and tell Martha to ready Dan's pack." He left with the messenger.

Shem pushed himself from the chair. "Since I have no wife, I will care for my things. I am ashamed of my countrymen who will fight for an idol but wouldn't fight against one."

"I must get to Martha before Joseph." Dan strode from the room. "She won't appreciate me sending word."

Kalif entered the bedchamber as Hadara laid Josiah in the cradle. "We will need a larger bed for him quite soon," she told her husband. "He grows so quickly." She looked at Kalif. "So, you leave?"

"Yes, at least I don't have to go to Jerusalem often." He enveloped her in his arms as he gazed on their sleeping son. "He *is* a big one."

"Look at his father." Hadara rotated to face him. "Of course, you have no idea how long you will be gone, but will you at least keep yourself safe?"

"Of course, I have much for which to live." He kissed her. "Now, I must pack to leave."

"I will help." She hurried to the chest where Kalif kept his clothes as he brought out a large pack that rode behind him on the horse.

When Kalif laid his pack by the door to the courtyard, he pulled Hadara close to him. "I will send word if we will be gone more than two days. I will miss you by my side, but if we are to keep our country worshiping Yahweh, I must help King Hezekiah."

"I know, but that doesn't mean I enjoy your trips, or that I don't worry one of those Moleck worshipers might decide to kill you." She brushed her hands over his face. "May the one true God keep you safe."

Stable workers met the men when they arrived behind the palace. "We will care for the horses and have your packs delivered to your rooms," one told them.

When Kalif, Dan, and Shem entered the door of the palace, guarded by soldiers inside and out, Aaron awaited them. "Come, the king waits for us in his advisors' room. There will be just the five of us. He wants this uprising kept as quiet as possible."

The men wound their way through the marble halls to a room one fourth the size of the throne room.

"Does the king not have a small room we could use?" Dan asked as they sat around a table in the middle of the room, where food and drinks waited.

"King Hezekiah will have more changes made after the business of the country is under better control. He doesn't care for too much opulence." Aaron lowered himself into a chair. "The king will join us in a few moments. Please drink and eat."

Shem took a seat before asking, "Has a High Priest been chosen?"

"The others want me to be, but the king wishes me to be his advisor. I asked another be selected for High Priest. More members of the Tribe of Levi are arriving every day. One will be blessed by Yahweh."

As he ate and drank, Kalif allowed his thoughts to wander, finally speaking aloud. "How can we destroy a rebellion without further dividing the country and make governing harder on the king?" He glanced at Shem and chuckled.

A servant opened a door at the back of the room, and the king entered. "Thank you, men, for coming so quickly. I hope you will be able to help me find a solution for our problem."

"I think Shem already has a solution, in a way." Kalif moved his goblet in a circle on the table top. "He would take prisoners and have them disappear." He lifted his goblet to the king's advisor. "If we can contact the 'silent soldiers,' we may cause so much fear among the dissenters that they will want nothing more to do with Moleck or any idol."

King Hezekiah leaned forward in his chair. "What are 'silent soldiers'?"

"When I was young and first in the military, a special group of soldiers were used for secret assignments. They dressed in clothing that allowed them to blend into the countryside, and they knew how to move silently." He chuckled. "Can you imagine our sending in enough of these silent soldiers to capture and tie up the opposition without a sound and move them to, oh, a ship which takes them to some other land and leaves them?"

"Terror would erupt, especially if the same thing happened more than once or twice in different places," Shem added. "And, I have the resources to cause many men to disappear."

"How do we find these 'silent soldiers'?" Hezekiah asked. "The plan wouldn't work unless we can obtain the right men."

Kalif nodded. "I will use some of my sources. If any silent solders are available, I will find them. How many men are taking a stand at Asdod, fifty?"

"Yes," Hezekiah replied, "Fifty to fifty-five."

"Then let me see how many soldiers I can find." Kalif rose. "I will begin now. Dan, will you come with me, please?"

Kalif led Dan through narrow winding streets into the poorest part of the city. As they walked, either man could have held his arms out and touched the walls of the homes and shops they passed, all which showed no signs of life. After following an unknown path for many minutes, Dan opened his mouth to ask Kalif when they would arrive, but his friend opened a door and stepped into a dimly lit area crammed with men and noise. Rough faces turned to stare at the newcomers before they continued with whatever they did before the interruption. Kalif pushed his way, followed by Dan, through the crowd to a counter where an enormous man filled mugs.

"Is Abel around?" Kalif asked barely above a whisper.

"Who be wantin' Abel?"

"Tell him Caleb needs to talk to him."

The man bent closer to Kalif's face. "You be Caleb?"

"Yes."

"Follow me." He lifted a section of the counter, reached to grab a customer's shoulder, and pulled him behind the counter. "Take care of business until I be back."

After closing the section, he pushed his way to a door in a side wall. He tapped a rhythm on the wood before opening it. The three men entered a room nearly dark but filled with several men.

The large man pointed a thumb at Kalif. "Says he's Caleb and wants a talk with Abel." He turned and walked back out the door, slamming it shut behind him.

"Caleb, that be you?" a voice from the darkest part of the room asked.

"Yes, it is. Abel?"

An elderly man hobbled into the dim light provided by one small fire pot. "Let me see." He grabbed Kalif's face and pulled it down where he could view it. "You done changed. Got fancified."

"I took over my father's business after my brother died. I had to look the part."

"Aye, you do that. What you need from an old bum like me?"

Kalif looked around at all the men within the light, knowing that more waited in the dark. "I need to have this between you and me, not anyone else, yet."

The old man clapped his hands, and bodies left through different doors until only the three remained plus one man who remained by the door to the inn next door. "Him stays," Abel proclaimed as he sat on a barrel. "Now, what be it you need."

Kalif squatted beside the man. "I have need of silent soldiers, if any are left. Are there?"

Abel rubbed his chin, covered with sparse tuffs of wiry hair. "There be some. How many you be needing?"

"I know there probably aren't that many left, but we could use a hundred or a few more, to help the new king."

"Help the new king, not that monster Ahaz?"

"Correct."

"Let me think a bit." He closed his eyes and rocked back and forth. "Me might know enough." He opened his eyes. "Where safe can the men meet up with you, and when they be needed?"

"They can meet me in the barracks area behind the king's palace. We need them as fast as possible. How long would you say until they could be there?"

Caleb pursed his lips and rocked some more. "Yeh, they be there not this comin' morn, but the next night after." He stared into the darkness. "I mayen be able to have the one hundern."

"So, I will wait at the barracks not tomorrow night but the next night, correct?"

"That be what I say. They be lookin' for Caleb." He stuck his thumb toward Dan. "Who he be?"

"This is my friend Dan. He also was a soldier but followed the one true God as we do."

"He be a fine man, then. Now, go out that there door," he pointed to the door to the narrow pathway road. "May the one true God go with you'ens."

Once back in the dark night, Kalif and Dan walked quickly toward the palace, saying nothing because the night can have ears. Once inside the palace, Dan took a deep breath.

"You weren't afraid, were you?"

"I know not to show any fear." Kalif shrugged. "I had too many assignments while in the military, dangerous ones if I were caught by any of the king's men. I had to learn not to show any emotion."

"I am glad we are on the same side."

Two nights later, Kalif, dressed in the military clothing he once wore, waited in the training yard in front of the barracks, Dan by his side. Close to midnight, figures began to slip into the dark training ground. Within half an hour, the men stood in military ranks, quiet and nearly invisible in their brownish and blackish clothing.

When Kalif faced them, one of the men stepped forward. "You be Caleb?"

"I was, yes, and you may use that name. This is my man." He pointed at Dan. "You are?"

"I be sergeant of these forces, name be Pace."

"Good, Pace. How many soldiers do we have?"

"With me, we got one hundern and four."

"Great, great. For tonight, you will stay in the barracks. Tomorrow we will discuss how to help the king dispose of dissenters. Do you need anything? Food and beverage will be served inside. Ten of the king's closest men will help you." He motioned to a man standing off by himself. "Sergeant Pace, this is Saburo, and he will be available to aid you anyway you need."

Saburo gave a salute to Pace. "Come with me, sir, you and your men. My men and I will settle you for the night."

The troops moved like a gentle breeze, no sound, little movement, and the training ground stood empty except for Pace, Kalif, and Dan. One of the silent soldiers moved from the shadows. "Kalif?"

Startled, Kalif spun to confront this unexpected man. "Amzi? What?"

Amzi chortled. "You never knew I was a member of this group? Most of the silent soldiers were also rebels. We did all we could to thwart Ahaz."

"I allowed Amzi to wait behind to talk, but we be needed to get sleep." Pace gave a salute, spun, and melted into the night.

"We will do the job, whatever it is." Amzi also disappeared.

"Come, Dan, let's get some sleep, too." Kalif started toward the palace.

"Imagine, Amzi a silent soldier. Amazing. Oh, well, we'll visit with Aaron and the king in the morning and then with our silent soldiers. The plot begins."

The next night

The silent soldiers departed the barracks as they appeared, one or two at a time without anyone knowing they left until the building sat empty of all except palace forces. Amzi and Pace melted into the night after everyone else disappeared. They moved not only silently but rapidly over the miles to the spot where they would convene before they removed the malcontents. During the day, the two hid in brushy areas and slept. When darkness arrived again, they continued on their way. The third morning, they found most of the soldiers hiding where they agreed to meet. After chewing dried meat and drinking some watered wine, they crawled under brush and slept.

Darkness fell, and the soldiers crawled from their hiding places and gathered around Pace. "We be less than a mile from our targets. We must have all the opposition tied and hooded and gone one hour after midnight. We be able to do our part. We be able to cause idol-worshipping maggots to disappear." He paused. "All be ready?"

A low murmur of agreement answered him.

"Then we be gone and know that Amzi be my second. He be most able."

Another murmur of agreement sounded, and the men dressed in their brown, tan, and blackish clothing slithered into the night. Less than an hour later, they circled the top of the bowl-like indention where the idol rested. Three campfires lit the area below them and revealed men wrapped in mantels and blankets huddled in sleep close to the fires. With a hand signal from Pace, the soldiers crept two by two to the edge of the encampment. Amzi searched the area for guards. The men willing to fight to defend the idol didn't even have guards for themselves.

Pace pointed to a man nearby, snoring loud enough to cover any sound made by a soldier. Amzi pulled a dark hood from a pocket and rope from another. Pace also removed rope and a strip of cloth from a pocket. They crawled to the sleeping man. Pace slipped the stip of cloth into the man's mouth as Amzi tied a rope around his neck, pulling it tight enough cut off the man's breath. When the man stopped thrashing around, they tied him up and pulled the hood over his head. Amzi glanced around the encampment. Each pair of soldiers had a man tied up, gagged, and hooded. The extra soldiers carried branches from bushes, waiting to do their job when the soldiers lugged the idol worshippers away.

One of the soldiers called to Pace, "Can we topple this monster?" He pointed at the statue.

"Do it."

The soldiers brought out more stands of rope, looping them over the head and arms of the statue. While some soldiers pulled on the ropes, others pushed from the back. The metal idol tittered several times before crashing forward to the ground. One arm broke from the rest of the statue, and one bent underneath. Soldiers removed ropes and returned to their prisoners.

Amzi and Pace stood together after the statue crashed to the ground, but rather than throwing their prisoner over his shoulders or helping to place the man over Amzi's, Pace motioned for one of the soldiers with a bush to join them. "I want Amzi to stay, see what happen when others find them be gone. He will brush out disturbance of the ground, and you be helping carry this prisoner to the ship."

Amzi took the bush from the other soldier. "Would you mind if I meet with Kalif after and give him a report?"

Pace nodded before he bent and picked up the prisoner, slung the man over his shoulders, and marched toward the sea. Amzi helped brush footprints and drag marks from the ground, with other soldiers doing the same. However, while the others followed their troops carrying prisoners, brushing away all traces of their activity behind them, Amzi used his branch to erase his footprints up the bank and to where brush and trees began. He threw his branch up into a tree and wiggled under a bush where he could spy on the now empty area where the idol lay tumbled and partially broken.

Kalif asked if he could lead the "official" troops that would create the diversion for the silent soldiers. With the king's permission, he rode at the head of troops dressed in the harness uniforms of the king. They timed their march so that they would arrive where the statue of Moleck rested at midnight or close thereafter. Dan rode beside him, and the men marched, making extra noise and often talking or singing.

Dan said, "Do you see them?"

"Yes, I've spied three so far. They try to hide, but they don't know how." He gave a low snort. "They joined us about five miles behind."

They rode in silence for another mile. "We need to slow down. We've traveled too fast the past two days." Kalif turned to watch the soldiers behind him. "We can't be in place too soon, need to give the silent soldiers time to be gone before we set up camp."

Dan rotated his horse so that he faced the troops. He raised a hand, a signal for them to stop in place. "Men, since we have a way to go before we camp, take time to eat and drink before we continue."

The men removed backpacks and dropped to the ground. They pulled out dried meat and wine skins.

Kalif swung from his horse, as did Dan. "Good idea, Dan. Do you need to eat, too?"

"No, I don't. That was the only excuse I could think of for us to stop. Soldiers are usually hungry."

The men walked their horses to the side of the rode where grass grew. As the horses nibbled on grass, Kalif and Dan sat on the ground close by. When men began to close their packs and to walk around, Kalif rose.

"Let's be on our way, Dan." He swung onto his horse as Dan mounted and rode to the head of the squad.

"In places, men," he called. The men took their places and arranged their packs on their backs.

Kalif told Dan, "Let's go at a slower pace. We don't want to rush."

A few minutes later, Dan remarked, "Our shadows are back. I was afraid we lost them by stopping." He chortled under his breath.

The troops marched through the evening into the gloom of night. Half way until dawn the leaders slowed the men more.

Dan whispered, "Shouldn't be long now."

"I know. Help keep an eye open for the place."

When Kalif saw the darker area ahead to the right of the road, he knew they had arrived. He saw no movement. He stopped his horse. "Dan, tell the men to make camp between the road and the sea. They are to build fires, too."

He dismounted and led his horse to a tree, where he tied the reins to a low branch. He slid down the trunk and leaned against it. "Now we wait. Owww. I'm getting old or the ground is getting harder," he muttered.

From where he hid, Amzi watched the three men who had followed Kalif and the troops walk around and scratched their heads. One shouted, "Where you be?" Nothing but silence answered.

He couldn't hear what they said as they huddled beside the broken statue, but their actions showed their confusion. They walked around the idol one more time before running toward the bank, right toward him. Amzi pulled back until he crouched against a tree. Once the men ran past, he followed. The three ran as quickly as they could through the dark, bumping into a tree or two, stumbling over rocks and brush. They headed for a small hut in a clearing, Amzi not far behind.

After the men entered the hut, Amzi crouched below a shuttered window that showed a narrow gap at the bottom. When he raised his body to peek through the gap, he saw a room with one table and six men plus the three newcomers.

"They be gone. I tells you they be gone." One newcomer kept repeating.

A man with gray hair and beard grabbed the first and shook him. "Be quiet. Let someone talk who can tell us what happened." He threw the other man to one side and circled the other two. "Did you warn our brothers that the king's army came? Did the army attack our men?"

The men looked at the floor.

"Answer me!" The elderly man slapped his hands on the table, and all the men in the room jumped, as did Amzi.

One of the three men who brought the news raised his head and stared at the elderly man. "King's men camped 'bout a quarter of a mile away from Moleck, but our men be gone. The statue dumped over and broken."

"Could you find signs of a battle?"

"No, couldn't tell in the dark, but only footprints I see be ours."

"We must search the area come morn." The gray-haired man walked to a corner of the room and dropped to the floor. He covered his head with his mantle and lay down.

Amzi crawled away and headed for the army camp. Once he reached the road, he allowed himself a good laugh. *The terror begins.*

Kalif awoke but kept completely still. He grasped his knife.

"Kalif, it's Amzi." The sound of Amzi's voice froze his movement.

"Do you know how close you came to meeting my knife?" Kalif asked as he pushed himself to a sitting position. "Did the plan work?"

"Better than we thought. Pace had me wait, and I hid and watched. I followed the ones following you to a hut where they reported that their men were gone." He stretched. "They will search the hollow where the statue lies. Oh, yes, the silent soldiers pulled and pushed it over. It's rather a mess."

Kalif peered at the silent soldier. "I brought you a change of clothes in case we met up again." He pulled his pack onto his lap and removed some clothing. "Here, you can change before light so no one will see you as a silent soldier."

When the sun rose, Kalif, Dan, Amzi, and ten soldiers stood at the natural entrance to the bowl and saw that the statue lay by itself. They waited but a moment before returning to the rest of the troops. The king's men ate more dried meat and drank from their wine skins before they began their long march back to Jerusalem.

King Hezekiah leaned back in his chair as he listened to the reports from the men sitting around the table. "I'm glad the plan worked. Shem, have your heard anything from the ship's captain about his passengers?"

"The message was coded, but the prisoners are now in a country where the people don't understand a word they say."

The king laughed. "Life may be different for the idol worshipers than they expected." He looked at Kalif. "Do you think we could adapt this plan for other areas? For example, we have the same situation at Geba, close to the Syrian border."

Kalif frowned as he thought. "I would think we could use the silent soldiers any way to cause the dissenters to disappear, if we can find a way to dispose of them."

"Just across the border not far from Geba is a walled enclosure where Syrian slave dealers 'store' their merchandise." Shem raised an eyebrow. "The slave idea has been used before."

"Pace agreed to be available any time needed. He can have a hundred silent soldiers within two days. Is there a job here he could have so he can live close by?" Kalif steepled his fingers.

The king looked at Aaron. "We need to find a head of household to take care of questions like this."

"I have found one who begins tomorrow. In the meantime, perhaps Pace could be one of our stable men, Kalif?"

"I will notify him before I leave. I must go home before everyone forgets who I am. Dan and Amzi will leave with me."

The king gazed at Kalif in silence before blowing a puff of air. "You have set up a way for us to handle the Moleck problem. However, we have one more problem. Shem, want to tell him?"

"One of the remaining Ahaz nobles is paying men to cause trouble. We need an idea of how to give him the fright of his life, but he is always protected with several men, even at night."

"Hadara will think I abandoned her and the babe." Kalif softened his words with a smile. "Where does this noble live?"

Shem squinted as he searched his memory. "Let me see if I remember. Were you familiar with the palace where Tzabar lived?"

Amzi burst out laughing. "Oh, no ... that's good ..." he said during guffaws.

Dan grinned. "Imagine that. Think you might help?"

"Amzi and Dan both are familiar with that place. Amzi more so than Dan," Kalif explained to the king and Shem. "So, Amzi, what do you think? *I* think I better send a messenger to Hadara and let her know I won't be home for a few more days."

"I have the perfect plan if the noble uses the right room for his bedchamber. Is there any way to discover which he uses?" Amzi asked.

Aaron and Shem nodded, but Shem answered. "How long would it take to dispose of him once we know which his bedchamber is?"

"One night. Many of the rooms have hidden passages and doors, and I know them all." Amzi leaned back still chuckling. "What if the noble disappears and is found in the vat when the main Moleck statue is brought tumbling down?"

Shem stood. "I know someone who will know, and he's right here in the kitchen. I'll be back quickly." His hoots of laughter could be heard as he left the room, causing servants to draw back as he passed.

Once told which room the noble used for sleep, and hearing the man barred the door from inside every night, Amzi rubbed his hands together. "All I need to know now is which night do you want the noble to disappear."

King Hezekiah tried to hide his smile behind his hand. "Uh, we have celebration day after tomorrow as we destroy the Moleck statue outside of Jerusalem. It's the biggest and most elaborate, and I like the idea of this particular noble being found inside the vat. Can you take him tomorrow night?"

Amzi nodded. "Oh, yes. Another nail of terror for those who insist on continuing the worship of a demon."

"What will you do with this man after he is 'found' in the vat?" Kalif asked the king.

"I will banish him from Judah for the rest of his life." King Hezekiah's voice held no hint of laughter.

Amzi and four silent soldiers slipped through the door hidden in the stable of Tzabar's former palace. One man carried a torch as he walked beside Amzi. They followed the passage between walls and up inclines, passing many offshoots and doors. Finally, Amzi raised his hand and pointed to an outline of a door in the passage wall. He stuck two of his fingers into notches and pulled. The door portion of the wall opened to reveal the inside of a cabinet. Amzi entered the cabinet, pushing clothes aside to reach the cabinet door. He released the door a crack and peeked into the room lit by one small fire pot in a far corner. Sounds of heavy snores filled his ears.

"The former cook said the master drank at least two jugs of strong wine every night. From the sound, our job will be easier." Amzi tiptoed to the door leading to an antechamber. "Yes, it's barred. Tie him, gag him, and put the hood over his head."

Within a quarter of an hour, the men had the noble in a cart, covered with bundles, and they headed toward the statue site south of the city.

The next morning, Shem, with his escorts, visited the noble's home. He gave the servant who allowed them inside an excuse, "The king wishes for Cymus to come to the palace."

"I'm sorry, sir," the servant mumbled. "Nobleman Cymus has not awakened this morn."

"Then awaken him."

"But, sir, we tried. He be not opening the bedchamber door, and it be barred inside."

Shem pushed by the man into the palace. "Get axes. We will break the door."

Several men welding axes and a battering ram crashed the door, only for them to find an empty room. They opened cabinets, looked behind wall hangings, and under the massive bed. The soldiers who guarded the noble and his servants stared at each other, at Shem, and some bolted from the room.

"What matter of demon action be this?" one of the servants demanded. "I hearded of Moleck followers disappearing, but I didn't believe."

"Believe now," another shouted as he ran.

Although Kalif didn't realize it, he stood at the spot where his wife stood years earlier when forced to observe the first infant sacrifice, the babe burnt in the hands of the statue below. King Hezekiah and his court sat on a platform directly below where he stood. Muscular men held ropes tied to different parts of the statue.

Boom! Bang! Boom! A banging resounded from the vat between the idol's hands. The priests of the one true God whirled from their spot between the platform and the statue to stare first at the king and then at the vat.

The king stood and announced, "See what is in the vat."

All of the men had dropped the rope ends when the banging began. Two ran to the vat and connected the ladders used by the Moleck priests to throw a victim in the metal container when filled with flames. They each hooked a ladder over the edge of the vat and scrambled up the rungs.

One man yelled, "There's someone in there." He and his partner reached as far as possible, but they couldn't grasp the prisoner's hands.

Another of the workers brought a length of rope and climbed a ladder to hand to the man at the top. One worker used the rope to climb into the vat.

"He be tied up," the worker called to those above. "I get him loose." In a few minutes he called again. "Pull him up, then me."

When both men stood on the ground by the vat, Cymus, in his bedclothes, turned frightened eyes to the people staring at him.

"Where ... what ..." he muttered as he staggered toward the platform.

The king studied him. "Were you so affixed to Moleck that you would die with his statue?"

"Die? No, of course not. Moleck is our god. He would not ..." He fell to his knees. "Moleck, have mercy on me."

King Hezekiah motioned for two soldiers to come forward. "Take this man to the lockup until he can be shipped to a country that will take him." He watched Cymus stagger so the soldiers half-dragged him away. The king turned to face the people watching on the banks of the valley behind him.

"If you follow any god other than Yahweh, you will be forced to leave, or perhaps you will disappear as others have. Only the worshipers of the one true God will live here." He rotated to face the statue. "Bring it down!"

As the statue crashed to the ground, the crowd roared. Moleck would not be welcomed in the land of Judah.

Chapter 44

The Farm Compound :: seven months later

Hadara walked from the kitchen through the inner courtyard. Josiah toddled from one divan to another and then to a table. "Hello, my sweet one. Look at you. You will be walking all over the place before long." She sat on a divan and scooped her son into her arms.

Josiah patted her cheeks. "Eema, Eema."

"Yes, Eema. I wonder where your abba is?"

"Abba, Abba." Josiah struggled to climb off her lap and to the ground. "Abba."

"Did I hear me called?" Kalif swooped up his son and held him against his shoulder. "How is my little man?"

Josiah thumped his father on the head. "Abba."

Hadara and Kalif laughed.

"I have trouble believing this child is less than a year old. He has passed his cousins in all areas," Mazza stated as she left her rooms in time to hear and watch the three she considered family. "He is most smart."

"Now, Mazza, he has Benjamin to teach him many things, while Benjamin thinks the other babes just babes." Kalif swung his son back and forth. The little boy giggled in delight.

Hadara reclined on the divan and watched her husband and son. "The one true God blessed me beyond measure," she mumbled. Her eyes closed, and she slept.

"Hadara? Hadara?" Kalif shook her and called her name.

She raised her eye lids. "Hard to waken." She let them lower again.

"Hadara, wake up, please."

"I ... will try." She struggled, but her eyes closed again. A splash of cold water hit her face, and she sat up spluttering. "What, what did you do?"

"You would not awaken, child, so I threw water in your face," her adopted grandmother answered.

"Eema," Josiah rubbed a hand over her face and shook it, spraying water from his fingers. His giggles increased. "Eema."

"Hadara, what is wrong?" Kalif used his mantle hem to wipe her face.

"I don't know. I feel so sleepy ..." Her eyes widened. "Ohh, the only time I've been this sleepy was when I was first with child, with Josiah." She smiled. "Oooooh ... Maybe I'm going to have another babe."

Mazza muttered as she carried a squirming little boy away for his nap, "Another one, too soon. I'm getting too old."

Kalif scooted Hadara over and sat beside her, holding her close. "Perhaps, we should find a younger nurse maid."

"Perhaps, if we could make Mazza believe it to be her idea." She lay against him. "How can we do that?"

"I'll think about the problem." He paused before asking, "Do you think having another babe now may be too soon? Especially since you had so much trouble with Josiah?"

"I don't know. I waited over twenty years between the first two. I will talk with Rachel, perhaps she will know."

"Hmmm ... how nice a normal life is."

She didn't answer because she slept again.

Kalef smiled as he stood and swept her into his arms. As he walked toward their rooms, Mazza opened the door to leave and held it as he carried Hadara through and to their bedchamber. Mazza followed and turned down the top covers so he could lay his wife down.

He stood gazing at Hadara. "I wonder how we'll manage. For the first several months, all she will do is sleep."

"I will watch after the little one, and the new babe when he arrives."

"I know you will do your best, but who will make sure Hadara takes care of herself? I can't be here all the time."

"Oh," Mazza murmured. "Yes, someone needs to watch over her." She looked at Kalif. "We really need a nurse for the babies. Let me think about this matter." She murmured under her breath as she left their rooms.

The next morning, Mazza helped Hadara arrange her hair. "Do you know Gafna, Dan's daughter."

"Mmm, yes, I have seen her around. She's already betrothed, isn't she?"

"Yes, but her parents want them to wait at least two years so her betrothed can be settled in his occupation. He is an apprentice currently." She sniffed. "Actually, they believe Gafna is too young yet."

"Too young? Girls often marry by the time they are thirteen or fourteen. How young is she?"

"She is thirteen and has cared for many nephews and nieces. I think she could be a help to us, especially since you have another babe on the way."

"Ah, you mean she could be a nurse for our babes?" Hadara patted her hair as she rose to face Mazza. "What a good idea. Thank you, Mazza. I don't know what we would do without you." She hugged her old nurse before walking away, hiding her grin.

Bethlehem

Tobias glanced at the long line of people still waiting to bring problems and concerns to him. Already he had sat on the hard rock at one side of the square for nearly half a day. He shook his head, wondering if the number of problems would decrease over time.

Abram motioned the next petitioner forward. The woman, tall and elegant but dressed in well-worn clothing, carried a child not more than a year old.

"Yes, what help do you need?" he asked.

"My husband was Lior, and I didn't know what he and his uncle tried to do to people until after they were killed. I have a house, but I have no way to make a living for me and my daughter."

A voice called from the back of the cluster of people, "You could always be 'nice' to men. They would pay."

Tobias stood and glared at the people standing around. "If I ever discover who said that, he will wish he had remained silent. I will not tolerate anyone in this community talking about or treating a woman in such a manner. Do you understand?"

A murmur of assent rippled through the group.

"Then, we need to help this woman find an honorable way to care for her child and herself."

"May I speak?" An older man moved through the mass of people. "My name is Hebran, and I have a small farm outside the village and grow olives. My business is pressing olives to make oil. I need a larger area to place my press. I have never had a wife or family, but I believe I could offer a home for this woman and her child, if she be willing to become my wife."

The woman swallowed as she examined Hebran. She gave a wobbly smile. "I am Jacoba, my daughter Dorina. Perhaps my house and yard will be large enough for a spot for your olive press?" She shrugged. "That could be my dowry."

Tobias looked at Hebran and at Jocaba. "Does this give an answer for both your problems?"

Both nodded.

"Then go together and decide the details. I will hope all works for you both." As the couple walked away together, he announced, "I will return in the morning and listen to your concerns again for half a day." He motioned for Abram and Amzi to follow him, and he strode through the crowd and along a road out of town.

"I believe we must set a time limit each day we listen to problems and limit the number of days. Any suggestions?"

Amzi agreed. "I also have work to do. I am supposed to help Kalif's father with the shop."

"I have told Simeon I would work with his sons with the harvests." Abram straightened his mantle.

The three stopped in the middle of the road and looked at each other. "Yes," Tobias admitted, "we need to limit the time we listen to petitions." He studied the ground. "Amzi, how much time a week can you assist me and still handle your job for Kalif?"

"Really not more than a half day.

"Abram?"

"The same for me."

Tobias gazed at each of the other men. "I could manage with one of you at a time. I could give half a day twice a week. What do you think?"

The others nodded. Amzi said, "My wife would be happier, too."

"Maybe I would have time to find a wife," Abram muttered.

Tobias and Amzi laughed.

"Let's head for home. Amzi, go visit your wife and baby boy. Abram, let's head for the farm and our mid-day meal." Tobias grinned. "We'll work on a wife for you after we eat. Actually, not until after I have time with my family."

"Tobias!" The men whirled to face the village. Raz and Philmon rode toward them and dismounted when they reached the three.

"Philmon! Raz!" Tobias wrapped one then the other in a hug. "What are you doing here? I thought you would be half way to the far East by now."

Philmon shook his head. "So did we, but the unease in Israel has resulted in bands of bandits attacking any group that may bring money to their pockets."

"We will have to plan different routes or something." Raz's scowl revealed his anger. "We travel with men who will fight but taking an army with us would be difficult."

"Our nation moves toward peace, and a country across our border becomes more unstable." Tobias turned to Amzi. "Since Kalif's and your business relies so much on Raz and Hemut's caravans, perhaps you should be a part of the discussion we'll have at the farm."

Amzi responded, "Of course I need to be there. I will tell Noma to pack what we need for us and the babe, and I will visit with Gideon. I can't leave him managing the shop by himself if Ruth is not well. However, I know he will work with us if he can."

"I need to get my wife, too, if she's welcome," Philmon added to the conversation.

"Wife?" Tobias and Amzi both asked at the same time.

"Where is she?" Tobias asked.

"She is with the caravan the other side of Bethlehem."

"Why didn't you bring her?"

"I did not want her to feel unwelcomed. She is the best of me."

Amzi interrupted. "I will be at the farm as quickly as possible." He rushed toward town.

"I will go on to the farm and let everyone know Philmon, his wife, and Raz are here and that Amzi and Noma will be joining us." Abram started toward the farm at a brisk pace.

"Let us go get your wife, my friend." Tobias thumped Philmon on the shoulder. "Raz, do you go back with us, or do you prefer to go on to the farm?"

Raz mounted his horse. "I will go with you. I have a camel loaded with some supplies for Hadara."

The night meal finished, everyone congregated in Kalif and Hadara's inner courtyard. Hadara welcomed Shebaon into her home as if a daughter. The elegant woman sat beside her husband, the torch light causing her ebony skin to glow.

Kalif asked Raz, "Have you any ideas of what to do to get your caravans through?"

"No, I thought smaller caravans of just horses might have a better chance, but the large shipments, like you need, must have camels to carry."

"We have enough inventory stored to last us several years, don't we, Amzi?"

"Yes, we have one large house filled, and where Noma and I first lived also full. We have at least five years' worth."

"Now if our other customers had been so wise." Raz leaned forward in his seat. "But, we have people in Egypt waiting for fine cloth and carpets."

Kalif studied his wife's brother a moment. "What if we provided your needs for now? We're already in business together, with your filling our orders. We could provide the inventory you need for now. What would you need to ship from the East?"

"Spices," Raz replied. "We could get large quantities of spices through with horses, too."

Zema entered the courtyard, stopped, and stared at Shebaon. Her husband bent his head to hers and whispered something. She shook her head, spun on her heel, and walked out of the courtyard. Fiaz smiled.

"I'm sorry, but my wife suddenly took ill. Please excuse us." He followed Zema out of the courtyard.

Simeon grimaced. "I have no idea what has happened to her. She was once a sensible child."

Several people laughed at Simeon's quip.

Amzi returned to the subject. "I wonder how long this 'unrest' will continue in Israel? We hoped we would have peace once King Hezekiah removed the Moleck worshipers, but any problems in Israel seem to spill into Judah." He stood and strode to a table of refreshments and poured fresh water into a goblet.

"But, that's not an answer to the caravan question."

"No, but at least we have a short-term answer, thanks to Kalif and his partners." Raz turned to Kalif. "Speaking of your partners, will your father agree? Gideon at times can be less than cooperative."

Amzi answered, "It was his offer. He often hears rumors before the rest of us, and he said if the Israeli problem stopped shipments of fine cloth and carpet, we should help."

Kalif laughed. "I never know what my father will do or support. I am glad, though, he agrees with this solution. So, Raz, will you have enough horses and men to adjust your caravans?"

"Yes, he does." Philmon gestured with one hand toward his wife. "My wife's father gave me a herd of twenty horses. We agreed to allow Raz to use them to keep the business going."

"Twenty horses?" Nava asked in surprise.

Shebaon tried to hide her smile. "Yes, I'm afraid he wanted rid of me."

"But why? You are so lovely."

"Ah, but I am female, the oldest of many. He had to find me a husband so he could marry off the rest, some who would give him important connections." She lifted one brow. "I would not accept just any man, and my father thought he would never dispose of me."

Philmon took her hand into his, which nearly swallowed hers. "What he didn't realize was I needed nothing but her."

Her smile at him softened the aloofness of her face and revealed her beauty as sternness had not.

"What items do you have on the camels at this time?" Hadara asked.

"We have linen, cotton, and Egyptian stone for the craftsmen in the East. We can store all of it until we can ship later."

"Why? Why not use the craftsmen here in Judah?" Nava entered from another room. "My mother makes beautiful cloth from both linen and cotton. My brother can take stone and engrave and sculpt it. They are but two people in this land with skills you could use."

Raz tilted his head. "You may have a solution. We could work with people here."

Different ideas came from others in the group. The discussion continued until late into the night. The new mothers would leave to care for their babes and return to participate in the family meeting.

When Philmon and Shebaon stood to leave to go to their room, Tobias joined them. "Philmon, how are you enjoying going with caravans?"

Shebaon looked away.

"I don't care for it as much as I thought I would." He touched Shebaon's arm. "She doesn't like that I'm gone so much."

"What if we could find something here? Perhaps you could organize the people the family could work with to use the materials they ship?"

Philmon glanced at Shebaon, who nodded before she said, "Perhaps that would give us a home. All have accepted me." She nodded again. "I think I could live here."

Chapter 45

Farm compound :: two months before barley harvest

Kalif slapped the rolled parchment against his leg as he walked from the outer courtyard into the inner one.

"You seem in deep thought. Is everything all right?" When he didn't answer her but walked by on his way to their rooms, Hadara raised her voice. "Kalif, is everything all right?"

"What?" His head jerked around. "Oh, I didn't see you." Kalif joined her on a divan while Josiah reached for him. He hugged the little boy and gave his wife a kiss. Handing her the parchment, he told her, "Read this."

As Josiah jabbered at his father, Hadara unfolded the parchment and read the message. After she finished, a smile brightened her face. "King Hezekiah wants all the tribes to return to Jerusalem for the Passover. Do you think they will come, with all the troubles in Israel and so many there still worshipping idols?"

"I, uh, don't know." Kalif moved his head to avoid his son's fingers poking into his mouth. "The celebration will be wondrous if it happens. The king definitely wants all of us to return to our practices and worshipping." He swung Josiah up and down. "But, will you be able to travel in one or two months, when the barley is harvested?"

"I think so. The babe should wait another four months or so. The sleepiness is over. I am sure I can travel to Jerusalem."

"Then I shall tell the rest of the family, and we will see how many will join us." He stood holding his son. "Come, Josiah, let's go see other people."

"Abba, Abba." The little boy patted Kalif's cheeks.

"Yes, my little man, Abba." He stopped his trek to the door. "By the way, where is Gafna?"

"I told her I wanted to spend time with my son, and she wanted to spend time with her betrothed. I'll keep him with me while you spread the news, if you wish."

"No, no, not at all. We will be back once we share the message." He swung Josiah to his shoulder as he left.

After daydreaming a short time, Hadara rose from the divan. "How quiet. Wonder where everyone is?" She walked toward the kitchen. "I'll tell everyone over here about Passover."

Caley looked up from the slab of roast meat he sliced and placed on a platter. "Mis ... Hadara, may I be of help?"

"I was wondering where everyone is."

"Young Abram came in just now and said ever body was to go next door. I said I be there when I finish this. We all goin' to eat together tonight." He glanced up from his work. "Din't no one tells you?"

"Not yet. Thank you. I'll see you next door."

As she walked from the kitchen, she heard Kalif calling her from the inner courtyard. She frowned at him when she reached him. "Oh, did you remember me?"

"I started to tell people and decided that one announcement would be better." He shrugged. "I hurried over as soon as I could. By the way, have you seen Philmon and Shebaon?"

"No, but I didn't check their rooms."

Kalif strode to the rooms the Ethiopian and his wife used and tapped on the door. Philmon opened it. "Yes, Kalif?"

"We're all going to have our supper next door. I received a message from the king I want to share with everyone."

"Shebaon and I will be there in just a short time." He grinned. "We have been working on her idea of finding crafts people here who can finish rough materials we ship. I married a very intelligent woman."

Kalif chuckled. "We both did. We will see you in a while."

When Philmon and Shebaon entered the inner courtyard next door, Hadara and Kalif stood inside the door waiting. "Come, let me introduce you to anyone you haven't already met." Kalif turned to move to the first group already sitting in the divans and chairs.

"No!" A scream split the mumble of conversations. Hadara stared around her husband's back to see who yelled. "No, I will not serve servants." Zema tried to push by her father.

"Zema, what is wrong with you?" Simeon grabbed her arms and held her so she couldn't leave, but she twisted away and walked toward the kitchen before her father caught her again.

"It is enough we must serve a woman who does nothing, yet she gets her own house, had the best rooms in our house. I will not lower myself to care for people who are servants. That ... that new woman is not quality, married to a servant."

Shebaon whirled and started toward the door, but Philmon wrapped her in his arms, not allowing her to leave even as she cried, "I want out of here."

"No, please, Shebaon, we will put an end to this behavior immediately."

Simeon called from across the courtyard. "Zema, you will apologize immediately."

"Apologize? Why? I am not a servant, yet I am expected to be."

Simeon's eyes squinted, and his breathing grew louder. "That woman you accuse of doing nothing was the wife of a very rich man, and she was our mistress. We were *her* servants. You have a roof over your head and are free to have a husband and family because of *her*. Those good people you call servants are wealthy. You insult good people, people who have cared for you. Kalif even saved you from being ravaged by a soldier. Yet, you insult his wife. You should be banished from this house and have to make-do on your own."

Zema glared at her father. "Philmon was a servant for Hadara. Servants marry servants. I am not a servant. I should be treated like the lady I am."

"No, daughter, you are confusing things. What's happened to you? You are not making sense."

"Simeon, please allow me." Fiaz took his wife and led her to the back of the courtyard. He held her in his arms and whispered in her ear as she sobbed against his chest. Hadara watched them as Rachel covered her face with her hands and ran to the kitchen. Others in the courtyard looked at each other, peeked at Zema and her husband, gazed at the group by the door. Simeon turned away from his daughter and her husband and walked back toward his former mistress.

"Philmon, Shebaon, Hadara, I don't know what to say. Zema has acted strangely for some time now, but Rachel and I had no idea she had such odd ideas." Simeon lowered his head. "We never tried to give our children and grandchildren any idea that we were the ones who provided the farms and houses. And, Zema is old enough to know. She served you, Hadara."

Hadara squeezed past Kalif and placed her hand on Simeon's arm. "Simeon, you made all this possible as much as I, you and your family. You cannot make a child something she isn't, and you have reared two other daughters and three sons who are all anyone could desire in children. Zema was once a sensible young woman, but I, too, noticed she has become stranger over the past years."

"Thank you, Hadara, but ... but ..." He raised his head and looked at Philmon and Shebaon. "I am humiliated that she talked about you as she did. We have never put people into classes and thought less or more of them. Philmon, she was in Tzabar's palace when you were. She saw that you were part of the family. Shebaon, please forgive us for embarrassing you."

"Simeon, I believe I rather scandalized your daughter when I helped with Josiah's birthing. I'm afraid she has been very uncomfortable around us since." Kalif clasped Simeon's shoulder. "Perhaps she would be happier elsewhere. Could we send her to a farm further from here?" He faced Philmon and Shebaon. "Please know her feelings are not shared by anyone else. As Simeon said, you are family."

"May we talk with you?" Fiaz asked as he and Zema rejoined them. "Zema has something to say."

Zema stared at her hands clasped at her waist. "I don't know what is wrong with me. I acted horridly. I think so highly of Hadara, and I insulted her." She forced her head up. "But, I insulted our guests even more. I am sorry. I don't know why I said what I did. Please, will you forgive me and not hold anyone else at fault? Sometimes I do things, say things I can't believe I did, things I don't really mean."

Shebaon took Zema's hands in hers. "You are forgiven by me. I can be a bit overbearing, and I hope I didn't cause you discomfort."

"Oh, no, ma'am. I felt awkward around you because you are so, so graceful and elegant and beautiful. You never said and did anything that I could blame for my actions. I … I …" Her tears and sobs returned. Fiaz drew her into his arms again.

"I will take her to our rooms. She hasn't been herself for many months." He kept one arm around her as he led her away.

Kalif glanced around the courtyard. "Shall we save the announcement until after we eat so we can recover from all this emotion?"

Tobias stood. "That might be wise, and since we have a shortage of help, I say we men serve supper."

Simeon shook his head. "That won't be necessary. We will have the meal served quickly."

"Simeon, go be with your wife. None of us are helpless, and some of us learned to handle many chores, right, Philmon?"

"Definitely, so, you women sit, and we will serve you."

Even with a sense of unease over the gathering, Hadara noticed all visited as they ate.

But, no one discussed the scene with Zema. She sighed.

After everyone finished eating, the women stared to gather the left-over food and dishes. Kalif stood and clapped his hands. "Wait, we will all help once we've discussed King Hezekiah's message."

All the women returned to their seats.

"Now that the king has cleaned the temple of idols and Moleck's priests, he has invited all the tribes to Jerusalem for Passover. Of course, the message has more detail, but that is basically the essence. I know that I and my family will participate, and I hope everyone else here will, too."

"Passover?"

"How long has it been?"

"I don't remember when we celebrated Passover in Jerusalem."

"Allow me to read part of the message which priests are taking across all of Israel and Judah:

> *Ye children of Israel, turn again unto the LORD God of Abraham, Isaac, and Israel, and He will return to the remnant of you, that are escaped out of the hand of the kings of Assyria.*
> *And be not ye like your fathers, and like your brethren, which trespassed*

against the LORD God of their fathers, who therefore gave them up to deso-lation, as ye see.

Now be ye not stiffnecked, as your fathers were, but yield yourselves unto the LORD, and enter into his sanctuary, which he hath sanctified forever: and serve the LORD your God, that the fierceness of his wrath may turn away from you.

For if ye turn again unto the LORD, your brethren and your children shall find compassion before them that lead them captive, so that they shall come again into this land: for the LORD your God is gracious and merci-ful, and will not turn away his face from you, if ye return unto Him."

Various comments popped up throughout the assembly. Hadara smiled as she and Kalif exchanged long looks. The niggling problem of Zema shifted to the back of her mind.

Two days after Kalif read the king's message, the Zema situation reap-peared. At the mid-day meal, as the extended family sat around the kitchen table in the back house, Philmon asked Tobias, "Do you know of any farm, a small one, close by that is available? Shebaon and I want to have a home of our own, but we want to be nearby."

Tobias glanced at his mother and Kalif. "I, uh, I hope you don't feel uncom-fortable –"

"No," Shebaon interrupted, "you have made us most welcomed."

"Until the other night?" Nava asked. "You both were gracious and tried to downplay how hurt you must have been."

"First," Philmon raised a massive finger, "let's discuss that night and put it behind us. Then we will talk about our needing a home. We were both shocked and upset by the woman's behavior, but we could tell she was disturbed and lashing out at everyone she could."

Shebaon nodded. "She seems very traditional, and apparently, some things in her life have changed drastically." She looked at Kalif. "I got the impression that she was more upset with you than with Philmon and me."

"Yes, she was." Kalif took a deep breath. "I rather shocked her when I helped with Josiah's birthing."

Tobias snorted. "Our family is not traditional by any measure, perhaps because we have depended on our women so much."

"You have shocked me at times," Mazza stated. "At first, I wasn't sure I liked what I saw Hadara becoming, but I realize that I envied her."

With another snort, Tobias said, "Eema didn't have much choice. But, now, I think I understand Shebaon and Philmon wanting a home of their own." He looked at his mother and then Kalif. "Who makes decisions as to building another house connected to the compound?"

"Actually, your mother." Simeon's voice started everyone. He stood in the door to the courtyard. "I am sorry to disrupt your meal, but I wanted to tell you

Fiaz is taking Zema away. He won't have any trouble finding work the way he handles animals, and he does love my daughter."

Kalif rose. "We will miss him. Is there any way we can find a place for him at one of the other farms?" He shook his head. "Would you ask him to wait until we've had time to consider how they can stay closer to her family?"

"I will ask." Simeon turned his attention to Tobias. "Your mother consults with Kalif and me, but she makes decisions." He nodded at each person before leaving.

"Eema, what do you think of adding another addition to the compound for Philmon and Shebaon?"

"Oh, I was afraid you wanted us to build a place for you and Nava." Hadara smiled before turning to Kalif. "What do you think?"

"I would agree, but perhaps we should ask them."

Chapter 46

Jerusalem :: Passover

Many people in Israel laughed and ridiculed the priests who delivered the Passover invitation. However, some came and joined the worshipers from Judah. The streets of the city teemed with people. Inns had no rooms left. Residents of the city invited relatives and friends to stay with them. The former palace of Tzabar, stocked by servants found by Shem, became the temporary home for princes and members of the king's administration, including Kalif, Hadara, and their family and friends.

Hadara sat on a divan in the main room in the former women's section of the palace. "I never thought I would return here."

Simeon glanced around the familiar room. "Nor did I. At least Shem allotted this wing to all of us. Some of the other occupants may not understand our relationships. Do you know when Kalif, Tobias, and other officials of our family will return?"

"No, no one told me. Perhaps, they didn't know. I was told by the servant in charge of this palace that the first night of Passover meal will be served after the sun sets and the blood is smeared on the door posts by the priests."

"Imagine, we can worship and celebrate Passover in public at last." Nava bounced her baby girl, Anna, on her lap. "King Hezekiah is a good man."

Noma entered from the balcony around the inner garden. "Gafna said she could manage watching the children. I'll take Anna down to the garden, if you want."

"She will soon sleep but thank you." As if on cue, the baby leaned her head on her mother's breast, yawned, and snuggled close. In seconds, she slept.

Hadara heaved a deep breath. "I never thought I could enjoy being back in these rooms. What a difference love makes."

For seven days and nights, the people worshiped and took sacrifices of cattle, goats, and sheep to the temple. The king and nobles provided the animals.

Many worshipers didn't know the procedure and the need to be cleansed before participating in giving a sacrifice. The Levites taught those who didn't know. After the seven days of worship and cleansing, the people enjoyed seven days of celebration. Though some pilgrims left the city after Passover, many remained. The city grew in number, and more homes had to be built.

The farm after the Passover

Hadara hugged Josiah and kissed his cheek. "Sleep well, my babe."

The little boy struggled to break the embrace. "Jos not babe. Jos big boy."

"I know, but can't you be my babe a little longer?" She put her son on his bed and pulled the cover over him when he laid his head on the pillow.

"For Eema." He pasted a sloppy kiss on her cheek when she bent over him. "Abba, no, big boy for Abba."

With a laugh, Hadara told him, "All right, my babe and Abba's big boy. Sleep, Josiah." A smile still covered her face when she walked from the child's bedchamber into the gathering room.

"You appear happy, my love." Kalif entered from the courtyard.

"I am. I have a grown son and his wife who is like my child, two grandchildren, a young son, another babe on the way, and most of all you. We have a king who worships Yahweh and has brought a period of peace." She whirled in a circle, both arms stretched out. "I am happy."

Kalif laughed as he stopped her spin and gathered her close. "We both have much for which to be thankful, but I most of all since I have you."

"Where are we going?" Nava asked as she and Tobias walked outside the compound.

Tobias took her hand and pulled her across the ground toward the animal pen and stable. "You will see. Be patient a little longer."

When they entered the stable, one of the farm workers held the reins of a horse with its harness and riding blanket in place. Tobias took the reins from the worker's hands.

"Thank you. I can handle everything now. I will also brush the horse and put him in his stall after we return."

The worker nodded. "Thank you, sir. I would return to care for the horse. I would be glad to."

"I know, but I don't know when we will return. Enjoy your evening."

The man nodded again before walking away. Tobias led the horse to stand by a large rock. "Come, let me help you onto the rock."

"You brought me here to climb a rock? I thought you were more romantic than that." Nava scowled at him, but with his help, she soon stood on top.

"Now stay there while I mount the horse. Then, I will put you in front of me."

"Oh, we're going for a ride?" She clapped her hands.

Tobias swung onto the back of the horse and guided it close to the rock and Nava. He wrapped an arm around her and set her across his thighs. With a gentle squeeze of his legs, he signaled the horse to step from the stable. He guided the horse across the stable grounds toward the harvested bailey field.

They rode in silence past the field and around an olive grove. Once they reached the top of a hill, Tobias reined the horse to a stop.

"Do you remember when we first met?" He nestled her closer to his chest.

"Of course. You were like a hero from stories. I couldn't believe your mother didn't consider you an adult." Her words and the smile in her voice reached him. "Philmon frightened me, so huge, like a mountain."

"We rode like this then, remember?"

"Yes, I do, and I fell asleep." She leaned her head against him. "I was such a child, but I knew I was safe in your arms. I was so correct, and I still am safe in your arms."

"I told my mother then you would be a great beauty, and *I* was right, great outward and inward beauty. Your beauty increases every day." He breathed in the scent of her hair. "The one true God blessed me greatly, but I'm not sure he blessed you that day. You have endured much as a result."

"Nothing that hasn't made me a stronger person. Everything I have and love is as result of your mother and you finding me that day." She turned enough that she could face him, her green eyes reflecting the brightness of the sun. "I would go through it all again to be able to be married to you and to have our children."

Tobias gazed over the land spread below the hill, the fields of grain, the fig trees in one area, the dates in another, the olive groves, and the different farm compounds. "From here, everything we can see belongs to the family through my mother, actually to Kalif now legally. However, he and Eema say that a large portion is mine, ours."

"How we live now is certainly different from our lives in Egypt." She leaned against him again. "That life also made us stronger, though." She sighed. "But, I'm thankful we have an easier life now."

They sat in silence. A bird called to another. A goat bleated somewhere in the distance. Past the field of ripening grain, a herd of cattle grazed on wild grass. A light breeze stirred Nava's hair, sending wisps across her face.

"We need to allow time for us, just you and me, and not allow life to take all our attention and energy." Nava felt her husband's heart beat against her back.

"Maybe we should take a ride like this regularly, just the two of us." Tobias brushed her hair from the side of her face.

Nava shivered as the sun dipped below the hill tops and the breeze increased. Tobias enfolded her in his cloak.

"We should return to the house, but I enjoy this quiet so much."

"Nava, would you like us to have our own house, separated from the others? Perhaps we could have more quietness."

"No, no, we have our own rooms, and no one bothers us unless for an emergency when we shut the door." She sighed. "I simply enjoy this time for us."

They watched the sun disappear. "I wonder how much longer we will have peace? I am glad King Hezekiah rid us of Moleck and we have no wars at this time." Tobias turned the horse's head back toward the compound. "I just pray that Yahweh will watch over us and allow the peace to last."

They rode in silence as the horse picked its way back to the stable. The stars provided the only light as they each allowed the quiet and hope for the future fill their minds.

Chapter 47

Aaron's house, Bethlehem :: 720 BC

The tale I shared was one of family and friends who lived during a depraved and immoral time. They faced difficulties and possible death, yet they continued. All, brave and strong in his and her own way, did what they felt needed done.

Life continued well under King Hezekiah because he did follow a moral path. All life wasn't perfect, but it was better with less overt wickedness and evil. The families added children; everyone grew older; the family prospered.

Now, I can leave this life knowing I did what I could, and I have shared the story of life and death, joy and sorrow, love and hate. All mysteries were not answered, but some questions will never be answered in life. Blessings upon those I consider my family and friends. May blessings and peace continue throughout your lives.

God's servant,
Aaron

Appendix

Author's Notes

Sources

Acknowledgments

Author Photo

Author Bio

Previous Books by Author

Author's Notes

Fact and/or Fiction

During the time period of this novel, research gave different years for various events, and they don't agree. According to one source, Ahaz would have had to be thirteen-years old when his son Hezekiah was born. Years of one king's reign overlapped the years of another's according to different sources. Therefore, I used the sources that worked better for this story.

Research never revealed time units or distance units during the 8th Century BC. Therefore, I used modern measurements in order to help the plot move forward without the reader having to figure times or distances.

Research revealed that potatoes and carrots (other than wild carrots) showed up in the Middle East during the 8th Century BC, but how they managed to move from South America to the Far East to the Middle East wasn't told.

The people used eggs only when found in nests of wild fowl, but geese and ducks had become domesticated to some extent. Therefore, I used my imagination having people discover eggs would add to food possibilities.

If any events or people seem familiar to any found in today's world, remember that evil and good have fought the same battles over and over throughout history. In modern days, some people discard, torture, and kill their children, even millions of unborn babies so far.

This story, fiction with a few facts thrown into the mix, tells us how heroes come from all sources of life. Many times, they simply do what is needed at the time

Sources

Associates for Biblical Research:
http://www.biblearchaeology.org/research.aspx
Fallon, M.B.: Kings of Israel and Judah in the 8th century, page 126
"Kingsof Israel and Judah in 8th century BC"

History World, "History of Judaism":
historyworld.net/wrldhis/PlainTextHistories.asp?ParagraphID=blg

Jewish History www.chabad.org "The Kingdom of Judah"
Kachelman, John L Jr., Kings of Israel: christianlibrary.org/authors
New International Bible, books of Samuel and Kings.

Acknowledgments

Many people helped me with this novel. I want to thank each and every one, and I hope I remember all of them.

Without editors, we would have no truly good writing. Thank you to the following who found all my many errors: Paulette Henderson, Sharon Worthy, and Dianna Street. More oversight was provided by proofreader Gene La Viness, proof copyeditor Wayne Harris-Wyrick, and Fiction Imprint Editor Rachel Peck. Pastor Mark Hollingsworth helped me by reading the manuscript and seeing that I didn't include material that would clash with religious thought.

Two writers whom I admired for years kindly read my rough manuscript (no, not my rough draft, but not my final version) and sent me a brief review to use on the back cover of the finished book. William Burnhardt, a best-selling author and one of the masters of mystery suspense, and the late Stan Toler, a best-selling Christian and inspiration nonfiction writer, gave the manuscript reviews that let me know I was going the correct direction. My heart is heavy because Stan passed away from cancer before he could see the finished and improved novel.

The fire on my cover comes from a photo my son Randy Zabel took during the burning of wheat fields after harvest. He graciously gave permission for it to be used.

Finally, I must thank Aidana WillowRaven for compiling the components for the cover and helping Dianna Street format *Burnt Offering*.

Biography

Vivian Zabel taught English and writing for nearly 30 years, but she has written herself since a child. When she shared her goal of becoming an author with a friend in the seventh grade, the friend laughed. She didn't share her desire with anyone again, but she worked to become an author.

She and her late husband married in 1961 and had four children, three who lived. As an Air Force brat, she traveled from Guam to Morrocco, and from Texas to Maine. But, Oklahoma was always home.

Zabel has been a member of OWFI since 2002 and the OWFI Grant Director since 2012. She was honored as the Lifetime Member in 2013. She and a friend founded an OWFI affiliate, Pen and Keyboard Writers, in Edmond, Oklahoma. Her home has been in the Edmond area since 1983.

As a former teacher, she finds the teacher in her continues to erupt. She often presents workshops and sessions at conferences concerning writing around the nation, including the Alaska Writers Conference and the OWFI conference. She has held workshops for different groups and for OWFI affiliates.

Zabel has attained her goal of authoring several books, which include YA books *The Base Stealers Club, Case of the Missing Coach,* and *Prairie Dog Cowboy.* She has four children's books released, *I Like Pink, Where Did Panther Go?: A Panther Adventure, A Baby Doll from Santy Claus,* and *Wave Excitement: A Louie the Duck Story.* Her novels are *Stolen* and *Midnight Hours.* Vivian also contributed to a book of short stories with another author and one of poetry with six others.

To learn more about Vivian Zabel and her books, go to her website VivianZabel.com.

Previous Books by Author

CHILDREN'S BOOKS:
(all ages)

The Base Steelers Club
Case of the Missing Coach
Prairie Dog Cowboy
I Like Pink
A Baby Doll from Santy Claus
Where Did Panther Go?
Wave Excitement

NOVELS & COLLECTIONS:

Hidden Lies
Midnight Hours
Stolen

CPSIA information can be obtained
at www.ICGtesting.com
Printed in the USA
BVHW040605100419
544914BV00038B/633/P